Every Window Filled with Light

A Weldon Novel

ENDORSEMENTS

Every Window Filled with Light by Shelia Stovall is a warm and delightful story of forgiveness and hope. Stovall skillfully paints a great word picture of her fictional little town of Weldon and peoples it with characters you will be glad to meet as you follow their stories. You'll love the generous heart of Emma and admire her resilience as she faces the challenges of life and love. If you like feel-good stories, then *Every Window Filled with Light* is a book you won't want to miss.

—Ann H. Gabhart, best-selling author of *An Appalachian Summer*.

A charming story of love and loss and love again. A gift for anyone who has journeyed through the shadows of grief and emerged into sunlight.

—Phil Gulley, author of the Harmony series.

What a sweet Christian debut! I thoroughly enjoyed getting to know this cast of small-town characters!

—Janet W. Ferguson, author, *For the Love of Joy*—a Coastal Hearts novel.

Every Window Filled With Light is a beautiful story of hope and new beginnings, filled with characters who come alive, and a deeper meaning that will resonate in readers' hearts. An excellent debut!

—Misty M. Beller, USA Today bestselling author

A lovely story of friendship, faith and forgiveness, restoration and redemption—with an engaging romance that will warm your heart. Shelia Stovall invites you into a community where broken people come together to help one another, with the charm of a small town and a deep message of how faith heals.

Shelia Stovall has created a charming community of characters who make you yearn for a visit and a piece of pie. *Every Window Filled With Light* tackles tough issues with warmth and wisdom.

A wonderful small-town novel full of caring souls you'll be happy to get to know. A heartwarming story full of faith, hope and love.

— Judy Christie, author of the "Gone to Green" series

Every Window Filled With Light is a masterfully woven story of friendship, hope, and fried fruit pies. The stories of Emma Baker, who longs for children and who sees no hope of that since her husband's murder, and Harley West, an abandoned teen who sees no hope for her future at all, come together in the small town of Weldon, Kentucky. Only God could have orchestrated the events in the lives of Emma and Harley along with those of a handsome young unmarried pastor. With God directing their paths, this is the story of how they all helped one another through seemingly impossible circumstances. The colorful characters and all those fried fruit pies will leave your mouth and your heart watering for more of the flavor of this small Southern town and its people. Filled with Biblical wisdom, this one is unputdownable. Highly recommended.

—Debra DuPree Williams, author, *Grave Consequences,
A Charlotte Graves Mystery*

Every Window Filled with Light

A Weldon Novel

Shelia Stovall

COPYRIGHT NOTICE

Cover and Interior Design: Derinda Babcock

Editor(s): Michele Chynoweth, Deb Haggerty

Author Represented By: Credo Communications, LLC

PUBLISHED BY: Elk Lake Publishing, Inc., 35 Dogwood Drive, Plymouth, MA 02360, 2021

Library Cataloging Data

Names: Stovall, Shelia (Shelia Stovall)

Every Window Filled with Light / Shelia Stovall

380 p. 23cm × 15cm (9in × 6 in.)

ISBN-13: 978-1-64949-169-5 (paperback) | 978-1-64949-170-1 (trade paperback) | 978-1-64949-171-8 (e-book)

Key Words: Small town life, Weldon: (KY imaginary place), Librarians, Foster-Care, Relationships, Values & Virtues, Forgiveness

Library of Congress Control Number: 2021935906 Fiction

And whatever you do, whether in word or deed, do it all in the name of Lord Jesus, giving thanks to God the Father through him. —Colossians 3:17

I dedicate this book to those who have endured a tragedy and are still waiting for God to use it for His good.

ACKNOWLEDGMENTS

Thank you to *New York Times* bestselling author, Lisa Wingate, and Judy Christie, who encouraged me to finish this story. Judy introduced me to her award-winning editor, Jamie Chavez who I consider a gift from God. Bless her heart for her patience with me as I learned how to be a writer.

Thank you to Julie Gwinn for starting the ACFW Middle-TN Chapter. I would have given up on the road to publication if not for the encouragement from Mary Keeley, my first agent, Tim Beals of Credo Communications, LLC, and my current agent, Pete Ford, Credo Communications, LLC.

God connected me with two talented critique partners, Kelly Liberto and Carrie Padgett. Many gifted writers have shared their wisdom at conferences. Thank you, Ann Gabhart, Ramona Pope Richards, Deborah Raney, Sarah Sundquist, Eva Marie Everson, and Steven James. There are too many authors to mention everyone. The most beautiful treasures of the writing journey are the friendships I've made along the way.

I am thankful to Deb Haggerty with Elk Lake Publishing and my editor Michele Chynoweth for sharing their skills and expertise.

Thank you to Sue Cline, who started the Hope Center for Women in Scottsville, Kentucky. Although this is a work of fiction, Sue Cline's ministry inspired me to create a fictional home for women in recovery, Freedom House. I will donate a portion of this novel's proceeds to the Hope Center.

I applaud the librarians with whom I work. All have shared in my struggles and successes, and so I extend a special acknowledgment to all librarians. It is a beautiful thing to open the door to learning and provide an escape hatch from the world's harsh realities. I hope you will introduce many readers to the delightful make-believe world of Weldon, Kentucky.

So much appreciation is extended to my family, and especially to my husband, Michael, who suffered through listening to me read this book aloud many times as I continued to polish the manuscript. I'm sorry for throwing a shoe at you when you fell asleep while listening to me.

And finally, a special thank you to you, dear reader, for taking a chance on me. I hope you fall in love with Weldon and the charming people who live there. Welcome to my dream.

CHAPTER ONE—EMMA

The albino python flicked its tongue next to Emma Baker's cheek. She shuddered but stood very still. Applause filled the Weldon Public Library's auditorium when Dr. Jones removed the reptile from around her neck. *Finally.* Assisting a wildlife biologist with his creepy critters was above and beyond the call of duty for any librarian. Emma covered her shaky relief with a broad smile and a wink at the audience.

Dr. Jones continued his monologue of corny jokes, and Emma stole a glance at the clock. When would this end?

"Let's thank my lovely assistant." Dr. Jones waved his hands with a flourish toward Emma.

She bowed and tightened her ponytail with a yank. The clapping and hoots of over two hundred kids intensified. Not bad for a small-town library.

A tall man wearing a fitted, black T-shirt leaned against the back wall and crossed his arms, exposing a tattoo of barbed wire encircling his muscled bicep. He swiped a dark curl behind his ear and seemed oblivious to the interested glances from several moms in the crowd. If not for the trimmed box beard, he could pass for Da Vinci's David come to life.

Dark eyes locked with hers, and Emma's pulse rate increased. Two years since Chris's funeral and her cloak of grief had stifled any attraction to the opposite sex … until now, surrounded by snakes, children, and small-town gossips. *Talk about bad timing.* She lowered her chin, and the sparkling ring on her right hand caught her attention. A heaviness pushed down on her. *Until death do us part.* There was no reason to feel guilt. Any breathing woman would react to this man.

The kids in front fidgeted, and Emma cleared her throat. "Th–thank you, Dr. Jones." *Of all times for her childhood stutter to resurface.* "Children, you're dismissed. Enjoy the rest of your fall break."

The stranger watched her while children swarmed away like minnows.

Emma turned her back to the dispersing crowd to thank Dr. Jones. Then she made her way upstairs and stopped at the circulation desk in front of the security monitor displaying twenty-four views of the library's property. Her senses remained on high alert as she attempted the impossible task of ensuring each child left the building with the proper guardian. The tension in her shoulders dissipated as the number of people inside the library decreased. One camera held her attention, and she meandered toward the back of the library.

At the last stack, Emma divided the books on the shelf and peeked through the opening. The lanky girl in the stained, sky-blue hoodie had been curled up in the chair all day, sleeping. Was that Harley? It had been weeks since she'd been in the library. Where had Harley been since school started? Poor kid missed the show. Emma removed her phone from her sweater pocket, turned, and walked directly into a hard, broad chest. The tall, dark, David-look-alike stranger stepped back and gripped her elbows.

"Excuse me." They spoke in unison.

"Are you all right, Mrs. Baker?" His inviting voice made her yearn to lean in, to wrap herself in the warm tones.

She blinked. "Y–yes." Emma slid her phone into her back pocket. But she didn't have a back pocket. *Good gracious.* She'd just shoved her phone inside the waistband of her pants. She slapped her palm against her hip to try to catch it, but the device slipped further down. She'd burn these slacks.

"I'm Luke Davis." He extended his hand.

Sweat broke out on Emma's forehead, but her palm remained glued to her backside.

"You are Mrs. Baker, aren't you?"

"Yes." Her voice sounded raspy.

She let go of the phone and shook his hand. A current of energy traveled up her arm, and she inhaled sharply. In all her life, she'd never had such a reaction to a man, not even when she'd met Chris.

She stood there, dumbstruck, then gulped in air.

"Is there a place we can speak privately?" His low voice implied intimacy.

Emma bit her lip when her phone slipped further down her back thigh. *Lord, have mercy.* She jiggled her right leg. The phone slid down to the bend of her knee, and she smiled without showing her teeth. If only the dratted thing would fall down the rest of the way. It didn't. With a sigh, she bent over and pretended to brush something from her calf. Finally! The onyx rectangle clattered to the floor.

She risked a glance up and saw a dimpled smile. *Snakes in a sack!* So much for being discreet. "My office is this way."

He chuckled, and she lifted her chin. A polite person would pretend he hadn't noticed.

A faint hint of cedar and wood smoke drifted on the air, and her insides melted. Heat coursed through her entire body.

When they entered her office, she waved towards a chair across from her desk. "Please, have a seat." She sat, clasped her hands in front of her, and squared her shoulders. It was never good when someone asked to speak with the library director privately. "What can I do for you Mister ... I'm sorry. Could you repeat your name?"

"Luke Davis. Please, call me Luke."

"And I'm Emma."

Luke beamed a smile, and her mouth went dry. The heat on her cheeks intensified.

Emma swallowed hard. "What can I do for you, Mr. Davis—um, Luke?" He wiped his palms on the worn fabric of his jeans and removed a folded envelope from his back pocket. "I lead a young men's Bible study on Wednesday evenings."

Emma crossed her arms and leaned back in her chair. He didn't look like the Bible study type.

His Adam's apple bobbed. "Winston Meador started attending our church last month after he left the juvenile detention center."

Emma sat up straight and gripped the chair arm. Winston Meador. The boy who killed Chris. Killed her husband. Killed her dreams. A chill washed through her. *Just breathe.*

After a few seconds, Luke spoke softly. "Are you okay?"

"I'll never, ever, be okay." Her voice was brittle as she enunciated each word.

"I'm sorry, but I promised Winston I'd deliver this." He placed the envelope on her desk. "He's not a bad kid. It was an accident."

Emma stared at her name, printed in a childish scrawl. She bit her trembling lower lip and fought to control her breathing as the ice in her veins transformed to lava. "A person doesn't accidentally stab a person with a switchblade. I want nothing from a murderer."

Luke cleared his throat. "It was an accident, and it was involuntary manslaughter. Not murder."

Anything to do with that hoodlum reminded her of all she'd lost and dredged up her buried grief and anger.

After a minute, Luke leaned toward her. "It might help you to read the letter. Maybe it's time to forgive Winston."

Her temple pulsed. *Forgive.* The moment he'd said the boy's name, the rage she thought she'd overcome burned through her.

Luke's dark eyes showed compassion. "It's been two years—"

"I know exactly how long it's been." She glared at the calendar and mentally calculated. "Two years, one month and five days." Her voice reverberated in the small space. On trembling legs, she stood. "Please go." She cringed at the pleading sound of her voice.

"I'm sorry I upset you." Luke stood. "If you ever want to talk about it, please call me." He placed a business card next to the envelope and walked away.

Emma dropped back into her chair and covered her face with shaking hands. Call him to talk about it? *Never.* She'd expected to have to deal with a snake today, but she hadn't anticipated him showing up in the form of a man who could be on the cover of *GQ*. Grief and anger twisted her insides every time she looked at her name on the envelope, and she was wilted to acknowledge she hadn't even come close to forgiving the boy who'd shattered all her dreams.

After a long time, she looked up. Almost five o'clock and she'd accomplished nothing. She shut down her computer and grabbed her purse. Her hand hovered over the envelope before she stuffed it into the drawer with the two others she'd received in the mail.

As was her habit, Emma walked all the hallways of the library before leaving. Behind the last stack, she stifled the urge to check Harley's forehead for fever. One of the closing staff members would wake the child in a couple of hours if she remained sleeping. If only Emma could take the scrawny girl home with her and fill her up with food. But Emma had learned long ago, wishes never came true.

CHAPTER TWO—EMMA

Emma parked in the drive and stared up at the old Victorian, every window dark. Clouds the color of concrete hung low in the air. She'd have to hurry, or she'd miss the chance to run without getting soaked.

A howl from her schnauzer broke the silence as she unlocked the antique back door. When she opened Pepper's crate on the sun porch, her beloved dog's chubby body vibrated. "Did you miss me?"

Pepper licked her palms, then her cheek, and she smoothed a hand over the dark, silky fur.

A few minutes later, with Pepper fed and secured in the backyard, Emma changed into sweats and prepared for a run. Images of the white envelope persisted in her head, but she forced them out.

Extending her leg on the front porch rail to stretch, she focused instead on her home. The house had always been white, but when she'd inherited it from Grandfather, Chris wanted to change the color to canary yellow. After his death, she'd hired painters with the hope of lifting her spirits, but something she thought impossible happened—the new sunny shade made her even sadder because he'd never see it.

On a street lined with bungalows, the oversized yellow house stood out—too massive to be anything except pretentious in a town the size of Weldon, Kentucky.

Emma had grown up in the old fortress with her mother and querulous grandfather, but most of the bedrooms remained empty. She feared anger would cripple her forever, just like it had Grandfather. And she didn't want to emulate her mother, the mayor of Weldon, who hid behind a mask of perfectionism. Meeting Chris, marrying him, had been her entrance into a life of freedom to be herself, to have a home overflowing with love and laughter, something sadly lacking from her childhood. They'd planned to fill the old house with children and dogs, but now ... it was the impossible dream.

Emma dropped her foot from the stretch and took off running. Wood smoke drifted on the air, and leaves cascaded around her. Luke Davis smelled of wood smoke.

Left foot. Right foot. Stretch long. Breathe in. Out. Don't think. Don't think. Don't think.

In the fading light, she could just make out the oak trees, with their still-clinging clumps of leaves. The familiar rhythm of her feet hitting the ground usually helped Emma block out all thoughts. But today each step echoed Luke's words. *Forgive, forgive, forgive ...*

Streetlights resembling antique gas lights illuminated the black ribbon of pavement that disappeared into the shadows. Several blocks later, a stitch in her side gathered, and she bent over double, breathing hard. Strands of her dark ponytail whipped across her face when she pushed up and straightened. Her shoulders slumped. *The cemetery.*

An invisible string pulled her to Chris's resting place, and she dropped to her knees. "Why, God?" she asked for the thousandth time. And received only the same silence as when she'd suffered her third miscarriage and lost any hope ever to carry a child to term. Emma rocked back on her heels, waiting. At last, she swiped her face with her sleeve.

Storm clouds gathered. The picture of the boy in the newspaper, the one who'd pled guilty to involuntary manslaughter, flashed through her mind. His sentence of two years in a juvenile detention center added fuel to the fire that burned through her. It wasn't nearly enough. Loneliness and heartache had stained her childhood, but she'd never known hate ... until now. A strangled sob at the unfairness of it all broke the silence, and she covered her face again with her hands, muffling the sound.

Thunder rumbled in the distance. If only Chris had followed his training and called the school resource officer instead of jumping into the fray, he'd still be with her. She pounded the ground with her fist and shouted. "Why didn't you wait for help?" Her shoulders slumped, and droplets of rain and guilt trickled over her. After several minutes, soaked to the skin, she shivered and slowly stood. Chris wasn't here. Only his empty shell. Feeling hollow and depleted of energy, she trudged home.

When she reached the gate of her backyard, Pepper greeted her with a yelp. Emma crouched down, and the dog licked her damp cheeks.

"Lord, help me," she whispered and buried her face in Pepper's soft fur. "I don't want to be like Grandfather."

After Chris died, she'd ranted like a three-year-old having a temper tantrum, and she'd felt utterly alone, abandoned. Months ago, she'd accepted the loss of her husband, and she'd thought she'd been making progress towards controlling her anger, but at the mere mention of the boy's name today, her smoldering fury burst into flames.

Somehow, she had to move on. Forgive and live. *But how?*

Four hours later, Emma rubbed her eyes. After quickly eating a microwave chicken tender dinner at home, she'd returned to the library to finish the financial reports that were due by the end of the week, but she'd spent the last hour staring at the envelope. With a sigh, she picked up Luke's business card. *Dr. Luke Davis—Associate Pastor, Westview Circle Church, Bowling Green, KY.*

Emma's mouth hung open. She'd attended a women's conference in that church's large auditorium. The megachurch had several pastors on staff, but this man hadn't looked like a preacher.

Still, he probably had a way with teens, and he certainly had crowd-drawing charisma. His dark eyes—they were compassionate. A deep yearning built in her chest. What was wrong with her? This man was nothing like Chris, who had been blonde and wiry, a runner, like her.

She placed her elbow on the desk and rested her chin in her palm. She'd raised her voice in indignation and anger—to a *pastor*! And here, in the library of all places.

Emma rubbed both palms over her face. If she ever saw Luke Davis again, she'd apologize.

A large thud sounded, and she jerked up straight. After a few seconds, her shoulders relaxed. It was likely just the library furnace kicking on.

As she gathered strewn papers on her desk, another noise sounded, and she froze. Was that a door closing? Her hand clicked open the security icon on her computer, and she squinted. Seeing nothing unusual, she turned away. *It's an old building, but still …*

A cursory search of the janitor's closet produced a broom handle for a weapon. Tiptoeing, she peeked around corners, ready to attack. Downstairs, she sniffed. That's odd. She shouldn't smell chicken soup when the library had closed hours ago. With trembling fingers, she tried the doorknobs of the meeting rooms and confirmed them locked. Satisfied no prowlers lurked, her tense muscles eased. "I'm going home," she said to no one in particular.

Almost as if in response, "Ah-choo!" echoed from the craft supplies closet.

Emma stepped back and sprinted toward the stairs.

The cool October air helped her clear her thoughts while she paced next to her car.

A Weldon police cruiser parked in front of the library. *Finally.*

Emma jogged toward it. The blue lights reflecting on the library windows instantly took her back to the worst day of her life, and the permanent ache in her chest expanded. She stopped. The police officer climbed from the cruiser.

Daniel. Her former classmate and Chris's longtime friend walked with purpose toward her.

"What's up, Em?"

She swallowed and gathered herself. "I came in after closing to finish a report and heard what sounded like a door closing, more than once. Then I heard a strange sound coming from inside one of the supply closets."

"Do you keep the closet door locked?"

"Yes."

"Did you check if it was locked?"

Emma looked down. "No. I ran."

"Good choice." Daniel looked around Emma's shoulder and peered into the library. "I'll check it out."

"Look at this." Emma opened the app on her phone showing the camera views and passed it to him.

Daniel ran his index finger across the screen. "The hallways are empty." He returned the phone to her.

"It's a big building." Emma pocketed the phone. "Let me show you where I heard the noise."

"Okay, but stay behind me." Daniel walked to the entrance, and Emma keyed in the security code.

When they reached the closet door where Emma heard the sneeze, she tugged at Daniel's sleeve and pointed.

Daniel removed his gun from the holster.

Emma gulped, shoved her key in the lock, and opened the door.

"Come out with your hands where I can see them." Daniel's tone was cold and precise.

A slight frame wearing a blue hoodie sat huddled in the corner.

"Harley!" Emma placed her hand over her slamming heart.

The girl lifted her hands in the air.

"You almost made me wet my pants." Emma pushed in front of Daniel. "For goodness sakes, put your gun down. She's a kid. I know her."

Emma and Daniel shared a look of concern. Daniel had been on duty when a *kid* killed Chris.

"I didn't take nothin'." Several long strands of Harley's dark oily hair had escaped from her messy ponytail. The frayed, dirty jeans she wore were too long, and the sweatshirt swallowed her slight frame. She looked like she had just woken up.

"Why are you hiding in the library?" Emma planted her fist on her hips.

Harley's shoulders drooped. "I got nowhere else to go." Her voice quavered.

Emma rubbed her temple. "Let's go to the break room, have a Coke, and we'll figure out what to do."

As the trio passed the circulation desk, Emma stopped and scribbled Harley's address and phone number on a piece of paper. A few minutes later, she placed a soda in front of the girl and sat next to her. "Where's your mother?"

Harley bit her lip.

Emma slid the paper toward Daniel. "This is her mom's cell phone number."

Daniel dialed and waited. "The number is disconnected or no longer in service."

Harley glared at Daniel. "I could have told you that."

Emma cocked her head. "Care to share her new number?"

"I don't know it."

"How did you get inside the storage closet?" Emma drummed her fingers.

The girl stared at the top of the Coke can.

After a minute, Daniel tapped the table with a pen. "We're not getting anywhere. I'll call social services."

Harley bolted for the door. Daniel grabbed her sweatshirt hood and pulled her back into the chair.

Emma placed her hand on the girl's bony shoulder.

"Running away is not the answer. I want to help you, but to do that, I need to know what's going on."

Harley's mouth set in a hard line, and she looked up at the ceiling. "Mom disappeared a few days ago with her latest jerk boyfriend."

A slow simmer built in Emma's stomach. "Where do you live?"

"We moved to Hadley last spring."

"That's over twenty miles from Weldon."

Harley shrugged. "I walked it in a day."

Emma rubbed her forehead. Surely Harley knew it was dangerous to walk the highway alone? "Why come all the way here?"

Harley's knee jiggled. "'Cause I thought it was a safe place."

A lump formed in Emma's throat. "How did you manage to get inside the closet?"

"A maintenance guy left a key in a door behind the elevator, and I grabbed it."

Emma made eye contact with Daniel. "That closet houses the mechanics of the elevator. The state inspector was here for the annual assessment yesterday. The same key opens all inside doors."

"Are you going to arrest me?" Harley's chin trembled. "I ate someone's food. I'm sorry."

Daniel scribbled on a notepad. "I'll call Child Protective Services."

"Who are you going to phone at this hour?" Emma glanced at the breakroom clock. "It's after eleven."

"Teresa Winslow will come. It's her job," he said in a clipped tone.

"Daniel—" Emma bit her lip. "May I speak with you?

14

Privately?" Her heart ached for Harley. What would it be like to have no one, not even a friend, to help if you were in trouble? She could only imagine.

"No." Daniel's voice was flat. "She might try to run again."

Emma stood, motioned toward the door, and he followed, keeping his eye on the girl, who glared back at him. Emma spoke just above a whisper. "Chris and I went through foster care training with Ms. Winslow. Maybe she'll let Harley come home with me."

Daniel scrutinized the girl with dirty hair. "That's a bad idea. You need to think about this."

Thinking is exactly what she'd been doing, ever since they'd discovered the huddled form on the closet floor. "It's only for tonight, and at least Harley knows me."

Daniel lifted a brow. "What about the charges?"

"It appears the closing staff accidentally locked a library patron in overnight. I'm not pressing charges."

"No way am I going to record that. Her mom might sue you."

"What are you going to report?" Emma crossed her arms.

"She admitted to hiding in the library." Daniel cocked his head.

"I'm not pressing charges." Emma lifted her chin.

"Suit yourself." Daniel scrolled through his phone. "I'm calling Teresa Winslow."

Emma paced, and Harley fidgeted in her seat while Daniel reviewed the details of their activities with the social worker and shared Emma's offer to keep Harley for the night. After a few seconds, he passed the phone to Emma.

"Hello, Mrs. Winslow. This is Emma Baker."

"Hello, Mrs. Baker. Sounds like you've had an exciting

night."

"Yes, ma'am."

"It's generous of you to offer to take the child, but I must refuse."

"But why?"

"I thought you'd decided not to foster any kids?"

"I don't know. I updated my certification last year, but Mother convinced me to withdraw my application." Mother had so many opinions, always, and Emma had let them and her grief rule her life for the last two years.

"What's changed your mind?"

A scared and lonely girl taking refuge in a library basement? "I have a big house, empty rooms. I think we'll be okay."

"This seems too easy a solution," said Mrs. Winslow. "She might try to run away."

"And go where? She hid here because she thought it was a safe place."

"That's certainly in your favor, but—"

"My house is better than a storage closet."

"Your house is lovely—"

Words tumbled from Emma's mouth. "Since Harley and I know each other, it might be easier for her to come home with me until you find her mother."

"We don't know how long it will take to locate the mother, and when the police find her, she might be facing criminal charges for child neglect. If the mother's not able to care for her daughter, it's better for the child if a family member takes her in."

"I see." Emma held her breath and looked at the preteen pretending to ignore her. *If Harley had another place to go, she wouldn't have hidden in the library.* "But if you can't find her mom, and there are no family members, what then?"

"I'll place her in a foster home."

"What about my home?"

Mrs. Winslow cleared her throat. "When did you complete your last training?"

"Last October."

"I'll be there in a few minutes. If you're really interested in fostering children, I'll stop by the office and pull your file."

"I am." Emma blurted.

Mrs. Winslow yawned over the phone. "In the meantime, you and Harley can spend a few minutes talking."

"Yes, ma'am."

"I'll see you within the hour."

Emma passed the phone to Daniel and addressed Harley. "Would you like to stay with me until your mother returns?"

Harley gave Emma a skeptical look. "What about your family? They won't like a stranger moving in."

"I live alone," said Emma. "Mrs. Winslow might allow you to stay with me."

Harley looked at the floor.

Emma returned to the table and sat in the chair next to Harley. "You're welcome to stay with me if Mrs. Winslow gives her approval." Emma leaned forward. "How does that sound?"

Harley shrugged. "I ain't got nowhere else to go."

Emma beamed. "I'd love having company."

The conversation dwindled, and Emma caught Daniel's eye. He shook his head back and forth.

Emma attempted to make small talk, but Harley remained mute, and Daniel continued to scribble in his notebook.

An hour later, Mrs. Winslow arrived in jeans and a wrinkled, white cotton blouse. Her silver hair, styled in a short, blunt cut, stuck up in the back. As she shook everyone's hand, she scrutinized Emma and handed her a packet. "These are the instructions for accessing the online training as well as other important information."

Emma stared at the serious woman who looked pale under the fluorescent lighting and took the extended envelope. "Thank you. I'll get to work on this first thing in the morning."

Mrs. Winslow sighed. "It is morning."

Emma tried to smile.

Mrs. Winslow looked Emma up and down. "I reviewed your file. Your foster care certification expires in a few days."

"So Harley can stay with me if you don't find her mom or a family member?"

Mrs. Winslow frowned slightly. "Complete the required continuing education so you don't lose your certification, then we'll talk."

Emma clasped her hands together, daring to hope. "I will."

Mrs. Winslow's face softened as she looked at Harley. "I've arranged for a very nice couple to look after you." Mrs. Winslow opened the library's entrance door. "They're waiting up for us."

Harley stood, glanced furtively around the room, then her shoulders sagged. Her boots scraped the floor as she followed two steps behind Mrs. Winslow, shuffling slowly as if she was headed for the gas chamber.

Daniel stood and scowled at Emma. "I hope you know what you're doing." He adjusted his holster.

Emma hugged herself. "I don't have a clue."

CHAPTER THREE—EMMA

While preparing for bed, Emma considered future room options for Harley. The bedroom suite she'd shared with Chris downstairs was the nicest, but it would be too easy for Harley to sneak out. Only three of the six bedrooms on the second floor had connecting bathrooms. When she and Chris first completed the foster parent training, she'd bought pink Hello Kitty bedspreads for a set of twin beds thinking they'd take in younger children. She could run to Target tomorrow and buy new bedcovers, but Harley would roll her eyes at the pink walls.

Her mother's old bedroom with the tower was too fancy for any reasonable person. Emma wouldn't dare remove the ornate French furniture. If she wanted Harley to enjoy the comfort of having the privacy of a bath connected to her bedroom, Emma would have to give up the room she'd moved into after Chris's funeral. It was the best choice for Harley.

Emma sat in a chair by the window and dropped her head in her hands. It was time to think of someone else for a change. Time to take a step forward. Time to return to her bedroom downstairs.

A few minutes later, lugging an armload of clothes on hangers, her feet grew heavier with each step as she walked toward the bedroom suite she'd shared with Chris. The antique glass doorknob felt cold in her hand, and a chill traveled up her spine when the hinges creaked. She gulped, squared her shoulders, and hit the light switch. The room smelled of lemon oil, and vacuum tracks covered the oyster-colored rug. Minnie, her housekeeper, must have cleaned it recently.

A taupe comforter with a bevy of pillows covered her king-sized four-poster bed. After removing layers of wallpaper, she and Chris had painted the walls to match a piece of green sea-glass she'd discovered on a sandy beach while on vacation. Pepper jumped up on the bed, circled twice, and settled herself.

Emma entered the walk-in closet and inhaled the faintest scent of Chris's sandalwood aftershave. *It's long past time to donate Chris's things to Goodwill.* Emma hung up her clothes and wiped a tear from her cheek. Pepper howled.

Emma scratched the dog's ears. At least she had Pepper for comfort, and even though her mom was often difficult, Emma knew Mother would walk through fire for her. Emma had Casey for a best friend, too, while poor Harley had no one. Her heart filled with loneliness and sadness.

She extracted her phone from her jeans pocket. It was late, but Casey would understand.

After the second ring, Casey answered. "Is everything okay?" Her voice held a hint of concern.

"I need to talk."

Casey yawned and Emma could picture her pretty red-headed friend sitting up in her pink silk pajamas with an expensive cream slathered all over her face. "Do you want me to come over?"

"No. It's cold out." The tightness in Emma's muscles eased as she shared the details of her day. When she remembered the zap of energy from Luke's touch, her mouth went dry. No way would she tell Casey about him. The mere thought of the man made her cheeks burn. Thank goodness Casey couldn't see her face.

Emma cleared her throat. "And so I'm going to complete the online courses, and if CPS doesn't find Harley's mother or a relative, I'll apply to be the girl's foster parent."

"Your mama will not like this one little bit."

Emma's mother had been against her and Chris fostering kids from the first time Emma mentioned it.

"That's why I'm not going to speak with Mother until I know whether or not CPS will place Harley with me."

"Smart."

Emma stretched. "Thanks for listening. I'll let you go so you can get your beauty sleep."

"That reminds me. I bought a new eye cream that made my crows' feet fly away. You should try it."

"Thanks, but I'd rather not mortgage the house for one of your potions. Good night."

"Skin care is an investment."

"Convince my banker, and I'll buy it. We'll talk tomorrow." Emma disconnected and fingered her silk drapes. God had blessed her with so much, but material things didn't count for much when loneliness filled your days and nights.

Casey's right. Mother will be annoyed. Dread pushed in on her.

She pulled back the bedcovers and ran her hand across the ice-cold sheets where Chris used to sleep. If only he were here. They might have a houseful of kids.

On the side table, she noticed the novel she'd started reading the day before Chris died. She'd left it on the bedside table, hoping she'd heal enough one day to finish it.

Her thoughts drifted to Luke Davis and the letter he'd delivered. If he weren't so sexy, she might take him up on his offer for counseling. The longing in her chest seemed a betrayal to Chris, and she fingered her wedding band. It was Chris's arms for which she yearned. Still, it encouraged her to realize her body had actually responded to the handsome Luke Davis like a normal woman. At least things were still working. *Too bad he had to be friends with her worst enemy.*

An hour later, Emma turned over for the umpteenth time. In the stillness, she whispered. "I forgive Winston Meador."

But her hard heart would not yield. She pounded her pillow, and Pepper growled.

"Sorry, girl." Emma smoothed her hand over the dog's head.

Emma wanted to forgive Winston Meador, but she just couldn't. Minnie's favorite Scripture came to mind. "I can do all things through Christ who strengthens me." If only he would! But he'd abandoned her.

She thought of Harley sleeping in a strange bed, in a new place, with nowhere to go. Something stirred inside Emma. Even though she couldn't help herself, maybe she could help Harley. At least she could give the child a safe place to sleep. *Why would a mother abandon her child?* A slow burn began to build in Emma's midsection, and she gripped the bedsheet. She refused to be like Grandfather. After taking several long deep breaths, she left the bed and pulled on her robe. In the kitchen, she turned on her laptop and started a pot of coffee. She was going to do this thing.

Early the next morning, Emma rubbed her eyes, and her stomach growled. Time to find something to eat. A bowl of cornflakes sounded good—but did she even have milk? She removed the half-gallon from the refrigerator and lifted it to her nose. Gagging, she carried it to the sink and poured it out.

Her mother might be right. How could she foster a child when she barely took care of herself? Then again, even with her poor shopping habits, Harley would be safer staying with her than living on the streets. Emma removed a notebook from her purse and started making a grocery list.

It was crazy the state required Emma to take twenty hours of continuing education annually to maintain her library position, but only mandated six hours of annual coursework to maintain her foster care certification and be an abandoned child's guardian.

While waiting for her bread to toast, she worked on a list of things to do. She'd wait until nine o'clock to call Tammy, the assistant library director, to tell her she wasn't coming in. Minnie, her housekeeper, wouldn't mind stocking her pantry.

Then she would plan to pay a visit to Mr. Wilson, the president of the library board of directors. Emma didn't want him to hear about Daniel and her discovering Harley hiding in the library from anyone but herself. It would be better to see Mr. Wilson in person. After these tasks were completed, she'd call the CPS office.

By this time tomorrow, she might have a foster child. A tiny spark flared inside her, and she placed her hand over her heart as it lifted. Maybe, there was hope for her after all.

At two o'clock, Emma sat in the parking lot, staring at the nondescript red-brick building that housed the CPS office. *It's showtime.* Emma corrected her posture. For once, she'd act like Virginia Willoughby's daughter.

Inside, Emma dropped into a black vinyl chair and studied the empty waiting room. A few plants would help soften the atmosphere, and almost anything on the wall would be more appealing than the sun-faded photograph of the former governor. Her phone vibrated, and she clenched her teeth. *Oh, no. It's Mother.* Every muscle in her body tightened when she hit the button to send the call to voice mail. Why was it she could stand up to almost anyone—except her mother?

After almost an hour, Mrs. Winslow came to the door and called to her.

Emma wiped her damp palms on her slacks. *There's no reason to be nervous.* She breathed in deeply.

"My office is this way." Mrs. Winslow pointed.

Emma sat down across from Mrs. Winslow and looked over the piles of folders on the desk. Did each one of those files represent a child? Could there be that many children in Weldon needing foster care?

Mrs. Winslow stared at her notes. "Harley said she hid in the library Monday night and was about to sleep over a second night but then you discovered her?"

"I can't believe no one caught her."

"It's a big building." Mrs. Winslow kept her eyes on the paper. "If you hadn't returned after hours, she'd still be sleeping in the library closet again tonight."

Emma pinched her chin. "What about her mom?"

Mrs. Winslow cocked a brow. "The police have been unable to locate her. It would help if Harley could remember their street address."

"That's nonsense."

"I agree. She also claims there are no relatives."

"Do you think Harley ran away from home?"

"If she did, her mother didn't report her missing. Harley shared very little information." Mrs. Winslow removed her reading glasses. "And I wonder how much of what she told me is the truth."

"Why would she lie?"

Mrs. Winslow's face looked fierce. "I'll tell you what I think, but only after I'm sure you're the one to foster Harley."

Emma gulped. "I understand."

"I called the school in Hadley and discovered she's not registered."

"Do you think her mother home-schooled her?"

"Not likely. What can you tell me about the child?"

"All I know is her name and that she often sits in the corner chair in the back of the library after school."

Mrs. Winslow picked up a paperclip and twisted it. "Let's call the library in Hadley. Maybe someone there knows something about her."

She dialed the Hadley library and hit the speakerphone.

Emma knew the library director and explained the situation. "I know you can't release confidential information about one of your library patrons without a court order, but of course, if Harley West didn't sign up for library services, there's nothing to share."

In a few seconds, they learned Harley didn't have a library card in Hadley, and when Mrs. Winslow emailed a picture of the girl to the director, she didn't recognize her.

"Thank you for your time." Mrs. Winslow disconnected and rested her chin in her palm. "Harley's lying about Hadley."

"Lots of parents won't take the time to sign their kids up for library cards."

Mrs. Winslow tapped her pencil on the desk. "But Harley said it's her habit to go to the library after school, and you've confirmed this."

Emma shrugged. "Several parents use the library for free childcare, but we don't mind if the kids are well behaved." Still, she knew Mrs. Winslow was probably right. There was no way Harley was walking twenty miles every day to get to the Weldon library.

"One of the few things I pried from Harley is she seems to like you."

"I know next to nothing about her."

"You knew her name."

"My staff and I make an effort to call all our patrons by name."

"Many would never have noticed her." Ms. Winslow's face showed no emotion. "We might find her mother tomorrow, or never. Do you think you can handle her for the long-haul if it comes to that?"

Emma bit her lip. "I don't know."

Mrs. Winslow tossed the mangled paperclip into the trash. "I'll find someone else."

"Wait." *It's just that Mother will be against it. But this is my decision.* She squared her shoulders. "I'll do it."

Mrs. Winslow's narrowed her eyes.

"I—I promise." *Breathe.* "It took a while for me to regain my footing after Chris's death." Her voice sounded more confident. "I won't back out on you."

Mrs. Winslow's face softened. "Carol Carter is waiting on my call to inspect your residence. As we already know your home, it's just a formality. Are you sure about this?"

"I am."

"I can give you temporary custody until the authorities find the child's mother." Mrs. Winslow dropped her chin. "And, I've not ruled out finding a family member."

"I understand." The knot in Emma's stomach tightened.

"If the child's mother shows up, call the police."

Emma's heart pounded. "Will the police arrest Harley's mom?"

"If what Harley said is true, she abandoned her daughter. Let the police sort it out."

"Okay."

"There's something else you need to know if you're going to be Harley's foster parent."

Emma sat up straight.

Mrs. Winslow's face turned hard. "Dr. Regina Anderson gave Harley a physical this morning and discovered bruises all over the child's body. Harley claims she fell down rickety steps."

A chill swept over Emma. "Oh, my."

Mrs. Winslow straightened the pile of forms and placed them in a folder. "I think someone beat the child, and she ran away."

"She can stay with me as long as she likes." Emma blinked back tears.

"Harley will remain under your care until the family court judge determines otherwise, and I'll make sure she sees the child's medical records."

Emma's nails bit into her palms. "I'll not allow anyone to hurt Harley." She forced determination into her voice.

Mrs. Winslow smiled. "Looks like you have a bit of your mother's spunk after all." Emma's chest swelled. Although her mother was prickly, she possessed an inner strength Emma envied. Everyone in Weldon respected her mother. Well, almost everyone. Arnold Alexander, a city council member, often challenged her. And then there was Grandfather. It made Emma sad to remember his acid tongue toward his only child, but his criticism fueled her mother's ambition to prove him wrong.

"When it comes to protecting a child, I can be just like her— pretty fierce." She felt a small smile play on her lips.

"Glad to hear it." Mrs. Winslow gave Emma a long look. "One of my staff members is at the Middle School with Harley. I'll send her a text and ask them to return here once they've finished meeting with the guidance counselor."

"Okay."

"You must take Harley shopping."

"Of course."

"We provided her with new underclothes, a T-shirt, and a pair of jeans this morning. She took the underwear but left the clothes on the bed. She's very proud." Mrs. Winslow made a note. "This will not be easy."

"I'll do my best."

"No one can ask for more." She shuffled a stack of papers. "Let's get to work."

Emma picked up a pen and wrote carefully as she completed the first form. *So what if her mother threw a hissy fit?*

When she signed her name to the last paper, Emma gulped. She was going to be a child's guardian.

A half-hour later, a petite woman wearing khaki slacks and a long-sleeved navy blouse escorted Harley into the office. Emma stood. How dreadful Harley had to endure a physical exam. She probably wouldn't appreciate a hug.

Harley's stared at the floor, her posture stooped.

"Mrs. Winslow agreed to let you stay with me." Emma did her best to sound upbeat. "It will be nice to have company."

Harley peeked up at her, her face crimson. "Really?"

Emma's voice softened. "I wouldn't say it if I didn't mean it."

Mrs. Winslow cleared her throat. "I texted Carol Carter, your social worker. She's on her way to your home."

"Ready to go, Harley?" Emma hooked her arm through her purse.

"Let's get outta here." Harley scuffed her boots on the floor as she walked out.

Emma parked her Honda in the driveway, and Harley looked up at the old Victorian with her mouth open. "How many people live here?"

"Just me and my dog, Pepper. Don't let her scare you. Howling is her way of expressing excitement."

"I like dogs."

"That's something we have in common." Emma smiled. "But I'll warn you—Pepper's distrustful of strangers. Don't try to pet her until she comes to you."

The social worker stood on the front porch, examining the ceiling painted to match a cloudless summer sky. She tightened the belt on her brown trench coat and lifted her hand.

"Carol must be freezing," Emma said. "I don't know why she didn't wait in her car."

Harley rolled her eyes. "She's probably been looking in your windows."

Emma gasped. "You're probably right." She rushed to the front porch and extended her hand. "Hello, Carol. I haven't seen you in ages." Her voice sounded too close to her mother's campaign voice. What was wrong with her? She needed to act normal.

"We don't seem to run in the same circles." Carol shook Emma's hand. "This is some house."

"It is grand, but … it's old. I'm still getting it updated." Emma gestured toward Harley. "This is Harley West."

Carol smiled. "We met earlier today. I had another appointment, or I'd have stayed with her while she met with the guidance counselor."

Harley remained mute.

Emma forced the antique key into the lock and pushed the massive front door open. When she hit a switch, light flooded the foyer. The elegant oriental rug's plush wool showed traces of vacuum tracks but still looked dated. The scent of baking lingered. Minnie must have arrived early in the afternoon.

"Wow," Carol said. "Look at that chandelier."

Harley and Carol both stood, mouths agape, while they stared up at the sparkling crystals.

"We rarely use the front entry," Emma said. "I forget how beautiful it is with the lights turned on." She placed her hand on the oak banister's carved finial and marveled at its shine. *Thank goodness for Minnie.* For the first time in months, Emma studied the bleached-out Depression-era wallpaper and bit her lip. It needed replacing, as did many things in the old house. After losing Chris, she had lost interest in updating her home, and she spent most of her waking hours at the library.

Carol's professional voice removed her from her reverie. "May I see where Harley will sleep?" The sound of Pepper barking emanated from the back of the house.

Harley dropped her backpack on the floor. "Can I go see your dog?"

"In just a minute. Let me give you a tour first." Emma started up the stairs. "I inherited this oversized antique a few years ago from my grandfather. It's a good thing the house came with a trust fund for maintenance, because I couldn't afford to keep it on my own."

"People like me don't live in houses like this." Harley's eyes were wide.

"What do you mean, 'people like you'? As far as I can tell, you're like the rest of us—two eyes, one nose." Emma turned right at the top of the stairs. "This way."

When they stopped on the threshold of the guest room, Carol stared into the doorway. "I love the soft gray shade."

"Thanks. Chris and I spent hours stripping the old wallpaper."

Harley followed Emma inside the room, then she opened the door to the adjoining bathroom and peeked inside. "Wow! My own bathroom."

"It goes with the room. Help yourself to anything in the bathroom closet." Emma crossed the room and opened a dresser drawer. "I left a couple of my T-shirts and sweatpants for you. They'll be a bit too large, but they'll do to sleep in until we can go shopping."

Harley's jaw stiffened as she circled the room. "This is bigger than our whole trailer."

"All the bedrooms are large, but there are few closets. You can hang your things in the chifforobe."

"In the what?" Harley frowned.

Emma opened the door of the walnut wardrobe next to the wall. "This is a chifforobe."

"I'll keep my stuff in my bag." Harley lifted her chin.

"There's a hamper in the bathroom. Put your dirty clothes in it, and I'll launder them for you."

"I'm used to taking care of my things."

Emma shrugged, "Suit yourself. After dinner, I'll show you the mechanics of the washer."

Carol and Emma shared a look of amusement. Emma held her hands loosely behind her back as she opened the other bedroom doors. "If you'd prefer one of these rooms, we can add fresh sheets," she offered.

Harley stared at the ornate French furniture in the one room and whispered, "No way. It looks like something in a movie."

"This used to be Mother's bedroom. It's too fancy for me," Emma said.

"It's lovely," Carol stretched her neck to get a better look. "It reminds me of the bedroom in the opening scene of *Roman Holiday*."

"Grandmother loved that movie. She might have used it for inspiration when decorating a bedroom for her princess." Emma led them down the long hallway. "This staircase will take you to the den in the back of the house." Pepper's howls grew more insistent as they walked down. "Let me introduce you to my schnauzer. She stays on the sunporch when I'm out."

Emma kneeled in front of the dog crate. "Sit." She unlocked the door, and a ball of black fluff bounced out and into her lap.

Harley dropped to her knees, and Pepper ran to her and covered her face with doggie kisses.

"My goodness," Emma gasped. "She's usually distrustful of strangers."

"Harley smiled. "Dogs know who to trust."

"Absolutely," Emma rose and opened the back door. "I'm sure she needs to go out." Pepper howled and scampered out.

"The back yard is fenced, so she'll be okay on her own."

"Can I go out with her?" Harley looked longingly out the window.

Emma glanced at Carol, who nodded.

"Sure." Emma grabbed a tennis ball from the table and tossed it to Harley. "She loves to play fetch."

Carol and Emma watched Harley throw the ball. "Be careful." Carol gave Emma a stern look. "Her mother might show up."

"Mrs. Winslow warned me to call the police if she does."

"It's standard protocol. You must get Harley a coat soon."

"I started a list and plan to go shopping with her tomorrow after school." Emma turned back to the window and gasped. In the backyard, her neighbor Mr. McCullough stood in front of Harley with a Super-Soaker water gun pointed at her. Harley stood, arms up, and Pepper danced in circles around them. The gate next to the driveway remained open.

Emma flew out of the door and yelled. "Mr. McCullough! What are you doing?"

He narrowed his eyes and slowly lowered the water gun. "This gal said she lives here. Is that true?" Mr. McCullough wore an unbuttoned black-and-red plaid flannel shirt with a white T-shirt covering his big belly. Red suspenders held up his faded jeans. Shooting squirrels with a water gun to keep them from robbing his birdfeeder occupied most of his waking hours. Mr. McCullough had been looking out for Emma since he had removed the training wheels from her bike. Before today, Emma appreciated his fatherly concern and laughed at his over-the-top neighborhood watch program, but today—she wanted to throttle him.

After making introductions, Harley and Emma returned to the house with Pepper in the lead. When Emma held the door open, the dog made a beeline to her food bowl, and Harley trudged inside, her cheeks flushed.

Carol planted her fists on her hips. "Is he dangerous?"

"No. Just over-protective." Emma divided her ponytail and tightened it. "It never crossed my mind Mr. McCullough might consider Harley a prowler."

Harley's eyes blazed. "He accused me of trying to steal your dog."

Carol placed her hand over her heart. "He almost gave me a heart attack."

"Me too." Harley hugged herself.

"Let's get back to business." Carol shuddered. "Emma, do you mind giving us some privacy?"

"No problem. I'll be in the kitchen if you need me."

"Thanks. Let's have a seat in the den, Harley."

Emma retreated to the kitchen, fed Pepper, and lifted the lid off the crockpot. The beef roast smelled heavenly. Then she noticed Minnie's elegant penmanship on a note placed next to the cookie jar.

Hi, Emma,

I'm sorry I couldn't stay to meet your new guest, but my church is having a fellowship meal this evening, and I promised to arrive early. There's a salad in the refrigerator.

An angel must have whispered in my ear this morning, because I baked an extra batch of chocolate chip cookies. You'll find them in your cookie jar.

I added a few things to your grocery list and taped the charge receipt to your refrigerator door.

Let me know if there's anything else you need. You know how I love to cook. I'll drop by one evening soon to meet the child. Tell her I added an extra cup of joy to the apple pie just for her. You'll find a box of vanilla ice cream in the freezer. I hope you enjoy your supper and the company.

You are both in my prayers.

Hugs and love,

Minnie

A smile spread across Emma's face, and she reached for the ironstone cookie jar. Eating just one wouldn't hurt. A few minutes later, Emma paused from setting the table when Carol walked into the kitchen. "Something smells delicious."

"Minnie left us a pot roast. Please, join us for dinner?"

"Thank you, but I can't stay."

Emma removed the lid from the antique cookie jar. "How about a cookie?"

"I shouldn't." Carol licked her lips.

"You won't regret it." Emma held the crock out to her.

Carol bit into a cookie and closed her eyes. "Mmmmm. This is homemade," she mumbled with her mouth full.

Emma passed the jar to Harley. "A gift from Minnie."

Harley hesitated, then snatched two cookies and crammed one in her mouth.

Emma cringed. Manners could wait. "My best friend, Casey, will join us for dinner. Do you think two cookies will be enough to hold you until six-thirty?"

Harley grabbed another one. "This'll do."

"Enjoy your dinner." Carol buttoned her coat. "I'll be in touch."

"Thanks for all your help." Emma's heart rate increased. She'd done it. She was responsible for a child.

She stood at the window, numb. The headlights of the government-issue sedan lit up Emma's yard as Carol backed out of the drive. Harley and Emma stared at each other. *Now what?*

CHAPTER FOUR—EMMA

An hour later, Harley sat in the corner, working on math problems, while Emma sat on the sofa rereading a book. Usually, reading small sections of her favorite books relaxed her, but not tonight. Casey should be here by now.

A car door slammed, and a few seconds later, another bang sounded.

Virginia Willoughby marched into the house without knocking. Her navy suit and matching pumps looked new.

Emma blinked and bolted up from the sofa. *Oh, no.* "Mother, what a surprise."

Virginia dropped her purse on the chair and planted her hands on her hips. "Something's wrong with your phone. I thought it would be nice to enjoy dinner together at the Triple D. Casey's just pulled in behind me. Perhaps she'll want to join us."

Casey rushed in, flinging off a long, eggplant-colored cape coat to reveal jeans with more holes than a slice of Swiss cheese. Her thigh-length aqua sweater almost draped off one shoulder. The furry Ugg boots looked more like something a teenager would wear than a thirty-five-year-old businesswoman. "Sorry I'm late."

Virginia's eyes landed on Harley. Her scowl transformed into what Emma called her campaign face. "Excuse me. I didn't realize you had company." She extended her hand and walked toward Harley. "I'm Virginia Willoughby, Emma's mother." She used her public voice.

Harley stood, gulped, and shook Virginia's hand.

"Young lady. When you meet someone, say your name with authority and grasp their hand. There's nothing worse than a handshake that feels like soft cheese."

"Uh-huh," Harley whispered. "I'm Harley."

Virginia dropped Harley's hand. "It's nice to meet you." Virginia smiled without showing her teeth. "You may call me Mrs. Virginia." She crossed her arms, turned to Emma, and lifted a brow.

"Harley's going to be staying with me for a few days."

Virginia's face blanched, and her eye twitched.

Casey sidled up next to Virginia and beamed her toothpaste-commercial-worthy smile at Harley. "And I'm Casey, but I'll give your arm a rest. Sorry to be so late, but I decided to change from my work clothes."

Harley's eyes widened, and she gasped. "You're Cassandra."

"I'm Casey. I left Cassandra in New York when I retired from the runway."

"You're famous."

"No one cares about an ex-model."

Harley's eyes found Emma. "Your best friend is a supermodel."

Emma wrinkled her nose. "She wasn't always this pretty. You should have seen those big teeth in second grade."

"And Emma's Minnie Mouse ears." Casey lifted a brow. "We had a little scuffle on the playground, and a week together in detention sealed our friendship."

Virginia's brow creased. "I'd say it's best not to share our past mistakes with an impressionable child."

"I ain't no child." Harley's face turned hard. "I'm almost thirteen years old."

Emma stepped between them. "Mother, would you like to join us for dinner? Minnie cooked a beef roast."

Virginia looked Harley up and down. "Thank you. It will give me the chance to get to know more about Harley," her mother lowered her voice, "and why she's here."

Emma squared her shoulders and lifted her chin, deciding there was no time like the present to admit the truth. "Harley needed a place to stay, so I updated my foster care certification."

Virginia's lips formed a tight line. "Well, then."

Minutes later, they settled themselves around the oak pedestal table. Harley kept staring at Casey, and Virginia studied Harley.

Virginia's voice sounded cold as she unfolded her napkin with a jerk. "Emma has the most beautiful dining room."

"But I prefer to eat in the kitchen," Emma said. After a quick blessing, she served the food. Harley kept her face down and stuffed roast into her mouth as if she hadn't eaten in weeks.

Virginia gave Emma a long look, then nudged her head toward Harley. Emma understood the silent command, and she froze, fork in mid-air. Harley had emptied her plate within two minutes.

"We have apple pie for dessert." Emma dabbed at her lip with her napkin.

"But it's good manners to wait until everyone is ready to enjoy the next course." Virginia said tersely.

Harley narrowed her eyes at Virginia.

Casey forked a piece of lettuce. "Emma asked me to go shopping with you tomorrow night, Harley. Tell me what you need. I might have some things in my shop you would like."

"I don't need nothin'."

"You need a coat." Emma kept her eyes glued to her carrots.

"And clothes for church," Virginia said.

"I sure ain't going to no church." Harley's voice sounded harsh.

"We can talk about that later." Emma winced as something sharp hit her shin. She realized it was probably her mother's heel.

"You can talk all you want, but I ain't going shopping." Harley glared.

Virginia's brown eyes were as hard as her shellacked hair. "Young lady." Her sharp tone made Emma grip her fork more tightly. "In this household, we speak to each other with respect."

"This ain't none of your business." Harley's eyes glittered.

"Mother's right, Harley. I know you've had a rough few days, but let's agree to be respectful." Emma thought her voice sounded too close to Virginia's.

Harley's cheeks turned pink, and she stared at her empty plate. "I don't have money for new clothes."

"Social services gave me funds to buy the necessities for you," Emma said.

"You keep their money." Harley pushed away from the table and scraped the floor with her chair.

Now what? Emma said with her eyes, shooting Casey an urgent look.

"Don't you want a second helping?" Casey asked Harley. "Minnie's the best cook in Weldon."

Harley looked longingly at the roast. After a few seconds, she scooted her chair back to the table.

"And another word of advice." Virginia's voice softened. "It's a sin not to savor food this delicious. For goodness sakes, take your time and enjoy it."

Emma placed another serving of roast beef and carrots on Harley's plate. The surly girl lifted a fork full of food and chewed in slow motion.

Virginia chattered about city business and volleyed questions to Harley, who answered with shrugs. When Emma placed a scoop of vanilla ice cream on a slice of apple pie, Harley's eyes followed the dish.

Emma turned toward Casey. "Can you leave the boutique around three tomorrow?"

"Sure." Casey held her palms out. "No pie for me, thank you very much. I had lunch with Daniel at the Triple D today, and he insisted I have a fried rhubarb pie."

"I told you, I ain't going shopping." Harley mumbled with a fork full of apple pie into her mouth.

"You aren't going," Virginia furrowed her brows. "Please remove *ain't* from your vocabulary."

Harley swallowed hard. "As soon as you remove that stick from—"

"I'm sure you don't want to do laundry every evening," Emma said.

"If you don't dress properly, the social worker will assume Emma's pocketing the money meant for you." Virginia coolly sipped her iced tea.

"Mother's right. I'd rather you choose your clothes, but I need to make sure you have what you need."

Harley muttered something unintelligible, licked her spoon, then pushed away from the table again.

"It's polite manners to ask permission to be excused from the table." Virginia sat ramrod straight.

Harley rolled her eyes. "May I be excused?" she said in a voice that mimicked Virginia's.

Emma dropped her head and swallowed a grin. "Yes."

The girl bolted up the stairs, and Pepper, who had been sitting under the table, streaked behind her.

"Really, Emma," Virginia placed her napkin on the table. "You cannot do this."

"Why not?"

"You hate confrontation."

"She didn't turn confrontational until you played twenty questions."

"I like her," Casey said. "And I think Emma's dealt with someone exactly like Harley for years."

Virginia frowned. "Who?"

"You." Casey pointed her manicured index finger at Virginia.

"Well, I've never!"

"You both have a sharp tongue, but you have a soft side too." Casey dabbed at her mouth with her napkin. "But you hide it, just like a turtle."

"Maybe a snapping turtle." Emma threw her napkin on the table.

"You two." Virginia stood. "I could just ... " Her face darkened.

Here it comes. Emma got up. "Thank you for joining us for dinner. You'll like Harley once you get to know her."

"I'd suggest you place anything of value in the safe."

"Mother. That's not fair."

"I'm calling the police chief the minute I get home to see if he knows something about the child's mother."

"He doesn't." Emma gave a condensed version of the previous night's activities and explained the police had failed in their efforts to locate Harley's mother or a family member. "When I asked Harley why she hid in the library, she said it was because she didn't have anywhere else to go."

"Poor little lamb," Casey's pretty features turned mournful.

"Little lamb my foot. More like a wolf pup," Virginia crossed her arms. "I can see your eyes are closed now, but you'll eventually see I'm right." She grazed Emma's cheek with a peremptory kiss. "Thank you for dinner." She turned. "And Casey—"

"Yes, ma'am."

"I'd appreciate it if you would try to talk sense into my daughter."

Casey winked at Emma and turned to face Virginia. "I told her she needed to think about this." Her hazel eyes were large and doe-like.

After Virginia left, Emma rubbed her shin and cleared the table. "Of all nights for Mother to pop in and invite me to dinner."

"That was awful. I almost turned around when I saw her car pull into your drive." Casey opened the dishwasher.

"Thanks for being in my corner tonight."

"I'll always be there for you." Casey hugged her.

Emma squeezed her back. No one could make a promise like that.

After they cleaned the kitchen, Casey grabbed her cape, glanced toward the stairs and lowered her voice. "Be careful. Daniel said taking in a kid like Harley is asking for trouble."

Emma cocked her head. "How would he know anything about the kind of kid Harley is, and a cop shouldn't be discussing police business." She crossed her arms. "Since when do you and Daniel Sheppard eat lunch together?"

"Don't be mad at Daniel." Casey clutched the cape and held it as a shield. "After you told me about your little escapade involving him, I thought it would be the perfect excuse to invite him to lunch."

"Any breathing man and a few dead ones would do almost anything to spend time with you. You don't need an excuse."

"Daniel's shy. Last week, the diner was crowded so Dot asked us to share a booth. I had a good time and hoped he'd call." Her mouth turned down. "But he didn't, so I used the excuse to find out more about Harley to convince him to meet me at the Triple D for lunch."

"He's a nice guy." Emma sighed.

"I know, and it's been a long time since a nice guy asked me out."

Emma arched her brow. Maybe Casey was finally healing too. For years, she had prayed for Casey to discover a man worthy of her love. Her best friend seemed to have a penchant for picking the wrong guys.

Two hours later, Emma paced around the sofa. She wanted to ask Harley if she could check her homework but suspected such a request would be rejected. She'd probably consider it none of Emma's business. What would it take for Harley to trust her, to know she only wanted to help?

Emma hugged herself. She could share that her Dad abandoned her, too. Sad they had that in common. Emma rolled her shoulders. She never talked about that with anyone. Not even Casey. At last, she trudged upstairs and knocked.

"Yeah." Harley's voice sounded harsh.

Emma opened the door. Harley lay on the bed watching television with Pepper curled up next to her. "Do you want me to check your homework?"

Harley rolled her eyes. "I ain't a first grader."

Emma sat down on the edge of the bed, picked up the remote and muted the TV.

"Hey!" Harley protested, still wearing the stained blue hoodie.

"Sorry, but I need to ask you a few questions."

"Like what?" Harley's jaw flexed.

"How are you settling in? The house can be intimidating."

"This is the nicest place I've ever stayed." The girl relaxed a little.

"Do you need anything? Help yourself to anything in the bathroom closet."

"You already told me that."

Emma fingered the soft fabric of the coverlet. "I happened to think you and I have more in common than you realize."

"Yeah, right. We're so alike." Sarcasm dripped from Harley's tone.

"You'd be surprised what we have in common. When I was your age, I used to hang out at the library too."

"I can see hiding out from your mom. She's a piece of work."

"Mother wasn't the problem. She spent much of her time working. I kept away from the house to avoid my grandfather. One never knew what might set him off."

"In a house this big, it wouldn't be hard to hide out."

"True. But his voice carried. Also, as you get to know people in Weldon, someone will likely mention this, so you might as well hear it from me—my dad walked out on us."

Harley gave her a long look.

"I wondered why a dad didn't show up with your mom tonight, but she's so old, I figured he must have already died."

Emma groaned. "Mother's not that old. My dad left town with his secretary." Emma remembered looking up the word *cliché* in her dictionary after hearing someone at church gossip about him. It had been a lonely time, and she'd been so hurt and embarrassed. Emma cleared her throat. "Then he died in a car crash."

"Bummer."

"Pretty much. My life's not been as perfect as you might think."

"I'll bet Mrs. Virginia didn't have creepy boyfriends."

"True." Emma suppressed a shudder and moved to the dresser and removed a pair of sweatpants and a T-shirt and placed them on the bed. "Are you sure you can operate the washer?"

Harley answered with an eye roll. "I ain't an idiot either."

"Right." Emma drummed her fingers on her thigh. "I'll leave so you can have a shower. I just wanted you to know I understand what it feels like to be left behind." She scratched Pepper's ear. "I guess I'll take this rascal out for a minute. Are you sure you don't need anything before I go to bed?"

"I'm good."

Emma lifted Pepper from the bed. "Let's go, little girl. You can come back up in a few minutes. Good night, Harley."

Emma could feel Harley staring at her back as she left. Harley spoke just above a whisper. "Mrs. Baker."

Emma paused and looked over her shoulder.

"Thanks for letting me stay."

"You're welcome. And call me Emma. We're going to become great friends."

Harley rolled her eyes again. "Whatever." But Emma caught the trace of a smile flicker across the young face.

"I'll be in the bedroom at the foot of the stairs if you need anything."

Later, as Emma prepared for bed, she wanted to kick herself for not asking Harley about the bruises after she'd commented on dealing with creepy boyfriends. There were terrible stories in the news about abusive men. What if a violent man had been the reason for Harley's mom disappearing? Maybe Emma should call Carol Carter. No. There really wasn't anything to tell.

She stood in the closet she'd shared with Chris trying to remember where she'd stowed his computer and phone. She'd add donating his things to Goodwill to her to-do list. That task should have been done months ago. It wasn't like her to procrastinate. She paused. She'd hardly given Chris a thought today. A wave of guilt washed over her, then she scolded herself. Chris would be proud of her. At least, she was no longer allowing her mother to run all over her. She smirked. *It's about time.*

CHAPTER FIVE—HARLEY

Harley took a long, hot shower, and scoured her skin, but she couldn't scrub away the rainbow of bruises covering her ribcage. Scalding water pounded her tender torso, and she winced. When the stream turned lukewarm, she leaned her face against the pristine, white subway tile and sighed. It felt so good to be clean.

A few minutes later, dressed in Emma's soft sweatpants and faded T-shirt, she returned downstairs to the laundry room, started the washer then tiptoed upstairs.

She lay under the luxurious bedcovers, inhaled a floral scent, and admired the moonlight streaming through the tall windows. Cocooned in softness, her body relaxed, and a deep yearning made her eyes water. Too bad she couldn't stay. What would it be like to live in a house like this forever—warm, safe, with food to eat every day? *Don't even think about staying for more than a few days.*

In four years, she'd be able to get a job legally. If only she could get hired at a fast-food restaurant, she wouldn't go hungry. Once she could work, she'd never ever steal again. But until that time, she had no choice.

For months, she'd slept on the stained futon in the rundown trailer that smelled of mildew and the overpowering cologne of Beau, her mother's latest man. She'd wanted to tell him if he'd take a shower, he wouldn't have to take a bath in cologne. The scar running down the side of his face, one eye completely white, caused her to shudder and look away the first time she met him.

Memories of his sweaty hands on her skin made her nauseous. Her hands fisted, and she wanted to hit something.

They'd lived in almost complete isolation for months in the countryside. Wild honeysuckle vines kept his rusted trailer anchored on the rocky ridge called the Devil's Half-Acre. Beau claimed his family had lived there for generations, producing the best moonshine in the area, and he'd expanded the family business to include meth. Her mother couldn't resist the free drugs he offered.

A chill ran through her, and she couldn't stop shaking. If only she'd hit Beau harder with the iron skillet. As he lay unconscious and bleeding at the temple, she watched his chest rise and fall. Her mother, passed out on the dirty sofa, couldn't save her now.

She squeezed her eyes shut, rolled over, and winced. *Don't think about Beau.* But she couldn't stop worrying about her mom.

Beau would come looking for her and the wad of cash she'd taken from his not-so-secret hiding place. If only she could buy a bus ticket to somewhere far away.

Harley wiped a tear from her cheek. She'd accepted the truth a long time ago:—her mom only cared about her drugs, and Beau kept her supplied.

Last night, for about one second, she'd considered telling the cop about her mom and Beau's drug business. The policeman didn't remember Harley, but she'd recognized him. He had talked to the kids at school last year at an assembly about the DARE program. She'd wanted to shout at him when he said he envisioned a world where kids could lead lives free from violence and substance abuse—they just had to make the right choices. It was a stupid thing to say. Kids didn't have choices. Their parents did. And her mom chose everything toxic.

Harley remembered her mom's constant warning—*Trust no one.* She bolted upright in the bed. What if Emma searched her bag?

Groaning, she threw back the covers, and her feet sank into the plush rug on the oak floor. In the dark, her fingers rifled to the bottom of her backpack until they found the money secured with a rubber band. Where could she hide this?

She crept down the hallway to the front bedroom, and the oak boards felt like ice to her bare feet. When she turned the glass knob, the hinge on the door creaked, and moonlight from the half-circle of turret windows lit the room. Her eyes landed on an antique vanity in the corner. She'd never seen such fancy furniture, and she hesitated before opening a drawer where she discovered old-fashioned curlers like her mamaw used to wear. No one would ever look here.

After hiding the bundle under the sponge-rollers, she tiptoed downstairs to the laundry room and moved her clothes from the washer to the dryer.

Yawning, Harley returned to bed and drifted into the memory ... or the dream—she wasn't sure which—that always comforted her. The woman with streaks of gray in her dark hair flipped burgers on the grill, and she placed the palm of her free hand on Harley's cheek. The aroma of charcoal and seawater drifted on the breeze, and the wind ruffled her hair. An endless ocean of blue filled the landscape, and she watched Mama run into the surf. Harley snuggled into the lap of the man with the big belly wearing a clean white T-shirt. He wrapped a hairy arm around her, and she'd inhaled the comforting scent of him. If only she knew their names instead of Papaw and Mamaw.

Somehow, someday, she'd get back there, to those people—to her happy place, her safe place. If only her mom would tell her where it was.

On Thursday evening, the price tag on the jacket in Harley's hand made her jaw clench. She couldn't afford this stuff. Her reflection in the floor-to-ceiling mirror amid the stylish mannequins made her insides shrivel.

Beside her, Casey rifled through the rack of coats. Her fuchsia minidress and thigh-high black boots made people look twice. Didn't she realize she'd left the Big Apple for Hokey-Pokeyville? Even if someone didn't notice her clothes, her perfume screamed city. Harley inhaled the lingering scent of something exotic. Very different from the light floral scent Emma favored. When Harley's mom took the trouble to wear perfume, Harley knew she planned to party and would likely return home with a stranger. Sadness welled up. *Don't think about her.* There was nothing she could do to change things. Nothing she could do to protect her mom.

Harley stole a glance toward Casey and Emma. They were so different from each other, but strangely, they kind of went together like chocolate and peanut butter. One of them was always elbowing the other, finishing a sentence, or teasing. Harley had always wished for a best friend.

Casey held up a black North Face down coat. "This will keep you warm."

Harley rolled her eyes. "If I wore that, I'd look like all the other clones at school."

"I get that." Casey's brows furrowed. "Are we going for preppy, grunge, vintage, boho, hippie, or gypsy? You tell me, and I'll put it together."

"What language are you speaking?" Harley frowned.

"Fashion slang. I love styling wardrobes." Casey rubbed her palms together.

"Focus, fashionista." Emma lifted a navy pea coat off the rack. "We're looking for a coat, not a wardrobe." She bit her lip. "Too preppy?"

Harley made a motion with her finger like she would gag herself. "Can we go to Goodwill?"

Emma scrunched up her nose. "The closest one is a forty-minute drive to Bowling Green, and it's already after six."

Casey pulled out a leather jacket. "How about this?" Her voice lifted.

"No, and I'm hungry." Harley crossed her arms in front of her. "I don't like anything in here, and I only have twenty bucks."

Emma rubbed her temple. "How about I hire you to walk Pepper every day. That will free me to go for a run."

"Maybe," Harley said.

"I'll pay you ten dollars a day."

"Ten dollars?" Harley's voice sounded overloud in the hush of the boutique.

"It's not easy money. Pepper hates to walk," Emma said.

"Okay. I'll do it." These people had no idea how rich they were.

"So it's a deal." Emma held out her manicured hand, and Harley compared them to her fingers with nails chewed to the quick. She slid her hands into the hoodie pouch and turned her back to them. "I'm leaving."

Emma followed her out of the store. "Let's go to Walmart to buy underclothes. They might have a coat you'll like."

"I like Dollar General." Harley opened the car door.

"They do have the best bargains," Casey said.

Harley narrowed her eyes. No way would she believe the ex-model Cassandra knew anything about shopping at Dollar General. Still, she wouldn't have thought someone like Casey would be from Hicksville and be best friends with the town librarian either.

A few minutes later, there they all were—Dollar General. Harley searched the discount rack and pulled off two sports bras—then she snatched a package of underwear. "This'll do."

While standing in the checkout lane, she studied a bin of jumbled items marked down. Her eyes lingered on a hair coloring kit. Beau wouldn't think to look for a blonde, but no way would Emma, aka Ms. Perfect, let her bleach her hair.

In half a second, her quick fingers slid the kit into her hoodie pouch, and then she removed a crumpled twenty-dollar bill—Beau's money—from her jeans pocket, to pay for the rest.

Her gut twisted when she passed the bill to the clerk. Then a weight settled in the pit of her stomach. She hated it when her mom made her steal things, and now, she'd done it with no one to blame but herself. Sweat beaded on her forehead.

Harley's skin prickled, and she locked eyes with Casey, who lifted a penciled brow. *Busted.*

Casey selected a hair coloring kit and took it to the checkout. After pocketing the receipt, she returned the box to the bin while Emma kept searching through the rack in the back corner. Casey looped her arm through Harley's, led her to the door, and spoke under her breath. "It would break Emma's heart to know you'd rather steal than accept her kindness."

Heat traveled up Harley's neck.

"Why would you filch something? Emma's pleaded with you to let her buy you stuff."

Harley wanted to hit something. These people would never understand she'd rather starve than ask anyone for anything. She been made to beg for money and humiliated when a classmate told everyone they'd seen her panhandling. Her mother beat her with a belt more than once when she'd refused to do it again. *Now what?* Harley snatched her arm away. "What do you want from me?"

Casey dropped her chin. "I want you to be nice and to give Emma a chance."

"A chance for what?"

"For happiness? Is that too much to want for someone who's been unhappy most of her life?"

Harley rolled her eyes. Sure, Emma hadn't had the perfect life Harley had pictured, but no one with everything Emma had should be bummed. Harley jutted her chin out. "I don't know how to be nice, and I sure don't know how to make someone happy."

"You're living with the kindest, most generous person I know. It shouldn't take you long to figure out how to be nice if you want to," Casey said. "That's the big question, isn't it? Do you want to be nice? Do you want a second chance? Because I will not give you a third." Her tone sounded menacing.

Emma rushed out of the store and placed her hand over her heart. "There you are. What are you two up to?"

"We're just talking," Casey gave a false smile.

Emma unlocked the car door. "You should have told me you were leaving the store."

"I'm sorry we scared you," Casey said. "I thought you saw us leave together."

"As long as Harley's safe, it's okay."

Harley buckled her seat belt. The box in her sweatshirt felt heavy. Casey asked the impossible. To give Emma a chance, she'd have to trust her. *No way.*

CHAPTER SIX—EMMA

On Saturday morning, Emma stood in the walk-in-closet and inhaled. The faint scent of Chris's sandalwood aftershave lingered, and she buried her face into a stack of sweaters on the shelf. It had been a mistake to ask Harley to help empty the closet … she wasn't ready.

She leaned against the wall, slid to the floor, and dropped her face in her hands. At least she could mark this off her list.

The week had been tension-filled, but she'd spent more energy focusing on Harley's needs than moping.

Harley sauntered into the closet and whistled. "Man! Look at all these clothes."

Emma gasped. "What did you do to your hair?"

"What does it look like I did?"

Emma stood up. "It's so short—and blonde."

"So? It's *my* hair."

Emma winced. "I'd have made an appointment for you at the salon if you'd mentioned wanting a new hairstyle."

"A waste of money when I can cut it myself." Harley touched a stack of folded T-shirts. "Are these going to Goodwill?

"Yes."

Harley removed a shirt from a hanger, folded it into a perfect rectangle, and placed it in a cardboard box.

"I thought you needed a board to fold shirts like that." Emma smoothed her palms over her jeans.

Harley shrugged. "Mom worked at a laundry, and I'd help her. With enough practice, you don't need a board." She pointed her chin toward a stack of hoodies. "What about those?"

"Everything goes."

Harley looked longingly at the stack. "But the one on top is a Tennessee Titans sweatshirt."

Emma shrugged. "That doesn't change the size. They'd swallow either one of us whole."

Harley huffed. "Never mind."

"If you'd like a Titans hoodie, maybe we can find one for you at the Goodwill store." Emma bit her lip.

"Yeah, and maybe there will be a diamond tiara you can buy for your mom there too."

They emptied the first shelf, and a tear rolled down Emma's cheek.

"Why don't you get out of the way?" Harley's voice softened. "I can do this."

"But—"

"Go." Harley pointed to the door.

"Thank you." Emma squeezed her shoulder. "Keep anything you want. Maybe we can have it altered."

"Really?" Harley's voice lifted.

Emma swallowed the lump in her throat. "I always mean what I say." And she left her to the task. She would not think about this.

While waiting in the den, Emma removed the black notebook from her purse, turned to her list and put a line through *Clean out Chris's closet*. Then she turned to the inside cover of the journal and read the rest of the list.

LONG RANGE GOALS
1. Build a family.
2. Stand up to Mother.
3. Run a marathon.
4. Write a book.

Emma picked up her pen and also lined through *Stand up to Mother* with a flourish. After a minute of musing, she wrote, *Be happy again* at the bottom of the list. Minnie told her time and again to choose to be happy. Her housekeeper was the most joyful person she knew. For years, she'd worked for Grandfather, the meanest man in Weldon, yet his hateful words would roll off Minnie like rainwater on a slicker. An invisible armor shielded her from the hurts of the world. What Emma wouldn't give to have Minnie's cheer and peace!

She sat there, lost in thought, with Luke's advice taunting her. *Forgive.* Gripping the pen, she pressed down hard and wrote *Forgive*. Acid filled her stomach.

Maybe she could still build a family of foster kids? No. She should focus on helping one child. This girl. Harley. Emma's thumb clicked the end of the pen, then she added, *Make Harley laugh* to her list and smiled. The child wanted a Titans jersey, but Emma doubted she'd accept a gift. Harley seemed to enjoy playing with Pepper in the backyard, but she couldn't get her a dog. That was a long-term commitment. Who knew how long she'd get to stay? Her mom might show up any day ... or never.

Emma imagined a Christmas tree overflowing with presents, and a new puppy. The old yearning for a family grew. She squeezed her eyes shut until the hopeless dream dissolved.

It was almost lunchtime when Harley shoved the last box into the back seat of Emma's Honda. Emma's breath caught, and she snatched Chris's favorite cashmere cardigan from the box. "I'm keeping this."

"It will swallow you whole." Harley shook her finger.

Emma stuck out her tongue, put the sweater on, and rolled up the sleeves, and she imagined Chris hugging her.

After a quick burger and fries at McDonald's, they drove to Bowling Green's Goodwill store. In a matter of minutes, they'd emptied the car of all Chris's clothes except the rescued cardigan and the confiscated hoodies.

The worker disappeared with the boxes. A wave of sadness washed over her; then she turned on her heel. *Don't look back. One step at a time. Breathe in. Breath out. Keep moving forward.*

They went inside, and Emma removed a shopping list from her purse and passed it to Harley.

"What's this?"

"The non-negotiables." Emma gave a tight smile. Too bad Casey had to work. She could have used some backup.

Harley crumpled the paper, tossed it in the trash, and rifled through a rack of clothes. "I know what I need."

Emma removed an envelope of cash from her wallet. "You've already earned thirty dollars for walking Pepper, and I'm paying you a hundred dollars for cleaning out the closet."

"A hundred dollars." Harley's mouth hung open.

"You earned it." She turned and walked toward the front of the store before Harley had the chance to argue. Emma's chest swelled. *Score one for me.*

While Harley shopped, Emma browsed, marveling at the store's low prices. No wonder Harley wanted to shop here. Two hours later, the clerk rang up a large stack of clothes—one hundred and eight dollars.

The items Harley bought made Emma cringe. Everything looked too large. She remained silent when Harley shoved her arms into a camouflage coat a boy might wear.

After placing the purchases in the trunk, Emma drove to a sporting goods store. "There's something else we need."

Inside the store, she went straight to a rack of Titans hoodies. "I think a Youth Large is the right size."

"That costs fifty bucks."

"Five days of walking Pepper." Emma held it out against Harley. "What do you think?"

Harley gulped. "Really?"

Emma nodded.

"Thanks, Emma."

"It's your money."

When they passed the *Welcome to Weldon* sign, Emma wanted to pump her fist in the air. Chris's clothes would be appreciated by some lucky shopper. And Harley finally had a coat, enough clothes to get through a week, and a Titans hoodie.

"How about pizza for dinner?" Emma asked.

Harley shrugged.

Why did everything have to be so hard? "Do you like pizza?"

Harley rolled her eyes. "You ain't figured out yet that I'll eat just about anything?"

Emma mimicked Harley's eye roll. "Fine. I'm ordering pizza with everything. I hope you like anchovies."

"Gross."

"Okay, no anchovies." Emma smiled, pleased she got a response at all. *Score another one for me.*

When they walked in the back door, Pepper howled from her crate. "I guess I'll go take Pepper for a walk after I put my stuff up." Harley trudged upstairs.

"Thanks."

"It's my job." Harley rolled her eyes.

Emma shook her head. She needed a run. After changing into a pair of sweats, she donned her running shoes. *Just breathe. One step at a time. One day at a time.* The familiar rhythm of her steps eased her tight muscles. Her feet pounded the pavement, then she paused and jogged in place for a minute. She would not go to the cemetery. When she turned to run the opposite direction, her heart felt lighter than it had since she'd become a widow. *One day at a time.* She repeated her mantra again, feeling hopeful.

Downtown came into view, and the lights of the library drew her when she rounded the corner. On Saturdays, it closed at five o'clock—as did most businesses on Main Street—but the Triple D drew a crowd for dinner. When she passed it, the smell of fried food drifted on the air. Emma admired the pile of pumpkins and gourds, arranged around an enormous shock of corn on the north corner of the square.

Someone called out. "Emma!"

She turned.

Mrs. Dot stood outside the Triple D, wearing her standard pink uniform, holding up a bag. Her white beehive had a blue pen stuck in it. "I fixed your favorite fried pie today."

Emma jogged up to her. "Raspberry?"

"You bet."

"Thank you."

"I haven't seen you all week."

"It's been crazy."

Mrs. Dot looked over the top of her reading glasses. "So I hear. When are you gonna bring that young'un over to meet me?"

"Soon, but she's shy."

"I don't like it when my regulars go missing." Mrs. Dot extended the white paper bag.

Emma took the bag and gave her a hug. "Thank you."

Mrs. Dot patted her back. "You take care of that child and yourself."

"I'll do my best."

Emma couldn't help but laugh. These were her people, and even though her family wasn't perfect, the realization she'd never be without friends in Weldon lifted her spirits. She clutched the bag of fried pies and sprinted home.

When she burst through the back door, she couldn't help shouting. "Harley, come down! We have fried pies!"

CHAPTER SEVEN—EMMA

Early morning light filtered through the kitchen's lace curtains and made intricate patterns on the oak floor. Emma, sitting at the kitchen table, cradled a cup of coffee. This discussion couldn't wait. Across from her, Harley crammed a spoonful of Cheerios into her mouth, and milk dribbled down her chin. The new haircut made her look boyish, but it didn't diminish her beauty. Emma passed her a napkin and pointed to her chin.

Getting Harley to church today would be more difficult than dragging Pepper outside while it rained. Emma squared her shoulders and lifted her chin. "We leave for church around nine-thirty."

"Pass."

"If you live with me, you go to church." Emma crossed her arms.

Harley's face darkened, and her knee jiggled. "I ain't got the right clothes for church."

Emma's heart softened. No adolescent girl ever felt she had the right clothes, but on this occasion, Emma agreed with Harley. Still, only her mother and a few of her cronies expected men to wear suits and women to be dressed in their best on Sunday morning. Emma pressed her lips together. She'd wear jeans to church today. "Anything you would normally wear to school will be fine."

"They'll stare at me." Harley pushed back from the table; her chair scraped the floor.

"Ignore them."

"People need to mind their own business." Harley dumped the rest of her cereal down the disposal and stomped upstairs.

"We leave at nine-thirty," Emma called out.

A door slammed.

An hour later, the familiar sound of Harley's boots clomping down the stairs made Emma stop pacing. She handed Harley a package. "I picked this up for you at Walmart the other day."

"What is it?"

"A Bible. *The Message* is written in contemporary language. I thought it would be a good starter version."

Harley stared at the book, her brows furrowed. After a few seconds, she tucked it under her arm. "Whatever."

They walked the three blocks to the church in silence. Harley lagged. "Where's your Bible?"

A heaviness settled over Emma. "Mine's broken. I should have picked up two."

"How do you break a book?"

"Not a pretty story." Two weeks after Chris's funeral, she'd turned to the Scriptures for comfort, but when she'd read the words, *In everything give thanks*, the next thing she knew, the Bible hit the wall with a thud. Later, when she'd retrieved it, the book fell apart in her hands, the spine broken. Guilt had flooded her and her "broken" Bible had remained hidden on the top shelf in the hall closet ever since. She'd remembered receiving her first Bible in a

66

ceremony at church as a child. Mrs. Reynolds, her Sunday school teacher had emphasized the importance of treating God's holy word with care. Wouldn't she be disappointed to know of Emma's tantrum?

Emma forced the memory of throwing her Bible from her mind. "We need to walk faster. If we're late, I can guarantee everyone will stare."

Harley rolled her eyes, but she picked up her pace.

When they entered the church, Emma pointed toward the front where Casey sat with Daniel Sheppard next to her. Jolene and Frank Bledsoe, Casey's parents, sat on the pew behind them. Emma scanned the crowd for her mother. Probably hobnobbing with people she thought important.

Emma slid down the pew, edged next to Casey, and leaned across her. "Hi, Daniel."

He turned. "Hey, Em." Then he glanced around her at Harley, who sat staring straight ahead, shoulders stiff and cheeks flushed.

Bessie Singer, a plump matriarch and meddler, turned around from her seat in front of them.

"Good morning, Mrs. Singer." Emma gestured with her hand toward Harley. "Let me introduce you to Harley West."

Mrs. Singer grabbed Harley's hand. "I've heard all about you."

"Harley, this is Mrs. Singer and her husband, Dr. Singer," Emma said.

"Umm ... It's nice to meet you." Harley tried to pull her hand back, but Bessie Singer held on.

"The kids call me Mrs. Bessie. I'm so glad Emma has company. She doesn't need to be in that big old house all alone."

Harley jerked her hand back.

"Perhaps you'll join our youth group. We have a praise band with drums so loud you'll think you're at a rock concert." Mrs. Singer smiled, and Emma noticed a dab of her coral lipstick stained her front tooth. "Do you sing or play a musical instrument?"

Harley's eyes widened, and she shook her head.

Dr. Singer patted his wife's shoulder. "Bess, you've scared the poor girl. Welcome to Loving Chapel, young lady."

Harley shrunk down into her coat.

Emma scanned the bulletin and stopped breathing as she read *Welcome, Dr. Luke Davis.* It explained that Brother Bob and his wife Eleanor were attending a ceremony for his nephew who was being commissioned as a missionary to Africa.

Emma kept her eyes focused on his name. *Holy Shittake Mushroom!*

Her mother's unmistakable voice making her way toward their pew made her stiffen. One would think it was an election year.

Virginia reached their pew and stared at Harley. "What have you done to your hair? And you're both wearing jeans."

"It's called a makeover," Harley said. "You should try it some time."

Virginia's nostrils flared. "Well, I've never."

"That's obvious with your Hillary Clinton dome."

Emma nudged Harley. "Stop it," she whispered.

Virginia mumbled to her daughter under her breath as she took a seat on the end of the pew. "Someone should have explained the dress code to our guest speaker and to you."

Music filtered through the sanctuary, and the congregants scattered to their seats. Luke Davis stood to the side of the choir, wearing starched jeans, a crisp white shirt with the collar open, and a tweed jacket that made his shoulders look even broader than when Emma had first met him. His cowboy boots reflected the light from the chandelier.

Virginia snapped open her bulletin. "Dr. Davis agreed to join us for lunch at Oak Grove."

Oh, no. Emma thought fast. "Harley and I plan to grab a drive-through burger," she said, wiping her damp palms on her jeans.

"Nonsense." Virginia looked Emma up and down. "Even though you're not dressed for fine dining, a table will be waiting for us."

Emma rolled her shoulders. She'd have to put *'Stand up to Mother'* back on her list.

Brother Bob, their regular pastor, always wore a dark suit and silk tie. Even on a weekday, he sported khaki pants and a sweater-vest with a tie ... never jeans. *I wonder what Mother's friends would say if they knew about Luke Davis's tattoo.* Emma stifled a laugh.

Everyone stood for the reading of Scripture, and heat traveled up Emma's neck as Pastor Davis read the words "Give thanks in all circumstances; for this is God's will for you in Christ Jesus" (1 Thessalonians 5.18).

She gripped the pew, sweat beading on her forehead. Of all the Scriptures, he had to choose. *Don't think. Just breathe.*

An hour and a half later, Emma drummed her fingers on her knee while Virginia parked the Cadillac in front of Oak Grove, a Civil War-era home transformed into a bed and breakfast that also featured a stellar restaurant.

"I don't know why Dr. Davis didn't want to ride with us." Virginia unfastened her seatbelt.

"Because he had a choice." Harley's voice drifted from the back seat.

Emma craned her neck. Luke's vintage white pickup sported a license plate featuring a frog with the slogan "**F**ully **R**ely **O**n **G**od."

"That cartoon plate is tacky, even for a pastor." Virginia opened her car door. "Still, I've heard good things about his work with troubled youth."

The four columns of Oak Grove exuded a feeling of permanence, and the white rockers on the front porch offered an invitation to linger. The restaurant of the bed-and-breakfast had even been featured recently in a *Southern Living* magazine article which touted Oak Grove as a must-visit destination for Southern food devotees.

Luke walked toward them with long strides. Emma gulped. *No preacher should be that good looking.* "Glad you could join us." Her voice sounded false.

Luke held open the front door. "It's nice to be invited."

"Ouch." Pain shot from Emma's heel.

"Sorry." Harley glared at Luke as she accidentally stepped on Emma's foot.

Emma winced. "It's okay."

"May I take your coat?" A staff person held out her hands.

Emma and Virginia passed their coats to her.

Harley kept her hands jammed into her coat pockets. "I'll keep mine."

The scent of roasted meat wafted through into the entranceway, and Harley's stomach growled. She wrapped her arms around her midsection as her cheeks turned pink.

Emma whispered. "It's okay. Everyone's stomach growls."

The hostess led their party to a round table dressed in a linen tablecloth and four place-settings of antique china covered in yellow roses. Virginia directed everyone where to sit.

Harley dropped into her chair and hunched into her coat.

Their waitress, Tippy, took their drink orders. "I'll be back in a sec," she said. All the servers at Oak Grove wore black slacks and white oxford shirts.

Virginia smoothed her skirt. "Dr. Davis, please do us the honor of offering a blessing?" She batted her eyelashes.

Harley rolled her eyes.

"Most people just call me Luke," the pastor said. He held out his hands, one to Emma and the other to Virginia. Emma reached for Harley's hand, but they remained buried in her coat.

Luke bowed his head. "Father in heaven ..."

Emma hardly heard a word of the prayer. Her ears started buzzing the minute Luke touched her fingers. When he said, "Amen," he gently squeezed Emma's hand, and she jerked it away.

Tippy delivered their drinks, and another server placed a bowl of creamy coleslaw in front of Virginia. She passed it to Harley. "I'll warn you to pace yourself and leave room for dessert. The Derby pie is something to relish."

Platters of fried chicken, meatloaf, and country ham arrived next, with bowls of green beans seasoned with bacon, whipped potatoes crested with droplets of butter, and a dish of glistening fried apples.

After emptying her tray, Tippy grabbed the basket in the center of the table. "Looks like y'all were hungry. I'll be right back with more yeast rolls."

Harley ate with gusto, and Virginia ran the conversation at the table.

An hour later, when Tippy placed a leather bill holder next to Virginia's dessert plate, Luke picked it up. "I insist on paying," he said.

"Nonsense," Virginia said. "You're our guest."

"I'm too old-fashioned to allow a lady to buy my lunch." He pulled his wallet from his back pocket and placed several bills inside the leather case. "Thank you for inviting me to join you."

Tippy returned. "Would y'all like a to-go box?"

"Not for me," Luke said. "I'll be sharing pizza with the men in my Bible study tonight."

Emma gripped her linen napkin. He'd be having dinner with Winston Meador.

Harley's eyes widened. "Heck, yeah. I want a to-go box."

"Sure thing, sugar." Tippy turned.

Virginia's index finger tapped a muted beat on the tablecloth and a line formed between her brows; then her expression transformed to her public face. "The Inn's walking trail leads to the river. Emma, why don't you take Dr. Davis for a walk?"

Emma's nails bit into her palms. Before she could speak, Luke stood.

"I'd love to see the grounds." He helped her with her chair. "Are you sure you and Harley don't want to join us?"

Virginia gave a tight smile. "It will be a chance for me to enjoy Harley's company."

"Yeah. Right." Harley snarled. "I'm sure we're going to be best friends." She mimicked Virginia's tone.

Oh, dear. Emma leaned down and whispered in Harley's ear. "Please do not taunt Mother. I mean it."

Harley gave her a wicked smile.

Why, she's enjoying aggravating Mother. Casey's right. They're cut from the same steel wool. After retrieving her coat at the desk, Emma headed out with Luke in tow. "The walking trail is this way." Her tone sounded sharp in her own ears.

When they stepped outside, she stuck her hands into her coat pockets. No way would she allow Luke Davis to touch her again. A breeze lifted her hair from her shoulders, and she inhaled deeply. She wouldn't think about his dinner plans, but her errant thoughts pictured Winston laughing amid a crowd of guys, enjoying life. Emma picked up a rock and flung it.

"Wow. That's some arm you have on you," Luke said.

"Oh, shut up!" Emma clasped her hand over her mouth.

Luke laughed. "That's almost cussin' for a librarian."

Emma rubbed her palms over her hot cheeks. "Please forgive me. I don't know what came over me."

Luke picked up a small stone and palmed it. "The atmosphere changed the minute I mentioned my Bible study group."

"Where I imagine Winston will be." Her voice sounded stiff.

"Let's pretend Winston is the monster you believe him to be—do you think your anger hurts him?"

Emma picked up another rock and threw it. "No."

"So you get you're the only one tormented by not controlling your emotions." Luke picked up a flat stone and fingered it.

They walked in silence until they reached the river, and Luke skipped the rock across the water. "There's a bench. Let's rest here for a minute."

Emma scooted to the edge.

Luke grinned. "I won't bite." He wiped his palms on his slacks. "Can I ask you a personal question?"

"You can ask, but I might not answer."

"Fair enough. You don't have to tell me the answer, but I want you to think about this."

"Go on." Emma lifted her chin.

"What's your biggest weakness?"

"You first." Emma sat up straight, feeling pleased with herself for volleying his question.

He stared at the water for a long time. At last, he answered. "I can't seem to keep to a schedule. When someone calls with a need, my first reaction is to drop everything."

"That doesn't sound like a weakness." Emma frowned.

"Tell that to the other person left waiting for me. It's one of the reasons I'm not married. I don't think I could balance being a pastor and having a family—when I feel it's my calling to work with underprivileged kids." He sighed heavily.

No room in his life for a family. How awful. Doesn't he get lonely? Empathy dissolved the wall she'd been attempting to build. One glance at him and her heart fluttered. Just her luck to be smitten with a man who didn't want a family, when all she'd ever wanted was a home with a kid hanging out of every window.

"I had a fiancée once though." He added softly.

Emma crossed her leg and tapped her toe anxiously on the hard earth, but didn't know what to say to that, so she remained quiet.

"Now it's your turn. What's your biggest weakness?" Luke turned to her.

"Mother would say I spend too much time with my nose in a book, and my best friend Casey would tell you I'm too hard on myself."

"I didn't ask what others think." Luke crossed his arms.

Emma chewed the inside of her lip. "It's a tie between controlling my anger and lacking the backbone to stand up to Mother."

Luke gave a wry smile. "I'd say very few people defy your mother's wishes, but I think Harley might be up to the challenge."

"Yes. I think Mother might have met her equal."

He chuckled. "So let's say controlling your anger is your biggest weakness?"

Emma shrugged. "Okay. I have anger issues."

"Do you know the secret to turning a weakness into a strength?"

"If I did, it wouldn't be my weakness."

"I hadn't guessed you to have such a smart mouth."

"I am a librarian."

Luke chuckled. "You are not the person you pretend to be."

"No one is."

"True." He sighed. "The secret of turning a weakness into a strength is to acknowledge it, and then to help someone else with the same problem. It's why I work with kids who feel unworthy and unloved."

Emma's mouth hung open. Was he saying he felt unworthy and unloved?

"Earth to Emma."

Emma blinked. "But how can I help someone when I don't know how to help myself?"

"You're the librarian. Look it up." Luke stood.

Emma wanted to throw something at him. "I'm sure Harley's ready to be rescued from Mother."

"I'd bet good money on it."

"You don't talk like a preacher."

"Finally, a compliment."

Emma studied him—his dark eyes looked directly into hers. Oh, she could drown in those dark pools. The desire to lean in and touch his bearded cheek made her fists clench. She could feel her cheeks blushing. *This is bad.* No way would she ever get involved with a preacher, a man with a tattoo no less, who didn't want to juggle his church duties with a family. She must be losing her mind. She needed to go for a run and focus on something other than her sinful thoughts. *Lord, have mercy.*

CHAPTER EIGHT—EMMA

Emma spent the afternoon reading while Harley played with Pepper in the backyard. The schnauzer never tired of chasing a ball. Didn't Harley's arm ever give out? After going for a long run, Emma showered, changed, and called up the stairs. "We leave for Casey's in ten minutes."

Harley stomped down. "Why are we going to her house?"

"Sorry, I should have mentioned it, but it's routine for me to share Chinese takeout on Sunday evenings with Casey, and we give each other manicures."

Harley looked like she'd swallowed sour milk.

"It will be fun," Emma said. "It's sort of our girlfriend time together each week."

"But we have leftovers from lunch."

"You can take your to-go box if you like, but I'm craving Chinese."

Harley glanced at her fingernails. "Do I have to get a manicure?"

"Why not give it a try? It might help you break the habit of chewing your nails."

Harley put her hands behind her back. "I don't chew my nails."

Emma cocked her head. It wouldn't help to argue. "My mistake. If you'll put Pepper in her crate, we can go."

Harley sighed. "Whatever."

When Emma pulled her Honda into Casey's drive, Harley's mouth hung open. "It's a normal house."

Emma studied Casey's bungalow. "What were you expecting?"

"I don't know, something more like your house."

"Chris and I used to live in a house very similar to Casey's, but smaller. I miss it—and the closets."

Harley shrugged. "If you don't have a lot of stuff, you don't need so many closets."

"Good point. Casey uses her spare bedrooms for closets. Shoes fill up one room."

"If she's so rich, why doesn't' she go get a manicure at a salon?"

"We enjoy painting each other nails."

Casey opened her front door in her bare feet. "You're late." A rip at the knee showed her creamy skin, and a low-cut oyster-colored boyfriend sweater clung to her curves.

Harley trudged up the front steps carrying her to-go boxes, muttering under her breath.

"What's that?" Casey asked.

"Supper," Harley scowled.

"Don't you like Chinese food?" Casey arched a brow.

"I guess, but I don't like to waste food," Harley growled.

Emma shrugged. "That's more for us."

After they'd stuffed themselves, Casey pulled out her manicure supplies. "Are you sure you don't want to try it, Harley?"

She shook her head. "Can I watch TV?"

Casey handed her the remote control. "Sure thing, hon."

Harley scrolled through the listings, then stopped on a drama about the witness protection program. Emma cringed at the language, but Casey winked at her.

Girl talk filled the next hour—Emma probed Casey about Daniel. "So you must have invited him to church."

"I did. And he's already asked me out for Friday night."

"Good for you."

Casey blew on her lavender polish. "What I'd like to know is how your lunch went with a certain good-looking preacher-man."

Emma concentrated on painting the nails on Casey's other hand. "Mother was the one who invited him to eat with us."

"What do you think about the preacher, Harley?"

Harley harrumphed. "If he's a man, he's no good."

"What makes you say that?" Emma and Casey shared a look.

"Experience." Harley turned back to the television.

Emma wondered again about the bruises from the doctor's report and the creepy boyfriend comment. Would Harley ever trust her enough to tell her the truth? It would take time, but Emma had patience. She didn't want to press Harley because of the social worker's warning from the first night that Harley might try to run away. For now, Emma would give her some space.

Emma tightened the top on the nail polish. "Pretty. What do you think, Harley?"

Harley barely glanced at Casey's hand. "It's okay."

"Are you sure you don't want to choose a color?"

"And make the princesses at school think I want to be like them? No thanks." Harley rolled her eyes. "I ain't like them."

Casey held her hand out and admired her nails. "Thank goodness for that. It kills me the way most girls your age copy each other's style. They come into the boutique wanting to buy the same outfit as their friends and ignore my good advice."

Harley frowned. "'Cause they're stupid."

Emma cringed at the hateful word. Didn't all girls want to fit in? She'd been so awkward at Harley's age, as had Casey with her wild hair yet to be tamed and teeth too big for her face. Thank goodness they'd had each other.

That's what Harley needed. A friend. A real friend, and Emma knew without a doubt she could be Harley's friend, if only she'd let her.

On Monday evening, Emma watched a YouTube video of Paula Deen and her son making speedy mini-meatloaves. Other than microwaving frozen dinners, Emma had no culinary skills. Chris had been the one who enjoyed preparing meals, and her job was to clean up afterwards. The desire to provide healthy food for Harley prompted her to scour the internet for easy meal plans. Emma bit her lip. The dish in progress called for fresh thyme, which she didn't have. A quick search of her spice rack revealed a jar of the dried herb. Emma dumped a handful into her palm and added it to the mixture of ground beef and chopped onions. She looked at the bottle again and squinted at the small print but didn't see an expiration date.

A knock sounded from the back door. "Yoo-hoo!" Minnie's cheerful voice made her smile.

"I'm in the kitchen," Emma filled the muffin tin with blobs of meatloaf.

"I never thought I'd live to see the day," Minnie beamed a smile. "You're cooking."

"I've turned on the oven before." Emma washed her hands, then placed the pan inside the oven and set the timer.

The powder-blue velour tracksuit Minnie wore complimented her caramel colored skin—a far cry from the ugly gray double-knit uniform Emma's grandfather had insisted his long-time housekeeper wear.

Minnie placed a sealed Tupperware container on the counter. "I baked chocolate-chip cookies, and I wanted to meet your girl-child."

Emma hugged her aged friend, inhaling the familiar scent of Esteé Lauder's Youth Dew perfume, and sighed. "Thank you for the cookies."

Minnie peeked inside the oven. "What are you baking?"

"Mini-meatloaves. They'll be ready in about twenty minutes."

"Uh, huh."

"It's Paula Deen's recipe."

"You can't go wrong there. I guess I'm old fashioned, baking mine in a loaf pan."

"But that takes over an hour."

Minnie tsked. "You're always in a hurry."

"Can you stay for dinner?"

"I don't want to impose."

"You could never do such a thing."

Minnie opened a kitchen drawer, removed an apron, and examined a boiling pot. "These potatoes are about to scorch." She turned the knob on the stove, and the flame disappeared. "Where is the child?"

"Upstairs. I'll get her." Emma went to the foot of the stairs. "Harley, can you come down? Minnie's here, and she brought cookies."

Seconds later, Harley's boots beat out a quick rhythm. Her worn flannel shirt almost reached her knees and a black knit cap covered most of her butchered hair.

Minnie folded her hands and rested them on her ample stomach, her dark eyes twinkling. "It's good to have the stairs making house music with the beat of a young person's steps."

Harley stopped in front of Minnie. "Your cookies are great."

"Thank you." Minnie extended her hand. "I'm Minnie Edwards."

Harley shook her hand. "I'm Harley West. Nice to meet you."

Emma's chest swelled.

"The pleasure is mine." Minnie let go of her hand. "Emma didn't tell me how pretty you are."

Harley looked away.

"Emma, you will need a new broom so you can sweep away all the young pups who will sniff around."

Harley rolled her eyes but smiled. "What kind of cookies did you bring?"

"Chocolate chip. What's your favorite cookie?

She shrugged. "I eat anything."

Minnie rubbed her jaw. "We'll just have to find out. I make a tasty snickerdoodle, and my sugar cookies will melt in your mouth." Minnie took the top off the plastic container. "Have a cookie."

"Thank you." Harley bit into it. "Mm. It's still warm."

"I'll bake some of my special recipes, and you and I can have a little experiment to decide which you like best."

"Hey! Maybe that's what I can do for my science project." Harley crammed the rest of the cookie into her mouth.

"You have a science project?" Emma sat up straight.

"Yeah. It's not due until after Christmas break, so I have a few weeks."

"I'll teach you to make cookies," Minnie said. "Then you can have all the science experiments you like."

"I'll help too," Emma said.

"No, ma'am." Minnie winked at Harley. "We want the child to get a good grade. But maybe you should join us … as a student."

"Why, if you're not going to let me help?" Emma stuck out her lower lip in a make-believe pout.

"So you can learn how to cook too. I won't be here forever, and you can't even make cornbread!" Minnie looked over her glasses at Harley. "Every self-respecting southern woman needs to know how to make biscuits and cornbread."

Harley's stomach growled.

"I heard that," Minnie said. "Let's finish dinner, and I'll work on a plan to teach you both how to cook everything southern."

They were about to sit down at the table when headlights showed in the drive. Within a minute, Casey entered carrying a pie with meringue piled high. "Mama sent me over with a chocolate pie to welcome Harley." Casey placed the pie on the counter.

"Just what we needed." Emma said cheerfully. "Now we can save Minnie's cookies for tomorrow."

"I'm eating cookies," Harley said.

"Why not have both?" Emma pulled out a chair.

"Now I know I'm living' right." Minnie leaned toward Harley. "Jolene Bledsoe wins a blue ribbon every year at the county fair with her chocolate pie."

"I'll call her later to thank her." Emma sat down. "Can you stay for dinner?"

"I've eaten, but I wouldn't say no to one of Minnie's cookies." She looked Harley up and down. "I love your grunge look. That's exactly how I dressed in New York when I wanted to blend in."

"I ain't believing that," Harley scraped the floor with her chair.

"No one ever recognized me with a knit cap on my head, but here in Weldon, it's impossible to disappear."

Harley frowned.

They settled themselves around the table and Emma cleared her throat. "Minnie, will you do us the honor of blessing the food?"

"It's my pleasure." Minnie took Emma's and Harley's hands and bowed her head. "Thank you, Father, for this day, for our friendship, and the love between us. Bless this food to our bodies so that we may be of service to you. In Jesus's name I pray, amen."

Gratitude infused Emma's being ... she was no longer eating a microwave dinner alone. But then she placed the first bite of meatloaf into her mouth, and bitterness blanched her tongue. "It's awful."

Minnie took a tentative taste. "Just a bit too much thyme."

"I should have used a measuring spoon."

"I'll bet Ms. Deen used fresh thyme and you used dry."

"I didn't think it would matter." Emma gulped her sweet tea.

"Dried herbs' flavors are concentrated, so you use less." Minnie patted her shoulder. "I've made the same mistake."

Harley popped half a mini-meatloaf in her mouth and gulped. "Just swallow it quick and it's not so bad." She crammed a bite of potatoes into her mouth, froze, and swallowed. "Forget the meatloaf. These potatoes are GOAT."

"I beg your pardon," Minnie said.

"Greatest of all time," Harley mumbled with her mouth full. She stuffed another spoonful into her mouth and closed her eyes. "Mmm."

"I whipped them with real butter and heavy cream," Minnie said.

Casey's face brightened. "I didn't realize these are your potatoes. I assumed they were Emma's favorite scorched version." Casey dipped her finger into Emma's potatoes and moaned. "Heavenly."

Emma drummed her fingers on the table. "Would you like a plate?"

Casey looked longingly at the mashed potatoes. "No thank you, I'm watching my weight."

For the first time, Harley joined the dinner conversation. Emma recognized Minnie's magic touch. While growing up, Emma had longed for Minnie's company at dinner, but Grandfather thought it inappropriate to eat with the help.

Every evening, Minnie had placed food on the table, grabbed her purse, and wished everyone a good evening. It had seemed to Emma every drop of joy left the house with her.

Thank goodness Minnie never held Grandfather's obnoxiousness against her. Instead, she'd showered Emma with love and chatter.

After savoring a piece of chocolate pie, Minnie glanced at the clock. "I best be getting on home." She placed her napkin on the table and stood. "But first, I'll help you clear the table."

"No, ma'am," Emma stood. "You're my guest. Thank you for staying and helping me finish dinner."

"It doesn't seem right to leave you with all this mess." Minnie waved her hand toward the table.

"I'll help her," Casey rubbed her palms together. "And I'll make her pay me in cookies,"

"I'll drop off a batch at your boutique," Minnie said. "It's been nice getting to know you, Harley. Are you free on Saturday morning to bake cookies?"

Harley shrugged. "I guess. What kind of cookies are we gonna make?"

"It's your science experiment. You tell me."

Harley bit her lip. "Maybe peanut butter. No. Change that. Maybe something with chocolate."

"Oh! I have a secret recipe for chocolate-peanut butter cookies."

Emma eyes widened. "I love those."

Minnie smirked. "Your favorite cookie is like your favorite book."

Emma frowned, confused.

"The one that's in your hand, that's your favorite."

"You've got that right." Casey laughed.

Minnie picked up her purse, which was the size of a small suitcase. "I'll be here at ten o'clock on Saturday morning to bake cookies."

Casey smoothed her hand over her hip. "Between Mama's pies and your cookies, I'll be broad as a bulldozer."

Minnie threw back her head and laughed. "I'll bet Daniel Sheppard will like seeing you with a little more meat on your bird bones." She opened her arms and gave Emma a hug, next Casey, then she stood in front of Harley with her arms open. Harley hesitated but gave a quick embrace. Minnie ambled toward the door.

Later, Emma reflected on the success of the evening. Even though the meatloaf had been horrible, she hadn't had such a good time in her home since becoming a widow.

It had been nice to see Harley eat at an almost normal pace, even though she'd yet to open up about her missing mother. Poor Harley. She must be worried.

CHAPTER NINE—EMMA

During the following week, tensions between Emma and Harley eased, and they fell into a routine. After school, Harley walked to the library, and later they'd leave for home together. After greeting Pepper and enjoying Minnie's cookies, they'd part ways. Harley entertained the chubby dog, giving Emma time for her daily run. Each evening. Emma made simple meals— grilled cheese sandwiches with canned tomato soup, burgers and fries, and frozen lasagna. For dessert, they enjoyed the chocolate-peanut butter cookies Minnie and Harley had baked on the previous Saturday.

The shared meals were quiet, even though Emma attempted to draw Harley into the conversation. After dinner, Emma convinced Harley to watch television with her in the den rather than scurrying upstairs. They watched the same series each evening—*In Plain Sight*. It featured a female US marshal helping people start new lives in the Federal Witness Protection Program. Emma sat on the edge of her seat and flinched at the coarse language, but Harley didn't seem to notice. Still, the main character exuded confidence and integrity, and men respected her. The federal agent reminded Emma of her mother. Of course,

Virginia never used foul language, but she still managed to win verbal battles with her sharp wit and tongue.

On Friday, as was her usual habit, Emma attended the weekly Rotary Club luncheon. Her job required her to be active in many community organizations, although she generally disliked networking and making small talk. Emma preferred real conversations with friends where she didn't have to worry about saying the wrong thing.

At this particular lunch, Bill Wilson, the president of the library board, motioned for her to come over. Next to him stood Luke Davis. Emma's mouth went dry. *Not again.*

Mr. Wilson said, "Hello, Emma. Allow me to introduce you to our guest speaker today. This is Dr. Luke Davis."

Emma smiled tightly. "I met Dr. Davis when he filled in for Brother Bob at church."

"It's nice to see you again." Luke extended his hand. "I thought we'd agreed you'd call me Luke."

Emma's breath caught. No one should be so darn good-looking. She didn't want to shake his hand but she couldn't be rude. His rough hand swallowed hers and her fingers tingled. "N-nice to see you too." *Breathe.*

"I wondered if I'd see you today," Luke said.

Across the room, Virginia wove her way through the crowd toward them. "Dr. Davis. It's so good to see you."

"Hello, Mayor Willoughby."

"Please, call me Virginia. Thank you for agreeing to speak to our little group on such short notice."

"I'm glad you called," Luke said.

Emma ground her teeth. *That woman.*

"Dr. Davis is not only a wonderful preacher, but he also teaches woodworking to at-risk youth," Virginia all but cooed to Bill Wilson. "I'm hoping someone from our community can replicate his program."

So that's why his hands were so callused. Emma linked her fingers behind her back.

Luke pointed to a table laden with hand-turned wooden bowls and platters. "Let me show you some of our work."

Emma ran her finger around the lip of a bowl. Had Winston Meador crafted one of these? She jerked her hand away. "They're b–beautiful." She gulped. "Are the artists the same men who attend your Bible study?"

He nodded. "A few, but Winston isn't one of them."

Emma stiffened. Could he read her mind? She picked up a large bowl. "This piece is exquisite. I've never seen wood like this." Random dark splotches of snowflake-like patterns covered the cream-colored wood.

"It's from a common maple tree. Those dark flecks were created by rot."

"It's so unusual." She rotated it in her hand.

"At first, I rejected the wood."

"But why?"

"I thought it too far gone, too damaged, but I wanted see if I could salvage something from the tree's former glory."

"So this unique speckling of the wood is from decay."

"Yes. That's nature's touch. I've learned the most unique pieces come from logs scarred by lightning and weather, but it takes patience and hard work to reveal the beauty. It can be the same with the young men with whom I work."

Emma swallowed a lump in her throat. "So you crafted this bowl?"

"Yes, ma'am."

"You're an artist."

He shrugged. "Just a simple carpenter. There's something about turning the wood that's healing for me, and for the men I'm counseling."

A bell-tone sounded. "That means we're ready to get started," Emma said.

"Maybe we can talk more after the program," Luke said.

"I'm sorry, but I'll be in a hurry to return to the library."

"I understand." Luke left her to sit at the head table.

Virginia took her by the elbow and whispered. "No one minds if you're a little late returning from lunch. After all, you're the one in charge at the library."

Emma's phone vibrated, and she glanced at it. *Weldon Middle School*. "Excuse me, Mother. I need to answer this."

She hit the accept button, and she stepped out the side door to the parking lot. "Hello?"

"Is this Mrs. Baker?"

"Yes."

"This is Patty Gamble, Principal Miller's assistant."

"Yes. What can I do for you?"

"I'm sorry to be the bearer of bad news, but as Harley West's guardian, we need you to come to the school."

Every muscle in Emma's body tensed. "Is Harley okay?"

"She's fine, but she and another classmate had a little cat spat. Mr. Miller instructed me to hold them both until the parents or guardians can meet with him."

"I'll be right there."

She walked with purpose to her car after quickly apologizing to the table for her sudden exit. A few minutes later, she stood in the office at the middle school, and Mrs. Gamble handed her a visitor's tag. "This way, please."

She led Emma to the principal's office, where Harley sat outside his door. In the next seat, Regina Alexander, a girl who also attended Emma's church, sat with one leg crossed over the other, her foot swinging.

Emma rushed to Harley. "Are you all right?"

"I will be, as soon as I give that lying, cheating—"

"She's a liar!" Regina's nostril's flared, her face crimson. She pushed a strand of blonde hair behind her ear.

"That's no way for either of you to talk." Emma sat down in the chair on the other side of Harley and squeezed her hand. Harley snatched it away, then slumped in the chair, her knee bobbing up and down.

After a few minutes, Mrs. Gamble returned with Regina's mother, Alecia. The scent of gardenias filled the air. In high school, Alecia and her pack of friends had teased and tormented Casey and Emma and christened them with the ugly nicknames Big Bird and Big Brain.

Sweat trickled down Emma's back. Alecia's mean streak had been wider than the Mississippi. Emma stood up, crossed her arms, and planted herself in front of Harley.

Principal Rod Miller rubbed his jaw, looked at Alecia, and then at Emma. "Ladies, if you'll join me."

Alecia looked perfect in a pair of black slacks and a creamy cashmere sweater. The soot-colored leather purse slung over her shoulder sported a Gucci insignia. Emma smoothed her hair with her hands and lifted her chin. She'd do her best to emulate her mother. No one would get away with bullying Harley.

The four entered the office, and Regina sat in a chair to the right. Harley dropped into a seat in the opposite corner. Alecia and Emma both stood erect in front of the principal's desk. "What's this about, Mr. Miller?" Emma asked.

"She's lying," Regina said.

Harley stared at the wall.

"Harley doesn't lie," Emma squared her shoulders.

Harley sat up straight and rubbed her sleeve across her face.

Alecia turned to face Emma. "I know you've always had a soft heart toward children, but this girl is dangerous."

"That's ridiculous," Emma said.

"Just look at her." Alecia narrowed her eyes.

Harley buried her hands in her camo coat.

"Choosing to shop somewhere other than the mall doesn't make someone dangerous. I'd say it makes her smarter than the average person."

"Her own mother abandoned her." Alecia extended her hand, pointing it at Harley.

Emma wanted to slap it down. "You don't know what you're talking about."

"Ladies, please have a seat." Mr. Miller dropped into his chair.

Emma moved to a chair next to Harley and Alecia sat in a chair on Regina's right, next to the office wall.

"Regina, perhaps we'll start with you." Mr. Miller gave her a long look. "Tell us why you're here."

"I don't know. She's the one who pushed me." Regina glared at Harley.

Mr. Miller's lips formed a thin line. "Security cameras are in every classroom and hall. Shall we watch the tapes together?"

Regina's eyes blazed at Mr. Miller.

"Have it your way." Mr. Miller turned to his computer screen.

"Wait." Regina bit her lip. Sighing, she turned to face her mother. "With dance practice last night, I didn't have time to finish my homework. When Harley left her worksheet on the desk, I took it without thinking." She cast her eyes down to her lap. "I'm sorry."

Mr. Miller tapped his pen on the desk. "Excuse me, but I think you owe your first apology to Harley."

Regina looked at her mother with a raised brow, then crossed her arms and leg, remaining silent.

"Taking someone else's work and turning it in as your own is a serious offense." Mr. Miller clicked his pen. "You signed the acknowledgment that signified you read and understood our school's handbook, which includes our policies."

Regina shrugged. "I guess."

Mr. Miller took off his glasses and pinched the bridge of his nose. "If you check the code of conduct section, it states a student cannot take part in school sports teams if caught stealing or cheating."

Regina rolled her eyes. "I don't play sports." Her smarmy tone made Emma grimace.

"The cheerleading squad is a sports team. Your actions disqualify you from cheering for the rest of the school year."

Both mother and daughter gasped. "That's unfair!" Alecia exclaimed.

"What's unjust is taking someone else's homework and then calling her a liar." Mr. Miller sat up straight and clasped his hands in front of him.

Alecia lowered her voice. "I'll take this to the school board."

"That's up to you, but I encourage you to think about it. Do you want an audience to watch your daughter helping herself to someone else's work? When people make bad decisions, there are consequences."

Mr. Miller dropped his chin and looked Harley square in the face. "The same goes for Harley. There are consequences for her poor choice."

"But she's the victim." Emma wiped her damp palms on her slacks.

"There's more that happened. Harley, would you like to explain the rest?" His face softened. "It will be better if you tell your side of the story."

Emma placed a hand on Harley's agitated knee. "Nothing you say can make me take her side." Emma jerked her head toward Regina.

Harley glared at Regina. "I went to sharpen my pencil. When I got back, I couldn't find my homework so I had to take a zero." Harley turned and looked out the window.

"Go on." Mr. Miller clicked the pen again.

"When she had the nerve to brag about it in the hallway, it made me so mad." Harley made a fist, and her eyes filled with tears.

Mr. Miller cleared his throat. "If Mr. Warren hadn't intervened, Regina's face might—"

"She had it comin' to her!" Harley yelled.

"Violence is never the right choice," Mr. Miller's voice was terse. "I know this seems unfair, but our school board also has zero tolerance for violent behavior. Regardless of what Regina said and did, it doesn't justify attacking her. I'm sorry, Harley, but I'm suspending you for two days."

"But under the circumstances, don't you think that's too severe?" Emma twisted her wedding band.

"My decision stands." Mr. Miller shuffled the papers on his desk. "Harley made a bad choice. In the future, I hope you'll choose to come to one of your teachers or to me."

"I ain't a snitch." Harley hunched into herself and stared at the floor.

"Harley can log onto her school account on Monday and collect homework assignments." Mr. Miller stood. "The suspension doesn't mean she's not responsible for the work."

"I understand." Emma squeezed Harley's knee.

Mr. Miller walked to the door and opened it. "Ladies."

Alecia's face turned a deep scarlet. She stood.

"But Mom," Regina wailed.

"We'll talk about this at home," Alecia's eyes glittered, and she strode from the room with her chin lifted.

"Thank you for coming." Mr. Miller glanced down the hallway.

Emma adjusted the strap of her purse. "Thank you for investigating the incident."

Principal Miller sighed. "Sadly, it's a big part of my job."

CHAPTER TEN—EMMA

Back in the car, Harley stared out the window.

Emma drove toward the library. What could she say? How could she help her? "I went to school with Regina's mother."

"Is she as mean as Regina?"

"When we were about nine years old, she cut Casey's braid because Mrs. Bessie asked Casey instead of Alecia to play the part of Mary in the Christmas pageant."

"What did Casey do?"

"She cried, but even with short hair, she still made a beautiful Madonna."

"Casey should have turned her bald."

"Striking back is not the answer."

Harley balked. "But you have to stand up for yourself."

Emma parked the car in the library's parking lot and rubbed her temple. "A boy standing up for himself in a fight killed my husband. An accident, or so he claimed, but ..." She shrugged.

Harley jerked open the car door.

Emma followed her. "You can start your homework in my office."

Harley glared at her. "I'm sick of being with you."

Emma squared her shoulders. "You will be by the time your suspension ends."

"What do you mean?"

"You're with me, by my side, through the weekend and your two days of suspension."

Harley's jaw dropped.

"Apparently, you need adult supervision." Emma hated that her voice sounded exactly like her mother's.

Harley threw her backpack on the ground. "You're not my boss."

"I'm your guardian." Emma planted her fist on her hips.

With clenched fists, Harley's arms vibrated. She squeezed her eyes shut.

Emma steeled herself for the explosion. *Harley and I have more in common than I thought.*

The expected rant didn't come. Harley took a deep breath, grabbed her backpack from the ground, and stomped toward the library.

"I'm proud of you," Emma called out.

Harley froze. "What?" She swerved around, her eyes wide.

"Just now, you controlled your temper. That takes real strength when you're furious."

Harley sniffed. "Can I have a Coke?"

The unexpected request made Emma pause. "Sure."

So they had the weekend together and Monday and Tuesday through the suspension. Emma had thought living with Grandfather stressful. If only she could retreat to her office, but no way would she reward Harley with an afternoon in her favorite chair. Maybe she should assign Harley a book to read. Emma felt a smile spread across her face. She'd find one on anger management for both of them to read and discuss. Her skin prickled. The last thing she'd expected to do was follow Luke's advice. The sneaky snake.

Two hours later, Emma glanced up from her work in the library to find Harley sitting across from her with her hands clasped behind her head, slumped in the chair, eyes closed. The book on anger management sat next to her, unopened.

"I suggest you get started."

Harley didn't open her eyes. "It's four days before I go back to school."

Emma leaned her elbow on the desk, rested her chin on her interlaced fingers, and her gaze fell on a stack of mail. She blew out a long breath and started sorting. Junk, bill, bill, junk. Her hand froze. Winston's handwriting on the envelope made her vision blur, then a fire burned through her.

"What's wrong?" Harley bolted upright in her chair.

Emma covered her hot face with her hands. "It's nothing."

"You're lying."

Emma cringed. No one had ever said such a thing to her. Her shoulders dropped. But Harley spoke the truth. "You're right." She rubbed her forehead. "It's a letter from the boy who killed Chris."

"How do you know it's from him?"

"The handwriting. This isn't the first one I've received."

"What did the other one say?"

"I didn't read it."

They sat staring at it.

Harley broke the silence. "We lived in the same trailer park."

"You know him?"

"Sort of. Sometimes we ended up walking to school at the same time."

Emma's gut twisted. "I'm sure he's sorry."

"Yeah, and my mom always said she was sorry, but that don't take away the beatings, or her sleazy boyfriend tryin' to corner me." Harley's eyes burned. "Or your husband being killed."

"So your mom beat you and her boyfriend ... " Emma couldn't say the rest.

Harley's face looked hard.

"Why didn't you tell the social worker?"

"What could she do about it? They're gone. GONE." Harley enunciated each letter. "Remember."

Emma pictured a slimeball pressing his ugly self against Harley. "I'm so—" No. She wouldn't say the word *sorry*. She blinked back tears. *Lord, give me the words.* She could almost hear Luke's voice. *Forgive.*

Harley might slug her if she mentioned forgiveness at this moment, but Luke was right. Somehow, they both needed to forgive, or anger would cripple them forever, just like Grandfather, who numbed his pain with alcohol. Perhaps some circumstance led Harley's mom, Anne West, to use the same poison. Emma couldn't let that happen to Harley. If Chris were still here, he'd know what to do.

"Let's go home." Emma turned off her computer, stuffed the envelope into her desk with the other mail and slung her purse over her shoulder. "I need a run."

They stopped at the circulation desk in front of Tammy. "I'm taking off early," Emma said.

"Good for you." Tammy gave her a thumbs up.

Emma strode toward the door, and Harley followed at a snail's pace. Hearing about Anne West beating Harley and men molesting the child tore at Emma's insides. She'd call and report this to Carol Carter.

No wonder Harley was angry. Never in Emma's life had she wanted to hurt someone, not even Winston Meador, but at this moment, if Harley pointed to a guy and said, "That's him," Emma would pick up a stick and chase him down. She drummed her fingers and waited for Harley to get in the car. They both needed counseling. Brother Bob might be able to help her. No. Harley would come closer to trusting a female counselor.

Harley slammed the car door and fastened her seatbelt in slow motion.

Maybe Brother Bob could suggest someone, Emma thought, but then the answer came to her. *Minnie.* No one had a more sympathetic ear or more wisdom than her. Perhaps she could add lessons for the heart while teaching them to cook. Yes, she'd ask Minnie to help. They both needed to learn how to replace their anger and bitterness with Minnie's joy. Emma smiled as she remembered Minnie's words. *Happiness is a choice. Only a foolish person chooses anything else, and I ain't that.*

For dinner, Emma picked up a rotisserie chicken from the market with a medley of steamed vegetables. It wasn't a terrible meal, but no one would ever call the food delicious. Too bad Casey had a date with Daniel. She could use the company and a sympathetic ear.

Emma sighed. She was glad Casey and Daniel seemed to be turning into a couple. It was far past time for Casey to have a serious relationship with the right kind of man.

Later, Emma sat alone in the den reading. Her home library only included her most beloved books. Reading snippets of favorite passages was like savoring a cup of tea with a cherished friend for Emma.

A car door slammed, and a few seconds later, Casey opened the back door without knocking, her eyes blazing.

Daniel followed her in. "Just cool off."

Emma's eyes widened. "What's going on?"

"Is Harley okay?" Casey threw her purse on the sofa.

"Of course. She's upstairs."

"Alecia Alexander spewed a slew of ugly things about Harley at the Triple D tonight." Casey narrowed her eyes.

"Oh, no." Emma put down her book.

"If Daniel hadn't been with me, I'd have tied her lying tongue in a knot." Casey paced in front of the fireplace. "Just thinking about what she said burns my biscuits."

I'm not the only one who needs a book on anger management. "What did Alecia say?"

"She called Harley dangerous."

"I guess she didn't mention her daughter took Harley's homework?"

Casey stomped around the room. "It's like I've been pulled by a vacuum right back to middle school. Her big-mouth daughter is not gonna get away with tormenting Harley the way Alecia and her bottom-feeder friends bullied us."

"Keep your voice down," Emma said.

Casey made a fist. "I'll knock both of them to kingdom come if she messes with you or Harley."

"Calm down," Emma said. "Mr. Miller dealt with Regina. He kicked her off the cheerleading squad. If you sit down, I'll tell you everything."

A few minutes later, Daniel patted Casey's knee. "I told you there was more to the story."

Emma's face softened. It seemed Daniel had changed his mind about Harley being trouble.

Casey was still angry, although her temper had cooled down a few degrees. "Alecia said that if I were any kind of a friend, I'd talk some sense into you."

"She's horrible." Emma tightened her ponytail.

"I told her I think about a dozen kids like Harley is exactly what you need."

"Thanks for that." Emma patted Casey's other knee. "But I'm learning that one is enough ... for now."

Hours later, Emma tossed and turned in her bed. It wouldn't take long for her mother to hear about Harley's detention.

Emma glanced at the alarm clock. It was too late to call her, but she'd get this task over with first thing in the morning. Four days with Harley by my side. Would their relationship improve or collapse? *Flip a coin.*

CHAPTER ELEVEN —LUKE

Luke awoke from a deep slumber as his phone rang on the bedside table. The digital alarm clock's fluorescent glow showed 2:15 a.m.. *Not good.*

He snatched his phone. "Hello. Luke Davis speaking."

"Luke. It's Eleanor, Bob Johnson's wife."

"Yes, ma'am. What's wrong?"

"Bob's going into surgery for an emergency appendectomy. Can you come?

"Yes, ma'am. Which hospital?"

"The medical center in Riverview."

"I'll be there within the hour."

"And Luke?"

"Yes."

"Pray while you drive. The surgeon thinks his appendix might rupture."

A heaviness pushed down on Luke's chest. *Oh, no. Father, help him.* "Already on it."

Two hours later, he sat holding Eleanor's hand silently praying.

The sleeves of the elderly woman's cardigan sweater were pushed up to her elbows. Strands of her salt-and-pepper hair had escaped from the usual tight bun at the nape of her neck. She squeezed his hand. "Before they took Bob into surgery, he said, 'Tell Luke, if he loves me, he'll feed my sheep.'"

The weight on Luke's shoulders doubled. "I'm not sure I'm cut from the right cloth for the Loving Chapel crowd."

Eleanor's face softened. "Nonsense."

The memory of his twelve-year-old self wearing dirty, secondhand clothes when he met Pastor Bob Johnson at church camp never left him. Abandoned by his mom on his grandmother's front porch, he'd lived a life of fending for himself. His grandmother made a living tending bar at a dive just across the state line and made it clear every day he wasn't her responsibility. The only reason she'd sent him to camp was because someone offered to pay his way. "Let someone else feed you," she'd said with glee.

He ran his hand through his hair. The people in Weldon would never accept him in the pulpit if they knew his pedigree.

A door swung open, and a doctor in green scrubs walked toward them with long strides, his mouth drawn down. Luke's gut twisted.

The physician's mask hung around his neck. He rubbed the stubble on his jaw and sat down next to Eleanor. "The appendix ruptured."

Eleanor gasped. "Lord, have mercy."

"I cleaned the abdominal cavity, and strong antibiotics are flowing through his IV."

Eleanor blinked rapidly. "May I see him?" Eleanor gripped Luke's hand.

The doctor nodded. "In a bit. He's still in the recovery room, and I'm going to move him to ICU. There's the risk of peritonitis, which can turn to sepsis."

Eleanor sat ramrod straight, her face white. "Are you a Christian, Dr. Connor?"

"I am."

"Then let us turn this over to the great physician." Eleanor turned to Luke. "Will you lead us in prayer?"

Luke kneeled in front of Eleanor and extended his palm to Dr. Conner, who took it and closed his eyes. Luke squeezed his eyes shut and waited a few seconds. "Lord, you tell us to come boldly to your throne of grace, that we may obtain mercy and find help in time of need. We are here, Lord, in need, feeling helpless and fearful for Bob's health, but we know fear does not come from you, and we are not defenseless because we have your power. We boldly ask for Bob's healing. Please give his doctors wisdom, and we ask of his caregivers to offer their very best to him. Be with Eleanor and meet her every need. Please provide her with your strength and fill her with your peace during this difficult time. Help us, Father, to act in a manner worthy of you. In all things, may your will be done. In Jesus's name, I ask these things. Amen."

Eleanor sighed. "Let's just hope and pray, for this one time, my will and His will are the same.

"Amen," Luke said.

CHAPTER TWELVE—HARLEY

Harley lay on her bed with her hands behind her head, staring at the ceiling. Minnie said she'd be by to bake cookies today. *Don't get your hopes up. She probably forgot.* A knock sounded on her door.

"Wake up, sleepy head. Minnie's here." Emma peeked inside.

Harley's spirits lifted. "In a minute." Harley rolled over and shoved aside Pepper, who gave a low growl. "Move over, you little varmint." Harley suppressed a smile. No way would she let anyone know she wanted to make cookies.

After a minute, she trudged to the bathroom and turned on the shower. Her stomach rumbled. A shower could wait. She quickly donned a faded T-shirt and sniffed the scent of the fabric softener. Clean clothes.

Emma had slipped a bundle of socks into her drawer, but Harley had ignored them even though her feet were cold. She lifted a pair and rubbed the soft yarn across her cheek. What were these things made of? She pulled them on and flexed her foot. *Who knew a pair of socks could feel so good?*

She walked into the kitchen and went straight for the cereal. Emma and Minnie sat at the kitchen table drinking coffee.

"Sleeping beauty is finally awake," Minnie said.

Harley winced at the lemon-colored velour track suite Minnie wore. It should be illegal to wear such a bright color.

"You look like you need a little pick-me-up." Minnie started singing "Walking on Sunshine."

Emma took the spoon from her coffee and pretended it was a microphone and joined Minnie.

Harley cringed. How could they be so cheerful?

They stopped singing and giggled.

"Y'all are crazy," Harley removed a gallon of milk from the refrigerator.

"No, ma'am!" Minnie hooted. "Crazy is feeling lonely and blue, and I ain't that." She broke into an old song Harley remembered hearing on the radio.

Harley placed her hands over her ears. "Okay, okay, I give up."

Minnie threw her head back and laughed.

Harley rolled her eyes and filled a bowl with Cheerios. "I need to eat."

She joined them at the table and started shoving cereal into her mouth, while Emma scribbled notes into a notebook.

"What are y'all doing?" Harley gulped a mouthful of cereal.

"I'm working on a list of food for Thanksgiving. Usually, I go to Oak Grove with Mother for Thanksgiving lunch, but I thought it would be nice to celebrate the holiday here, with all the fixings."

Harley lifted a brow. Emma could barely make grilled cheese sandwiches without scorching them. She shrugged. At least there were always microwave dinners in the freezer. They wouldn't starve.

"What do you want to add to the menu?" Emma lifted her pen.

Harley bit her lip. "I've never had a real Thanksgiving meal, like what's on TV. Turkey with real dressing."

"It's on the list." Emma held her pen at the ready.

"Speaking of lists, I made a list of my favorite cookies and wrote down the recipes for you in a notebook." Minnie dug through her enormous purse. "I thought it might help you figure out how you are going to turn baking cookies into a science project."

Harley took the binder from Minnie and thumbed through the pages. "Some of these look complicated."

"Not at all." Minnie clasped her hands in front of her. "The key to good baking is to follow the instructions, step-by-step and to measure the ingredients."

"I guess I can do that," Harley studied a handwritten recipe.

"There's no guessing in baking," Minnie dropped her purse onto the floor with a thud. "And you have to have patience. You can't hurry cooking and end up with something decent to eat."

Harley kept turning pages. *It must have taken Minnie a long time to put this together.* "What type of cookies are we baking today?"

Minnie stood and removed a box of butter from the grocery bag on the counter. "Oatmeal-raisin cookies."

"I have butter," Emma said.

"This is unsalted butter, and it needs to be at room temperature." Minnie set it aside. "I'd say it's about ready. Let's gather the other ingredients while the oven heats up."

Minnie opened the kitchen drawer and removed three aprons. "Ladies, let's get to work."

An hour later, Harley removed the first batch of cookies from the oven and placed them on a wire rack. Her mouth watered.

"They have to rest for ten minutes." Minnie filled a cup with fresh coffee. "Then we'll have our own experiment. We'll see who can eat the most cookies."

Emma's pocket vibrated, and she removed her phone. "Hi, Mother." She turned her back to them. "If you'd give me the chance to explain." Emma walked toward the front of the house. "Harley's fine. Of course, she didn't start it." Her voice faded.

Harley sat down hard at the table and Minnie patted her hand.

"It will be all right, hon."

"So you heard."

"Emma said you had a little trouble at school."

"But it wasn't my fault. It's not fair."

"Honey, you're talking to a black woman who's lived her whole life in the South. Life is not fair, but let me tell you what makes it better." She paused. "Freedom."

Harley huffed. "What does freedom have to do with Regina stealing my homework?"

"You are free to choose your response—in every situation. I've learned to choose kindness and happiness."

"No one chooses to be happy if someone steals from them."

"That's a natural response, but think about this. If you allow someone to ruin your day, you've given them power over you."

"So. What should I have done?" Harley crossed her arms.

"Told the teacher your work disappeared while you were at the pencil sharpener."

"But she wouldn't have believed me."

"You don't know that, and Emma mentioned the school's camera showed exactly what happened. Always tell the truth and whatever the outcome, refuse to allow it to ruin your day by meditating on good things. Don't allow someone to steal your joy."

"But how?"

"My mother and grandmother were domestic workers for many unhappy people—impossible to please."

"They should have quit."

"They had to work to provide for us children. My father died when housing tobacco in a barn. The rafter broke and he fell to his death."

Harley's gasped. "That's awful."

"Mother and Granny were grateful for the work and felt blessed to live in a peaceful household with a supper table filled with food and surrounded by people they loved."

"But you shouldn't have to take crap from anyone."

Minnie smiled. "If you want to discover happiness, learn to ignore unpleasant people and forgive. Don't let their dirt stick to you. Walk around it."

"You have to stand up for yourself."

"That's pride talking, honey." Minnie gave a long sigh. "I had a long battle with pride." Her face looked mournful. "We'll talk about that later." She rose from the table. "I expect those cookies are ready to eat. Let's have one."

Harley grabbed a cookie and bit into it. Every muscle in her body relaxed when she tasted the melded flavors. "Wow!"

"We'll make snickerdoodles next week," Minnie said.

Emma joined them. "Sorry to be so long. Mother had a few questions."

"We heard," Harley said. "I guess everyone in town is talking about me."

"Nonsense, just the gossips in Alecia's circle. Don't worry about it. Folks don't know you, but they know the Alexanders can be ..." She wanted to say ugly. "Difficult. Don't think you're the first person to be their target. We'll walk into the sanctuary tomorrow with our heads held high."

"And be nicer than nice to them—act like the sweet Lord Jesus." Minnie patted Harley's hand.

"That'll aggravate them." Emma giggled.

"I hate to leave good company, but I need to be getting on home. First, let me show Harley something." Minnie reached for her purse, removed a small Bible, and adjusted her glasses.

"I've been thinking about our conversation, and this Scripture came to mind. It might help you understand my advice. *For freedom Christ has set us free; stand firm therefore, and do not submit again to a yoke of slavery.*

Minnie took off her glasses and cleaned them with a napkin. "You said it was important to stand up for yourself. I'm hoping you'll learn to let Jesus stand up for you. He's the real reason I'm free to choose my response in any situation. I'm free to choose happiness, no matter how I'm treated. I'm free to shield myself from hateful words and evil people. Their words cannot penetrate the armor of God. I'm free to choose to love my enemies, no matter what they do, and that, my friend, really irritates that ol' devil. Thanks to Jesus Christ living in me, I am free."

Harley crossed her arms in consternation. *What does free really mean?*

That evening, Harley wrapped her arms around herself as they walked downtown to the diner. Dot's Deluxe Diner glowed in pink neon. "So this is the Triple D"

"Yes, ma'am." Emma smiled. "The fried pies we enjoyed the other night came from here.

A woman whose name tag said *Dot* greeted Emma with a hug. "It's about time you brought this young'un to meet me." The waitress extended her hand to Harley. "Folks around here call me Mrs. Dot."

Harley squared her shoulders and clasped Mrs. Dot's hand just as Mrs. Virginia had demonstrated. "I'm Harley West. Nice to meet you."

Emma's chest seemed to swell as she passed a brown paper bag to Mrs. Dot.

Mrs. Dot looked over the top of her onyx cat-eye glasses. "What's this?"

"Minnie helped us bake oatmeal-raisin cookies today." Emma beamed a smile.

Mrs. Dot's face brightened. "No one ever gives me treats! Thank you, hon." She took the offering and slid it under the counter. "I'll save these for later." She escorted them to a booth and removed an order pad from her pocket. "What can I get you to drink?"

Harley ordered a Coke, and Emma asked for sweet tea with lemon. "I'll be right back."

Harley studied the dinner menu, waiting for Emma to order. Everything looked good.

She looked up from her menu to find Emma gazing at her. "You know what, that pixie cut is growing on me. You remind me of Katie Perry. She used to wear her hair in a similar style."

"Oh, brother. She's like ... ancient." Harley rolled her eyes, but she secretly felt good about what Emma said.

"I knew I'd find you here." Mrs. Virginia's voice broke through her musings.

Emma stood and grazed Mrs. Virginia's cheek with a kiss. "Why aren't you at the country club?"

"I'm on my way, but first, I wanted to tell you the news."

"Why didn't you call?"

"I tried, but the blasted call went directly to voice mail."

Emma bit her lip. "Uh, oh. I can't remember when I charged my phone last. I'll bet its dead in the bottom of my purse. What's wrong?"

"Let me sit down." Mrs. Virginia slid in the booth next to Emma. "Have you heard about Pastor Bob?"

"I haven't talked to anyone today except you, Minnie, and Harley." Emma removed her phone from her purse. "It's dead." Emma dropped the phone in her bag. "After baking cookies, we went to the library to check out cookbooks."

"Cookbooks?" Virginia frowned.

"I haven't told you, but I'm cooking a traditional Thanksgiving dinner."

The crease in Virginia's brow deepened. "You won't have time."

"Of course—"

"I volunteered you to organize the community Thanksgiving meal for Eleanor."

Emma's jaw dropped. "What?"

Mrs. Dot arrived at their table with their drinks. "I saw Virginia slip in so I added a sweet tea."

"Thank you, Dot." Virginia lifted the glass to her lips and sipped.

Mrs. Dot removed the pen from her beehive and held out her order pad. "What'll it be girls?"

"I'm not staying. I dropped by to tell Emma about Pastor Bob," Virginia said.

Dot looked sympathetic. "Bill Wilson told me about him. Poor Eleanor."

"What about Pastor Bob?" Emma asked.

Virginia and Mrs. Dot took turns sharing what they knew.

"Eleanor called me because she couldn't reach you," Virginia said. "She asked for you specifically to take over organizing the community Thanksgiving meal, and I said you'd be more than happy to do that for her."

"Doesn't anyone remember I have a landline?" Emma sipped her tea. "Maybe Harley will help me."

Harley held her palms out. "No way."

"We'll talk about it later." Emma said.

"I need to go," Virginia stood and left a few dollars on the booth table. "Others are expecting me. I'll call Eleanor and tell her not to worry."

She pecked Emma's cheek. "Enjoy your dinner. And Harley, your hair looks very nice this evening. The color suits you."

Harley narrowed her eyes. "I still ain't helping."

"If you stay with Emma long enough, you'll learn we serve."

"Serve who?"

"Each other. Eleanor needs Emma's help, and Emma could use your support." Virginia left the diner as quickly as she'd appeared.

Harley rolled her eyes.

Mrs. Dot lowered her reading glasses. "You never should

have said, *I ain't doing it*. When I say those words to her, I know I'm doomed." Then she winked. "If y'all don't order soon, we're likely to run out of food."

Harley ordered a double cheeseburger with fries.

"My mango fried pies are going fast." Mrs. Dot held her order pad at the ready.

Harley leaned across the table toward Emma. "Can I have dessert too?"

"Of course," Emma said.

"I liked that raspberry fried pie Emma brought back." Harley licked her lip. "Do you have any of those?"

"Nope." Mrs. Dot clicked her pen. "I make a different flavor every week."

"They're all wonderful," Emma said.

Harley shrugged. "I ain't never had a mango anything, but I'll give it a try."

Emma ordered and fiddled with her straw.

When their food arrived, Harley forced herself to eat slower, more mannerly. It seemed they'd eaten all day between the cookies and pizza delivery for lunch so she wasn't starving after all. The morning with Minnie had brightened the day, and Harley actually felt for once that her stomach wasn't in knots. Maybe even a little hopeful and happy.

When their fried pies arrived, Harley bit into the crusty goodness and moaned. "Man! Mangos are the best."

"Just you wait," Emma said. "Cranberry is my favorite."

"You said raspberry was your favorite."

Emma shrugged. "Minnie would say my favorite fried pie is—"

"The one in your hand." Harley rolled her eyes. "Wonder what flavor Mrs. Dot will fix next week?"

"We'll just have to come back and see," Emma said.
"I could get used to this." Harley patted her tummy.
Emma grinned. "Me too, hon. Me. Too."

CHAPTER THIRTEEN—LUKE

Luke sat in his boss's office and rubbed the stubble around his beard. He'd driven straight from the hospital to meet with Steve Watts, the head pastor of Westview Circle Church in Bowling Green, Kentucky. With three ancillary pastors on staff, Luke appreciated how they supported each other in ministry. As Luke explained to Pastor Steve about his previous night's vigil with Eleanor, the weight on his shoulders seemed to grow heavier.

"You must help Bob, and it will be a great opportunity for you to take the next step toward leading a congregation of your own."

Luke scratched his head. "I'm not the right guy for Weldon. I feel as if everyone is talking about me."

"I can guarantee you they are. That's the way it is in a small town."

"That's why I like Bowling Green. In a city of seventy-thousand, it's rare for someone to notice me."

Pastor Steve leaned back in his chair and steepled his fingers under his chin. "You're wrong. There's always someone watching and waiting for a preacher to make a wrong step. "

"But the congregation at Loving Chapel is so formal. It's like stepping back in time twenty years, maybe forty."

"Bob could have called on any number of men. Why do you think he asked specifically for you?" Pastor Steve lifted a brow.

"I don't know." Luke had failed at the first small church he'd pastored, and they were progressive. To step into the pulpit of a small-town church where everyone expected a perfect preacher with a spotless past? *No way.* He'd been down this road and blown it.

He liked being an associate pastor for a large congregation where no one paid too much attention to the ancillary staff.

"Bob believes in you, and so do I." Pastor Steve's voice sounded confident. "One thing I've learned is when we feel as if we're pushed outside our comfort zone, God's at work. What's really hindering your decision?"

Thoughts of Emma crossed his mind. He wasn't ready to tell anyone about his attraction to her. During their conversation after lunch last Sunday, she'd looked so beautiful sitting on the bench, and for a few brief seconds, he considered reaching for her hand. Then she'd turned her tear-filled eyes toward him, and he'd wanted to kiss away the hurt he'd caused. He wiped his palms on his jeans. "Not anything I'm ready to talk about."

Pastor Steve gave him a sympathetic look. "Let me pray for you."

During the prayer, Luke's burden drifted away. He owed so much to Bob, but more than that, he owed his salvation to Jesus. The scripture Eleanor had quoted came to mind. *If you love me, feed my sheep.* He wouldn't make Bob ask again. He'd do it.

When Pastor Steve said, "Amen," Luke looked up. "Thank you."

"I'll be praying for you."

"I'm counting on it."

Pastor Steve opened his planner. "Let's go over your schedule and figure out how we can rearrange things so you can take care of Bob's congregation."

Luke gulped. "I don't want to abandon the young men in my Bible study nor the guys in the Rocky Hills Juvenile Detention Center. Since I started going weekly, we're making real progress."

"You will be busy, but that's a good thing." Pastor Steve grinned. "My granny always said, 'No rest for the wicked and the righteous don't need none.'"

"I'm far from righteous."

"Not with Jesus, Brother. Not with Jesus."

An hour later, Luke strode toward his truck with a lighter step. He had a sermon to prepare for tomorrow, but first, he'd call the head deacon. Eleanor had given him the name and number of Tim Pitt, and the names of others who were sick or in the hospital that needed a visit this week. She'd said the deacons would step in and help.

He removed her list from his shirt pocket. How in the world could he get everything done? *Lord, you're going to have to take over, and if you don't mind, step on it!*

Luke sipped cold coffee and grimaced. For hours, he'd drunk too much coffee as he attempted to prepare an uplifting message of hope. When he spoke the words aloud, his sermon sounded trite. He sat in his one-bedroom apartment and stared at the wall. At last, he closed his laptop, bowed his head, and waited in the silence.

The old burden he'd given to the Lord repeatedly settled on him—the hurt and shame of being the kid no one wanted washed over him. A long sigh escaped.

He'd lay it all out for the congregation and tell them about growing up with a grandmother who tended bar, and his mother who'd disappeared without a trace.

The Scripture from the previous sermon came back to him. *In everything give thanks ...*

Luke often gave thanks for the rough circumstances from which he'd emerged because it allowed him to help other fatherless young men discover their heavenly father and their true worth.

The angst dissipated the moment he'd decided he would flat out tell the congregation at Loving Chapel everything. Maybe there would be someone in the crowd who needed to hear his testimony of what God had done in the life of an abandoned boy. The more he thought about it, his confidence grew.

"Thank you, Father." Luke went to bed. God would give him the words he needed tomorrow morning. He glanced at the clock. Make that *this* morning.

At nine o'clock on Sunday morning, Luke sat at one end of the conference room table with the twelve deacons of Loving Chapel. The head deacon, Mr. Pitt, sat at the other end of the table and said, "If Pastor Bob wants Dr. Davis to lead us, that's good enough for me."

A bald man, whose name Luke thought was Dennis, leaned forward. "I make a motion to appoint Dr. Davis interim pastor."

Another voice chimed in. "I'll second the motion."

Mr. Pitt stood. "All in favor?"

Only one deacon didn't raise his hand. A middle-aged man in a black suit sat in his chair rigid with his arms crossed and eyes narrowed.

"Motion carries," Mr. Pitt said. "Meeting adjourned."

Men shook hands with Luke as they filed out. The graying but stately man who'd failed to support Luke's appointment glared at him, then stood and made his way to him, his chest puffed out under his expensive suitcoat and tie.

"I'm sorry, but could you tell me your name again?" Luke extended his hand.

"I'm Arnold Alexander." The older, well-dressed and rather pretentious looking businessman spoke in a gruff voice as he narrowed his eyes and ignored Luke's hand. "I remember your grandmother—meaner than a rabid dog, and she cussed worse than any man I know."

Luke gave a tight smile. "Sounds like you knew her well."

"Well enough to know it's unlikely a grandson of hers could be a man of God."

"It's often hard for me to believe too. How is it you knew her? Were you one of her customers?"

Mr. Alexander's face turned purple under his starched white collar. He stood there, mouth open like a fish pulled from the water. When he didn't comment, Luke turned and left him standing there.

But Luke immediately regretted his words. He'd tried to tell Steve he wasn't the right preacher for Weldon. Luke squared his shoulders. It was rare for Bob to ask a favor. He wouldn't let him down.

Thirty minutes later, Luke stood at the door of the church greeting the members. The second looks from many in the congregation made him smile. He searched for Emma's face and he wondered what her reaction might be to seeing him. When she stood in front of him, his breath caught. The single men in Weldon were probably wearing out her front door knocking. He inhaled a soft floral scent.

"Are you surprised to see me?" Luke asked, giving her his best smile.

"Not really. We heard about Pastor Bob at the diner yesterday." Emma placed her purse on a table by the coat rack and started removing her coat.

"It seems we keep running into each other," Luke said. "Let me help you." He reached for Emma's coat. "What's new with you, Harley?"

Harley glared at him. "The principal kicked me out of school for fighting."

"Been there. Done that." Luke chuckled.

"It's just for two days," Emma said, "And she didn't get into a fight, she only shoved someone."

Harley muttered under her breath, "If she messes with me today, she'll wish she hadn't."

"She doesn't mean that." Emma said.

"Just watch me," Harley narrowed her eyes.

"I will," Luke said. "Thanks for the warning."

"Welcome to Loving Chapel." Emma shook his hand.

The moment she touched his hand he resisted the magnetic pull. *Did she feel it too?* It didn't matter. His past experience proved romance and ministry didn't mix.

A flash of pink lace against her skin under her crisp white blouse made him inhale sharply. Luke swallowed hard, leaned in and whispered in her ear. "You have a button undone."

She looked down, and crimson traveled all the way to the roots of her parted hair. Her palm flew to her chest and she rushed away.

Luke walked in the opposite direction out the front door. He hoped for a brisk breeze and cold rain. *Lord, have mercy.*

CHAPTER FOURTEEN—EMMA

Emma slid into the pew next to Casey, who elbowed her. "I guess I know what's got you all hot and bothered?"

"I don't know what you're talking about." Emma opened her bulletin.

Casey lifted a penciled brow and looked back over her shoulder. "Liar, and in the church of all places. I watched you and the preacher and your little square dance."

Emma wanted to walk out and leave, but tongues would wag. She couldn't believe Harley hadn't noticed her blouse undone. And to top off the morning, she'd received a scathing glance from her mother while trying to button her blouse.

Twice she'd made a fool of herself in front of Luke. Goodness, he must think her a bumbling exhibitionist.

A few minutes later, Emma forgot about her embarrassment as she listened to Luke's sermon, mesmerized. The picture he painted of a lost boy of twelve, at a crossroads when he'd met Pastor Bob, chilled her. Violence and abuse stained his childhood, yet he'd escaped thanks to Pastor Bob's intervention. She hoped she could be that person for Harley.

After hearing Luke's story, she remembered his comment about why he worked with kids who felt unworthy and unloved. As a parent, Virginia had many failings, but her strong love for Emma could never be questioned. Hearing of the good created by Luke's troubled past made Emma reflect on the teaching that God could take our very worst experiences and turn them around for His good. But what good could ever come from her husband being stabbed to death? *No way could God turn that to His good.*

The next morning, Emma and Harley drove to the library in silence. "Looks like someone has the Monday morning blues," Emma remarked as she parked her Honda.

Harley remained silent.

When they walked through the library's staff entrance, Harley said, "See ya," and turned toward the back of the library.

"Wait," Emma dropped her chin.

Harley turned.

"Sorry, but you're with me today." Emma gave a tight smile. "I told you Friday you would be by my side through the detention."

Harley's face turned dark, and her nostrils flared.

"This way." Emma turned and strode toward her office.

"Whatever."

Emma's shoulders relaxed and she greeted the other staff members and told them Harley would be with her today.

"That's great," Tammy said.

"It's better than listening to my teacher, old man Barnes, say the same things over and over," Harley said.

"I'll bet." Tammy winked at Emma.

In her office, Emma opened her briefcase and removed a small laptop. "I finally found it in the coat closet." She passed it to Harley. "It's not been updated in two years. I'd suggest doing that first thing."

"Wow! Thanks." Harley stared at the slim silver computer, then looked back at Emma. "It's a Mac."

"I like PC's, but Chris preferred Apple products."

Emma dug through the case and retrieved Chris's phone. "It's ancient, but I called and had it activated."

Harley fingered the device. "I don't have anyone to call."

Emma lifted a brow. "But I might want to call you, and you can still download free games and other apps. I'll trust you with my credit card number."

"If it's free, why do I need that?"

Emma shrugged. "I don't know, but it's required."

"Thanks," Harley pocketed the phone.

"You're welcome." Emma ripped a paper from her planner.

"What's this?"

"I looked at the library's online courses and discovered *Anger Management 101*. These are the instructions for how to log on with your library card.

Harley's faced turned hard.

"Detention is not a vacation day. Now let's get to work."

Harley scowled, then she glanced at the laptop and back at the list, her lips pursed in concentration.

Emma pointed to a small round table with two chairs in the corner of her office. "You can set up over there."

Harley muttered something under her breath while she plugged in the computer.

"Here's the login password." She handed Harley another piece of paper and turned on her computer. "I'm going to the break room for coffee. Do you need anything?"

Harley kept her eyes glued to the computer screen. "Nope."

Two hours later, a knock sounded at Emma's door, and Tammy said, "Luke Davis is here to see you."

Emma gripped her pen. "Harley, do you mind giving us a minute? You can hang out in the breakroom." She dug through her purse. "Here's some change for the pop machine."

Harley stood and stretched. "What's the preacher doing here?"

"Probably church business. Now scoot."

"He sure doesn't look like preacher." Tammy smirked. "Let's give them their privacy, Harley."

Emma glowered at Tammy. *Now what?* She smoothed her hair.

Seconds later, Luke stood in her doorway wearing faded jeans and a black V-neck sweater over a T-shirt. His neatly trimmed beard drew her eye. Butterflies tickled her stomach. She sat up straight and clasped her hands in front of her.

"I come bearing gifts." Luke placed a bakery box on her desk.

"Good morning, Dr. Davis."

He cocked his head. "You sound like your mother. My friends call me Luke."

"But you're my pastor."

"Interim pastor." He opened the box. "Have a muffin."

Emma inhaled the sweet scent of the lemon-poppy-seed muffins. "I love these."

"Yes. The lady at the counter said you'd like them, and a dozen should be more than enough to share with the other library workers."

Emma cringed. News of Luke asking about her preferences would travel through Weldon faster than high-speed internet. "Thanks."

"I guess you're wondering why I'm here?"

"As are my staff, and everyone in the bakery."

"Ouch." Luke shrugged. "Sorry about that."

"It's just the way it is in Weldon," Emma bit into a muffin. "Mm. These are the best."

"I visited Eleanor this morning. Pastor Bob has a high fever."

"Oh, no."

"They're keeping him in the ICU."

"That doesn't sound good."

Luke sighed. "Eleanor's worried about him and a host of other things."

Emma savored the burst of citrusy flavor as empathy for Eleanor filled her. "What can I do to help her?"

"I'm glad you asked." He removed a piece of paper from his pocket and pushed it across her desk. "I need a volunteer to organize the church's float for the Christmas parade, which is the first weekend in December, decorate the church for the holidays, and direct the children's Christmas pageant."

"Wow," Emma studied Eleanor's neat cursive penmanship. "Even if Pastor Bob was healthy, Eleanor shouldn't have to be in charge of all this stuff."

"I thought the same thing. Any idea who might volunteer to help?"

Emma bit her lip. "I might be able to talk Casey into the Christmas pageant. Let me think about it."

"I guess there's no use hoping I can leave this list with you."

"I've already agreed to organize volunteers for the community Thanksgiving meal, and I've just taken in an abandoned kid."

"Involving Harley in church activities will be an opportunity to make her feel included." He smiled.

Emma hated to admit he was right. No way would she tell him she and Harley talked about the book on anger management yesterday. She swallowed the last bite of her muffin and brushed the crumbs from her slacks.

Luke gave her a pleading look. "You know everyone in the congregation and their talents. I can't even keep all the deacons' names straight."

"Our congregation is mostly senior adults. There are many willing to help, but few able." Emma wiped her lips with a napkin.

"I guess that's why Eleanor asked me to see you."

"Maybe." Emma sighed. "I'll take the list so I can think about who else might lend a hand, but I can't take over everything."

"I understand." Luke shifted in his seat and stared at her lips. "I've a long list of shut-ins to visit, so I can't stay." He stood and extended his hand. When he clasped Emma's palm, goosebumps covered her arms, and she blinked.

He let go and continued to stare at her lips. "Thank you, Emma."

She tried to act normal, so she beamed a smile. "I'll stop by to see Eleanor this evening. I'm sure she'd enjoy something from the Triple D for dinner."

"That sounds like a great idea."

He turned to go, then stopped and scratched his beard. "Um, you have a poppy seed stuck right here, between your teeth." He pointed to his front tooth.

Emma covered her mouth with her hand as he left her. She just stood there, eyes closed. At last, she dug through her purse and pulled out a compact and dental floss. When she stared at her reflection, her cheeks turned bright pink. The poppy seed made her look like she had a giant cavity between her front two teeth. She covered her face with her hands. If it were possible to die of embarrassment, she'd be dead. But her racing heartbeat after spending time with a too-handsome preacher indicated she was anything but. She pounded her desk. *Stop thinking about him.* But she couldn't.

Later that afternoon, Emma pushed a cart through Walmart, while she and Harley selected snacks and a variety of items to fill a care package for Eleanor. Next, they picked up her mother at the City Center, and made a final stop at the Triple D for a carry-out dinner.

During the twenty-mile drive to the regional medical center, Virginia kept up a nonstop tirade about city councilman Arnold Alexander blocking her efforts to have a new subdivision developed.

Virginia fumed. "There's a dire need for starter homes, but Arnold is against anything that might cut into his rental property revenue."

At the hospital, they found Eleanor in the ICU waiting room. The antiseptic smell made Emma shudder.

A dozen chairs lined the wall of the small room surrounding the flat-screen television hanging on the wall.

Eleanor sat in a corner chair knitting a scarf. When they entered the small space, she dropped her work, stood, and leaned into Emma. "My hero. I knew I could count on you."

Virginia patted Eleanor's back. "Just tell us what needs doing."

Emma hugged Eleanor and inhaled the sweet scent of talcum powder. "I'm glad to help." *Liar.* If she failed to recruit others, the projects would be hers.

The pasty color of Eleanor's face wasn't normal. It seemed their pastor's wife had aged years since Emma had seen her two weeks previously. "How is Pastor Bob?"

"Not good."

"Everyone is praying," Virginia said.

Harley remained in the doorway, clutching the overstuffed gift bag, and Eleanor walked around Emma to her. "I've been looking forward to meeting you."

"I'm Harley." She shoved the bag forward. "This is for you."

"Why, thank you." Eleanor almost dropped it. "The kids at church call me Mrs. Eleanor."

Harley crammed her hands deep into her coat pockets and stared at the floor.

Eleanor placed the bag in a chair and rifled through it. "My goodness, you've included all my favorite snacks." She removed a bottle of water. "Just what I needed." Eleanor sipped a drink of water. "Let's sit down."

She patted the chair next to her. "Harley, sit here."

Harley looked longingly toward the television, sighed, and complied.

Emma placed the bag bearing the Triple-D's logo on the side table. "Mrs. Dot sent chicken and dumplings with all the fixings, and a fried cherry pie."

"I love cherry," Eleanor said.

"That's what she said." Emma crossed her legs.

Eleanor chatted and told Harley about being Emma's childhood Sunday school teacher. "You wouldn't know it to look at her, but she's very competitive."

Harley frowned. "That don't sound like Emma."

"No one could beat my daughter at Bible drill," Virginia sounded smug.

Emma cringed at the memory. It had been her mother who'd made her memorize all those Scriptures. She'd cared little for winning the trophy other than pleasing her mother, which still seemed impossible.

"I've forgotten almost everything," Emma said. "I guess it's the old cliché—use it or lose it."

"Nonsense," Eleanor said. "When you need a particular Scripture, it will return."

The verse that tormented her came to mind. *In everything give thanks.* Emma gave a tight smile. "Maybe you're right."

Eleanor lifted her chin. "I know I'm right. These last two days have been tortuous, and just when I think I'm going to have a breakdown, I say, 'when I am afraid, I put my trust in you. In God, whose word I praise. In God I trust, I will not be afraid.'"

"Psalm 56:3!" Emma blurted.

"That's right. See? I told you. I just say those words over and over, and I'm comforted." Eleanor looked at the clock. "I can't see Bob until seven, and then it's only for fifteen minutes. Let's go to the cafeteria where there's a microwave. We can talk and eat.

As the hands of the clock inched toward seven o'clock, they prepared to leave.

Eleanor stood. "I've had a constant stream of visitors today, and when they asked what they could do for me, I told them to help you. Just put a signup sheet on the bulletin board."

"I will," Emma said. "Thank goodness I have Harley to help."

"And me to supervise," Virginia said.

"And there's a handsome preacher at your beck and call too." Eleanor winked.

"He brought muffins to the library today," Harley said.

Now, she speaks. Emma forced a smile. "Just take care of yourself and Brother Bob, and try not to worry.

Eleanor stuck up her index finger. "Do not be anxious about anything, but in every situation, by prayer and petition, with Thanksgiving, present your request to God."

"Philippians: 4:6," Emma said.

"You haven't forgotten a thing." Eleanor squeezed her hand. "Be nice to Luke. He's what I'd call husband material."

Emma shook her head. "But I'm not pastor wife material."

"For once, you might be wrong." Eleanor lifted a brow.

Why is it, everyone thinks I need a man in my life? Emma wanted to groan out loud. *Lord, help me.*

CHAPTER FIFTEEN—EMMA

The next two weeks passed without incident. Minnie's cooking lessons resulted in several successful meals as she and Harley worked together in the kitchen. Last night, Harley had softly hummed as she whisked the glaze for the pork chops. It lifted Emma's spirits to see Harley using earbuds to listen to music with the phone app.

Emma pushed the cart through the grocery toward the meat department, where she hoped to find two twenty-pound, fresh turkeys. She hadn't expected there to be a crowd in the store on a Tuesday evening. Then again, it was Thanksgiving week.

They'd spent Saturday afternoon baking pans of cornbread and sheets of biscuits under Minnie's watchful eyes. She insisted they take the opportunity to practice their baking skills as stale biscuits and cornbread made the best dressing, and they needed a mountain of breadcrumbs to make enough dressing for the community feasts.

Emma stopped the cart in front of the spice section. Minnie's brine recipe called for kosher salt. Studying her list, Emma backed into another customer. "Excuse me." She turned and looked into the sapphire eyes of Becky Swanson, the young math teacher whose classroom had been next to Chris's.

"Hello, Becky. How are you doing?" Emma smiled.

Becky wrinkled her pink nose. "To be honest, not so well. I'm getting over a cold."

"I'm sorry to hear that."

The chubby toddler in the carrier said, "Want cookie."

Emma's heart softened. "I haven't seen you since you had your baby. She's precious."

"Goodness, Leslie's almost two years old." Becky dug into a box of animal crackers and passed one to the child.

Emma swallowed the lump in her throat as she thought of everything she'd lost. Chris, her ability to have a child. Her voice sounded croaky. "I haven't been getting out much, other than to work." Harley stood next to her, motionless, staring at the waxed tile floor.

"By the way, this is Harley West." Emma placed her palm on Harley's shoulder. "She's staying with me for a while. Harley, this is Becky Swanson. She teaches geometry at the high school."

"Nice to meet you." Harley lifted her chin and extended her hand.

"It's a pleasure to meet you too." Becky wiped her nose with a tissue. "But it might not be a good idea to shake my hand."

Harley nodded.

"Is your mother still in Germany?" Emma adjusted her purse strap.

"Yes. I won't see her again until next summer."

"What are you doing on Thanksgiving Day?"

"I always have papers to grade, so I won't lack for something to do." Becky's mouth turned down.

"Our church is hosting the community Thanksgiving dinner. Why don't you join us?"

"Oh, I don't think so."

Emma tilted her head to one side. "Why not?"

Becky looked away. "I haven't come up with the requisite husband. Church people might frown on that."

"You sound like someone from the dark ages."

"That's because living in Weldon is like stepping back in time. I often hear people whispering."

Becky's eyes looked so sad, Emma leaned in and gave her a hug. "That's usually the person trying to deflect attention from themselves."

"You might be on to something," Becky said.

"Please come. No one should spend the holiday alone, and I could use the help because I'm the one organizing volunteers this year."

"That sounds like a job and a half." Becky brushed a crumb from Leslie's chin.

"It's not been too bad with Harley's help, but I could use an extra set of hands."

Becky bit her lip. "I might not be much help with a toddler on my hip."

"Some of the teenagers will entertain the children in the nursery."

Becky's brows lifted. "It would be nice to have an adult conversation. At school, I'm surrounded by hormonal teens, and at home, it's just baby-talk from Leslie."

Emma's spirits lifted. "Do you know how to roast a turkey?"

"No way." Becky took a step back.

"You can't blame a girl for trying." Emma shrugged. "How about a pumpkin pie?"

"Now that I can handle."

"Great. Come by Loving Chapel around ten o'clock Thursday morning. I'll save an apron for you."

"Thanks, Emma. I was feeling a little sorry for myself."

Emma patted her shoulder. "I'm glad I ran into you."

Becky pushed her cart down the aisle, and Leslie waived. Emma lifted her hand, gazing after the chubby baby. *If only. No. Don't go there.*

"What are we waiting for?" Harley's surly tone broke through her reverie.

"Just thinking," Emma vowed to be thankful for what she had. Harley's company had made such a difference during the last few weeks. Worry tiptoed up her spine. It would be hard to adjust when Harley's mother showed up. Then again, maybe she wouldn't. Guilt flooded her. *How terrible it would be for Harley if her mom remained missing.*

"Come on." Harley's irritable tone broke into Emma's thoughts.

Emma cleared her throat. "Sorry.

"I'm hungry."

"Okay. But we'll need to deliver the turkeys to the church first. Afterward, we'll head to the Triple D."

Harley rolled her eyes. "You're addicted to those fried pies."

"It will be cranberry tonight." Emma licked her lips. "Ms. Dot only makes that flavor during Thanksgiving week. I love cranberry fried pies. They might be—"

"Your favorite."

Emma giggled. "You're catching on." She remembered her vow to choose to be happy and not worry about tomorrow's trouble.

The notebook containing her lists remained open in her purse and she turned to the inside front cover where she'd written her long-range goals. *Learn to be happy.* After digging out her pen, she marked through the goal and sighed. Happiness never lingered long in her life. *Don't be such a pessimist.* No matter what happened, she would choose to be happy. Minnie was right. Only a foolish person chose to be anything else.

"You're doing it again," Harley said.

"What?"

"You've gone off to La La Land, and I'm starving,"

"Sorry. I hope the church secretary remembered to leave the side door unlocked for me."

"I'm going to die of hunger if we don't eat soon."

Emma opened a box of Triscuits. "Have one."

"We haven't paid for those." Harley's eyes bulged. "Are you trying to get me arrested?"

"Nonsense." Emma bit into a cracker and returned the notebook to her purse. Harley clutched at the hem of her sweatshirt and furtively looked down the aisle.

"Honey. The manager knows me. He won't mind I opened the box of crackers before checking out." She passed the box to Harley. "Have one."

"No way."

Casey had told Emma about Harley pocketing the hair-coloring kit during their first shopping excursion. She made Emma promise not to confront Harley. It still mystified Emma as to why Harley stole the kit. Perhaps this was a sign Harley's days of shoplifting were over. Lord, she hoped so.

CHAPTER SIXTEEN—LUKE

Luke rubbed his back and winced. He'd recruited Ben and Garret from his Bible study to help him set up tables in the fellowship hall. It discouraged him no one from the youth group signed up to help. He hoped Emma had better luck recruiting volunteers to cook the community Thanksgiving meal.

Mrs. Bessie, the head of the decorating committee, had given him a sketch of the floor plan of how she wanted the tables arranged.

A cold breeze blew in when the side door opened. Emma and Harley trudged in lugging grocery bags. He quick-stepped to help them. "Those look heavy. Let me help you."

"I've got it," Emma said. "But if you could open the kitchen door, I'd appreciate it."

Luke stepped around her and held it open.

"Now the refrigerator door," Emma said.

Harley followed her.

After placing the turkeys in the commercial refrigerator, Emma dug through her purse and removed a slim black notebook. "Harley and I thought we'd prep and roast the birds here because there are two ovens."

Emma tucked a piece of her dark hair behind her ear, and Luke inhaled her floral perfume. He longed to move in closer. Instead, he crammed his hands in his pockets and stepped back, resisting the urge to touch her. "That's a great sweatshirt."

"I've had it for years." Emma looked down at the word *Thankful* embroidered with orange thread on the olive fleece.

If only she'd look at him. "Can we help you with something?"

"No, thanks. Minnie says to bring the brine solution to a boil, let it cool overnight, then tomorrow morning, I'll stop by and put the turkeys into the mixture to soak."

"Who knew roasting a turkey was so complicated?" Luke stroked his beard.

"Not me, that's for sure," Emma opened a cabinet and scanned the shelves.

His two helpers slouched into the kitchen shoving each other. "We finished setting up the chairs," Ben said.

"Thanks," Luke said. "Let me introduce you to these two knotheads. The dude wearing the crooked cap is Ben, and the Titans' fan is Garret." He waved his hand toward Emma. "Guys, this is Mrs. Baker and Harley."

"Call me, Emma." She extended her hand. "Thanks for helping."

Harley took a step back and remained mute.

"Thanks to these fellas, I might get home at a decent hour tonight." Luke slapped Garret on the back. "I promised them pizza. Care to join us?"

Emma bit her lip. "Thanks, but we're headed to the Triple D."

Luke clutched his stomach. "Those fried pies are the best."

"This week's special will be cranberry." Emma sighed.

"Before coming to Weldon, I'd only heard of fried apple or cherry pies," Luke said.

"No one ever knows what flavor to expect except Thanksgiving week. That's when she always makes cranberry pies." Emma removed a large pan from the cabinet. "I make sure to never miss out on those."

"How about it, guys? Want to try a fried cranberry pie?"

Ben lifted his shoulder. "If you're buying."

"Let's make it a party," Luke said. "My treat."

"We'll still be a few minutes." Emma turned her back to him and started filling a pan with water. "I'm sure you don't have time to wait for us."

"The guys wanted to play air hockey," Luke said. "We'll hang out in the game room until you're finished." Emma gave a half-smile and looked over her shoulder at him. "Okay."

Harley muttered something under her breath.

Luke placed his hands on both boy's backs. "Come on, you two. Let's see which of you is the best, and I'll take on the winner."

He left whistling, and then he pictured the face of Amy, the woman who'd thrown her engagement ring from him into a mud puddle. It surprised him the old ache wasn't there. He'd refused to accept a luxury home from his future in-laws, and she'd refused to live in his studio apartment. The relationship ended with her claiming he loved God more than her—and she was right. Her family, long-time members of the first church he'd pastored, were also significant contributors to the church's budget. Luke resigned before being asked to do so.

A sense of regret washed over Luke. Emma and Amy both came from wealthy families. Someone like Emma, the daughter of the mayor, wouldn't be interested in a guy like him from the wrong side of town with nothing to offer except his heart.

Luke held the door of the Triple D open. Emma entered first and Harley followed her, closely staring at the black and white tile floor. The guys were shoving each other. Luke frowned and gave them a serious look he hoped communicated *behave.*

Mrs. Dot's eyes twinkled. She elbowed Emma and said, "I knew you'd be by for a fried cranberry pie." Mrs. Dot whispered something, and Emma's face turned his favorite shade of pink.

Mrs. Dot led them to a large round table set for six. "This should work." She took their drink orders. "I'll be back lickety split, so be ready to order."

Emma ignored the menu. "I'm having the beef stew."

When Mrs. Dot returned and distributed drinks, she stood at the ready with her order pad.

The teens ordered double cheeseburgers and onion rings, and Luke matched Emma's order of beef stew with cornbread. While they waited for their food, Emma drummed her fingers on the table. "What's the update on Pastor Bob?"

Luke's stomach tightened. "Not good. He's critical."

"Critical?" Emma's eyes widened.

"His infection turned septic, and the antibiotics don't seem to be working." Luke wiped his palms on his thighs.

"Oh, no. And I don't think I've even prayed for him today."

"Eleanor's considering moving him to Vanderbilt, but she's worried the stress of transporting him is too risky."

"That's terrible. I should have stopped by the hospital." Emma chewed her lip.

Luke spoke softly. "No one understands more than Eleanor. You've been busy. Did you get someone to volunteer to direct the Christmas pageant?"

"Casey finally gave in," Emma said. "And her mom will be in charge of the costumes."

"That's great," Luke said. "What about the Christmas parade float?"

"I called everyone I know who might be an option, but no one wants anything to do with a project involving small children, live animals, and walking the two-mile parade route beside the float."

"I'll help," Luke said.

"Can you build a manger scene for a wagon bed?"

"Consider it done."

"Your truck will be perfect to pull it."

"You can ride shotgun." Luke brightened.

"No. I'll need to walk next to the float in case a lamb or kid tries to escape. Daniel Shepherd agreed to walk on the other side."

"That's great." Something ugly prickled Luke's thoughts. He'd remembered the handsome man sitting on Emma's pew. Luke stared at the floor. *Father, forgive me.*

The boys ignored their conversation while they attempted to tackle a peg board game.

"Give me that thing!" Harley reached across the table and grabbed it. Within seconds, she cleared the triangle of pegs.

"How'd you do that?" Garret asked.

"Simple," Harley said. "I ain't stupid."

Emma cringed and squeezed Harley's knee. "A kinder word, please."

"Slam!" Ben said.

"I like a woman with a smart mouth," Garret said.

"Like a smart woman would have anything to do with you!" Harley crossed her arms and stared out the plate glass window, her knee jiggling.

Luke watched as Emma squirmed in her seat and looked at her activity tracker. She was probably counting the minutes until she could escape. *At least he'd get to see her on Thursday.*

Mrs. Dot delivered their food, and the conversation ended. The guys wolfed down their burgers. When Mrs. Dot placed their pies in front of them, Luke bit into the buttery crust and the tangy cranberry flavor exploded in his mouth. *Heaven ... or close to it.*

Emma bit into her pie, and the red filling stained her lips. Luke swallowed hard. When he tore his eyes away from her mouth, he met Harley's steely gaze. Luke had the uncomfortable feeling she could read his mind. Lord, he hoped not.

CHAPTER SEVENTEEN—EMMA

On Thanksgiving Day, Emma and Harley were in the church kitchen at five o'clock in the morning, waiting for the oven to heat. Emma passed Harley a pair of rubber gloves. "First, we rinse the birds and soak them in fresh water for thirty minutes."

Harley looked at the instructions. "We have to smear butter all over these things. Gross."

Forty minutes later, Emma shoved the oven door closed. "Do you think they'll be fit to eat?"

Harley threw her plastic gloves in the trash and washed her hands. "We followed the instructions, and I watched you like a cop on a stakeout. It ain't our fault if they make people puke."

"Six others agreed to roast turkeys and deliver them by ten o'clock." Emma read from her notebook. "I hope everyone shows up."

Harley's stomach growled.

"I have the answer for that." Emma opened a bakery box. "How about a cinnamon bun before we peel potatoes?"

"Now, you're talking."

Emma placed two of the pastries on a paper plate and set the timer on the microwave.

Harley removed the sticky note on the box and scowled. "The preacher left these for us." She wadded up the paper and threw it in the trash.

Emma shrugged. "So?"

"I don't trust him."

Emma licked creamy icing from her finger. "Who do you trust, Harley?"

"Not him. I don't care if he is a preacher."

"Why not? What's he done to make you suspicious?"

Harley's eyes narrowed. "He's always watching you when he thinks nobody's looking."

"Nonsense."

"I've watched men watch my mom, and I can tell he's up to no good."

Emma inhaled the sweet scent of the rolls. "You're right. He's trying to make me fat. I've gained three pounds in the last month." She bit into the gooey pastry and sighed.

Harley rolled her eyes. "It's all those fried pies you eat."

Emma licked the heavenly icing from her lip. "Mrs. Dot claims there's a fruit for every season, and I've never tasted a fried pie I didn't like."

A few minutes later, Emma groaned at the five large bags of potatoes.

"We're fixing all those?" Harley's eyes bulged.

"No. We're starting. Others will show up. I hate to mention it, but we need to dice onions for the five pans of dressing."

"How many people are we feeding?"

"Last year, we served about one hundred and seventy people, so I've planned enough food for two hundred."

Harley sat down hard on a stool. "I always wanted a traditional Thanksgiving meal, but I ain't so sure about it now."

"It will be worth the effort, I promise."

"We'll see."

At ten o'clock, women talking, cooking, and laughing filled the kitchen. Emma thought they sounded like a gaggle of geese. Becky arrived with a pumpkin pie and became wide-eyed at the assembled crew. Emma greeted her with an apron. "Welcome."

"Wow," Becky said. "Looks like you have plenty of help."

"There's more to do than you can imagine." Emma admired Becky's clinging russet-colored sweater. The hem reached mid-thigh, and her walnut-colored leggings enhanced her perfect figure. Standing next to her, Emma realized she still wore the sweatpants she'd grabbed when she'd rolled out of bed at four-thirty. She'd planned to return home to change, but time had slipped away. She smoothed her hand over her messy ponytail.

Becky removed Leslie's coat to reveal a black-striped top that featured a tom turkey, with a burnt-orange fluffy skirt. Her black tights featured tiny pumpkins.

"What an adorable outfit," Emma touched the ruffle.

"It's fun to dress her." Becky's face seemed to glow.

"I'll bet." Emma's heart squeezed.

After getting Leslie settled in the nursery with two high-school girls, Emma said, "Let's go help Harley finish cutting the cakes and pies."

"Okay." Becky followed her.

When they found Harley in the fellowship hall, she'd just placed the last slice of a three-tiered chocolate cake on a plate, then she picked up a crumb and sampled it. "This is the best job ever."

Emma grabbed a plastic fork, swiped it across the empty platter, and scooped up left-over icing. The dark chocolate melted in her mouth. "Mmm. This cake is sinfully good."

Becky copied Emma's actions. "Wow. You're right."

Emma handed her a pie server. "How are you at cutting pies?"

Becky bit her lip. "I think I can handle it."

Emma pointed to a table laden with pies. "Thanks. There's no way I'm going to tackle Mrs. Bessie's perfect mile-high meringue."

Harley handed Becky a pair of rubber gloves. "If you mess up, just eat the evidence."

"That's great advice." Becky pulled on the gloves. "Thanks."

"If you'll excuse me," Emma said, "I need to see what's going on in the kitchen."

When she turned around, she ran right into Luke's broad chest.

He steadied her. "There's the woman who's earned a jewel for her crown."

Emma inhaled the scent of cedar and stifled the urge to step closer. "Harley's the one who deserves a prize. She's been right here with me through the whole thing, keeping me on track."

"How's the chocolate cake?" Luke asked.

"How'd you know I sampled the cake?" Emma licked her lip.

"You left some of the evidence right here." Luke touched her chin with his thumb.

Emma leaned in, then jerked back, and swiped at her chin. "It was just a crumb."

"You deserve the whole cake." Luke's voice sounded raspy.

Minnie walked into the kitchen, followed by a deacon carrying a platter of turkey. The skirt of her cranberry-colored A-line dress flared when she circled the room. "Happy Thanksgiving." A jaunty hat featuring pheasant feathers tilted on her head.

Meanwhile Mrs. Bessie and Wynonna Peterson were busy carving the turkeys she and Harley had roasted. "Happy Thanksgiving," they said in unison.

"Oh, my, that smells wonderful," Minnie said.

Luke inhaled and closed his eyes. "This is torture for a starving man."

Miss Bessie lifted her knife. "Would you like a sample?"

"Yes, ma'am," Luke said.

"I wouldn't say no either." Minnie took a proffered piece of turkey, nibbled, and closed her eyes. "Mm. Emma, your turkey is wonderful."

"How did you know I cooked that turkey?"

"I'd know your platter anywhere," Minnie said.

Luke grabbed a paper plate. "I missed breakfast."

Miss Bessie placed a large piece of white meat on his plate.

"Thank you." Luke didn't bother with a fork. "This will sustain me while I'm delivering lunch to the shut-ins."

Emma removed her phone from her pocket and showed Minnie the selfie she'd taken with Harley and their birds after they removed them from the oven.

Minnie hugged her. "I'm so proud of you! And you've organized an army of people to help." She looked through the pass-through window to the fellowship hall. "I can guess who dressed the tables. Bess, you could start a business."

"No, thank you. Taking care of Doc is all the job I want."

Minnie's gaze stopped on Becky. "Who is the young woman cutting pies? I thought I knew everyone at Loving Chapel."

"That's Becky Swanson," Emma said. "Chris's classroom was next to hers." Her heart ached a little at the mention of his name. "Let me introduce you to her. Her little girl is being entertained in the nursery."

"Maybe we can convince her and her husband to join us on Sunday morning," Luke suggested.

Emma whispered. "There's no husband."

"All the more reason to make her feel welcome," Luke said.

"Of course," Emma agreed.

On the way to meet Becky, Luke stopped at the table where Harley worked. "Thanks for helping."

She didn't look up from slicing the cake. "I'm used to working for my keep."

"A good habit," Minnie interjected.

Becky looked up from slicing a pie when the trio approached her.

Emma said, "Becky, I'd like to introduce you to our interim pastor, Pastor Luke."

Luke extended his hand. "Welcome to Loving Chapel."

"Thank you." Becky removed the rubber glove and shook his hand.

Emma placed her hand on Minnie's back. "And this is my long-time friend Minnie Edwards."

"Welcome, young lady, and thank you for pitching in to help." Minnie beamed a smile.

"You're welcome," Becky said. "I'm glad Emma invited me."

"I'm a visitor too. I go to Alpha Baptist, two streets over," Minnie said. "Next year, we'll be hosting, so consider yourself already invited."

Becky bit her lip. "Thank you."

"Emma says you have a daughter," Minnie said.

"Yes, ma'am, Leslie will turn two next month."

"A Christmas baby! What a blessing. There's nothing I love more than a little one. I'm reserving the seat next to you right now, so I can entertain her while you eat."

"That's so nice," Becky said.

Luke cleared his throat. "I hope we see you on Sunday morning."

Becky smiled but didn't answer.

Luke looked longingly at the table. "I hate to leave good company, but Emma has me on the list to deliver take-out boxes."

"I understand," Becky said. "Speaking of assignments, I should get back to cutting pies."

Luke left them, and the three women watched him go.

"My goodness," Becky said. "If I'd known preachers looked like that, I'd have already been attending church."

"If I was forty years younger, I'd be sitting on the front row every Sunday shouting 'Amen!'" Minnie emphasized the long "a" sound.

Emma felt tongue-tied as all eyes turned to her.

Minnie elbowed her. "I've noticed this preacher looks at Emma the way Harley looks at my cookies. One of these days, he might just try to take a bite out of her."

Becky giggled. "I thought he might lick the chocolate right off her chin."

Emma's jaw dropped. "You knew I had chocolate on my face and didn't tell me?"

"I didn't want to embarrass you," Becky said. "I thought Harley would say something."

"Thanks a lot." Emma pretended to pout.

Virginia walked into the fellowship hall and marched straight toward Emma. She did not look happy.

Emma lowered her voice. "Uh-oh." Then she straightened her face. "Happy Thanksgiving, Mother. Have you met Becky Swanson?"

Virginia gave a tight smile and extended her hand. "Hello, I'm Virginia Willoughby, Emma's mother."

"Becky teaches geometry at the high school," Emma said.

"We're so glad you could join us." Virginia looped her arm through Emma's. "If you'll excuse us."

Virginia led Emma to a corner. "What in the world are you wearing?"

"I haven't had the chance to change. Harley and I started at five o'clock, and we've hardly had a break."

"Tell me what to do. I'll take over while you go home and change."

Emma blew out a breath. "There's a list of volunteer assignments on the bulletin board in the kitchen."

"Let's go add my name to the top of the list as the supervisor."

Emma clenched her teeth and followed her mother to the kitchen. Not one compliment. Had she not noticed the counters overloaded with food, the stunning table decorations that could stand up to the scrutiny of Martha Stewart? Not to mention the four tables filled with every kind of dessert imaginable! And now, just as they were about to open the church doors to feed the community, her mother planned to swoop in and be the one to welcome everyone.

Emma removed her apron and flung it on the counter. "There's the bulletin board."

Virginia lifted her reading glasses hanging on a chain around her neck. "I don't see Minnie's name here."

"Her church will host next year, which means she'll be the one to organize everything, and she's already roasted a turkey for me. There's nothing else for Minnie to do but enjoy the day."

Virginia gave her a sour look. "Go. You look like a homeless person."

"I'm leaving."

Emma found Harley standing in the corner, arms crossed. "I'm done."

"Me too," Emma said. "I'm going to run home for a shower. Do you want to come?"

"It's almost time to eat." Harley's voice sounded incredulous.

"We've been snacking all morning. Don't tell me you're still hungry."

Harley's chin gutted out. "No way, no how, am I leaving just when we're about to eat."

"Okay," Emma's shoulders drooped. "I hoped we could eat together with Minnie and Becky."

Harley rolled her eyes. "Okay, I'll wait to eat unless the food starts running out. If that happens, I'm getting in line."

"Thanks, I'll hurry."

Minutes later, Emma released Pepper from her crate and the pup covered Emma with doggie kisses. After a moment, she opened the back door, and the little dog scampered out, barking all the while.

Oh, how her feet ached. Nothing would suit her more than a soak in the tub, but she would not leave Harley waiting.

After a dash through the shower, she dried her hair and decided to leave it down for once. In the closet, she surveyed her clothes. Minnie's cranberry dress and Sunday hat made her want to dress up, but she also wanted to avoid making Harley feel underdressed. She settled on a moss green cashmere sweater with a longer hem and leggings. After adding a navy and green plaid wrap scarf and ankle boots, Emma stared at her reflection. The fried pies and eating regular meals since taking in Harley had helped her regain some of her curves. At least she no longer had bones sticking out.

After adding mascara and lip gloss, Emma felt ready to celebrate the holiday. At the back door, she whistled, and Pepper came running. Emma tossed a doggie treat into the crate, and the front doorbell rang. Emma clicked the latch, and Pepper howled.

Who in the world could that be? Everyone Emma knew was sitting down to Thanksgiving lunch or at the church helping. And anyone who knew her well would know to come to the back door.

Emma peeked out the window, and she stopped breathing; her legs trembled. Winston Meador stood on her porch holding something. *The nerve.* A heaviness settled in the pit of her stomach.

She placed her hand on the doorknob, and the doorbell rang again. Pepper's bark echoed through the stillness. It was time to face the devil.

With a jerk, Emma turned the knob and yanked open the door.

Winston stood motionless, his mouth open, face pale as the coconut cake she'd watched Harley slice.

Their eyes locked, and neither spoke. His dark eyes filled with tears, and he placed the letter on the cast iron love seat to the right of the door. The boy gulped and stepped back. Words tumbled from his lips. "Mr. Baker said to tell you if he didn't make it, he would be okay and that he'd see you in heaven." Winston ran his sleeve across his cheek. "He said other stuff, but you'll have to read it in the letter." He turned and ran to the rusty pickup truck parked in front of her house. Tires squealed, and the truck lurched forward.

Emma dropped into the seat and picked up the letter. Chris's last thoughts had been of her. She covered her face with her hands. Someday, she would read Winston's letters, but not now, not with Harley waiting for her. She sniffed. *In everything give thanks.* The Scripture reminded her of Luke, and suddenly she was angry at him. She'd bet he'd put Winston up to this. Her insides burned and she pounded her fist with her knee.

CHAPTER EIGHTEEN—LUKE

Luke returned to the church from making food deliveries to the shut-ins on his list. Tantalizing aromas filled the air, and his stomach growled. Contemporary Christian music played in the background. Almost every chair held a guest, and Luke's chest warmed when he noticed Mr. Pitt sitting with a man in a threadbare shirt and dirty cap. Other faces in the room looked familiar, and for the hundredth time, he wished for name badges.

A few people lingered around the long buffet. Emma's recruitment efforts had resulted in an excess of food for the community meal. He'd have to find her and congratulate her on the success of the event. His gaze landed on her, and his mouth went dry. She'd changed from her sweatpants, and for once, her hair was down, but the tightness around her lips concerned him.

The young woman whom she'd introduced to him earlier laughed and elbowed Harley. He searched his mind for her name, but gave up.

Luke filled his plate, and scanned the room for an empty seat.

"Pastor Luke. Come sit with us." Minnie motioned for him to join her. A blonde-haired baby sat in a highchair at the end of their table, and she mimicked Minnie's gesture and waved too. Who could resist that sweet face? Her cheeks were plump and rosy, and what looked like sweet potatoes stained her chin.

Luke sat down in the empty chair and couldn't help but glance Emma's way. "I'll be the envy of every man in Weldon, sharing a table filled with beautiful ladies."

Minnie threw her head back and laughed. "And I'll be the talk of the town, sitting next to the most eligible bachelor in Weldon."

Emma didn't share in the laughter. She didn't even crack a smile.

Minnie's brows furrowed, and she patted Emma's hand. "Are you feeling okay, hon?"

"Just a little overtired," Emma said.

"Don't worry about the clean-up," Luke said. "I can help with that."

Emma glared at him. "I think you've helped enough today."

Uh-oh. What had he done? His hunger left him.

Minnie and the baby kept everyone at their table entertained while he emptied his plate. He kept trying to make eye contact with Emma—to seek understanding, but she looked everywhere but at him.

Luke cleared his throat. "Ladies, I'm going to visit the dessert table. May I get something for you?"

"I'll help myself," Harley said, and she strode to the pies.

Becky sighed. "I'll have to take a dessert home for later. I couldn't eat another bite."

"No, thank you," Emma said in a clipped tone.

Luke crossed his arms. "I think I'll wait for a while too. Care for a walk, Emma?"

"No, thank you, I've had enough exercise today."

Luke adjusted his posture. "We can talk about what's upset you here in front of everyone, or you can walk with me to the sanctuary. The choice is yours."

Emma's eyes blazed. For the first time, he glimpsed a hint of her mother.

Minnie reached across the table and placed her hand on Emma's. "I think a walk outside in the cool air is exactly what Emma needs."

Virginia studied her daughter closely. "I agree with Minnie."

Becky's eyes were wide, and Emma smiled at her. "Sorry to leave good company, but there's something I need to discuss with Dr. Davis ... privately."

"So we're back to Dr. Davis." Luke rolled his eyes.

Once outside, the cool breeze lifted Emma's hair, and she pushed a strand behind her ear. Luke touched her elbow, and she jerked it away.

He pointed. "Let's walk around the building." When they turned the corner, they came upon several kids in the fenced playground, taking advantage of the sunshine.

Emma stared straight ahead and kept walking.

Luke sighed. "Let's see if anyone's in the prayer garden."

When they reached the gate, Luke fiddled with the latch and opened it. "Let's have a seat."

"I'd rather stand."

"What have I done to upset you?"

Emma planted her fists on her hips. "My worst enemy showed up on my doorstep!"

"Who?" Then he winced. "Winston."

"Yes, Winston." Emma's voice sounded spiteful.

Luke scratched his beard. "I had nothing to do with him visiting you."

"How did he know where I lived?"

"Probably Google or a phone book." Luke ran his hands through his hair. "I felt terrible about not inviting the guys from my Bible study to come today, especially after they helped me set up the tables, but I couldn't invite everyone and leave out Winston."

Emma picked up a rock and flung it. Tears filled her eyes.

Luke didn't know what to do, how to help. *Lord?*

"Winston said Chris asked him to tell me that if he didn't make it, he'd be okay, that he'd see me in heaven." Emma sank to a bench and covered her face with her hands. "Then he ran off before I could say anything."

Luke gulped and sat down beside her. He knew all of what Winston had to say to her, but it wasn't his place to speak. There would be healing for her if she'd read the letters, but he couldn't make her. Only she could help herself.

She ran her sleeve across her cheek.

They sat and watched a gust of wind sweep through the leaves on the ground.

Emma sniffed. "I don't want to be angry all the time."

"Satan really is like a crouching lion, waiting to devour. These dark emotions don't come from God."

"I can't let go of the anger. I can't forgive him. I've tried."

"Maybe you should stop trying to do this hard thing and let Jesus do it for you."

"But how?"

"Surrender. Every time you think about Winston, or whatever is upsetting you, first ask God to forgive you and then lift a prayer for the person causing the unhealthy emotions."

"But it will just be words."

"At first, yes. When a wound is deep, forgiveness can be like a drop of water dripping on a boulder, but as you allow

Jesus to take over, it gathers strength and begins to flow and His living water eventually frees you. It's a process. We have to come to the end of ourselves and let go. I've learned that when I'm at my weakest, completely empty, He fills me. It's not just words."

Emma dug a tissue out of her pocket and wiped her tears. "Minnie's said for years if you pray for someone often enough, you learn to love them. That's how she experienced joy every day while working for my grandfather. He had a mean streak."

"I'm sorry," Luke said. He placed his hand over Emma's. "Let me pray for you." He closed his eyes. He resisted the desire to pull her to him, to hold her and protect her from the hurts of the world. Guilt washed through him. She needed a pastor, not a man. He'd have to take his own advice, and let Jesus take over. At last, he prayed. "Thank you, Father, for loving us." He paused again. "Help Emma to search her heart and thoughts and pour out any evil You reveal so that You may fill her with the fruit of Your Spirit. I ask that you help Emma love Winston as You love him—unconditionally. Soften her heart, Lord. Help her to forgive him. I don't know how You are going to turn this terrible thing to your good, but I trust You. May Your will be done in all things. In the name of Jesus, I ask these things. Amen."

When he lifted his head, his cheeks were damp, too, and she stared at him. A tenderness washed through him, and his heart ached for her.

"Thank you," Emma dropped her chin to her chest. "I'm sorry I spoke so harshly to you."

"Comes with the job title."

Emma frowned and searched his face.

"Meddler," Luke said. "Pastors are always meddling, which is how I've ended up being between you and Winston."

Emma gave a half-smile. "Pastor Bob is a meddler too."

"I know. He's the one who introduced me to Winston."

"Sounds like something he'd do."

Luke looked into the distance. "I don't know how Bob keeps up. There are so many needs."

Emma smiled. "He has Eleanor as a helpmate."

"Yes, and she's a force of nature, but Bob's illness is taking a toll on her."

"Poor thing." Emma sniffed. "Let's go in and fix a plate for her."

"Great idea," Luke extended his hand and helped her up, but he didn't let go of her hand. How he longed to wrap his arms around her. He resisted the urge and savored the feel of her skin. Peace washed through him ... but then he heard the sirens.

Luke held the church door open for Emma, and a pale-faced Becky met them at the door. "I've got to go." The young mother's voice trembled.

Minnie followed, holding Leslie in her arms. "Emma, go with Becky. I'll watch the baby."

"Go where?" Emma asked.

"My neighbor called and said my apartment complex is on fire." Becky wrung her hands.

Luke's pulse rate increased. "I'll drive and Emma will pray." He pointed. "There's my truck."

Emma gasped when they turned onto Becky's street. A police barricade blocked the road. When Luke opened the truck door, the acrid scent of smoke filled his nostrils. At one end of the complex, hungry flames licked up through the roof.

Becky pointed. "My apartment is in the middle." She sprang from the truck and darted toward the barricade. Emma scampered behind her.

Fire devoured Becky's curtains, glass shattered, and a wave of smoke rolled from the window. The bucket of the firetruck rose higher above the roof and a fireman sprayed water directly onto the blaze through the hole in the roof. Other firefighters on the ground sprayed water on Becky's unit. Emma shuddered.

Becky stared with her mouth open, tears streaming down her face, and Emma grabbed her hand and pulled her back. "Don't look."

Beside them, Luke prayed.

Becky jerked away from Emma, bent over double, and vomited.

It felt unreal to watch the scene unfold. A firetruck from a neighboring community arrived, and the police pushed the crowd back. Other anxious friends and family members gathered, desperate to find their loved ones. People clung to each other amid the crowd.

A wave of sadness washed over Emma's face while the fire devoured the building.

Two hours later, smoke hovered over the skeletal remains of the apartment complex and it seemed all of Weldon stood on the perimeter, stunned.

"Let's go. There's nothing we can do here. Luke ushered them back to his truck.

Inside the vehicle, Emma rubbed her cold hands while Becky stared into space.

"I-I don't have anywhere to go." Becky spoke just above a whisper.

"You can come home with me," Emma squeezed her knee.

Luke's heart softened at Emma's impulsive invitation. She probably hadn't thought about Harley's reaction to having another houseguest.

"I've lost everything." Becky's mouth hung open.

Emma hugged her. "You have Leslie. Everything else is replaceable."

"What have I done to deserve this?" Becky slumped forward, covered her face with her hands and sniffed. "I guess losing an apartment can't compare to losing a husband."

Emma gave a sympathetic smile. "Loss is loss, and it hurts. I've had two years to learn to focus on my blessings instead of my losses, while you've barely had any time."

Becky touched her temple. "I can't even focus—to process what we need to get through the night, much less the next few days—the necessities."

Emma clutched Becky's hand. "Let's return to the church for Leslie, and then we'll figure out which bedroom in my house suits you best.

"Are you sure?"

"I've never been surer of anything in my life."

Becky spoke through hiccups. "I need to make a Walmart list."

Earlier in the week, Luke had fumed about the big-box store opening at five o'clock on Thanksgiving Day. Now, he lifted a prayer of thanks.

Emma squeezed Becky's hand. "No one other than Santa Claus is better at making a list and checking it twice than I am."

"She's right." Luke started the truck. "I've noticed Emma making a list more than once."

Becky stared ahead, and the hiccups softened.

Luke wished he had the words to make things better.

Emma helped Becky fasten her safety belt and turned toward Luke. "Can you take us back to the church, then to my house?"

"Yes, ma'am. Anything you need."

Luke wondered again about Harley's reaction to a houseguest. The girl seemed distrustful of everyone. He'd hate to be the one telling her the news.

Luke watched Emma usher Becky into the Victorian mansion. The sheer size of it gobsmacked him. He'd assumed such a pretentious home belonged to someone like Arnold Alexander. Never in a million years would he have guessed this was Emma's home.

Emma assured him she had everything under control so he returned to the church to help with the cleanup.

After putting the last of the tables away, he finally made it to the hospital with a to-go box for Eleanor. When he entered the ICU waiting room, his spirits sank lower at the sight of Eleanor's downturned lips and slumped shoulders. Eleanor noticed him, and her brows lifted. "How did the Thanksgiving luncheon go?"

"Great! Emma organized an army."

Eleanor gave a weary smile. "I knew she wouldn't let me down."

"And she has another new houseguest—actually two more."

"Really?"

"A fire burned down an apartment complex in Weldon. Eight families lost everything."

"Oh, no."

"Several members of the church took up an offering for them."

Eleanor's face relaxed. "That's sounds like Loving Chapel. We have our petty squabbles, but when someone's in need, our church lives up to its name."

"One of our luncheon guests, a young mother, lost her home."

"Poor thing. What's her name?"

Luke looked toward the ceiling. "Becky ..." He shrugged. "Her baby's name is Leslie, and Emma invited them to stay with her."

"More people to love. That's exactly what she needs."

"I think so too." Luke studied her face. "What about you? How are you holding up?"

"Soldiering on, but I'm worn to a nub, and Bob's completely unresponsive."

A sense of helplessness covered Luke. *Lord, have mercy.* "Have you decided about transferring him to one of the big hospitals in Nashville?"

"That's all I've been thinking about."

"Let's pray together." Luke gripped her hand and closed his eyes. Tears threatened, and the stress of the past week pressed in on him. His thoughts and feelings had become overwhelmed by Emma.

He sat in the stillness next to Eleanor, whose eyes were closed, lips moving. His friend and mentor should be foremost on his mind. *Father, forgive me.* Memories of Bob praying with him through his rebellious teen years flooded his thoughts. Luke would be forever grateful for

Bob's intervention. He'd stepped into the fray, been a father figure to him, introduced him to his Heavenly Father, and made him understand God loved him unconditionally.

Luke closed his eyes and squeezed Eleanor's hand and silently prayed. *Father, help us. Please give Eleanor wisdom as to what You would have her to do. We're both feeling abandoned and drowning, but I know You are with us. We need Your guidance and strength. I'm losing hope in this situation. Forgive me. I'm floundering without Bob's counsel. Maybe that's part of the problem. I've relied on him, when I should be relying on You. I'm sorry. Thank You for reminding me that You are the only thing I need. I surrender everything to You. Whatever the reason for our suffering, I trust You. Thank You for all that You have done and will do. May Your will be done in all things.*

Once he'd prayed those words, the heaviness of his heart lifted. "Amen."

When he opened his eyes, Eleanor blew her nose into a tissue, then said. "Be still and know that I am God."

"So He spoke to you."

She nodded. "I'm staying put, for now. I don't know. Maybe, I imagined it. Did the Lord give you any idea what to do?"

Luke bit his lip. "I'm afraid I did most of the talking and didn't give him the chance."

Eleanor patted his knee. "That sounds like me, but I'm out of words. I'm getting a whole new understanding about Peter saying 'the spirit helps us in our weakness. We do not know what we ought to pray for, but the Spirit Himself intercedes for us through wordless groans.'"

"Amen," Luke said. Oh, how he wished he could comfort her, but he had no words either.

On the drive back to Weldon, the sense of hopelessness blanketed him again when he passed Emma's grand home. An ache formed in his gut. Emma and Amy shared more similarities than he'd imagined. Only hopeless idiots repeated the same mistakes.

CHAPTER NINETEEN—HARLEY

Harley pushed a cart in Walmart and Emma stood behind her, list in hand. They'd left Ms. Swanson under Minnie's ministrations. Harley was glad Mrs. Virginia stayed at the church to supervise the clean-up and left-over food distribution. Harley had had enough of taking orders from Emma's mom for the day.

Harley stopped their cart in front of the toddler bed and cocked her head. "There ain't no way all this stuff is fitting in your car. We might get the highchair in the back seat but that's about it."

Emma pinched her chin. "You're right. Too bad Pastor Luke had to deliver food baskets. I'll call Casey."

"She drives a Mustang," Harley crossed her arms.

"And she's been spending a lot of time with Daniel. He drives a truck, and if he's not there, she has five brothers home for the holiday. Someone will be in a truck." Emma dialed her phone and spoke overloud. "I need help." A few minutes later, Emma disconnected, smiled, and sighed. "Daniel will help us. He and Casey are on their way to the boutique so Casey can pick out some clothes for Becky."

"What if Ms. Swanson can't afford them."

"I'm sure they'll be a gift." Emma leaned on the shopping cart. "I'm about beat." She picked up a pair of pink toddler-footed pajamas which made her smile, and a dreamy looked crossed her face. "This is precious."

Harley rolled her eyes. "If you're going to moon over everything like that we'll be here all night."

Emma tucked a stray hair behind her ear. "You're right. "She grabbed a few items. "Let's get to work."

An hour later, Harley crammed her hands into her jeans pockets. The checkout line looked endless. What if Ms. Swanson opened the drawer in the tower room with the curlers and found the sock full of money? If only she'd chosen the room with the twin beds, but no... Emma had insisted she take the big room at the front of the house because it had a nicer bathroom. Somehow, she would have to sneak in there and get Beau's money.

"Are you okay with everything, Harley?" Emma asked with concern. "You look worried."

Harley chewed her thumbnail. "It's just that ..."

"Go on," Emma said.

Harley sputtered. "I think it would be better if Ms. Swanson took my room. It's bigger, and the little bed would fit under the window."

Emma squeezed Harley's elbow with compassion. "You don't have to give up your room."

"But I could take the tower room. It don't matter where I sleep as long as it's warm."

"The bed in your room is more comfortable." Emma twisted a strand of her hair. "But if it's really what you want ..."

Harley perked up. "Maybe I could put a Christmas tree in the tower."

Emma's face brightened too. "What a great idea, and I can call Bentley's furniture store first thing in the morning.

I'm sure Mr. Bentley will deliver a new mattress. Maybe we should buy a new bedroom suite that fits your personal style."

Harley rolled her eyes. "I ain't got no personal style."

"Yes, you do." Emma craned her neck and looked toward the cashier. "Why don't you hurry and pick up a pre-lit Christmas tree for the tower?"

"We got enough stuff to load."

"I'm not setting foot in this store tomorrow! Let's seize the moment."

Harley pressed her lips together. Spending money on something she didn't need was foolish. "How much do you think one of them trees costs?"

Emma shrugged. "Whatever the price, you've earned it. We've been on our feet for over twelve hours, and we still have a youth bed to put together. Go! Get the tree you want."

What would it be like to spend money like that? Emma hadn't looked at the prices while they'd loaded the carts. Still. She wouldn't take advantage of her. "No. That's okay."

"Please," Emma's voice sounded whiny. "Think of what it will look like. I want a tree in the tower."

Harley bit her lip. "Okay, I'll be right back."

She walked faster with each step. Never in a coon's age could she have imagined living in the princess room with her own tree. She'd never admit it to anyone, but she liked the fancy room.

What would her mom think about her living in such a place? She ached at the thought of her mom. She hoped she had food and was not staying high all the time. For weeks, she had searched the streets of Weldon for her mom's face. Tears filled her eyes, and she swiped at them. The brief bubble of excitement fizzled.

She wished her mom could be like Emma, someone nice to everyone, who helped people instead of conning them.

Harley had watched Emma deal with people in the library. It didn't matter to her if someone asked a million dumb questions or if they smelled bad, and sometimes people were downright hateful, but Emma never exchanged ugly words with anyone. Sometimes, her lips would form into a tight line, but she'd keep her cool.

Harley wanted to forget about her mom and stop worrying about her. It wasn't like her mom ever worried about her. She hadn't even reported her missing. If she had, the nosey social worker would have said something. Then again, maybe Beau had hurt her because Harley had taken his money. Worry niggled at her. Maybe she could go back and hide out in the woods and try to catch a glimpse of her mom. It was a long walk back to Rocky Hills. *Still ...*

They finally made it back to the house. It took forever to unload the cop's truck and move her things to the tower. Harley sat on the cushioned seat that circled her new bedroom and her gaze lingered on the lights of Weldon. With the leaves gone, she could follow the streetlamps all the way to the square. Icicle Christmas lights hung from the roof of the house across the street. She wrapped her arms around her knees, rested her chin, and looked over her shoulder at the tall bed and the padded headboard. It seemed a dream to be here.

Her gaze lingered on the vanity. Maybe she could sneak some of the cash into Ms. Swanson's purse. Harley remembered her mom having the same vacant look when they were down to no money and no options. Becky Swanson might turn to drugs like her mom. Harley chewed her nail. If only there had been someone like Emma to help them.

Instead, her mom turned to worthless men who lied—and Beau was the biggest creep of them all. She squeezed her eyes shut. *Don't think about him.*

A chill blanketed her, and Harley snagged a crocheted afghan from the chair and wrapped it around her shoulders. Maybe all people weren't bad. The folks at the church had passed a basket around taking up money for people at the fire, and the cop had shown up tonight with Casey. When he'd asked her to help him put together the bed for Leslie, Harley had wanted to run. But they'd worked together in silence. Her hands trembled as she imagined Emma opening the drawer with the money. Harley had barely been able to breathe, thinking about what she might say if they did.

Daniel had stared at her shaking hands and said, "You never need to be afraid of me, Harley." Harley had swallowed hard and tried to smile. He might be okay—at least he didn't give her the creeps. But he was a cop, and cops couldn't be trusted.

CHAPTER TWENTY—EMMA

Emma soaked in the clawfoot tub and sighed. Never in her life had she had such a day. Her back ached, and she flexed her swollen foot.

It seemed unreal a mother and child lay asleep upstairs, and Harley was ensconced in the tower room with Pepper for company. She missed having her beloved pet snuggled next to her, but no one knew better than she the comfort of cuddling the little dog.

Emma had asked Becky if she had a special friend she could call, and she'd said she had no one close by, and she didn't want to call her mom in Germany until she could speak to her without breaking down.

When Chris had died, innumerable people had waited in line for hours to offer her their condolences. It seemed everyone in town had wanted to hug her, to touch her, to do anything that might help. But no one could bring back Chris. Emma knew, without a doubt, if she needed help, she only needed to lift the phone, and many people would drop everything and come. Poor Becky, to be so alone in the world, and with a baby.

Emma left the cooling water, slipped into flannel pajamas, yawned, and stretched. Somehow, she had to stop her brain from thinking, from worrying, and get to sleep. The library only closed for federal holidays, and because several of her staff asked to be off, she'd committed to help cover the front desk the next day. So much for being the boss. She always worked the days around holidays and usually it wasn't a problem.

She would just have to visit the furniture store tomorrow. Maybe on her lunch break. If only she could stay with Becky instead, but she couldn't do that without ruining someone else's day. Thank goodness Minnie insisted on spending the day at the house to ensure Becky had everything she needed.

With the chaos of the grueling shopping spree, Emma had only spoken briefly with her mother about her growing household. But it was long enough for Emma to recognize her mother's displeasure by her curt tone. The thought of having another conversation with her made her groan.

The letter from Winston on the bedside table drew her attention, and she pictured his boyish face and tear-filled eyes. Her chest tightened. Luke had asked her to pray for Winston. She picked at a thread on the coverlet. It couldn't hurt. With eyes closed, she held her breath for a few seconds then let go. *Father, forgive me. Help me forgive him as You have forgiven me. I'm sorry that I'm so weak.* A fragment of hardness in her heart softened. She opened her eyes. Maybe, she should follow Luke's advice to stop trying to do this hard thing and let God do it.

She closed her eyes and tried again. *Thank You, Father. Thank You for my home and for giving me the chance to put it to good use. Be with those who lost their homes.* She bit her lip. *Thank You for placing Harley, Becky, and Leslie in my care, and help me make them feel welcome ... like family.*

She paused. *Please, help me keep them safe.* There she went again, trying to do God's job. *Please Father, keep them safe.*

Emma yawned. Never in her life could she remember being this tired. *Help me to forgive Winston Meador. Amen.* On the edge of sleep, she imagined hearing Minnie's voice whisper 'but those who hope in the Lord will renew their strength. They will soar on wings like eagles; they will run and not grow weary, they will walk and not be faint.'

She remembered the feel of Luke's callused hand holding hers. It had felt so right. Her lips curved into a smile. And then she slept deeply.

The next day Emma sat at the kitchen table cradling a mug of coffee, her notebook open in front of her, when Becky crept down the stairs with Leslie on her hip.

"Good morning." Emma sipped her coffee. "Did you sleep well?"

"Not really, but Leslie never whimpered."

"How about a cup of coffee?"

Becky tucked a strand of her long blonde hair behind her ear. "Sounds wonderful, but first let me get Leslie some milk. You wouldn't have Cheerios, would you?"

"It's Harley's favorite." Emma removed the yellow box from the pantry.

"Do you have a plastic bowl?" Becky strapped Leslie into the new highchair.

"I picked up a child's dish set just for her last night. Let me rinse it out."

Becky adjusted the highchair's table. "You and Harley must have been like a whirlwind in Walmart."

"It was Harley mostly," Emma said. "Stealthy as a cat, she somehow slipped through the masses to get the best buys."

"You've been so generous." Becky smoothed her hand over her white terrycloth robe."

Emma opened the package of sippy cups and rinsed one. "It's a blessing to help you."

After getting Leslie settled with cereal, Becky accepted the mug of coffee from Emma. "Thank you."

They sat in silence, watching Leslie finger Cheerios with her chubby fingers. Pepper sat next to the highchair, on high alert for spillage.

Becky looked at Emma's notebook. "I should put together a list of things to do." She blew out a long stream of air. "But the thought of starting over, finding an apartment, and buying furniture is making my head swim."

"Why not take the day to settle in? There's plenty of time for lists." Emma bit her lip. "I wish I could stay with you today, but I'm on the work schedule, and I'd hate to call in someone who has plans."

"I'm surprised the library's open today."

"Unless it's a federal holiday, we're open, and our regulars count on us. I know some spend the day with us because they can't afford to keep their homes warm, and I suspect a couple are homeless." Emma sipped her coffee. "I like to think of our reading area as a community living room where everyone feels welcome."

"I'm embarrassed to admit, I haven't visited Weldon's library because I use an e-reader."

"We have the latest digital books too."

"It's not likely I'll have time to read anything in the near future."

"Maybe that's exactly what you need to do today. I can't tell you the times when escaping into the pages of a good book is the only thing that's kept me sane."

"Really?"

"Absolutely. A few of my old favorite books are lying around. Help yourself."

"I might try to read when Leslie takes a nap."

"Minnie will be here soon. Just enjoy her company and get used to the house."

Becky glanced around the room. "It seems a dream to be living in a home like this."

Emma smoothed Leslie's hair. "It seems a dream to have you and this beautiful girl eating Cheerios in my kitchen—

and Harley too." Her shoulders dropped. "Last year, I didn't even put up a Christmas tree."

"Leslie and I spent the holidays alone too."

"Let's make this Christmas one to remember forever. We'll add a wreath to every window, and a tree in the front parlor. Last night, Harley picked out a tree for the tower. I bet she'll have it up before the end of the day."

"She's so quiet. Are you sure she's okay with changing rooms?"

"She's the one who suggested it."

"How long has she been with you?"

"A little over a month." Emma refilled her coffee mug and glanced up the stairs. "Harley's mom abandoned her, and I found her hiding in a storage closet at the library. Turns out she'd spent the first night alone in the dark, then I discovered her the second night when I came in after hours."

"Poor thing."

"Her company's been good for me, and having you two will be great too. I've always wanted to fill this house with a family."

"You've treated me like family." Becky reached across the table and squeezed Emma's hand. "I've always wished for a sister."

"That's something we have in common." Emma's voice trembled. "So I will treat you like family and leave you to get your own breakfast."

"Don't worry about us."

Emma tore a sheet of paper from the notebook. "Why don't you and Harley work on a grocery list?"

"Let me buy the groceries this week. You've done so much."

"Okay." Emma said. "We can take turns cooking."

"That sounds great," Becky said.

"You may not think so after you eat my food. Minnie's cooking lessons have helped. At least the turkeys Harley and I roasted turned out okay."

"The entire event was wonderful, until my neighbor phoned."

Emma rinsed out her mug. "Make yourself at home, because it is your home."

"Thanks."

"There're eggs and bacon in the fridge."

"I'll just have toast, but thank you."

An hour later, Emma's peeked into the tower room at Harley. Pepper, snuggled by her side, lifted her head and growled.

"Shhh." Emma returned downstairs, grabbed her coat and waved to Becky and Leslie, still in the kitchen. "Minnie will be here soon. Y'all have a good day."

"You too."

Leslie waved her chubby little hand. "Bye bye."

Emma's heart melted, and she waved. "Bye, sweet pea." She couldn't believe she'd return home to this adorable face.

Emma stepped outside and the cool air refreshed her, but her legs still ached. Maybe a walk would help stretch her tight muscles. The temperature hovered around freezing, but there wasn't a wind. A light frost made everything look pristine, and the early morning sunlight made the grounds sparkle. A walk would clear her head.

"You're out early this morning."

Emma jumped at the sound of Mr. McCullough's gruff voice.

She placed her hand over her pounding heart. "Good morning. I'm headed to the library. What are you doing out so early?"

"Feeding the squirrels."

"I thought you hated them."

"It's my new strategy for keeping the varmints out of my birdfeeders. See this little platform?"

Emma looked closely at the tree where he pointed. "It's a squirrel feeder. I leave a dried ear of corn here each morning hoping they'll leave my bird seed alone."

"That's a great idea."

He hooked his thumbs through his red suspenders under his Carhartt coat, a big grin on his face. "Harley suggested it."

"Really?"

"Yeah. She's a good kid. Most afternoons, she listens to my old army stories while you go out for a run."

"She's never mentioned it," Emma said.

"Oh, she's quiet, always watching. Makes me wonder what she's watching for."

"Probably her mom," Emma said.

"Yeah. Some people." Mrs. McCullough's jaw turned hard.

Emma turned to leave, then paused. "Oh. I have another houseguest."

"You opening a boarding house?"

"No. Nothing like that. Did you hear about the fire yesterday?"

"Yeah. Some knucklehead tried to deep-fry a frozen turkey."

"I'm sure he feels terrible. Anyway, one of the residents who lost her home is staying with me. She has a toddler."

"That's mighty nice of you."

Emma shrugged. "Having company is good for me."

"I'll be watching for her and do my best to make her feel welcome."

"Thank you, and maybe leave your Super-Soaker at home."

"I've put the dadburn thing away. I felt terrible for scaring Harley."

"It's forgiven," Emma said. "And I appreciate that you watch over us."

"It gives me something to do."

"I thought your volunteer work at the trailer park kept you busy."

"It only took me about six months to get things in order. Now I spend most of my time looking for things to fix"

"I know they appreciate you handyman skills."

He stomped his feet on the ground. "I'm 'bout to freeze, so I'll head back inside."

Emma waved. "Have a good day."

"You too, hon."

In mere minutes, she reached the library. The scent of roasted coffee filled her nose when she opened the breakroom door, and every muscle in her body relaxed.

"Coffee's almost ready." Jasmine, a part-time staff member who also attended community college handed her a mug.

"Thanks," Emma smiled. "Looks like you'll be supervising me today." She loved working the circulation desk and reshelving books.

Jasmine giggled. "Yeah, right."

"I hardly ever get to work the desk. If a new patron comes in, you'll have to retrain me on the software to issue a library card."

"I think you'll be able to figure it out," Jasmine said.

The moment Jasmine unlocked the front door, a string of people entered. Emma's spirits lifted. She loved working among the stacks. She wouldn't let anything bring her spirits down today.

CHAPTER TWENTY-ONE—EMMA

That afternoon, Emma sniffed the familiar scent of Chanel, her mother's signature perfume. Virginia rounded the corner. "There you are!"

Oh, no. This can't be good. Emma forced a smile. "Mother. What a surprise. Thanks for supervising the cleanup yesterday."

"I didn't have a choice, did I?"

"Sorry, but my hands were full with Becky at the apartment complex."

"Yes. I know. When I stopped by your house to check on you and your houseguests, I couldn't believe it when Minnie said you were working today."

"Why not?"

"Because you have houseguests."

Emma straightened the books on the shelf and kept her face turned away from her mother. "Becky will stay with me until she finds a new place. She's more like a housemate than a guest."

"What do you know about this young woman?" Virginia spoke under her breath.

"She's very nice."

"Where does she come from? Who are her people? Why did she settle in Weldon?"

Emma held up a hand to interrupt the spew of questions. "The same reason we stay, she likes it here."

Virginia lifted her chin. "But what's her background? Where's her family."

"Becky is a teacher. Her mother serves in the military and is currently stationed in Germany."

"But she has a baby and no husband. Where's the child's father?"

"I don't know, and that's not our business." Emma huffed.

"Really, Emma. You can't take in all these stray people!"

"Why not?"

"You're acting irresponsible."

"Mother, you know better than anyone there are few decent rental properties in Weldon. I couldn't leave Becky and her baby standing on the street."

"But there are agencies to help people."

Emma squared her shoulders. "Have you ever wondered why God blessed us with so much, and others with so little?"

Virginia's face turned a dark hue. "I've worked my entire life."

"Yes, but Grandmother's money gave you a very nice cushion."

"And Father left his estate to you." Virginia's eyes turned hard. "What's your point?"

Emma bit her lip "I didn't want Grandfather's money, and you insisted I take over the house."

Virginia waved her hand. "I care nothing about his estate. Why are we talking about our finances?"

"Because I believe the reason God blessed us with so much is so we can bless others."

Virginia's gasped. "It would surprise you to learn what I give to charities, but that's no one's business but mine."

"Writing a check is good, but it's not a sacrifice to either one of us."

"I'm not discussing my benevolence with you or anyone for that matter." Virginia's voice sounded cold, but her eyes blazed. "However, I have something else to discuss with you. Privately." She emphasized the last word. "Let's go to your office." She turned and marched with her head held high.

Emma followed. "I'm short of staff today. If Jasmine calls, I'll need to go."

Virginia strode into Emma's office as if it were hers. *The nerve.* Emma took a deep breath. It surprised her when Virginia didn't sit in the chair behind the desk.

Emma sat down with a thump and crossed her arms. "You have my attention, Mother. What is it you want to say?"

Virginia's cheeks flushed, and she fiddled with her purse strap. She glanced out the office window—then she faced Emma with a piercing gaze. "I hired a private investigator to find Harley's mother, Anne West." She looked defiant.

Emma's jaw dropped. "A private investigator!"

"His name is Luther Warren. When I worked at the bank, I had to call on Detective Warren more than once. He's the one who discovered an employee laundering money for drug dealers."

"Why won't you allow the police do their job?"

"They've had no results, so I hired Luther." Virginia's lips formed a tight line. "He wants to interview Harley on Monday afternoon, after school."

Emma covered her face with her hands.

"Harley needs to be with her mother," Virginia said.

"Who might be living with an abusive man!"

"Maybe we can get her the help she needs."

Emma's cheeks burned, and she wanted to throw something. A knock sounded.

"Sorry to interrupt." Jasmine bit her lip. "But I need your help."

Emma smiled tightly. "Yes."

"There's a lady at the desk who's wearing a trench coat and muddy house slippers. She's confused."

"Sounds like you're needed." Virginia stood. "Try to restrain yourself from taking in this confused person."

Emma narrowed her eyes.

"I'll phone later." Virginia left without another word.

Now what? At the front desk, she greeted a woman with white hair, matted on one side.

"May I help you?" Emma said.

"This is an emergency."

Emma stood behind the counter. The scent of menthol salve permeated the air. "What's wrong?"

"I need to speak with my sister." She rifled through her purse. "Call this number. I'm being held against my will."

Emma took the piece of paper from the shaking hand extended to her. The old Walmart receipt had a phone number written on the back, but the spidery scrawl made it impossible to decipher. Closer scrutiny revealed a dirty ruffle of a nightgown showing under the hem of her oversized trench coat.

"If you'll have a seat, I'll make the call in my office. Could you repeat your name again?"

"I'm Pernie Ann White."

"Mrs. White, I'm Emma Baker." Emma caught Jasmine's eye. "This is Jasmine. She'll sit with you while I make the call."

Emma went to her office and dialed the nursing home. "Do you know a Mrs. Pernie Ann White?"

196

"Yes, she's missing. The police are looking for her."

"She's here, at the library." Emma peeked outside her office door. "I'll watch her until someone arrives."

A few minutes later, a commotion ensued in the library when a nurse and aide came to retrieve their disoriented patient. Emma's spirits sank lower. That would be her someday, alone in the world and no one but paid attendants to care for her.

Emma returned to her office and called the social worker, Carol Carter. After informing her about her new houseguests, she shared the information about Virginia hiring the private investigator who wanted to interview Harley.

"I'll drop by and meet Ms. Swanson this afternoon and ask her to sign a release form so that I can obtain a copy of the school's background check," Ms. Carter informed her.

"I'll let her know to expect you," Emma said.

"Also, I want to be present during the detective's interview," Carol said.

"Mother said he'd like to visit with Harley Monday afternoon, after school."

"I'll be at your house by four o'clock."

"I'll relay that information to Mother and ask her to let the investigator know."

"If he finds Anne West, the police will arrest her for child neglect." Carol's voice sounded hard.

Emma wanted to go home and pull the covers over her head. She started to dial Casey but paused. It was the busiest shopping day of the year. Emma bit her lip and sent her a text. "Can you come over for dinner tonight?"

Thirty seconds later, Emma's phone pinged with a thumbs up emoji."

Emma functioned on automatic pilot through the afternoon, shelving books and keeping to herself. Her thoughts were in a whirl. So much for having a good day in the stacks.

That evening, as Emma approached her house, she stopped and stared at the tower. Lights from the fiber-optic Christmas tree changed colors every few seconds. The aqua color looked unusual for a Christmas tree, then the shade melded to blue, purple, pink, and back to aqua. In the evening fog, light shined from Becky's bedroom upstairs too. Emma's heart lifted, and on a whim, she fumbled for her phone and dialed.

"Hello?" Harley's voice sounded unsure.

"Harley, It's Emma. I love the tree in your window."

"Yeah. I put it up this afternoon. I think it looks pretty wicked."

"Have you seen it in the dark?"

"Not yet."

"Come down."

A minute later, Harley joined her on the sidewalk and Emma wrapped her arm around Harley's shoulder.

"Wow." Harley stared at the tower window. "That's sick."

"I hope that means you like it?"

Harley rolled her eyes.

Emma ruffled Harley's hair.

"Hey!"

"It's going to be the best Christmas ever."

The aroma of baking filled the air when she and Harley walked in the back door. Becky sat at the kitchen table with Leslie in the highchair, eating graham crackers.

"Chocolate cake." Emma pointed to the counter. "This can't be my kitchen."

Harley shrugged. "Minnie said I needed to learn to bake a cake."

"Someone delivered a box of left-over turkey from yesterday's feast, so I put together a turkey pot pie." Becky wiped her hands on an apron.

Emma savored the moment. "Casey's joining us for dinner. Is there enough for one more?"

Becky wiped a crumb from Leslie's cheek. "There's plenty and I'm glad she's stopping by because I need to know how much I owe her for the clothes."

"Your money's no good." Emma said.

"She can't donate a whole wardrobe to a stranger."

"It's hardly a whole wardrobe, and she can afford it. Believe me, she loved selecting items for you."

"But I'm a stranger to her," Becky said.

Harley opened the cookie jar. "They'll wear you out trying to give you stuff. Might as well save your energy."

Emma blinked. Harley had contributed to the conversation without coaxing. She inhaled the delicious aroma coming from the oven, and her stomach rumbled. She'd wait until later to tell Harley about the detective. No way could she steal the joy of this moment. For now, she would enjoy the festive atmosphere.

At six-thirty, Casey burst through the back door without knocking. She flung off a crimson wool cape to reveal black velvet slacks with a clingy, sparkly gold sweater with a boat collar. A gold clip retrained her mass of curls into a high ponytail. Large gold hoops hung from her ears. She lifted her pert nose in the air and sniffed. "If dinner tastes as good as it smells, I might move in too."

"Sorry, but there ain't enough room for all your shoes," Harley said.

"And we sure don't have enough counter space in the bathroom for all your cosmetics." Emma raised her palm in the air, and Harley smacked it.

"Thanks a lot." Casey elbowed Emma. "I could see your tree from a block away. It looks great."

"That's Harley's doing," Emma said. "I'm hoping she'll help me decorate the house tomorrow."

"I ain't got nothing else to do." Harley shrugged.

Becky bit her lip. "Or perhaps you don't have anything else to do."

Harley scowled.

Becky's shoulders almost touched her ears. "Sorry, but the word 'ain't' is like fingernails on a chalkboard to my teacher ears."

Emma waited for a sharp retort but Harley only rolled her eyes. Would she regress to silence again?

"Before we can decorate, we'll need to buy fresh red ribbon." Emma removed her notebook from her purse.

"I'll take a pass on another trip to Circus-mart," Harley tossed a dishtowel on the kitchen counter.

"Admit it. You had fun yesterday," Emma said. "You were my hero, wading into battle, returning victorious."

Becky lifted Leslie from the highchair. "You're all heroes. I can't thank you enough for everything you've done."

"It's our pleasure," Casey said. "We single gals have to stick together."

Becky's eyes grew teary. "It's been a long time since I've had girlfriends."

Casey hugged her. "There's no better friend than Emma.

"But her mom is a piece of work," Harley muttered. "Watch out for her."

"I'll do my best to stay on her good side," Becky said.

"Impossible, because porcupines have prickles on all sides." Casey lifted a brow. "But she has a good heart, although she'd rather die than let anyone know."

Emma sighed. Her mother had a soft side, even though she rarely revealed it. Maybe, she had Harley's best interest at heart. If the private detective found Anne West, Emma vowed to do all she could to help her, for Harley's sake. She'd do anything to remove the angry look that often crossed Harley's face. Whatever happened, she'd make sure Harley knew she'd always be welcome in her home.

Emma tossed and turned through the night while she envisioned different scenarios in which she told her mother off for meddling. She flung the bedcovers back and paced around the room. *When at night I cannot sleep, I read a Psalm, instead of counting sheep.* The memory of Minnie's whimsical rhyme made her pause. Her Bible remained hidden in the hall closet. How many months had she ignored it?

On tiptoes, Emma crept down the hallway. Stretching, she felt underneath a stack of quilts. Her fingers touched the familiar shape, and she retrieved her Bible with the broken spine. The worn leather felt comfortable in her hands when she caressed it. Maybe a conservator could repair it. First thing on Monday, she'd call a shop in Atlanta and arrange to send it to them.

Chill bumps covered her arms when she returned to her bedroom, so she pulled on Chris's old cardigan, curled up in the winged back chair, and thumbed through the psalms. Different verses made her pause, and the knots in her shoulders eased. "Blessed are those who take refuge in him." She read on. "In peace I will both lie down and sleep; for you alone, O Lord, make me dwell in safety." She turned the page.

Within minutes, her lids were droopy, and she placed her broken Bible on the side table next to Winston Meador's letters. *Please forgive him for me.* She paused. *And please help Anne West. Thank You for allowing my home to be a refuge for Harley, Becky, and Leslie. I don't know what to do, so I'll leave it to You. May Your will be done.* Peace covered her like a warm blanket, and she crawled into bed. Maybe there was hope for her after all.

CHAPTER TWENTY-TWO—EMMA

After spending Saturday decorating the house for Christmas, Emma wanted to spend the afternoon resting. If only she hadn't asked the church secretary to post a notice in the bulletin requesting children taking part in the Christmas parade to be at the church for costume fittings at two o'clock today.

Oh, well. Emma shook herself from her reverie and rolled her shoulders. It would be another sleepless night if she didn't tell Harley before bedtime.

Emma and Harley drove the short three blocks to church just before two o'clock. Luke was there to unlock the doors.

"Thanks for taking this on," Luke said as he pocketed the keyring.

Emma shrugged. "It will be fun."

"As fun as a toothache," Harley grumbled.

Luke gave Emma a sympathetic look. "I'll be in Bob's office if you need me."

"We'll be fine." Emma led Harley to the costume room.

It took over three hours of wading through clothing to get everyone dressed for their parts.

Her troop of characters was traditional—Mary, Joseph, three wise men, four shepherds, four angels, and a plastic baby Jesus.

The last shepherd, ten-year-old Jeremy, had just tied the sash on his robe when Luke joined them amid the jumble in the fitting room. "How's it going?"

Emma adjusted a piece of cloth on the boy's head and tied a piece of rope around it. "Great. We're almost finished."

"Do I really get to hold a baby lamb?" Jeremy admired himself in the mirror.

"That's the plan." Emma handed him a shepherd's crook.

"Shut up!" Jeremy said with enthusiasm.

It seemed unwise to Emma to have live animals on the float, but it was a tradition. "So you'll have the wagon bed ready for this crowd?" Emma glanced at Luke.

"Yes, ma'am," Luke said, "I ordered hula skirts from Oriental Trading Company to edge around the wagon bed, and I retrieved old barn wood to build the manger. It's not my first three-ring-circus. There's nothing for you to do but show up."

"Right." Emma exhaled loudly. "Nothing for me to do." She studied the mass of costumes scattered across the room, and she helped Jeremy remove his robe and headdress. "Be here at three o'clock on Saturday."

"Yes, ma'am," Jeremy said. "My mom said I should meet her in the choir room."

"Okay," Emma hung his costume on a hanger. "Thanks for coming."

Luke picked up one of the rejected costumes on the floor. "Looks like you could use help."

Emma folded a piece of burlap. "Harley's around here somewhere."

"How is Harley?"

"Okay, I guess."

"How's she's handling your new houseguests?"

"She seems to enjoy playing with Leslie."

"That little sweetheart could melt the hardest of hearts."

"There's nothing hard about Harley's heart." Emma's tone sounded sharp.

Luke stopped in the middle of folding a sheet. "I didn't mean to imply—"

"Sorry, I'm a little touchy about Harley, and I'm tired of hearing whispers when we go places."

"I know the feeling," Luke said.

"Looks like a tornado struck in here." Harley stepped out from behind the door.

So she'd been there the whole time. Emma hung up another costume.

"Hi, Harley." Luke's voice reverberated in the small room.

"Hey."

"Are you going to be on the float?" Luke asked.

"Heck, no."

"You'd make a great angel."

A vinegar look crossed Harley's face. "Yeah. Right! The last thing I want is more people staring at me."

"Me too." Luke gave a tight smile.

"So I heard." Harley narrowed her eyes.

Luke smoothed his beard. "Looks like you have good help, Emma, so I'll head over to my workshop and finish the manger. He stopped at the door and lifted his hand. "See you Saturday."

"Not if I see you first," Harley muttered.

Emma bit her lip and kept working. When the room almost cleared, she said. "You don't like Pastor Luke."

Harley scowled. "I don't like most people."

"But why?"

Harley shrugged. "Because they don't like me."

Emma lowered her voice. "I like you."

Harley kept her face down.

"And so does Minnie, and Casey, Becky—and Leslie adores you."

"What about Mrs. Virginia?" Harley's jaw hardened.

Emma stared at the ceiling as if the right words might appear. "She'd never admit it, but I know she enjoys sparring with you, and I like how you stand up to her. Few people have the backbone to do that."

"But she doesn't like me." Harley's voice sounded angry.

"With Mother, trust has to come first, but give her time. Once you prove yourself, you'll have a warrior friend forever."

"A warrior?" Harley frowned.

Emma lifted a brow. "Just ask the city council members. She loves Weldon and fights hard for improvements."

"She just likes to boss everyone around."

"True, but she stands up for what she believes is the right thing to do." Emma tugged at her ear. "Speaking of that ... Mother is concerned about your missing mother."

Harley kept her face down. "So what's she gonna do about that?"

"She's not happy with the lack of results from the police, so she's hired a private detective."

Harley stilled.

"He wants to speak with you."

"Why?" Harley gulped. "I ain't heard from her."

Emma shrugged. "It can't hurt, and I'm sure you're worried about her."

Neither spoke for several seconds, then Emma couldn't stand the silence. "I've been thinking about this a lot. It's not normal for a mother to abandon her child unless there's a very good reason."

"Yeah, like she hated having me around."

"Or maybe she left with the man you were living with to protect you. I've not forgotten about your bruises."

Harley glared at her. "I fell."

"I haven't noticed you being clumsy. Maybe you took a tumble after someone pushed you."

Harley's jaw hardened. "It don't matter if this guy finds her. All my mom cares about is her drugs."

"Why didn't you share that with the social workers—or me for that matter?"

"'Cause it ain't nobody's business."

"Don't you want to find your mom?" Emma placed her hand on Harley's elbow.

Harley shrugged away and remained mute.

"The detective and Carol Carter will stop by tomorrow afternoon to meet with you. He'll have questions."

"But I don't know anything!" Harley shouted.

"Then it will be a short conversation." Emma resisted the urge to give her a hug. "Let's go home. I need a run."

"Are we going to Casey's for Chinese?"

"Yes." Emma bit her lip. "I should have mentioned it to Becky."

The drive to the house was silent. When they opened the back door, Pepper greeted them with a howl. Wonderful smells drifted from the kitchen.

"Something smells delicious," Emma said.

"Meatloaf will be ready in about an hour," Becky said. "It's been ages since I made one. Let's hope it tastes good."

"I should have mentioned it, but it's our habit to share Chinese takeout with Casey on Sunday evenings."

"Oh." Becky's nose scrunched up. "I shouldn't have assumed you didn't have plans."

"I'll just call her and have her come over here. It's not a big deal." Emma hung up her coat.

"Are you sure?" Becky bit her lip.

"She loves meatloaf." Emma patted her shoulder.

Harley grabbed Pepper's leash. "I'm going for a walk." And she left them.

"Is everything okay?" Becky asked.

Emma explained the pending meeting with the detective and the social worker.

"Poor kid," Becky said.

Emma rubbed the back of her neck. Harley's comment about her mother loving drugs gave her a sinking feeling. Harley often reminded her of her mother. Grandfather had said terrible things to Virginia when he drank. Had Harley suffered from the same mistreatment? Emma swallowed the lump in her throat. She could still hear him rant and slam doors. Why they'd stayed after grandmother died remained a mystery to Emma.

Emma called Casey, who showed up a few minutes later, lugging a large plastic container.

"What's all that?" Becky asked.

"Manicure supplies." Casey placed the tote on the coffee table.

"It's what we do on Sunday evenings," Emma explained.

"I've never seen so many colors of nail polish," Becky said.

Casey beamed her award-winning smile. "Are you up for a manicure?"

"Sure." Becky picked up a bottle of pink polish. "It's like I'm a teenager again at a sleepover."

When the back door opened, Pepper streaked to her food bowl while Harley hung up the leash. Virginia walked in behind them, dropped her purse on the sofa, and Pepper growled.

"That's enough out of you." Virginia pointed her finger at Pepper.

The schnauzer showed her teeth, then scampered upstairs on Harley's heels.

"Mother, what a surprise." Emma smoothed her hair.

Virginia's gaze followed Harley up the steps. "Yes, I thought I'd stop by before you left for Casey's to see if your houseguest needs anything."

"How nice of you," Becky said. "Thanks to Emma and Casey, I don't need a thing."

Virginia sniffed. "Something smells delicious."

"We're changing our routine for tonight," Emma said. "Becky made a meatloaf. Would you care to join us?"

"I wish I could, but I'm meeting a friend at the club." She removed an envelope from her bag and handed it to Becky. "As there's little rental property in Weldon, I had an idea. This is a Habitat for Humanity application."

"But that's for low-income families," Becky said.

Virginia sighed. "It's already a shame a teacher's pay is so low. As a single mother, you might qualify."

Becky bit her lip. "I hadn't thought about being able to afford to build a house."

"The purpose of the program is to help low-income families build and purchase modest homes. It's not a quick fix, and it can take several weeks to process an application, but it's the perfect long-term solution if you have patience and a willingness to learn how to use a hammer."

"Thank you," Becky said appreciatively.

"You're welcome." Virginia turned toward Emma and lowered her voice.

"Is Harley ready for tomorrow's interview?"

Emma nodded.

"Good. The sooner we find her mother, the sooner we can help both of them."

"Harley said her mother only loves drugs."

"As I suspected." Virginia shrugged. "When Luther finds the woman, we can determine the best course of action."

Casey lifted a penciled brow. "So you're on a first-name basis with the detective?" Her tone was sweeter than one of Mrs. Dot's fried pies.

Virginia gave her a sour look. "I've known Luther for years. In fact, he's the friend I'm joining for dinner."

Emma couldn't resist teasing her. "You're going on a date!"

Virginia harrumphed. "Nonsense. We're old friends." She emphasized the word *friends*. "Let me know how tomorrow's interview goes."

"I'm sure it will be confidential," Emma said.

"You're the child's guardian so I'm sure you'll be clued in." Virginia made *tsk*ing sounds and picked up her purse. "I must go, or I'll be late."

"Enjoy your date." Emma kissed her mother's cheek.

Virginia blushed. "It's dinner with a friend."

Casey winked at Emma. "That's also called a date."

Becky stared out the window and watched Virginia's Cadillac back out of the drive. "Your mother is so ..."

"Something else." Casey's penciled brow arched.

"Tell me about it." Emma popped her knuckles. Her mother liked to control everyone and everything. She hated to admit the Habitat application for Becky was a good idea, but it shredded her hope of stitching together a patchwork family. Soon she'd probably be all alone again. She borrowed a word from Harley—*Bummer*.

CHAPTER TWENTY-THREE—EMMA

On Monday morning, Emma stared at a thermometer then glanced at Harley's flushed face. "You have a slight fever. When did you start feeling bad?"

"I woke up puking?"

"Yes ... so best to stay in bed. I'll bring you up some juice and Tylenol."

"Thanks."

"It won't take me but a few minutes to pick up some files from the library. I can work from home today."

"I ain't a baby. I don't want you hovering all over me."

"I won't hover."

"Yes, you will. I'm just gonna stay in bed." Harley rubbed Pepper's soft ears. "Pepper will keep me company."

Emma bit her lip. "Maybe, I should take you to Dr. Singer."

Harley crossed her arms. "I ain't goin' to no doctor. My mom says doctors make you sick so they can make more money."

Emma lifted her head to the ceiling. "Fine. But if you're not better in the morning, I'm taking you to Dr. Singer."

A few minutes later, Emma passed Harley two pills. She swallowed them, emptied the glass of juice, and rubbed her sleeve across her face. "This will probably make me puke again. Happy?"

"I'll leave this plastic basin on the floor next to the bed in case you need it."

"I'm feeling better." Harley pulled the covers up to her chin. "I'm going back to sleep." She closed her eyes for a few seconds, then cracked an eye open. "You're hovering."

"Sorry." Emma looked at her watch. She supposed it wouldn't hurt to check in at the library. "I'm going. Call me if you need anything or if you start to feel worse."

"I can't because I'll be asleep."

Harley closed her eyes, and Pepper rested her chin on Harley's calf.

"Okay. I'm going." Emma backed up and closed the door softly.

Emma returned downstairs just in time to see Becky's car back out of the drive. *Rats!* She'd wanted to ask Becky if she thought Harley would be okay alone. The perfect answer popped into her head, and she dialed Minnie.

After a brief conversation, Minnie agreed to spend the day at Emma's sorting out the pantry. She'd planned to tackle that task Wednesday but said she could do it today.

"I'll be there as soon as I shower and stop by the Piggly Wiggly," Minnie offered in a cheerful voice. "This calls for a batch of my chicken noodle soup."

Relief flooded Emma. "Thank you. I'll come home for lunch and have a bowl."

"I'll look forward to seeing you."

Emma drove to the library with only a twinge of worry. She lifted a silent prayer of thanks for Minnie.

Emma's phone rang at almost ten. It was Minnie. Emma snatched up the phone. Before she could say a word, Minnie yelled into the phone. "The child's gone!"

Emma paced in front of the fireplace. Casey and Minnie sat on the sofa while Scotty Davis, a young policeman took notes. "When did you last see Harley?"

"About seven-thirty. Then I had a shower and went to the library."

Minnie stood. "I got here around eight-thirty and went upstairs to let her know I was here. When I went up at ten o'clock to take her temperature, I discovered the pile of clothes shaped to look like a body under the covers."

"Maybe she just snuck out to hang out with her friends. Let's call one of them."

Emma shook her head. "She doesn't seem to have any friends. At least, she's not mentioned them to me. She's only been with me a few weeks."

Minnie twisted her apron. "She must have slipped out while I ran the vacuum."

"Is anything missing? Do you keep money around the house?" The officer looked to Emma.

"I just keep pocket change." Emma said. "I haven't noticed anything missing."

Minnie cleared her throat. "There's been a package of bacon in the refrigerator for weeks. I thought about making BLTs the other day because it's getting close to its sale date. Did you cook it Emma?"

"No."

"It's gone."

"Why would she take a package of bacon?"

Minnie shrugged. "Why would the child run away?"

Virginia's white Cadillac pulled in the drive.

Emma closed her eyes. "It's Mother."

Seconds later, Virginia strode in and crossed her arms. "I know where she is."

Emma rushed to her. "Where?"

"She's on Highway 100 headed toward Rocky Hills. Luther's following her."

"The detective?"

"Yes. He's been watching the house. He suspected she might try to run away, knowing she'd have to answer questions this afternoon."

"So, he watched her leave?"

"Yes. She took a bicycle out of the garage."

"Chris's old bike?"

Virginia shrugged. "I don't know. Luther said she took off right after you left this morning. He's been following her because he thinks she'll lead us to her mother"

Emma's temple throbbed and heat spread throughout her body. "How dare you?" Emma knew her voice sounded harsh but she couldn't stop her temper toward her mother from flaring. "How dare he? Harley is not your responsibility. She's my responsibility. If anything happens to her, I'm holding you to blame."

Virginia lifted her chin. "I trust Luther. The child is going to her mother. What harm could there be in that?"

"She had bruises when she arrived!" Emma shouted. "She ran away."

Virginia's face blanched. "You never mentioned that."

Emma's phone rang. She glanced at the display. It was Luke. "Luke, I can't talk now. Harley's missing."

"I think I know where she is." Luke said tersely. "I just left the juvenile detention center in Rocky Hills and passed a biker wearing a coat like Harley's. At first, I didn't think anything of it, but I don't know. Something tugged at me so I turned around. There's a white sedan following the rider ..."

"That's probably the detective Mother hired."

"She's just turned left on a gravel road, and the sedan pulled over. I'm going to ask him what's going on." He disconnected.

A minute later, Luke called again. "I'm here with Detective Luther Warren. He's confirmed it's Harley on the bike. We're on Highway 100, about four miles West of Rocky Hills. I've pulled up Google maps and it looks like this is a long driveway that leads to a trailer. We're going in after her. Call the Rocky Hill's sheriff's office."

"Ok, I'm on it."

"And I need you to do one more thing."

"Yes. Anything."

"Pray."

CHAPTER TWENTY-FOUR— HARLEY

Harley opened the package of bacon and crept toward the two sleeping Rottweilers. A thick chain connected them to the corner of the trailer. Beau had never named the dogs, but Harley secretly called them Max and Buster. Black Max lifted his head, a low growl rumbling from his chest.

"Hey, guys. It's me and I brought you some food." She threw each dog a piece of bacon and their jaws snapped the meat from the air.

The first time she'd asked Beau if she could let the dogs off their chains, he'd ignored her. The second time she'd asked, he'd slapped her so hard, the side of her face stayed swollen and bruised for days. After that, she did her best to keep out of his reach.

Harley scanned the area. Beau's old rusted truck wasn't in the drive, and her racing heartbeat slowed. *God, if you're real, keep Beau away. Help me and Mom get out of here alive.* She bit the inside of her cheek and crept to the back of the trailer and looked for something to stand on so she could peek in the window. After stacking up old tires, she climbed up, peered inside and gasped. Her mom lay sleeping on the stained sofa. Something close to hope bubbled up in Harley.

Maybe, she could convince her mom to leave and they could get away before Beau got back.

Harley sprinted around the trailer and pushed open the front door. "Mama!" she called and dropped to her knees in front of her mother's face. Her mother's skin looked leathery, and there were blisters around her mouth. Harley gulped, and her mom opened her eyes and squinted. Harley gasped when her mother opened her mouth and revealed missing teeth.

The stench of her mother's breath made her gag, and she turned her head, but the trailer smelled like cat urine and rotten eggs. Burnt spoons and rolled up pieces of paper were strewn on the wooden crate. Harley removed a bottle of water from her pack and held it to her mother's lips. As she drank, some of it dribbled down her chin. When the bottle was empty, Harley wrapped her arms around her mother. "We've got to get out of here."

Anne sat up and dropped her head in her hands. "I need a minute."

"We might not have a minute. I'll help you." Harley tried to pull her up. "Come on, Mama. We can hide in the woods."

Her mother looked confused. "Hide in the woods?"

"If we can get out of here, I can call someone who will help us."

The dogs barked, and Harley froze, then she shouted the only words Beau ever said to them. "Shut up!" The dogs whimpered. In the distance, she could hear an engine. Harley wanted to run, but she couldn't leave her mom to Beau's cruelty. She tugged on her mother's arm. "We've got to hide." Her mother stood, swayed, and Harley put her arms around her. As they walked down the concrete block steps, her mother stumbled, and they both tumbled to the ground. A white pick-up truck parked in front of them.

Harley scrambled up and stared. *It couldn't be.* The aluminum plate on the front featured a green frog. *Pastor Luke.*

"Help." Harley waved her arm in the air.

Pastor Luke's door flung open.

"We need a doctor," Harley said. "But we've got to get out of here. Beau might be back any minute."

Another older man exited the passenger side of Luke's truck, a phone to his ear.

Harley dropped to her knees next to her mom, and cold mud soaked through her jeans. "Mama, it's okay. Pastor Luke will help us."

The man with white hair spoke with a gravelly voice. "The sheriff should be here any minute. I've asked for an ambulance."

Her mother curled up in a fetal position and cried. Harley didn't know what to do.

The preacher took off his denim jacket and placed it over her mom, then he knelt on the ground next to them. "It will be okay, Harley."

But Harley knew it would never be okay because the cops would arrest her mom when they went inside. What a mess. *How had Pastor Luke found her—and who was the man with him? Why couldn't people just mind their own business?* Harley swiped at her cheek.

A few minutes later, the wail of sirens broke the silence, and a sheriff's deputy parked behind Pastor Luke's truck. An ambulance arrived, and an EMT bent on his knee next to her mom. She fought him, crying and cursing, and she raged at Harley too.

Harley put her hands over her ears and squeezed her eyes shut. It seemed as if the devil had taken possession of her mom. Anne's panic gave her extraordinary strength but then the deputy intervened and helped subdue her.

It took a few minutes for the ambulance workers to secure her mom to the gurney with the aid of the two deputies who read her mom her rights over the barrage.

"Lord, have mercy," Pastor Luke said.

Harley sat on the ground, hugged her knees to her chest and hid her face. Shame flooded through her. She'd just wanted to warn her mom. Harley hadn't expected to find her in such a pitiful condition. The soiled, stained clothes covering her mother's skeletal frame and her leathery skin pock-marked with sores made Harley shudder. Never in a million years had she imagined it getting so bad. She shouldn't have left her mom to fend for herself with Beau.

Thirty minutes later, Harley waited with Pastor Luke in the yard while the police circled the trailer with yellow caution tape.

Emma's blue Honda skidded to a stop in front of Harley. Casey jerked open the passenger side door, but Emma jumped out of the first and sprinted toward her. Minnie and Virginia climbed from the back seat of the vehicle.

Emma grabbed Harley in a hug. "Are you okay?"

Minnie wrapped her big arms around them both, and Harley inhaled the comforting scent of her perfume and gulped. The tears she'd been fighting broke through, and Casey patted her back. "It's okay, honey."

Guilt pressed in on Harley. Her mother had been living in filth all these weeks while she'd been living in luxury, with food to eat every day.

At least Emma hadn't witnessed the pitiful state of her mom and the inside of the trailer.

Harley ran her hand across her face. "My mom is sick."

"Luke said they took her away in an ambulance. I'm sure she'll get the medical treatment she needs," Emma said.

"Will she go to jail?" Harley asked.

Emma rubbed the back of her neck. "I don't know, honey."

Virginia's lips disappeared into a grim line. "Luther reported there is a meth lab in the trailer."

What would Mrs. Virginia think about her now? Harley hung her head. If she could run off, and hide, she would.

"Let's not worry about that right now." Emma clutched Harley's hand.

Harley sniffed. "Mom's still on dope." Harley ran her sleeve across her cheek. "I'm done with her."

"Amen to that," Virginia said.

Minnie dug around in her purse. "The Lord don't give up on no one." She removed a package of tissues and passed it to Emma first, then Harley. "And I don't either."

"Amen to that." Emma dabbed at her cheeks with the tissue with one hand and gripped Harley's with the other.

Harley looked at her backpack still holding Beau's money. When he found out she'd led the cops to the trailer, he'd hunt her down for sure. She'd be dead before Christmas.

Luke cleared his throat. "Ladies, I'll leave you to sort things out."

"When you said you were following Harley, it was an answer to prayer." Emma gripped Harley's hand harder. "Thank you."

"No thanks necessary," Luke said. "I'd say it's a case of God looking out for Harley. I'm just glad He got my attention."

The hairs stood up Harley's arm. She *had* sort of prayed and asked God to help her.

"Definitely," Casey said.

Harley watched him leave. Pastor Luke had seen the worst of her mom and heard the ugly string of words, yet he'd knelt on the ground and prayed over her mother as she cussed him and everyone else. He'd also prayed over Harley, something no one had ever done. Maybe he wasn't all bad.

CHAPTER TWENTY-FIVE—EMMA

That evening, Emma sat in one of the club chairs, arms crossed and her knee bouncing up and down. Across from her, Virginia sipped a cup of chamomile tea. "Mrs. Rivers should be here in a few minutes."

During dinner, her mother informed them she'd invited a woman who'd opened a home for women recovering from addiction to stop by around seven o'clock. Would her meddling never end?

Becky excused herself with Leslie and scampered upstairs, while Minnie remained, sitting on the sofa next to Harley.

Virginia held the cup out and studied the blue flowers. "Mother loved this pattern, but I can't recall the name."

"It's Moonlight Rose," Minnie said.

Emma wanted to throw the cup at her mother.

Harley jutted out her chin. "Why do I have to talk to this woman?"

Virginia sipped her tea. "Patsy Rivers wants to rescue your mother."

"No one can do that." Harley voice sounded angry.

"I'm inclined to agree with you. However, let's see what Ms. Rivers has to say." Virginia placed the teacup and saucer on the coffee table.

"What's so special about her?" Harley glared.

"I'm not sure, but over a dozen women struggling with addiction have come through her program. They've found jobs and support themselves today, but most importantly, they've managed to stay drug-free." Virginia emphasized the last two words. "Don't think you're the only person in this household to deal with addiction."

Harley narrowed her eyes.

Virginia lifted her chin. "My father was an alcoholic."

Emma couldn't believe her mother had just shared their darkest secret.

"It's not the same as a druggie." Harley clenched her fist.

Virginia shrugged. "It took years for me to understand addiction is a disease."

"Why did you stay with him?" Harley scowled.

"I promised Mother not to abandon him, and I keep my word."

Harley glared at Emma's mother. "I hate my mom."

Virginia face softened. "Yet, you returned to her."

"I just wanted to ... " Harley stared at the floor.

Headlights beamed in the drive. "That will be Patsy Rivers," Virginia said. "Let's put on our best manners."

Harley rolled her eyes.

Emma opened the back door. A short woman with white hair, spiked with gel, stood in front of her. "You must be Ms. Rivers."

"Call me Patsy." She extended her hand.

"I'm Emma Baker. Thanks for stopping by."

After the introductions, Patsy settled herself in the leather club chair opposite Virginia, and her gaze wandered around the room. "This is a house and then some." Patsy's country accent reminded Emma of Dolly Parton. Emma guessed her to be from the Appalachian region.

"Yes, ma'am," Emma said. "I inherited it from my grandfather."

"Smack dab in the middle of town." Her gaze lingered on the stairs.

"It's convenient. I often walk to work."

"My home is out in the boondocks, sort of in a secret location so my guests' old friends can't find them. The women I take in spend time sheltered from the world during their first few weeks of recovery, but later, when they start new jobs, it's nice for them to be in town."

Virginia cleared her throat. "Can you tell us about your home and your program?"

Patsy beamed a smile. "It's not a program, it's a calling. It all began with me starting a Bible study in jail. One of the women who'd accepted Jesus had nowhere to go upon her release except to return to the people who got her hooked on drugs. After a lot of time arguing with God about why I couldn't take her in, I finally gave in. Then, there were more women, and my little house wasn't bigger than a shoebox. I prayed for weeks for an answer." She paused.

Emma sat on the edge of her seat. This woman knew how to tell a story.

"You will never believe what happened next."

"Tell us," Minnie said.

Patsy's face glowed. "A widow left me a large property with the perfect house, but I needed furniture."

"Thank you, Jesus!" Minnie clasped her hands together.

"There's more." Patsy sat up straight.

"Keep talkin'," Minnie said.

Patsy jumped up. "A television ministry featured our story on their show, and the next thing I knew, a lawyer created Freedom House as a nonprofit organization. Someone else set up a website, and donations flooded in."

Harley stared wide-eyed, her knee jiggling all the while Ms. Patsy talked.

"There are rules at Freedom House, but it's free, and I offer encouragement, love, and support while the women heal and reclaim their lives." Pasty grinned.

Virginia lifted a brow. "What do you think is the reason for your success when so many who enter rehab fail?"

Patsy squared her shoulders. "At Freedom House, we focus on the heart, mind, soul, and spirit. We study the Bible, and the women share their stories with each other. There is no judgment at Freedom House, only love, and loads of encouragement as we all learn together about God's unconditional love and forgiveness, and how God can use our past mistakes to his good. It's because they find Jesus that they live in freedom from their addiction."

Virginia narrowed her eyes. "But I understood you provided training for jobs?"

Mrs. Patsy nodded. "We do, but that comes second to teaching them how to live for Jesus."

Harley looked doubtful. "I don't think my mom's gonna want anything to do with Jesus."

Mrs. Patsy shrugged and sat down. "We won't know if we don't introduce her to Him."

"Will you visit Harley's mother in the hospital?" Emma asked.

Mrs. Patsy shook her head. "I'll ask the ladies who attend my Bible study at the detention center to approach her and invite her to join us. Sometimes it takes a while. "

Virginia cleared her throat. "Luther introduced me to a criminal attorney this afternoon. I asked him to represent

Ms. West." She clasped her hands in front of her. "Mr. Tate believes a judge will be lenient if your mother will work with the authorities to help locate the man who owned the property where they discovered the meth lab."

"Mom won't be a snitch." Harley crossed her arms.

"The right attorney might convince a judge to release her within a few weeks if she's willing to enter a qualified rehabilitation program," Virginia said.

"My mom ain't gonna want nothing to do with rehab." Harley's eyes brimmed with unshed tears.

Patsy frowned. "It's mighty nice of you to hire her an attorney, but she needs to stay in jail long enough for the ladies in my Bible study to connect with her. Let's pray for God to make that happen."

Minnie patted Harley's knee. "I'll promise to keep her in my prayers, and I'll ask the women in my Sunday school class to pray too."

Emma's heart softened. "And I'll pray."

"Let's go to the Father," Patsy said. "When two or more are gathered in His name—"

"He is here with us." Minnie bowed her head.

Harley fidgeted when Emma squeezed her hand.

Patsy's booming voice reverberated in the room. "Lord. Thank you for loving us enough to send Your Son to rescue us. We need Your help. Please carry Harley's mom through this dark night while she fights the demon of drug addiction. Give us time, Lord, to help her. We can do nothing without You. Give us wisdom, courage, and Your strength. Open the door for us, Father. Help us help her. I claim victory in the name of Jesus, amen."

No one spoke, and they sat in silence. At last, Virginia said, "Thank you for coming."

"It's my pleasure, and thank you for your generous donation to Freedom House."

Virginia's jaw hardened, and her eye twitched.

Patsy stood and brushed her jeans. "I hate to rush off, but I need to get back to Freedom House."

"Thank you." Emma stood and gripped her hand.

Patsy's eyes twinkled. "Let's go to lunch one day soon. God planted a little seed the moment I crossed your threshold, but I need to let it germinate for a few days and make sure it was the Lord speaking and not Patsy getting ahead of Him."

"I'd love that."

Patsy brows lifted. "You're the librarian, right?"

"Yes, ma'am."

"Why don't you come out to our house one day and tell the ladies about library services?"

"I'll be happy to," Emma said. "Maybe we should add your home to the bookmobile schedule."

"That's a great idea," Patsy said. Her gaze landed on the grandfather clock. "Oh no—I need to go." She hugged Emma. "I'll be calling you. And Harley, I'll be praying for you and your mama."

Harley just stared at her.

Later that night, Emma knelt at her bedside. She pictured the rundown trailer where Harley's mom lived, the half-starved dogs with the heavy chains. A shelter worker had taken away the poor things. Never in her life had she witnessed such poverty. Never in her life had she been this angry with her mother.

Her muscles tensed, and acid burned through her. No. She would not succumb to this. *In everything give thanks.* Emma lifted a prayer of thanks for sending Luke and the detective to rescue Harley and for Ms. Patsy's program. As she spoke her gratitude for each blessing aloud, the burning ember extinguished. When she could think of nothing else for which to be appreciative, she remained motionless for a long time, wilted from the heaviness of the day. She lifted Anne's name and Winston's. *Help them, Father. Help me love them as you love them.* Peace washed through her. "Thank you, Jesus. "Emma stood and rubbed the cramp in her leg. She felt compelled to go upstairs and check on Harley. If only she could protect the child from more heartache. *Impossible.*

Emma knocked on Harley's door and found her sitting in the tower's window seat, behind the multicolored Christmas tree changing colors.

"How are you feeling?"

Harley shrugged. "Sad."

"At least we know your mom is receiving medical treatment."

Harley sniffed. "She said awful things to me. She called me a ... and said she hoped I would ..."

Emma swallowed the lump in her throat. Oh, how she wished she had words that could erase Harley's pain and find a way to shield her from the hurt. "Drug addiction is not a problem with a quick solution. We need to keep praying for your mom."

"Humph. I heard Ms. Patsy, but y'all don't know my mom. She's hopeless. I realized that when she cussed everyone who tried to help her."

Emma rubbed her temples. "I'm sorry."

"Why are you sorry? It ain't—" She bit her lip. "It's not your fault."

"No one is hopeless, and prayer helps. I thought I was hopeless, always so angry and bitter, but since I started praying for Winston Meador, I've realized my heart is starting to change."

"What's that mean?" Harley looked at her confused.

Emma searched for the words. *Father, help me.* "When Chris died, I blamed God for not protecting him. Angry doesn't begin to describe how I felt. But I've learned my fury separated me from God."

"I still don't get it?"

"I felt like God abandoned me, but I was the one who stopped reading the Bible and stopped praying."

Harley gave her a long look.

Emma wiped her damp palms on her jeans. "Prayers are powerful, and when I began lifting petitions for someone I considered my enemy—I know it seems impossible—but I began to care about him."

Harley dug her hands into her armpits. "I sort of prayed today, before I went to the trailer."

"And what happened?"

Harley shrugged. "It didn't turn out like I expected, but I'm still here."

"That's an answer to my prayers."

"If God's in charge, why didn't He do something to keep my mom from becoming a druggie? For that matter, why does He let bad things happen?"

"That's a hard question, but I think the answer is God gives each of us free will. We are free to make choices, even when they harm us and others get caught in the wave."

Harley turned away from Emma and stared out the window.

"We shouldn't judge. When dealing with difficult people, especially at the library, it helps me to think everyone is doing the best they can."

Harley shrugged. "That's like ... sticking your head ... um, in a groundhog's hole."

"But what if it is the truth? We don't know what others have experienced. Sometimes it's mental illness or other issues. One of Minnie's favorite sayings is 'But for the grace of God, there go I.'"

"What does that mean?"

"It means without God's blessings and favor, I'd be walking in their shoes."

Harley rolled her eyes.

"Let's pray for your mom."

"Saying a bunch of words ain't gonna help."

"It won't hurt." Emma placed her hand over Harley's rough one

After a moment's silence, Harley said, "Please help my mom get off the drugs."

Emma held onto Harley's hand. "Amen."

"People like you don't get it." Harley dabbed at her cheek with her shirttail.

"I think we do more than you know. Mother shared our darkest secret tonight. Believe me, we understand what it's like to live with an addict."

"I ain't gonna be like y'all and put up with it. I'm done with Mom."

"Everyone makes mistakes, and everyone deserves forgiveness."

Harley chewed her nail and looked out the window. "I'm sorry I lied to you this morning."

"I would have helped you."

"You'd have called the cops."

"The police are not the enemy."

"They are where I come from."

Emma's shoulders drooped. "You have nothing to fear from the police, unless you break the law."

"I stole a hair-coloring kit from the Dollar Store."

Emma lifted a brow. "Casey said she paid for it."

Harley looked away. "So she told you? I should have known." Her tone sounded menacing.

"She's my best friend, and she's your friend, too, Harley."

They sat in silence for a long time, then Harley sighed. "Why are you so good to me?"

"Because I love you, and I care about you. You'll always be welcome in my home. I hope you know that."

Harley gave her a long stare, and then reached for her and gave her a strong hug that Emma melted into. It would rip her heart out to lose Harley, but Emma knew the young girl's happiness and well-being depended on her mother's recovery to health. Every possible outcome included heartache for someone. *Lord, give me strength...*

CHAPTER TWENTY-SIX—EMMA

On Saturday morning, Emma sat at her kitchen table, dreading the day. What if a child fell off the float today and was injured? Her coffee grew cold, and the muscles in her shoulders tensed. *Stop imagining the worst. It's gone off without a hitch for years.*

Attending the annual Christmas parade used to be one of her favorite traditions. Anyone willing to pay the ten-dollar entry fee could take part, and Chris never missed being in the lineup. He'd purchased an exact replica of a Buddy costume from the *Elf* movie. Those yellow tights never failed to make her laugh out loud. Her manly man would skip around and pass out candy canes to adults and children.

Emma corrected her posture. The festive event might pull her and Harley out of their dark moods.

Thank goodness for Becky and Leslie's company this week. The toddler's antics lifted their spirits during the evening meals, and Emma appreciated Becky's interest in Harley's homework. She'd winked at Emma and claimed it unethical for a math teacher to live under the same roof with a student and not check her homework. Harley groaned and griped, but she listened to Becky's instructions. After reviewing math worksheets, Becky moved on to other subjects without missing a beat. Becky's tactics impressed Emma.

Last evening, they'd all accepted Casey's invitation to join her and Daniel for the Friday night catfish special at the Triple D. It seemed everyone in the restaurant stopped by their table and said something kind to Harley. When Luke walked into the diner, Mrs. Dot escorted him to their table as if she'd been instructed to do so, and Emma scooted her chair over without being asked.

The meal had been fun, and some of the knots in Emma's shoulders disappeared through the laughter.

Emma dumped her cold coffee in the sink and refilled her mug. Time to put on a happy face. She would not meditate on the past nor worry about Harley leaving. Stewing on it solved nothing. *What if "it" never happened and Harley got to stay with her?* Her heart constricted. That was a selfish thought. Harley needed her mom to recover.

Emma savored her coffee and closed her eyes. It would be a good day, and nothing could tarnish the joy of Christmas and the hope it offered.

The familiar sound of Harley's boots clomping down the steps made Emma smile. "Good morning! You're up early."

"Pepper needs to go out." Harley put on her camo coat and pulled the black cap over her ears.

"I'll go with you." Emma rose and grabbed her coat.

"Whatever."

When Emma stepped outside, she gasped. The hoarfrost left the landscape looking every bit a fairyland and their warm breath created a fog around them.

Pepper tentatively stepped forward, shaking her paw after each step. Emma giggled. The dog sniffed at a mole's burrow, dug, and looked up with a mustache covered in mud and dirt.

"Stop that," Emma commanded, but Pepper ignored her and kept digging. Then she rolled in the freshly dug dirt.

"Come!" Harley said. Pepper hesitated, but then obeyed. "You're a mess." Harley reached down and brushed the schnauzer's mustache. "Now you'll need a bath."

Hearing the word *bath*, Pepper lowered her ears and growled.

"If she keeps this up, you'll deserve a raise," Emma said.

"Silly dog." Harley scratched Pepper's ears. "That's all right. I like taking care of her."

"How do you feel about your mom's situation?"

Harley blew out a breath. "I try not to think about it. I'll bet everyone in town is talking about her."

"That's part of living in a small town."

"I don't know why they have to put the arrest reports in the paper." Harley's jaw hardened. "It was bad enough y'all had to see where we lived. Now everyone at school will know about my mom." She kicked a rock on the path in front of her.

Lord, give me the words. Time seemed to stand still while she studied the shimmering ice and searched for words of comfort. At last she said, "Nothing will make this easy, but I know from experience that when you go through something like this, you'll discover your true friends."

Harley's hunched shoulder stooped further. "I ain't ... " She gulped. "I don't have any friends."

"You'll never find more loyal friends than Casey and Minnie. Don't forget Becky—and Mr. McCullough likes you too. I hope you count me as someone you can trust."

"I hadn't thought of y'all as my friends."

"We are. Mother may seem hard, but I know she'd walk through fire for you. Did you see the look on her face when we arrived at the trailer?"

"Yeah. She looked like she might whoop someone."

"And she would if she thought someone meant to harm you." Emma looped her arm through Harley's. "It's freezing out here. Let's go in."

A flock of cardinals covered their back yard. Their scarlet feathers glowed against the frost of the morning. "Wow!" Harley exclaimed. "Have you ever seen anything like that before?"

"Cardinals! A sign of good luck! Maybe this is a signal the tide has turned. Here's to *A Red Bird Christmas!* That's a great Christmas book written by Fannie Flagg. You should read it."

"You and your books." Harley smiled and shook her head.

Luke's white pickup truck pulled the Christmas float into line in the high school parking lot. Emma looked at her watch and bit her lip. Four o'clock. The child to play the part of the Virgin Mary still hadn't shown up. Emma's phone vibrated and she hit the button.

"Is this Emma?"

"Yes." Emma placed her hand over her other ear.

"It's Kirsten Williams. I'm sorry, but Bethany's sick, so she won't be able to play the part of Mary after all."

"Oh, no." Emma's stomach dropped.

"I should have called you earlier, but she kept saying she felt better."

"Sounds like she's not."

"It's a stomach bug. You do not want the gory details."

Emma sighed. "I hope she feels better soon."

"Me and you both," Kirsten said.

Emma rubbed her palms over her face. *Now what?* The parade wouldn't start for another hour, but that didn't leave much time to find someone to fill in.

"What's wrong?" Harley said.

"Bethany Williams, aka the Virgin Mary, is sick." Emma gave Harley a piteous and pleading look.

"No." Harley shook her head. "No way am I riding on the float with a bunch of little kids."

"Please," Emma's voice sounded imploring. "We can't have a nativity scene without Mary."

"I ain't got a costume." Harley chewed her nail.

Emma looked at her closely, then tried to hide a smile. "It won't take but about ten minutes to run to the church, but we'll have to go on foot because of the traffic. I'll owe you forever," Emma grabbed Harley's arm. "Let's go, but first we need to tell Luke." She stopped and shouted to Luke, who held a baby lamb. "Can I have your church keys? Bethany's sick and we need a costume for Harley to fill in for Mary!"

He smiled. "We had the new electronic locks installed a few days ago. All you need is the code." Luke leaned in, his lips touching her ear, and she shivered. He whispered, "1812. The year they founded the church. It's on the plaque next to the door in case you forget."

Emma mimicked Harley's usual eye roll. It would only be a matter of days before everyone in town knew the secret code. She left Luke and a parent in charge of the rowdy kids and the lambs on the float.

Almost an hour later, Harley sat on the float surrounded by the others. With her blonde hair covered by a wig of long dark hair, Harley resembled the girl who'd first come to live with Emma.

Ovaleta Mayhew, Mrs. Dot's sister, trotted up to Emma and handed her a piece of paper promoting the Sassy Creek Christmas parade. Sassy Creek was a small community about ten miles from Weldon."

"We'd love to have Loving Chapel's float in our little line-up."

Emma bit her lip. "I doubt I can fit another event into my schedule.

"I heard you took in a little girl, and a young mother with a toddler."

Emma nodded and pointed. "That's Harley."

"She looks sweet."

Emma lifted a brow. *I'll bet no one has ever called Harley that before.*

Ovaleta leaned in. "And I also heard about a good-looking interim pastor."

Emma shook her head. "You and your match-making schemes. It didn't work last year when you tried to fix me up with Seth Davis."

"You let Pastor Seth get away. I hope you won't make the same mistake twice."

"I didn't make a blunder. Seth's completely smitten with his new fiancée."

"I hope you'll reconsider the parade." Ovaleta fluffed her white curls. "I'm going to be Mrs. Claus, and Roy's going to be Santa. We'll be riding in Weldon's antique firetruck."

"That sounds perfect, but I'm afraid I can't make any promises. I'm sure you'll have plenty of entries as it seemed everyone in Sassy Creek was in the parade last year."

"They were. That's why we decided the people who live on the east side of the road will be in the parade this year, and folks who live on the west side of the road will cheer. They'll swap places next Christmas. Last year was a mess and a half, but somehow, God worked it all out."

"He always does." A shrill whistle pierced the air.

"Everyone ready?" Seth shouted from his truck.

"I've got to go." Emma hugged Ovaleta. "Merry Christmas."

Ovaleta whispered. "That man is good looking. Don't let him get away."

Emma pushed back from the hug. "I don't know who's the biggest meddler, you or your sister."

Ovaleta's shoulders touched her ears. "Probably a tie, but Dot's less subtle."

You're both about as subtle as a tank. But Emma smiled at Ovaleta's cheerful countenance. The parade started, and the route passed through the square, then down Main Street. Harley waved at the crowd and Emma walked beside the float. For the first time since she'd been living with Emma, Harley acted like a kid, but Emma still had not heard the girl laugh. She wished Anne West were here to see her daughter instead of in the hospital ... or maybe she was in jail by now. The thought of Anne in a prison cell made her picture Winston Meador locked up. Poor kid. Surprised at the sympathy she felt for Winston, she lifted another prayer. *Thank You, Jesus.*

Something squished under her sneaker. Emma groaned. The Arabian horses following the high school marching band had littered the street with tokens of their appreciation, and she'd stepped right into the middle of one of their gifts. She remembered her vow from early this morning. Nothing would ruin this day, the Christmas season, and the hope it offered. She shoved her hands in her coat pockets and lifted her chin. It doesn't matter. No one will notice. *Horse hockey.*

Emma watched proudly as Harley rode in the center of the best float in the parade, surrounded by angels, a real baby lamb cuddled next to her. They passed Emma's house, and Becky, Mrs. Virginia, Casey, and Minnie waved and called out to them. The Christmas tree in the tower shined out on Main Street, and Emma thought their home to be the prettiest in town.

The parade route circled back toward the high school parking lot. This day would be a memory Emma would keep forever.

But Emma was suddenly distracted when she saw Harley jerk her head to the side of the float and her eyes open wide. Emma followed Harley's gaze toward a man wearing a dark leather jacket with a do-rag and black sunglasses, looking totally out of place amid the town's festive folks and charming atmosphere.

Harley turned back around and looked down at the lamb as she pet it.

Quit overreacting, it was nothing. Emma reminded herself not to let her imagination or fear take over, but she couldn't help a motherly instinct that rose inside.

CHAPTER TWENTY-SEVEN—LUKE

Luke turned off the bedside lamp and heaved a sigh. Exhaustion washed over him, but it was a good kind of tired. The parade float turned out better than expected, and his chest swelled at the memory of Emma claiming it was perfect. What a trooper she'd been through the entire event. Nothing had rattled her, not even the last-minute substitution for the sick child, the bleating lambs, nor walking the two-mile parade route with manure caked on her shoe.

He'd kept track of her by using the side mirror of his truck as she walked beside the float. So many people from the crowd called out greetings to her and to him throughout the journey. He was beginning to feel at home in Weldon, and his heart warmed.

It seemed unbelievable the girl riding on the float was the same one he'd rescued in Rocky Hills on Monday. Over and over, he couldn't stop thanking the Lord for intervening.

On Thursday evening, he'd stopped by the hospital to visit Anne West, and she convinced him there were truly evil people in the world.

Harley's mom and his mom had so much in common. The old anger bubbled up, and once again, he surrendered.

Search me, God, and know my heart; test me and know my anxious thoughts. See if there be any offensive way in me and lead me in the way of life everlasting. He repeated the Scripture passage from Psalm 139 over and over until peace infused him. He then lifted a silent petition for Anne West and his mother.

His phone dinged, indicating a text message. He snatched it. Only bad news came this late in the evening. The text was from Emma.

> **"The float looked great. You went above and beyond what we normally do. Be sure to turn in your expense receipts to the church secretary so you can get laid."**

Luke's mouth hung open. His cheeks warmed. He pondered the last word. She'd never say something so crude. Another text came through.

> **If the budget committee complains you spent too much on the supplies, let me know, and I'll take care of it.**

His eyes widened. *Control your thoughts.* The phone dinged again.

> **PAID, PAID, PAID Stupid auto correct. you should be paid, reimbursed for your expenses, not LAID.**

Luke burst out laughing. Another ding.

> **If I'm not at church tomorrow, it's because I've died of embarrassment. Please delete this string of texts.**

Luke chuckled again. *Poor Emma.* He yearned to put her at ease. He hit the call button. After five rings, Emma answered. "Don't even look at me tomorrow. I'm likely to burst into flames."

"I knew immediately it was a typo or something was amiss." He held back a laugh.

"I'd never—"

"I know. Don't worry about it."

"So you deleted the text?"

"I will the moment we hang up if you promise me you won't fret about this."

"You're asking the impossible."

"We're friends. Right?" Luke held his breath and waited.

Her voice was just above a whisper. "Yes."

"Good. I've sent messed up text messages too. Everyone does."

"I guess, but if anyone found out."

"They won't. Trust me."

"Okay. Thanks for understanding." Emma's voice sounded almost normal.

Luke yearned to keep her on the phone so he steered the conversation to Harley and her transformation. Then they talked about Brother Bob's influence in his life and how Emma might be filling the same role for Harley. When he heard Emma yawn, he knew he needed to let her go. "Sorry to keep you up."

"I enjoyed talking with you. You gave me some good advice."

"You're doing great," Luke said.

"Right back at you."

An awkward silence fell over them.

"I guess I'll say goodnight." Luke gulped. "Sleep well."

"You too."

Luke lay on his back with his hands behind his head for a long time thinking about Emma. It had been years since he'd ended the day with a conversation with a woman, and he'd enjoyed every minute. He liked every second spent in Emma's company. This was a problem, but he couldn't seem to help himself any more than his grandmother could resist alcohol.

Luke visited the hospital the next morning to give Eleanor an update on the parade and the events that had occurred with Harley, but it turned out the pastor's wife had an update for him as well.

The heavy weight that pressed down on Luke's shoulders crumbled when he looked into the alert eyes of Pastor Bob. Eleanor sat next to his bedside, the smile on her face bright enough to light up the darkest night.

"The newest antibiotic worked," Eleanor crowed.

Bob lifted a hand. "What do you think about my new room?"

Luke pulled a chair from the hospital room's corner next to Eleanor. "Love it."

"It's nice to be out of the ICU waiting room." Eleanor smiled.

"Tell me about my flock." Bob hit a button and the bed lifted him to an upright position.

"No," Eleanor sounded fierce. "You need to rest and recover. Luke has everything under control."

Luke rubbed the back of his neck. "I've never felt more helpless in my life."

"That's good," Pastor Bob gave a weak smile. "Because that's when you let the Lord take over."

"Amen to that," Luke said.

"Let me pray for you," Pastor Bob said.

Luke's chest warmed. "I'd appreciate that, and please include Harley, her mom, Anne West, and Emma Baker."

Pastor Bob's brows drew together.

"Harley's the teenager Emma took in," Eleanor said.

Luke's shoulders dropped. "I visited Anne West's hospital room the other day." He rubbed his palms over his face. "She's an addict in withdrawal."

"Lord, have mercy," Eleanor said.

Luke's heart ached for the woman who looked skeletal and for Harley, who would surely suffer nightmares. Anne West had appeared so helpless, but then when the ambulance drivers tried to help her, she'd fought them, and spewed a vomit of words that matched her deplorable condition.

He was so thankful God had pulled him from his thoughts to notice the camouflage coat and for the detective on Harley's heels—and grateful there would be no more meth cooked in the rusted trailer.

Brother Bob's prayer lifted him from his dark thoughts. The soft words of his mentor and friend flowed over him like warm water, washing away the sludge and muck of the past few days. Hope for Harley's mother replaced despair. *Lord, You know what she needs. Please provide it.*

On Sunday morning, Luke sang "O Come, O Come, Emmanuel" with the congregation while it felt like moths multiplied in his stomach. He experienced this sensation every time prior to standing in the pulpit. With Bob on the mend, he figured he would soon be leaving, and he was surprised the thought made him a little melancholy.

His gaze landed on Emma and the pew she almost filled now with people from her home. When their eyes connected, her cheeks flushed pink and she turned away. He wished he could somehow help her forget the silly text message ... though it had been a long time before he had fallen asleep last night due to his errant thoughts. *Father, forgive me.*

The song ended and Luke stepped into the pulpit. "Did you pay attention to the words? *God with us.* They reminded me that God is with me. He saved me and he can rescue you too. I came to Jesus in filthy rags, and He's clothed me in His righteousness. I have many failures. I'm a liar. I've coveted what others possess. I'm a man with sinful thoughts. But I have hope because God sent His Son to save me."

Luke ignored his notes and allowed the Holy Spirit to take over. His skin prickled and the air in the room seemed charged with electricity. Yes. God had something to say this morning. If God could use him, even with all his failings, He could use anyone.

CHAPTER TWENTY-EIGHT—EMMA

On Monday afternoon, Emma sat in her library office staring at the spreadsheet on the computer screen when her assistant knocked on her door. "Carol Carter is here to see you."

The hairs stood up on the back of Emma's neck. "Th—thanks." *Breathe.* "Please show her in." Emma stood.

"Sorry to drop in without calling," Carol said.

"No problem. Can I get you a cup of coffee?"

"No thanks. I just left the courtroom. Anne West pleaded guilty to cooking meth, and the judge sentenced her to five years in prison."

A wave of sadness washed over Emma, then her treacherous heart lifted. "So I'll have Harley for five years." She knew her voice sounded upbeat but she couldn't help it. Hope and joy at the news swelled her heart at the prospect of Harley being able to stay, tinged with a little bit of guilt. She shifted in her seat and averted her gaze. How selfish could she be?

Carol cleared her throat. "Thanks to her plea agreement, the judge showed leniency and she'll be eligible for parole in a year."

Emma clasped her hands in front of her, her joy fading. "Th—that's good news."

"The judge showed great compassion by agreeing to allow her to serve her time here in the county jail so she can have regular visits with Harley."

Emma nodded, her stomach aching. "Maybe that will give Ms. Rivers time to get through to her."

"I've heard about her home, but I'm skeptical in this case. Anne West must prove she can stay clean, care for herself, and take care of her daughter before she recovers her parental rights." Carol's jaw turned hard. "In the meantime, Ms. West wants to see Harley, and it's my job to schedule regular visitations."

"What if Harley doesn't want to go?"

"We won't force her, but through my years of social work, something I've learned is that kids always love their parents. It doesn't matter if the parents neglected them or abused them."

Emma nodded and blinked. "Just tell me when and where to take her." Her voice came out in a croak.

"I'll take her and supervise the first visitation. We'll see how that goes before we make other plans."

A numbness blanketed Emma.

Carol closed her notebook. "If it's okay with you, I'll stop by this afternoon and speak with Harley."

"Of course."

Carol's expression looked like she'd just bit into an aspirin. "Please encourage Harley to give her mom a chance."

Emma's throat constricted.

That afternoon, Emma and Harley sat at the kitchen table across from Carol Carter, who gave a semblance of a smile. "The authorities transferred your mother to the county jail, and I'd like to set up regular visitations."

Harley crossed her arms, and her knee bobbed under the table.

Ms. Carter explained the details of her mom's plea agreement, in which she waived her right to a jury trial.

Harley gulped. "Five years."

"Or maybe as little as one year, depending on the parole board's decision," Carol said.

"Did the cops tell you how crazy she acted?" Harley leaned her elbows on the table and covered her face with her hands.

"That was the effect of the drugs," Carol closed her notebook. "She's clear-headed now, and she's asked about you."

Harley's face paled. "I don't want to see her."

"Your mother has the right to visitations, and it's my responsibility to make that happen." Carol closed her day-planner.

Emma squeezed Harley's shoulder. "Let's give her a chance."

Harley shrugged her away. "If you want me out of here, just say the word."

Emma softened her voice. "I love having you here."

"Then why do you want to send me back to my mom? You saw the dump where we lived. Just ask the preacher about the ugly things she screamed at me."

"As much as I'd love for you to live here forever, the goal of the foster care program is to reunite the child and parent. I made a promise to help make that happen, and if your mom can't get her act together, you know you're welcome to stay."

Harley shoulders slumped and she stared at the floor.

"But I've been praying for you *and* your mom," Emma continued. "The more I've prayed, the more I've come to care about both of you."

Harley rolled her eyes. "If she knew that, she'd laugh in your face or cuss you out, depending on her mood." She crossed her arms. "I've had enough of her cussin's."

Carol gripped her pen. "No one will be verbally or physically abusive to you."

Harley scraped the floor with her chair and she pushed away from the table. "I need a walk. I'm taking Pepper out."

She grabbed Pepper's leash and the little dog scampered to the door. Harley slammed it behind her.

"Don't let her fool you," Carol said. "She may be angry with her mom, but she still cares for her."

"I feel helpless." Emma sighed heavily.

"Welcome to my world." Carol stood.

Late that night, the phone on Emma's bedside table vibrated, and she opened her eyes. The clock showed 12:22. *Nothing good ever happens after midnight.* She snatched the phone. "Hello."

"Is this Emma Baker?"

"Yes."

"This is Scotty Jepson with the Weldon Police."

"What's wrong?" Emma's heart stuck in her throat. *Something's happened to Mother.*

"Isn't Harley West the kid that ran away last week?"

"Yes. I'm her foster parent."

"Do you know where she is?"

"Upstairs." Emma clutched at her throat.

"No, ma'am. I'm staring at her. She's in a Jeep Cherokee registered to you."

"What?"

"We're parked on Highway 31W South, at the city limits. She has a flat."

"I'll be right there."

"Yes, ma'am."

Emma placed her hand over her pounding heart. She'd never considered Harley knew how to drive. And to take Chris's Jeep. Emma couldn't remember when the vehicle had last been started. The tires were probably dry rotted. Casey had encouraged her to sell it, but the thought of seeing someone else drive the vehicle around town, a constant reminder of Chris, was something she hadn't wanted to experience.

Emma grabbed a pair of jeans and her hands shook as she fastened them. When she got her hands on Harley, she'd ... *What?* What would she do? What could she do? Might Carol Carter remove Harley from her home? Tears filled Emma's eyes. She might lose Harley.

Twenty minutes later, Harley sat in the passenger seat of Emma's Honda. Emma stood in the cold next to Officer Scotty. "Thanks for calling." Her tone was clipped.

Scotty sighed and jerked his chin toward Harley. "Seems like this girl is determined to run. It's not your fault."

Emma swallowed the lump.

"I'll have to make an official report. If I were you, I'd call Social Services first thing in the morning."

Emma nodded.

"What about your Jeep?" Scotty pointed his flashlight at it.

"I'll call a wrecker service and have it towed."

"Want me to wait with you?"

"No. We'll be fine."

A few minutes later, Harley sat in the passenger seat of the Honda while they waited for the tow truck. Emma drummed her fingers on the steering wheel. "Where were you going?" Her voice sounded cold in her own ears.

Harley stared out the darkened window.

"Why?" Emma pounded the steering wheel with her fist.

Harley swiped at her cheek. "I don't want to see my mom."

"Is that what this is all about?"

Harley shrugged.

They sat in silence until the wrecker showed up. Emma gave him a slip of paper. "After you change the tire, just tow it to this address and leave it in the drive."

The return ride to Weldon was silent, and Emma's thoughts drifted to Luke. He had experience working with troubled kids, and she had no idea what to do. She'd almost lost Harley tonight. She gripped the steering wheel to keep her hands from trembling. First thing in the morning, she'd call him.

When Emma parked in the driveway, she asked the question again. "Where were you going?"

Harley let out a long sigh. "To the beach."

Emma's jaw dropped. "That's over six hundred miles." Her pulse pounded at her temple.

"I think I have family there." Harley's voice sounded defeated.

Finally, an answer. "Who?"

"Mamaw and Papaw, but all I remember is the beach. I don't remember their names."

Emma's entire body trembled. "Why didn't you tell the social workers you had family?"

Harley shrugged again, and Emma wanted to shake the answer out of her. Silently, she focused on controlling her breathing. After a minute she said, "I'll help you find them if you'll promise me something."

Harley stared straight ahead, her chin jutted in the air.

"I'll help you find your grandparents if you promise me you won't run away again."

Harley gave a brief jerk of her head up and down.

"No, ma'am. That will not do. I need to hear the words."

"I promise, I won't run away again," Harley's voice was just above a whisper.

As they trudged to the back door, someone shined a flashlight in Emma's face and a booming voice startled her. "Who goes there?"

Emma shielded her eyes with her hands. "It's Emma, Mr. McCullough."

"Everything okay?" His gruff voice made her cringe.

She felt anything but okay, but the last thing she wanted to do was stand in the cold and tell Mr. McCullough about Harley's escapade. "Everything's fine," Emma covered her eyes with her sleeve. "You're blinding me with the light."

The light shifted away and Emma blinked. Mr. McCullough marched toward them wearing striped pajamas and leather house slippers. He held his Super-Soaker in one hand and a flashlight in the other. "Do y'all know what time it is?"

"Yes, sir."

"I guess you have a good reason for waking up the entire neighborhood."

Emma wanted to tell him he was the one yelling, but she gave a tight smile. "I'm sorry we woke you. Goodnight, Mr. McCullough." And she left him standing on the walkway.

When they entered the house, Pepper let out a howl. Harley dropped to her knees in front of the crate and released the door. The dog covered Harley's face with slobbery kisses.

Emma leaned against the doorframe and crossed her arms. "I guess I should be thankful you didn't run off with Pepper."

"I ain't—I'm not a thief. Not anymore."

"I know that." Emma silently counted to ten. "Let's sit down for a minute."

Harley dropped to the sofa and Emma sat in the club chair and extracted her notebook from her purse. "Tell me everything you know about your grandparents."

Harley stared into space, her lips turned down. "There's hardly anything I remember about them. Just wisps of a dream. I remember Papaw smelled good."

"Have you asked your mom about them?"

"She won't tell me. I've asked her before."

"What makes you think they're still out there?"

"Because I'd know if they'd died. I'd remember something that important." Harley bit her lip and glared. "And my mom's good at lying."

Emma rubbed her cheeks with her palms. "I'll call Mother in the morning and get the private detective's contact information and hire him to find your grandparents."

Harley winced. "Are you going to tell Mrs. Virginia about tonight?"

"She'll likely learn about your little adventure first thing in the morning because the police chief reports to her."

"Oh, no," Harley said.

"Whether or not you believe it, Mother cares about you, and so do I."

"I know," Harley said in barely a whisper.

"Then why did you run?"

"I don't know."

"You can trust me."

Harley gave her a long look, and then she looked at her backpack.

"You're not still thinking about running away, are you?"

"No, ma'am." Harley whispered. "Can I go to bed?"

Emma nodded and Harley snatched the backpack and bolted upstairs with Pepper on her heels.

Instead of going to bed, Emma sat on the sofa and stared into space. What could she do to make Harley trust her? How could she make her feel safe and wanted?

Harley would likely be with her for at least a year, maybe longer. That is, if Mrs. Winslow didn't remove Harley from her care. She'd call Carol Carter first thing in the morning and tell her Harley promised not to run away. Emma sighed heavily. Perhaps, she could offer Harley something that would make her want to stay put.

Emma bit her lip. Maybe, it was time Harley had her own dog. The more she thought about it, the more she warmed to the idea.

She opened the cover of her notebooks and looked at her long-term goals. *Make Harley laugh*. Emma went to bed determined to make that goal a reality.

CHAPTER TWENTY-NINE—EMMA

Emma called Carol Carter, the social worker, first thing the next morning and told her everything, including Harley's admission of looking for her grandparents. Emma also explained she'd offered to hire a private detective to find Harley's grandparents, contingent upon Harley's promise not to run away again. Carol agreed to interview Harley's mom again to see if she could pry information from her. Thankfully, the social worker didn't mention removing Harley from Emma's home.

Just before noon, Emma gathered her thoughts while waiting for Luke at the Triple D. She glanced at the clock and yawned. Her eyes itched and she snatched a napkin from the dispenser. *Ah-choo!* She didn't have time for a cold.

"God bless you," Luke said as he slid into the booth. "Sorry I'm late."

"Thank you." He wore a blue flannel shirt with sleeves rolled up at the wrist. A white triangle of fabric drew her eyes to his throat. Specks of sawdust rested on his left shoulder and she reached across the table and brushed them off.

His lips curved into a smile, and a yearning built in her chest. She blinked rapidly and sat up straight. Luke was her pastor, and he was here to help her figure out how to gain Harley's trust. *Stop thinking sinful thoughts.*

Emma cleared her throat. "Sorry to take you away from your work."

"Are you kidding? I'd never pass up an opportunity for a fried pie. What's the flavor today?"

"Pineapple."

Luke's brows lifted. "Interesting."

Mrs. Dot stood before them, pen at the ready. "Don't y'all make the cute couple?" She winked at Emma.

Emma picked up a menu even though she knew every item on it.

"You can see by Emma's sour-grape face, we're not a couple, but a guy can always hope," Luke said.

Mrs. Dot elbowed his shoulder. "I'll be hoping too. Ovaleta said y'all made a good team on Saturday."

Emma's ears burned. She huffed and rested her chin in her palm. It would be best to ignore that comment. "I'll have sweet tea with lemon and the chef salad."

"And I'll have the Manhattan plate with sweet tea," Luke said.

After Mrs. Dot delivered their drinks, Luke gave Emma a serious look. "I'm not so foolish as to think your invitation to lunch is about anything but church business. Something's up—and the dark circles under your eyes make me think it's serious."

Emma shredded her napkin. It would be best to get straight to the point. "Harley tried to run away last night. She stole my husband's Jeep but had a flat tire before she reached the county line."

Luke's jaw dropped. "Whoa. I didn't see that coming."

Emma related the previous evening's details.

"I'm not surprised she can drive," Luke drummed his fingers on the table. "Kids who grow up with little supervision gain adult skills early, but I'm shocked she took off."

"Me too. She said she ran because she didn't want to see her mom."

Luke's brows furrowed. "Her mom needs serious help, but—"

"You've worked with troubled kids. Do you think there's something else going on?"

He stroked his beard and stared at the tabletop for a long time, then he cleared his throat. "Have you ever been driving someplace, lost in thought, and you ended up turning at the wrong place because your brain was on autopilot. Maybe you planned to go to the grocery store but you ended up at the library?"

Emma shrugged. "Sure. Everyone has."

Luke went into great detail describing brain development, the establishment of neural pathways and synapsis. *Why is he giving me a biology lesson?* Emma fidgeted in her seat.

"When we repeat an action, over and over, we develop a synapsis, or an automatic response. Harley's lived in and survived terrible conditions. I think one of her automatic responses is to run when threatened, maybe even to hide. It could be a behavior she's learned from her mom."

Emma stilled. Harley had cut her hair, bleached it, and she dressed like a boy. Was she hiding from someone? "She said she ran because she didn't want to see her mom."

Luke brushed away the shredded napkin. "Yet she rode a bike over twenty miles on a cold December day to check on her. That took determination."

Emma remembered the bruises the doctor reported seeing when she'd first taken her in. "Maybe this has something to do with her mom's boyfriend. He's still out there."

Luke lifted a brow. "You might be on the right track. Ask her about him."

"I'm way in over my head."

"Welcome to the club. God can heal you and Harley, but first, you both have to ask him to take over."

"What do you mean 'heal me?'"

Luke sighed. "It's the same thing for you, but a different trigger and response."

Emma crossed her arms and hugged herself. "Go on."

"Every time you see or think about Winston, you get angry."

She felt her jaw stiffen and her body tense.

He lifted an index finger. "Hear me out."

"We've already talked about this." Emma clenched her fist. "Yes. I have an anger issue when it comes to Winston, but I'll have you know I've been doing a better job of controlling my thoughts since our last conversation."

Luke gave her an encouraging smile. "Good for you."

Her heart softened a bit. "It's getting easier."

"Eventually, if you keep working to control your thoughts, it will wear away the synapses."

Emma crossed her arms. "I didn't ask you to lunch to talk about me. You're here to help me figure out how to help Harley."

Luke dropped his chin. "The more you share your struggles with her, the more she might reveal to you."

"She said she lived in the same trailer park as Winston, and sometimes they walked to school together. I can't tell her what I really feel about him."

Luke placed his hand over hers. "Why not? It's real. No one's perfect."

Emma bit her lip. *Try telling that to Mother.*

"She's probably not aware running seems to be her automatic response. Talk through it and give her another option."

"Such as?"

"Trusting you to help her. She's probably never had someone she can count on."

"The social worker said kids always love their mom."

Luke's eyes looked so sad. "But we can't always count on the people we love."

"There must be something we're missing."

"I think you're on to something about the boyfriend. Ask her point blank if she's afraid he'll turn up on your doorstep." Luke leaned back and gave her a long look.

Mrs. Dot plopped two plates in front of them and they both jumped. Emma's salad looked puny compared to Luke's plate—a mountain of mashed potatoes next to a pile of roast beef on sour dough bread, everything smothered in gravy.

Luke reached for a fresh napkin and unfolded it. "If I eat all this, I'll be worthless the rest of the day."

Mrs. Dot looked over the top of her onyx cat-eye glasses. "Why don't y'all share?"

"That's a great idea," Luke said. "Then I'll have room for a fried pie."

"I've been gaining weight." Emma's mouth watered.

"And that's a good thing." Mrs. Dot turned. "I'll be right back with two empty plates. It won't hurt the padre to eat something healthy."

"That woman!" Emma pretended to fume.

"Temper, temper." Luke wagged his finger.

He was asking for it. She refocused her gaze on his plate and licked her lips.

When she looked up, she noticed his eyes seemed to smolder.

That evening, Emma knocked on Harley's door. "Room check."

Harley slumped against the overstuffed headboard and looked up from the computer cradled on her lap. "What's that supposed to mean?"

"It means I'm hoping there will be no more late-night excursions."

"I promised I wouldn't run."

"And I promised to help find your grandparents."

Harley sat up straight.

Emma sat on the edge of the bed. "Ms. Carter is going to see if she can get information about them from your mom. Also, Detective Warren requested an interview with your mom."

Harley closed the laptop, her lips turned down. "She'll never help."

"But why?"

"I don't know but I've asked her about them before."

"And what did she say?"

"She said they were dead to her."

"That's not the same thing as being dead."

"I know."

"Tell me what you remember."

"I've already told you all I know." She turned her head and stared at the changing lights on the Christmas tree. "I remember I felt safe with them."

A wave of sadness washed over Emma. "Do you feel safe here?"

The only sound in the room was Pepper softly snoring. Harley remained silent.

"I had lunch with Pastor Luke today."

Harley rolled her eyes. "Don't make me puke."

"Did you know he's a counselor?"

"Like a shrink?"

"Like someone who helps people work through their problems."

Harley glared at her. "Were you talking to him about me? Are you saying I'm a problem?"

Emma held her hands out palms up. "No. Nothing like that."

"Then what?"

Emma gulped and did her best to explain her anger issues.

"Why are you telling me all this?" Harley crossed her legs on the bed and her foot jiggled.

"Because maybe you have automatic responses that are unhealthy too."

"I get mad sometimes." She looked away.

"There's something else I want to ask you about."

Harley's jaw looked like stone.

"This is twice you've run away. I'm guessing you run when something threatens you."

Harley stared at the changing lights of the tree.

"Does this have something to do with your mom's boyfriend?" Emma placed her hand on Harley's jittery leg.

"He's still out there."

Emma withdrew her hand. "Tomorrow morning, I'll call a security company and have an alarm installed. Also, I'll deliver you to school and pick you up. I won't let someone hurt you."

Harley's face looked sadder than Emma ever recollected. So much for her goal to hear the child laugh.

Emma gulped. "Something else I wanted to talk with you about is a dog."

Harley's brows furrowed. "A dog?"

"Yes. Now that we know you'll be with me for an extended period, I think it might be a good idea for you to have your own dog."

"Really?" Harley's voice lifted.

Emma nodded. "What kind of puppy do you think you'd like?"

"I want Buster and Max."

"Buster and Max?"

"The dogs at the trailer. The cops told me they were taking them to a shelter."

Emma's stomach dropped. Those dogs seemed downright dangerous.

Harley's face brightened. "They are the best dogs ever."

Emma blew out a long breath. "Okay. We'll make calls first thing in the morning."

Harley spontaneously hugged her tightly. "Thank you. Thank you. Thank you. I've been so worried about them."

Emma hugged her back. "You should have said something."

"I didn't think you'd want anything to do with rottweilers."

"It wouldn't have been my first choice, but I trust your judgment."

Harley released her. "They were my only friends for weeks."

"Sounds like they'll make great guard dogs." Emma tried to sound enthusiastic.

"No. They're afraid of Beau. He treated them awful."

Her wariness dissolved. "Poor babies. Don't worry. We'll rescue them."

Emma's mother's face would have a permanent scowl when she learned of the rottweiler rescue. She hoped Becky would be okay with the dogs being in the yard. How in the world had she gotten herself into this mess? Thank goodness the yard was fenced in, but was it enough space for two rottweilers? The image of them joining her on her daily runs made her smile. People would talk, but that was normal for Weldon.

CHAPTER THIRTY—EMMA

The next morning, Emma hung up the phone and sniffed. No doubt about it, she had a cold. *Just my luck, with Christmas only days away.* The two rottweilers had been easy to locate because Rocky Hills only had one animal shelter. The staff person faxed the adoption paperwork and accepted her credit card for payment. After having a small surgery this afternoon, they'd be ready for pickup tomorrow. Emma drummed her fingers on the desk while the worker lectured her on the responsibilities of pet ownership.

Her next call was to the security company. When she disconnected, she marked it off her list and lifted her mug to her lips. She cringed. *Nothing worse than cold coffee.* Before she had the chance to go to the break room, her phone rang. Thirty minutes later, she disconnected from Patsy Rivers, who'd invited her to lunch—today. She rolled her shoulders. It was unlikely to be a quick meal.

She sent Harley a text so she wouldn't worry about the dogs. They'd need to go to the farm supply store this afternoon and purchase two dog houses. With a sigh she opened her moleskin notebook and made a list. *Crates, dog houses, leashes, collars, food bowls, chew toys, dog biscuits.* No way would all this stuff fit in her car. Maybe it was time she traded Chris's Jeep in for a truck with a king cab. She pictured her mother's scowl and smiled.

Emma dialed Casey. "It's about time you called me."

"Hello to you too. The phone lines goes both ways."

"The boutique's been slammed, and I've been spending my evenings at Christmas pageant rehearsals because someone roped me into being the director."

"That would be Eleanor."

"That would be my best friend," Casey shot back.

"And you've been spending more time with a certain policeman." Emma leaned back in her chair and relaxed. Finally, after all these years, her best friend was dating a good guy.

"He's good company."

"And apparently better company than me and my crowd."

"You know that's not true. Are you free for lunch?"

"Rats. I just agreed to have lunch with Patsy Rivers."

"Oh, I'd love to meet her. I've heard so many good things about her work."

"You're more than welcome to join me, but it might be an extended visit because I plan to tell her guests about library services."

"Can't do it. Gina would kill me if I left her shorthanded for more than a half hour."

Emma clicked her pen. "Maybe we can get together this afternoon. That's why I called. Do you think Daniel might bail me out again? I need someone with a pickup."

"Don't tell me you're taking in someone else?"

"Sort of." Emma told her about Buster and Max.

"Two rottweilers? Are they dangerous?"

"Harley says they're big babies."

"Wish we could help you, but Daniel sleeps during the afternoon when he's on the night shift. I'd hate to wake him."

"Snakes in a sack," Emma said.

"Pastor Luke has a truck," Casey's tone sounded sugary sweet.

"He's the last person I want to call."

"And why is that?"

Emma remained mute for a few seconds.

"As much as I'd love to needle you further, I have to go," Casey said. "Customers are waiting."

"We'll get together this weekend for our manicures." Emma rested her elbow on her desk.

"I'm counting on it."

Emma stared at the wall across from her desk for a long time. *You're being foolish. If Pastor Bob had a truck and you needed help, you wouldn't hesitate to call.*

She bit her lip and dialed. It wouldn't hurt to ask for help.

By the time Emma ended the phone call with Luke, it was time to leave for Freedom House. Emma grabbed her laptop and shoved a stack of library cards into her bag. In her haste, she almost left without the directions. Patsy had warned her a GPS would lead her in circles through the hollows.

Thirty minutes later, Emma's Honda idled as she studied her notes. The rhythmic swish of the windshield wipers lulled her into a stupor as she looked for the tree with a horseshoe nailed upside down. She rolled down the window; a cool mist hit her face and a chill settled over her.

This had to be the driveway according to her odometer, but she didn't see the marker.

While giving Emma directions, Patsy explained some people considered an upside-down horseshoe bad luck, but she used it to symbolize her guests pouring themselves out when they crossed her property line so Jesus could fill them.

Emma thought Minnie a bold witness, but compared to Patsy, she was as mild as dish soap. Put those two together, and they'd move mountains.

There it is! Tree bark camouflaged the rusted color of the horseshoe. Turning left, she followed the taper of gravel through the forest.

The hedgerow cleared and a two-story log cabin with a dog trot in the middle came into view. The roof extended over a wide front porch extending the length of the structure. To the right of the home, a large pond reflected the gray sky and a raft of white ducks paddled on the surface. The yard backed up to a sprawling woodland meadow where Emma noticed two deer staring at her. When she opened the door of her sedan, they skittered toward the forest.

While Emma followed the flagstone walkway, she admired the cedar wreaths on the windows. Woven willow-tree chairs lined the front porch. A flock of starlings erupted from the bird feeders hanging on tree branches.

The front door opened when Emma's foot hit the porch step.

"Welcome to Freedom House." Patsy wore a sweatshirt featuring Snoopy dressed in a Santa costume. Her white spiked hair seemed to brighten the gray day.

"Thank you for inviting me," Emma said, stepping into the warm entranceway.

"It's our pleasure. Ladies, this is Mrs. Baker, the director of the Weldon Public Library."

Six women stood in the foyer in front of a cedar tree covered in hand-made Christmas ornaments. All wore jeans and holiday sweaters or sweatshirts. Each woman extended her hand when Patsy introduced them. When she reached the last guest, Patsy said, "Debra made lunch today."

"We take turns cooking." A pencil-thin woman extended her hand. "Nice to meet you, Mrs. Baker."

"Please call me Emma." The scent of spices lingered. "Are we having tacos?"

"Enchiladas."

Emma guessed Debra to be around twenty years old. A rubber-band kept her long blonde hair secure at the nape of her neck. The edge of a tattoo peeked from the cuff of her sweatshirt sleeve when she shook hands.

"I love Mexican food."

"Debra's gifted in the kitchen," Patsy said. "She's been teaching others how to cook too."

"I could use a few lessons myself." Emma smiled.

Debra looked away. "I'm happy to show you a few things."

Patsy led the troop to the dining room and directed Emma where to sit.

After blessing the food, Patsy clasped her hands in front of her and it reminded Emma of her mother chairing a board meeting. "There are two reasons I asked Mrs. Baker here today."

Emma remembered one of her mother's favorite sayings: *There's no such thing as a free lunch.*

"I'd like each of you to tell Ms. Baker about yourself." Ms. Patsy lifted her chin. "And then she will tell us about the library services."

The women took turns sharing their stories. Emma surmised their ages ranged from their early twenties to their late forties. Little bits of her heart ached while she listened. They came from different socio-economic backgrounds and a variety of family situations; a couple of them had even lost custody of their children. The one thing the residents had in common was a prison record and that they had the feeling that everyone had given up on them and considered them a hopelessly lost cause until Patsy had stepped in and introduced them to the One who saves.

Debra served flan for dessert. Emma had no appetite but she couldn't refuse. When she spooned the first bite of the custard into her mouth, the caramel flavor made her sigh. "Delicious. You're a chef."

Debra's face glowed. "Thank you. It's the one thing I'm good at."

Patsy reached across the table and patted Debra's hand. "That's not true. We've all learned to be better cooks with your teaching skills. Plus, your gentle manner of sharing about Jesus is very effective." Patsy looked squarely at Emma and lowered her voice. "Sometimes my boldness can put people off."

Emma smiled. "We each have different styles and gifts,"

Patsy sat up straight. "That's exactly what we learned last week when we studied First Corinthians, Chapter Twelve."

When everyone finished with dessert, Patsy placed her napkin on the table. "It's time to get to work." She stood. "We'll leave the dishes for later. This way to our computer lab."

Patsy led Emma to the den. A table with three laptops sat in the back corner. Emma issued library cards to everyone then showed them the résumé-writing software. The residents kept their eyes on the computer screen as Emma scrolled through the selection of online classes available and practice tests for the GED exam and college entrance exams. It was almost two-thirty when Ms. Patsy escorted her to the door.

Emma tightened her coat. "I hate to rush off, but I need to pick up Harley from school."

"This won't take but one more minute." Patsy walked with her to the car.

Emma dug her keys out of her purse, wishing she were on the road.

"As you can see, we're in a remote location."

"Yes, ma'am."

"It's perfect for the early days of recovery for my guests, but when the women prepare to reenter the workforce, transportation is an issue."

"It is a long drive."

"Debra's been with me for over a year, and Ms. Dot offered her a job at the Triple D."

"It's my favorite restaurant," Emma said. "Ms. Dot is a character but she's a sweetie."

Patsy gulped. "They want her to cook for the early morning shift, which means she'll need to be at work by five o'clock."

"That's early."

"It is and I'm willing to drive her, but I had a thought. Your home is only about three blocks from the square. Would you consider renting her a room?"

Emma stilled and she remembered the old dream of seeing every window of her home filled with light. Her breathing slowed and her mouth went dry. "M—maybe." Of all times to stutter.

"If you're worried about her past, she insists on being drug tested every week."

Emma gulped. "You know I'm a foster parent."

"I know Mrs. Winslow, the head of social services, well because two of my residents are hoping to regain their parental rights. Debra's one of them."

"There's a young mother who lost her home who also lives with me."

Patsy lost her smile and her shoulders hunched.

Emma gulped. "I'll speak with Harley and Becky tonight. If they're open to meeting Debra, I'll call Harley's social worker."

Ms. Patsy wrapped her arms around Emma and squeezed tightly. "Thank you."

"It's not a yes, yet." Emma looked at the time on her activity tracker. "I really need to go. Thank you for lunch."

Patsy seemed to stand taller. "And thank you for telling us about all the library has to offer. Most of these women have never stepped foot inside such a place."

Emma's heart softened. "You're more than welcome."

As she drove home through the drizzle, a small headache pounded at her temple. Now, to find her way back to Weldon. Emma started considering how and when to share Ms. Rivers' request with Becky and Harley. *Lord, help me.*

CHAPTER THIRTY-ONE—EMMA

Emma followed the line of cars snaking through the school's pickup line. The familiar green coat stood out amid the crowd of teens.

Harley threw up her hand, jogged to the car, and jerked open the door. "Can we go get Max and Buster?"

"Sorry, but the shelter won't release them until tomorrow, and we need time to get ready for them." Emma sniffed and dug a tissue out of her pocket. "The farm supply store should have everything we need."

Harley rubbed her hands together. "Let's go." She turned and faced Emma. "No way will dog houses fit in the car."

"That's why Pastor Luke agreed to help us. He'll be at the house in a couple of hours. That will give me time for a run and you time to exercise Pepper."

Harley's knee jiggled but she didn't comment.

Later, when Luke's vintage white truck pulled in the drive, Harley stopped pacing and rushed to the back door. Emma still in her sweats, looked out the window and smiled at Harley running towards him.

Emma turned back and faced Becky. "Are you sure you're okay with Debra taking one of the extra bedrooms? Maybe you should meet her before deciding."

"It's your home and if not for you, who knows where I'd be living. No way could I deny her the chance to start over."

"It might be a good idea for her to meet us first to make sure she wants to live here. Patsy was the one who made the request." Emma tugged at her ear. "If you don't mind, I'd like to take Harley to dinner alone and ask her what she thinks about the idea."

"That sounds like a great idea," Becky bounced Leslie on her hip.

Emma and Luke rushed to catch-up with Harley who almost jogged to the door of Tractor Supply. They found her in the pet supply aisle.

Harley stood in front of a dog house that looked like an igloo and chewed her thumbnail. "They're over a hundred dollars."

"A good dog is worth his weight in gold," Emma moved to a more expensive cedar model. "They deserve the best."

"Thank you." Harley grabbed her in a hug and then gave her a wide smile that reached her hazel green eyes. Emma thought her heart would burst from happiness. That was two hugs and a smile Harley had offered freely. It didn't matter to Emma if she emptied her bank account.

Emma sniffed and removed a tissue from her purse. She would not cry and spoil the moment. "We'll need a cart and a dolly."

"I'll get the cart." Harley took off.

"And I'll get the dolly." Luke squeezed her shoulder when he passed.

Emma reined in her emotions. Maybe she wasn't doing as bad as she thought as a foster parent.

Later that evening, Emma looked at the size of the miniature barn-like structures set up in the back corner of her yard. Thank goodness Luke agreed to help.

The minute the dog houses were secure in the backyard, Harley unloaded their purchases from Luke's truck.

Mr. McCullough opened the gate. "Hey, neighbor. What's going on over here?"

After introducing Mr. McCullough to Luke, Emma explained the reason for the cedar buildings.

"Nothing better for a kid than a good dog."

"I'd forgotten you like dogs."

His bushy eyebrows met and formed one. "I don't trust a person who don't like dogs. Something's wrong with their heart." He sighed. "I still miss old Alvin."

"Goodness, it's been years." Emma blew her nose into a tissue.

"I'd just turned sixty-five went he departed for the Happy Hunting Ground. The odds of me outliving another dog was too slim to risk it."

Emma patted his shoulder. "You are more than welcome to share our dogs."

"I'll help Harley train them. Rottweilers, huh?" He scratched the stubble on his chin.

"I'd appreciate the help," Emma said.

"I'll be looking forward to meeting them." He turned to Luke. "Nice to meet you, preacher. You get tired of all the pomp and circumstance at Loving Hope, you can join us at Bethel Hill. We're pretty casual."

"Thanks." Luke shook his hand. "If the next business meeting is as quarrelsome as the last one, I might take you up on that offer."

Mr. McCullough cackled. "I'll look forward to seeing you, then." He waved and walked across the yard towards Harley.

Luke turned to Emma. "How about we head over to the Triple D and give people something to talk about."

Emma's heart warmed, then she sneezed three times in a row. "I think I'm coming down with something, and I need to speak privately with Harley."

Luke's rubbed his beard. "I'm glad you two are making progress. Did you ask her about the boyfriend?"

"Yes. Security alarms will be installed on Monday."

"That's a good idea." He patted his stomach. "I already had two fried blackberry pies today, anyway."

"I love that flavor," Emma said.

"We'd hardly settled Bob into his recliner when Mrs. Dot showed up with a box of his favorite pies."

"That doesn't surprise me."

"Apparently, blackberry is his favorite."

Emma turned her head and sneezed. "Excuse me."

"Bless you," Luke gulped. "

Emma burrowed into her coat. *Just a group of friends having dinner. Nothing wrong with that. Still ... People would talk, and he's my pastor.* She sneezed again, which helped her decide once and for all. "I—I don't think so."

Luke's face dropped and she placed her hand on his sleeve. "I've got so much going on—Harley, the dogs, and I might have another guest soon."

Luke dark eyes filled with compassion. "I thought something was worrying you. Let's sit down for a minute and talk." He brushed leaves off a nearby bench. "I'm your pastor. You can tell me anything."

For a minute, Emma just sat there. When she spoke, words tumbled from her lips and her burden seemed to lighten. The rottweilers combined with a toddler in the house worried her. Then she described her experience at Freedom House and her worries about Patsy Rivers's request. And Anne West was constantly on her mind. Emma let out a long sigh. "Wouldn't it be something if both Harley and Anne could live under my roof one day? Am I crazy to think such a thing?"

Luke placed his hand over hers. "Let me pray for you before I go."

His words blanketed her in peace and her fears dissolved as quickly as the morning's frost when the sun broke through.

After Luke said amen, he wrapped his arms around her and rested his chin on her head. The lingering scent of cedar comforted her and she relaxed into his warm chest. Oh, she could rest here forever. Then she remembered—*this was a bad idea*. She extricated herself from his arms and stood, feeling bereft as cold seeped through her jacket.

Luke sighed and stood slowly. "Y'all have a good evening." He strode to his truck, his shoulders rigid.

It took all Emma's willpower not to chase after him for another hug.

How had he broken through the wall around her heart? His back profile was lit by the streetlight, and she admired the cut of his Levis, sinful thoughts crossing her mind. *Thank goodness Protestants didn't have to confess their sins to their pastors*. The thought made her ears burn.

Inside the house, Harley arranged the dog supplies in the butler's pantry. "I can't wait for the big guys to get here."

"They'll need exercise," Emma said. "Maybe I should start taking them out on a leash when I run in the afternoons."

"Would you?"

"It's a plan." Emma bit her lip. "They might not be up to it for a few days because of their surgery."

"What surgery?"

Emma described responsible pet ownership and the neutering operation Buster and Max had to undergo.

"Poor guys," Harley frowned.

Emma patted her shoulder. "They'll be fine."

"You've got that look on your face again,"

"What look?"

"There's a line between your brows that gets deeper when you're about to tell me something bad."

"There is something I need to ask you, but it's not bad."

Now Harley had a line between her brows. "I shoulda known it was too good to be true to have a day where everything went right." She sat on the floor of the cupboard and wrapped her arms around her legs.

Emma sat down next to her and squeezed her knee. "Nothing is wrong. I need to ask your opinion about something."

"Why does it matter what I think?"

"Because you live here, and you're important to me." Emma explained Debra's situation.

"So she's really clean?" Harley narrowed her eyes.

"Yes. And she voluntarily agreed to weekly drug tests."

"What about her kids?"

"I need to speak with her about that situation."

Harley narrowed her eyes. "So?"

"I told Patsy it's not only my decision. We're a family, s— sort of. I told her I'd have to ask you and Becky."

"Have you asked Becky?"

"Yes. We talked while you were playing with Pepper this afternoon. She said it might be like having another sister."

"Another sister?" Harley looked confused.

"To Becky, you're sort of like a little sister, and I'm kind of a big sister."

Harley's eyes widened. "Really?"

"Really."

Harley chewed her nail. "Did Ms. Patsy say anything about meeting my mom?"

Emma shook her head no.

"I guess it's okay if someone else moves in."

"There's still one more person to check with." Emma gently pulled Harley's thumb away from her mouth.

"Who?"

"Ms. Carter. There's no way I'd jeopardize losing you without getting her approval first."

Harley rolled her eyes. "This ain't—isn't—none of her business."

"She cares about you and has as much responsibility for your safety as I do."

"Whatever."

Emma stood. "I'm feeling achy. Do you mind settling for cheese toast and tomato soup for dinner?"

Harley shrugged. "Sounds good."

Emma rubbed her temple. She'd been dreading this conversation since Patsy mentioned taking in Debra, but it had gone better than she had expected. Why did she always expect the worst? She hadn't always been this way. Losing Chris had changed her. It was time to live expecting the best, not the worst. Now to speak with Carol. Dread washed over her again and she remembered Luke's lecture about triggers and responses. *It will be fine.* Then she pictured her mother's scowl. *I can do all things through Christ who strengthens me.* Where had that come from? Maybe Eleanor had been right. Scripture had a way of coming back when we needed it. Emma sighed. She'd need more than Scripture when she faced her mother next.

CHAPTER THIRTY-TWO – EMMA

On Thursday morning, a dull headache throbbed at the base of Emma's skull and her nose dripped like an irrigation system. Two tablets helped control the symptoms of her cold, but her lids felt heavy. If only she could spend the day sleeping, but commitments forced her out of bed. Unless her body ended up on display at Johnson's funeral home, she'd keep moving.

No way could she disappoint Harley by postponing rescuing the dogs, nor could she miss her appointment with Carol Carter.

Emma borrowed her mother's strategy for forging through a difficult day—dress to impress and fake it. Her mother insisted no one should see a weakness. The silky lining inside her black wool slacks caressed her skin. This was a day for cashmere, so Emma slipped into a cobalt blue turtleneck that hugged her curves. After applying makeup to conceal her pink nose, Emma squared her shoulders and filled her lungs with air. *Forward, march.*

When she arrived downstairs, Harley stood at the sink, rinsing a cereal bowl. "Everything's ready for this afternoon. The leashes and crates are on the sunporch."

"There's coffee." Becky zipped Leslie's pink coat. "Time to go, little miss."

Emma's voice sounded croaky. "Have a good day."

"Are you feeling okay?" Becky cocked her head.

So much for her strategy to fool everyone. "Just a little head cold." Emma sniffed, grabbed a tissue, and looked at the clock. "I'd better grab a to-go mug. I hadn't realized the time."

When she stopped the car at the school's drop-off line, Harley jerked open the car door. "Have a good day!"

Emma sat there, mouth open upon hearing the cheerful words. A car honked behind her, but she remained sitting still and she felt a slow smile spread across her face. It wasn't her imagination. Harley was happy.

An hour later at the library, a knock sounded at her office door. Emma looked up from her work. Her assistant stood at the doorway with Carol Carter by her side.

Emma stood. "I'd shake hands, but I'm coming down with a cold." She sneezed into a tissue.

"You look terrible." Carol scrunched up her nose, then she sat down and opened her briefcase. "I visited Ann West."

"Did you learn anything?"

"No. She said she didn't have any family relations." Mrs. Carter's lips turned down. "She wants to see Harley. I told her I'd bring her by for a visit on Saturday morning."

"That's when she and Minnie usually bake cookies."

"Surely, that can be rearranged."

Emma palmed Chris's glass paperweight on her desk. "You're right." She cleared her throat. "There's something else we need to discuss." Emma told her about her luncheon at Freedom House.

Carol cocked her head. "If everything I've heard about Ms. Rivers' program is true, I like the idea of one of her graduates being around Harley."

"Good." Emma nodded.

"It might encourage Harley to be around a recovering addict who is maintaining a steady job and staying clean." She emphasized *and*.

"I hadn't thought of it that way." Emma studied the melding of blue, gray, silver, and the touches of crimson in the hand-blown paperweight. "Ms. Rivers said Theresa Winslow is familiar with Debra as she hopes to regain custody of her children."

"I'll talk with Mrs. Winslow to see what she says about this woman. If she gives a good report, I'll call Patsy Rivers and set up an appointment to meet the woman who's interested in renting a room." Carol closed her briefcase.

"Do you think it possible Anne West might follow in Debra's footsteps?"

Carol's face turned down. "Don't get your hopes up."

Emma's temple throbbed. If only she could go home and pull the covers over her head.

"I'll see you Saturday around eleven o'clock." Carol stood.

Emma pushed herself up and a wave of dizziness washed over her.

After Carol left, Emma stared into space. If Debra passed Carol's scrutiny, she would have another houseguest, but which room would work best? The other bedrooms available didn't have a bath connected to them, but Debra would still have her privacy.

When it was almost three o'clock, Emma trudged to her car. Harley would be eager to rescue her dogs. She looked at her activity tracker. In two hours, she could finally do what she'd wanted to do all day. Go to bed.

The sight of Luke's truck in the drive made her spirits lift. When Emma parked, Harley turned to her. "I'll let Pepper out and see if Mr. McCullough will watch her." She jumped out of the car and bolted to the house.

Luke stepped out of his truck, and Emma admired his broad shoulders. Had she really leaned into them yesterday? *Goodness.* Even sick, her insides melted at the sight of him. This was seriously bad.

Harley jogged to them. "Mr. McCullough said he'd exercise Pepper for me. Let's go."

"Hello, to you too, Harley." Luke touched her shoulder and she flinched.

"Sorry—" Luke raised his hands palms out.

"It's okay." Harley looked away. "I didn't mean to jump."

Emma was surprised when Harley stepped up into the truck first and scooted to the middle. "Let's go. They close at four o'clock."

Once settled with her seatbelt fastened, Emma leaned her head against the window and fell asleep.

"We're here," Luke said.

Emma sat up and winced at the crick in her neck.

Luke's brows furrowed. "You look terrible."

"Thanks a lot." Emma rubbed her eyes. But she was too tired to be defensive. Plus she saw the look of genuine concern cloud Luke's dark brown eyes. *Or was that something else?* Maybe her cold was fogging her brain a bit too much. She shook her head to clear it.

"Why don't you wait here? We can collect the dogs." Luke opened his truck door.

Emma dug a tissue from her bag. "Thanks."

Harley rolled her eyes impatiently. "The dogs are waiting."

Luke exited the truck and Harley scooted out behind him.

Emma's teeth chattered.

Luke climbed back into the cab and placed his palm on her forehead. "You're burning up."

"I'm freezing."

He started the truck and turned the heater up. "We'll be quick."

"Thanks," Emma said.

Harley disappeared behind the shelter's front door.

Luke slammed the truck door and sprinted towards the building. Preachers were not supposed to be built like that. She blew her nose and hoped he'd lost his knack for reading her mind.

Luke carried the empty dog crates inside the house and Emma followed, while Harley kept watch over the hounds in the back yard. Once the crates were secured on the sunporch, they walked to the row of windows. It looked like Harley was introducing the dogs to Mr. McCullough. Who would have thought her grumpy old neighbor would become best friends with Harley?

"Hope you feel better soon," Luke gently touched her shoulder.

"Thanks, and thank you for helping us."

"I owed you one since you talked Casey into taking over the Christmas pageant."

Emma blew her nose. "Speaking of which, I'm supposed to help her tomorrow afternoon, but that's not likely going to happen."

Luke placed his thumb under her chin and lifted her face. "You look worn out."

Emma stared into his dark eyes, leaned into his touch and gulped, mesmerized by his stare. His face so close to hers. She closed her eyes, and held her breath, yearning for his lips to touch hers. Instead, he whispered, "Go to bed."

He left her feeling wanting as he waved and walked out the back door to his truck.

Becky sauntered up next to her with Leslie on her hip. "Dang, I thought for sure he would kiss you or maybe offer to tuck you in."

Emma jumped. "Were you hiding behind the door?"

"Yes."

Emma elbowed her. "You're worse than Casey"

"I'll take that as a compliment." Becky adjusted Leslie. "Wow. Those dogs are big but so thin."

Emma bit her lip. "Do you think I made a mistake?"

"No. I trust Harley. If she say's they're okay, they'll be fine."

Emma lunged toward the tissue box and grabbed one. *Ah-choo!* Her eyes watered and she felt on the verge of another sneeze but it didn't materialize. After blowing her nose, she said, "Best stay away from me."

"I'm around germy kids all day long." Becky backed up. "But Leslie's a different story."

Emma tossed the tissue in a wastebasket. "I'm going to bed. I've felt worse as each hour passed today. If I hadn't promised to pick up those dogs, I'd already be in bed."

"Sounds like a good idea. I'll get out the Lysol and take care of dinner."

Emma started toward her room, but stopped. "Oh, I need to speak with Harley first."

"You look like you're about to drop. When Harley comes in, I'll send her up to see you."

A few minutes later, Emma stood in her bathroom in her pajamas searching her medicine cabinet. After taking two cold tablets, she crawled under the covers, and closed her eyes. *Finally.* Someone knocked on the door and Emma struggled to open her eyelids through the fog of sleep.

Harley stood over her, brows furrowed. "Becky sent me up to see if you needed anything."

Emma succumbed to the desire to close her eyes. "Sleep," she mumbled.

On Friday morning, Emma, feverish, ached all over. It was the flu. Thank goodness she had Becky to deliver Harley to school. Emma slept through the entire day and only stayed awake a few minutes while Minnie watched her drink a glass of juice and eat a bowl of her homemade chicken noodle soup.

"Everyone else is going to the Triple D for the Friday night catfish special." Minnie said.

Emma's brain was foggy. "There's something I need to tell Harley." She yawned.

Minnie *tsk*ed. "I'm sure it can wait."

CHAPTER THIRTY-THREE— HARLEY

Harley removed a cookie sheet from the oven and paused as a car door slammed. She turned to the kitchen window. Carol Carter's white sedan sat in the drive. "Oh, no. It's the social worker. What's she doing here?"

Minnie looked over her shoulder. "Probably checking on you. Isn't that her job?"

Harley threw the oven mitt on the counter as the front doorbell rang. "You'd think she had something better to do on a Saturday. She stomped to the front of the house and halted. Emma would want her to act nice. Harley squared her shoulders, then opened the door.

"Hi, Harley. Ready to go?" Ms. Carter wore the same trench coat. Her brown hair was pulled in a tight bun.

Harley's stomach dropped and her pulse raced. Was she taking her to live somewhere else? "G—go where?"

"Didn't Emma tell you? I scheduled a visit with your mom today."

Harley wanted to sigh in relief. She wasn't being taken away, but then she pictured seeing her mom in the ambulance cussing her. Harley crammed her fist into her armpits. Sweat broke out on her forehead. "Emma went to bed Thursday night, and I haven't seen her since. Becky said it might be the flu."

"Oh, no. Poor thing. I knew she didn't feel well Thursday. She must be very ill if she forgot to mention I'd scheduled a visitation with your mom."

Minnie joined them. "You're just in time. We're making Danish wedding cookies."

Carol looked at her watch. "We need to be going. I'm already behind schedule and Harley's mom is expecting us. I'm sure she's anxious to see her."

Harley's chest tightened. Did her mom really want to see her? For an instant her spirit lifted, then she remembered all the lies. "Do I have to go?" Her voice was dull.

Ms. Carter's face looked sympathetic. "I'm not going to drag you kicking and screaming." Her voice softened. "Don't you want to see her?"

Minnie patted her shoulder. "I'm sure she'd like to sample your cookies."

Harley rolled her eyes. "Like they'd let us give her home-baked cookies that could be laced with drugs."

"Oh." Minnie's eyes widened.

"You can buy her snacks at the jail's commissary." Ms. Carter's voice was overly bright. "Or we could take her plastic pencils with stationary so she can write you. She might like a magazine."

A heaviness pushed down on Harley's shoulders. "Give me a minute." She trudged upstairs and removed some cash from her sock drawer. This was money she'd earned. No way would she touch Beau's dirty money still hidden under the curlers. She sat on the floor and hugged her knees to herself. Why couldn't she forget her mom? Then she sat up straight. Maybe she could use Beau's money to bribe her to tell her something about her grandparents. A longing built in her chest. She sighed, then pounded her fist on her thigh. She hated her. Harley wiped a tear from her cheek.

An hour later, she sat in the county detention center. The room, just a small box really with walls made of gray cinder block, smelled of bleach. Ms. Carter sat in the corner in a plastic folding chair looking at a magazine, pretending she wasn't paying any attention. She didn't take off her beige trench coat. Maybe that was a sign they wouldn't be here long.

Her mom reached across the stainless steel for Harley's hand. "Why did you run away?" She'd chewed her nails to the quick, just like Harley.

Harley spoke low. "You know why I left."

"You disappeared, and when Beau found out ... " She glanced at Ms. Carter.

"Beau is the reason I left."

"I was so worried."

Harley leaned away from the table and crossed her arm. "Then why didn't you report me missing?"

Her mother rolled her eyes. "Call the cops?"

Harley's knee jiggled. At least her Mom had on clean clothes, but the jumpsuit the color of Orange Crush made her skin look sallow.

"I like your hair. The blonde suites you. If I bleach my hair and cut it, people will think we're sisters."

"I'm letting it grow out." Harley held out a green plastic bag. "We bought you some things."

Anne's face brightened as she snatched the bag and rifled through it. "No cigs." Her shoulders dropped.

"You're welcome." Harley slid the twenty-dollar bill across the table. "You can buy your own cancer sticks."

Her mom lowered her voice. "I'll ... "

Harley scooted her chair back and narrowed her eyes. "What? Smack the snot out of me?"

Anne tore into a bag of Doritos, and Harley grimaced as her mom crammed chips into her mouth, talking all the while, asking questions about school, then gave her a sly look. "I'll bet you have a boyfriend," she said in a sing-song voice.

Of all the things she didn't want. Harley rolled her eyes and shuddered. For an instant she thought about telling her mom about her good grades, no thanks to her making her miss months of school. But her mom never asked her about her grades. Harley wouldn't tell her about her science project either. Her mom would laugh at her baking cookies. Harley crossed her arms. She sure wouldn't mention rescuing Buster and Max.

After a few minutes of useless chatter, her mom leaned in close to her and mouthed, "Where's the money?"

Harley narrowed her eyes, leaned forward and whispered, "Where's Papaw and Mamaw?"

Her mother's nostril's flared and her eyes burned into Harley as she grabbed the hoodie, pulled her close and whispered in her ear. "Dead, just like you'll be if you don't give Beau his money."

Mrs. Carter was standing over them in an instant. "Let go of her." Her voice sounded menacing.

Harley jerked away. Her mother hadn't changed. A chill washed through her and her eyes filled with tears. She must have been crazy thinking her mom would change, might get off the drugs and be able to live with her on Main Street. She turned her head so her mother wouldn't see her face. She'd use any sign of weakness against her. The only thing her mom wanted was the money, and Harley would make sure she never got it because it would be the same as giving her a bag of drugs.

The dirty money kept her feeling trapped with nowhere to turn, Harley realized. *It was time to rid herself of it.*

Mrs. Carter adjusted her purse strap. "It's time to go." Her posture was ramrod straight.

Harley pushed her hands against her thighs and pushed up."

"I just wanted to be closer to my girl." Harley's mom whined. "Can't I hug her?"

Mrs. Carter looked at Harley and she rolled her eyes. *If that's what it takes to get out of here without a fit, fine.*

Harley just stood like a stone while her mom did a little performance and hugged her tightly. Harley's muscles tensed hard in her arms when her mother whispered in her ear. "Beau will track you down and sell you to the highest bidder if you don't give him his money."

Harley did her best to keep her face blank of emotion. All the more reason to have a bonfire tonight. He might get her, but she'd make sure he wouldn't get the cash.

When her mother released her, Harley looked her in the eye. "I won't be back." Her voice was flat.

She turned on her booted heal, lifted her chin, and did her best to emulate Mrs. Virginia's confidence. The first thing she'd do when she got home was destroy the last connection she had with her mother and Beau. Her jaw clenched so hard it ached.

Don't look back, she told herself. The desire to return to her mom and say she was sorry was so strong, she had to grip the door handle to keep from turning.

Her mother had once said her parents were dead to her. She gulped and squared her shoulders. *Like mother, like daughter.*

Beau was out there somewhere, but she wouldn't run. An idea sparked and she paused.

When she stepped outside the jail into the sunlight, a cold wind blew into her face and she breathed in deeply, savoring the clean air. Running was not an option. It was time to hunker down and protect the ones she loved. Beau would come and she'd be ready.

CHAPTER THIRTY-FOUR—EMMA

Emma remained quarantined in her room due to her fear of spreading the virus.

Her heart warmed when Becky peeked in and announced she and Harley were leaving for church. Emma wished she could be there. And she'd be missing the Christmas pageant tonight.

After they left, Emma raided the refrigerator of juice and ice.

Vaguely, Emma remembered Minnie sitting on the side of her bed yesterday afternoon and telling her about Carol Carter's unannounced arrival. She couldn't believe she'd failed to warn Harley. Remorse washed through her.

How had the visit with her mother gone? Emma yawned and couldn't keep her eyes open. She succumbed to the lethargy and closed her eyes.

The scent of cut grass and apple blossoms wafted on the air. Bees swarmed the flowering trees. A carpet of wildflowers blanketed the meadow, and she realized she wasn't alone. When she turned her head, she gasped. Chris sat next to her, his large, tan hand caressed the side of her cheek. A sense of peace filled her when she looked into his gray eyes.

Chris stroked her hair. "It's time."

"Time for what?"

She leaned forward, inhaled his sandalwood cologne, wrapped her arms around him and his lips touched hers, but then pain slammed into her shoulder.

Emma's eyes flew open. She lay on the floor, her body aching, and tears spilled. If only she'd been able to hold him, to have the presence of mind to tell him how much she loved him. But it was a dream. It wasn't real. She pounded the floor with her fist and sobbed.

After returning to the bed, she wiped her cheek with the edge of the sheet and picked up the packet of letters from Winston Meador and sniffed. *It's time.*

Emma turned her attention to the ring sparkling on her right finger. She removed it and held it up to the light. She'd kept every promise to love and to cherish. She'd finally come to realize having feelings for someone else didn't diminish her love for Chris. Emma placed the ring on the bedside table next to the stack of letters. *It's time.*

On Monday morning, Emma felt better, but she stayed home for the security system installation. She'd breathe easier once it was in place.

Becky had promised to drop Harley off at the Middle School before taking Leslie to daycare.

Taking a shower depleted her energy so she wrapped up in Chris's cardigan and stared at the stack of letters and her ring next to them. *It's time.* The dream seemed so real. Real or imagined, the truth sank in. It was past time to let go of the anger and bitterness.

After a brief respite, Emma went downstairs for a cup of coffee. A stack of mail lay on the counter along with a box with the book conservator's return address. *My Bible.* She ripped open the package. The familiar feel of the worn leather comforted her when she hugged the book to her chest. How was it possible she'd gone so many months without this solace? No wonder she'd been angry all the time, had failed in her battle to forgive.

A car door slammed, and she glanced out the window. Her mother's Cadillac gleamed in the morning sunlight. Emma unlocked the back door and opened it. "Good morning." She buzzed her mother's cheek.

"How are you feeling?" Virginia looked her over from head to toe.

"Much better, thanks."

"Good." Her mother was all business.

"I'll be leaving town this morning, and it might be a few days before I return."

"But Christmas is Saturday. Where are you going?"

"Gulf Shores, Alabama."

Emma's jaw dropped. "To the beach?"

Virginia sat down on the sofa and smoothed her slacks. "Luther believes he's located Harley's grandparents." Her face looked like stone.

Emma's stomach fell and she sat down hard on the couch next to her mother.

"Already! But how?"

"Anne West's prison record left a trail of bread crumbs for Luther to follow."

A sense of indignation flooded Emma. "Wait a minute. I hired him to find Harley's grandparents. Why hasn't he reported this to me?"

"Because you've been sick and didn't answer your cell phone. When he phoned me, he asked if he should check them out, and I agreed to pay his expenses to do so."

Emma crossed her arms. Her knee started to jiggle.

Virginia sat down on the sofa next to Emma. "Do you want to hear the rest?"

"Yes"

"At the age of fourteen, Anne West was arrested for shoplifting. It was from these records Luther gained the name and address of her parents."

Emma leaned forward and dropped her head into her hands. It surprised her when she felt her mother's arms around her.

"You were the one who asked Luther to track down these people."

Emma leaned into her. "Harley deserves to know her grandparents."

Virginia's eyes narrowed. "But do they deserve to know Harley?"

"What do you mean?"

"That's why I'm going, to check things out." Her face looked fierce. "There's no way I'll send the child to live with hoodlums."

"But I'm obligated to tell CPS if I locate her closest relatives."

Virginia threw her hands up in the air. "I made no such promise. I'll keep my findings to myself if I discover they're outlaws."

Emma grabbed a tissue and blew her nose. "You're always so negative. They might be wonderful."

"And if they are, you'll suffer. No matter what we find, there will be heartbreak for someone."

"Harley cares for me, and for you too. Finding her grandparents won't change that."

"But what if they're thugs?"

"She said they made her feel safe. We owe it to her to do all we can to help her find them."

Virginia stood, and then her voice broke. "We might lose her."

Emma's heart softened to see her mother vulnerable. Virginia gazed out the window and she narrowed her eyes. "What is Randall McCullough doing in your yard with two of the ugliest dogs I've ever seen?"

"He's training them." Emma sniffed.

Virginia lowered her glasses and looked over the top. "He must have lost his mind to take in dogs at his age—and why is he in your yard?"

Emma gulped. "They're Harley's dogs."

Her mother's mouth remained open. "They're the dogs from the trailer, aren't they?"

"The very same."

Virginia shook her head back and forth. "And people warn you about the terrible twos. If anyone knew the life-long worries of parenthood, humans would become extinct."

"They're sweet dogs." She would not tell her mother she might have another new guest soon. *Lord, help me.*

Virginia looked at her watch than peered out the window. "Luther will be waiting."

"So the two of you are traveling together?" Emma couldn't suppress a wry smile.

"Don't give me that look. We're two old friends, business acquaintances on a business trip. There will be two hotel rooms."

Emma pecked her mother's cheek. "Your secret's safe with me."

"I have no secrets."

Emma gave her mom a smile. *Of course you don't, because no one can keep a secret in Weldon.*

When the workers from the security company arrived, they mapped out her property for the new alarm system. The technicians attached sensors to each downstairs window along with motion activated outdoor lights. The possums would light up her yard all night long. While the technicians worked, Emma yawned, curled up on the sofa and thumbed through her Bible. The repair was almost invisible, but when she rubbed her index finger along the binding, she could feel the scarred leather, a permanent reminder of how broken she'd been.

She wished the workers would leave so she could read Winston's letters in peace. *It was time.*

CHAPTER THIRTY-FIVE—LUKE

Luke sat in a worn plaid recliner that matched Bob's and leaned back. "It was great to see you sneak in yesterday, but I noticed you escaped before I dismissed the congregation." Luke thought back to Sunday's service and smiled.

He'd lifted his voice with the congregation while most struggled to keep up with the contemporary song he'd asked the choir director to lead that morning. Jeremy Camp's "Walk by Faith" never failed to stir his heart, and he hoped it would lift the spirits of the congregation, even though many stared at the screen, lips unmoving.

But then everyone's heads had turned as the door at the back of the sanctuary had opened and Pastor Bob made his way to the last pew with the aid of a walker, Eleanor by his side. Luke's had felt his chest swell to see his friend who'd passed through the dark valley and come out victorious. He'd closed his eyes and lifted his hands to the words, "your broken road prepares your will for me," not minding if his voice was off-key. Luke didn't care what others might think of his worship while he praised God with a full heart.

A few minutes later, he'd stood behind the pulpit, and his eyes had connected with Harley's. He'd lifted a silent petition for Emma's return to health, and without missing a beat, he prayed, *"Father, Take Over. Give me the words that will save."*

He'd borrowed the words from the song. "The broken road led me to this pulpit today. Walking by faith is difficult. Through the weeks of praying for your pastor, his job responsibilities overwhelmed me, and I felt helpless. Then I remembered from where my strength comes. I can do nothing without God, and neither can you. We are helpless without him."

Harley had just stared straight ahead.

"With all my heart, I pray that if you do not know Him, if you doubt his existence, that you ask Him to open your eyes and draw you to faith," he'd continued. "God does not need us to accomplish His will, but He allows us to be a part of His plan. But many times that plan looks like a road filled with landmines. Still, He will lead you through. God desires a personal relationship with you. Do you lack friends? He is the one friend who will never fail you. Men and women will always let you down, but not Jesus. It's through the shattered places of our hearts He enters and heals. Is your heart cracked? Is there an empty place in your soul that needs filling?"

Harley had shifted in her seat.

Luke hoped and prayed for Harley's broken heart to be healed by the Savior."

Bob's words removed Luke from his reverie. "I loved being there, but the thought of being swarmed by the crowd left me feeling weak."

Luke cleared his throat. "When do you think you'll be ready to take over again?"

Bob stared at the gas logs in the fireplace. "I won't be returning."

Luke sat up straight. "What?"

"I'm retiring."

"But—"

"For years, Eleanor and I have wanted to travel, but it's impossible with the responsibilities tied to Loving Chapel."

"You deserve a break, but retirement?"

"Yep."

"I feel sorry for the poor man who'll have to fill your shoes."

Neither spoke for a long time.

"I want you to consider applying for the job." Bob picked up a mug on the side table.

"Me? For the Loving Chapel crowd? Your illness addled your brain."

"They've become attached to you."

"Arnold Alexander never misses an opportunity to point out my shortcomings."

Bob threw his head back and laughed. "The permanent thorn in my congregation!"

"I'm not the right guy for the job. I'll stay as long as you need to recuperate but ... why don't you take a few more weeks and think this through?"

"While lying in the sick bed, the Lord placed other desires on my heart."

A heaviness pressed down on Luke's chest. "It's hard to argue with that."

"Don't think Eleanor and I haven't prayed this through and through."

"Will you stay in Weldon?"

"Probably. I'm thinking about the mission field. First on the agenda, after my strength returns, I plan to lead a short-term team to Africa, to support my nephew's efforts. That will keep me out of the new pastor's way."

"I'm sure whoever takes over will appreciate any support you can give him. I've not had a day of rest since you became ill."

"That's why a preacher needs a wife by his side, to shield and protect him."

They sat in silence. A deep yearning built in his chest. What would it be like to have Emma by his side? The pretentiousness of the oversized house didn't seem to fit her personality and she kept surprising him at every turn as she added people to her household. Life with Emma Baker would be anything but boring. It would be a full-time job keeping her from overextending herself.

"Let me pray for you," Bob said.

"I'd appreciate it."

"That's another thing about having a good wife. I know I'm always covered by Eleanor's prayers."

Luke looked away. Had Bob guessed his thoughts? Usually, Bob's prayers made him feel better, but his request for him to consider being the full-time pastor for Loving Chapel weighed him down. He couldn't do it.

"Amen." Bob weakly squeezed his hand.

"Thank you." Luke left his recliner and hugged his friend.

"Are you going to apply?" Bob's gaze seemed to pierce through and read his thoughts.

Luke rubbed his jawline. "I'll think about it."

"Pray about it with an earnest heart. Not like Moses telling the Lord all the reasons he couldn't lead the Israelites."

"But I don't feel adequate."

"And the right preacher never will. The perfect pastor for Loving Chapel will rely on the Lord to take over."

Luke stared at the carpet. He'd need to talk to his boss at Westview Circle Church, Pastor Steve, about this new turn of events. The feeling of unworthiness washed through him again.

"I can see by the look on your face you're already thinking about why you can't do it. Let me remind you, Satan is a liar," Bob said gently.

"You know me too well," Luke said, feeling guilty and ashamed.

"Well, it's enough to know that you can do it, you can do anything with Jesus, and Jesus is with you."

"Amen." Luke felt like a concrete truck had just unloaded on his chest.

CHAPTER THIRTY-SIX—EMMA

The security workers pulled out of the driveway as Harley arrived home from school along with Becky, who had been her ride, and baby Leslie in tow. Emma drummed her fingers. The letters would have to wait.

"She's alive," Harley said sarcastically.

Emma sipped from her glass of juice. "Almost."

Leslie reached for her. "Oh, no," Becky said. "Let's give Emma another day." And she carried the baby to the kitchen.

"Mr. McCullough's been working with your dogs all day," Emma told Harley. "I let Pepper out to join them, and he even has her minding."

"He's excited about training them." Harley dropped her backpack.

"I hadn't realized you two had become such good friends."

Harley shrugged. "He likes dogs better than people, just like me. That's why he was so upset the first day we met. He thought I was stealing Pepper."

"Surely not."

"He's okay," Harley said. "I'd better help him, but first I want a cookie."

"I think I'll go lie down for a nap," Emma said, already feeling exhausted again. "Watching the security team wore me out."

In her bedroom, Emma stared at the stack of letters. This wasn't the time.

She pulled the covers up to her chin wondering what sort of people her mother would find in Alabama. Mother was right. Whatever happened, there would be heartbreak—and just when she thought hers might be healing.

On Tuesday morning, Emma sat on the edge of Harley's bed and looked at the thermometer. "One-hundred and three."

"Thanks for sharing your crud with me." Harley covered her face with her arm and sneezed.

Emma narrowed her eyes and placed her palm on Harley's forehead. "You didn't drink a hot beverage so you could fool me again and cut class, did you?"

Harley sneezed. "I ain't that stupid. I feel like crap thanks to your germs."

"I'm sorry. Maybe I should take you to see the doctor."

"No telling what kind of disease I'd pick up in a doctor's office."

Emma shook out two tablets from a bottle. "Acetaminophen should bring down your fever."

Pepper whined and Harley swallowed the pills with juice and wiped her mouth with her sleeve. "She needs to go out."

"I'll take her and check on the other two fur babies." Emma stood. "Need anything else?"

"Nah. I'm going back to sleep." Harley rolled over and mumbled. "Thanks for the pills."

"You're welcome."

Outside, the trio of canines chased each other in the backyard. Emma took advantage of being alone and dialed her mother. She couldn't believe she'd slept through the night without angst over what her mother would find in Alabama.

The call went to voice mail. *Drat.* After leaving a brief message, she disconnected, then called Tammy and reviewed the library's work schedule. The two decided the library wouldn't suffer if Emma took off until after New Year's Day. After all, the holidays were the slowest time of the year for the library, and Christmas was only four days away.

Emma disconnected the phone and went out into the backyard. Pepper dropped to the ground in front of her. The little dog yipped and the two larger dogs dropped to their bellies, panting. Across the fence, Mr. McCullough filled his birdfeeders.

"Good morning," Emma called.

He finished his work and walked to the fence "Are you over the crud?"

"Yes, but now Harley's down."

"Poor kid." Buster and Max jumped up and rested their front paws on the top of the fence. Mr. McCullough scratched their ears. "Sit."

The dog's rumps immediately hit the ground, their chins up. He reached into his pocket and tossed them each a treat, which they caught in midair. Pepper howled. Mr. McCullough wagged his finger at her. "Hush."

She whined.

"Sit," Mr. McCullough wagged a finger.

Pepper howled again, but sat down.

"This little missy is stubborn and likes to complain when she's made to mind"—Mr. McCullough tossed her a treat—"just like Harley. But they're sweethearts once they trust you."

"Thanks for being Harley's friend."

He shrugged. "She's a good kid. I don't think anyone's ever paid too much attention to the girl."

Emma chewed her lip. Maybe she'd treated Harley too cautiously in an attempt to give her space. "She appreciates your help training the dogs."

"It goes both ways. She helps me fill the birdfeeders and feed the squirrels."

"I've been wondering what to get her for Christmas. Maybe I'll get her a birdfeeder for our yard and a supply of food for it."

"Too late, I already bought her one."

"Rats. Any other ideas?"

He scratched his jaw. "Nope. If I were you, I'd ask her."

"Do you think she'd tell me?"

"Harley doesn't volunteer information, but she'll answer a direct question unless she thinks it's none of your business."

Emma thought about her conversations with Harley and realized he was right. She scratched Pepper's ear. "Is your son coming home for Christmas?"

"Nope. I'll visit him in Louisville on Christmas Eve, then they're headed to his wife's family in Cincinnati for Christmas Day."

"I'd love to fill up my dining room table on Saturday. Why don't you join us for Christmas lunch?"

Mr. McCullough's face lifted. "I'd like that."

When Emma and Pepper returned to the house, Pepper made a beeline up the stairs and Emma followed. By the time she reached the bedroom, the dog was already on the bed next to Harley, who snored softly.

Emma quietly shut Harley's bedroom door and thought about who else she might invite to lunch. Maybe Pastor Bob and Eleanor ... and Luke? Was it too forward to invite him to lunch? The thought of him being alone on Christmas Day made her sad. He didn't seem to have any family. Casey would spend the day with her family, and Minnie would travel to her sister's home in Nashville.

If her mother really managed to locate Harley's grandparents, it would be a reason to celebrate, so why did she feel so low?

A few minutes later, she curled up in the chair in the bedroom and wrapped Chris's sweater around her. With trembling hands, she picked up the stack of letters, then placed them on her lap. She couldn't do it. *Could she?*

Her gaze fell to her Bible and she thumbed through the pages to the book of Psalms and read, "Be strong and take heart, all you who hope in the Lord."

Lord, give me strength to do this. Her hands shook while she unfolded the first letter. The childish scrawl softened her heart. *I can do all things through Christ, who strengthens me.* After saying that over and over, she looked at the letter.

> *Dear Mrs. Baker,*
>
> *I'm sorry for being too scared to face you to tell you this stuff. You probably hate my guts and I don't blame you.*
>
> *I didn't mean to hurt no one, but I was afraid the other boys were going to kill me. After the*

accident, I held my hand to the cut and tried to stop the bleeding. While we waited for the ambulance, Mr. Baker told me he forgave me, and he said it would be okay.

Mr. Baker made me promise to tell you he loved you and that if he didn't make it, he'd see you in heaven. I've let him down by being such a wimp.

Then he started talking about Jesus and said I needed to ask you or his preacher, Pastor Bob, to tell me about the One who saves. Because of Jesus, Mr. Baker said he'd spend eternity in heaven, so not to worry.

Pastor Bob came to visit me in jail that first night, and he kept coming. Then he brought Pastor Luke to meet me, and he started a Bible study at the detention center.

It might make you feel better to know I suffer. I ain't slept a whole night without nightmares since the accident.

I hope you'll forgive me even though I don't deserve it.

Sincerely,
Winston Meador

Emma wiped her face with the sleeve of her sweater. Chris forgave him immediately. If only she'd been able to do the same.

Father, please forgive me for my stubbornness. I forgive him. Thank you for helping me find the way out of the darkness.

After a long while, she picked up her phone and dialed Luke. When he answered, she said, "I need to see Winston Meador."

"So you read the letters."

"Only one. Will you bring him to see me?"

"I will."

"Harley's sick in bed, so I'll be home all day."

After they disconnected, Emma opened her Bible. To get through this day without a meltdown, she needed sustenance.

Minnie arrived at noon with a covered stew pot. "Homemade chicken noodle soup. The cure for all that ails you."

After Minnie placed the pot on the stove, Emma gave her a hug and leaned into her.

"What's wrong, sweetheart?"

"Luke will be here with Winston Meador at two o'clock."

Minnie squeezed her hard. "I knew the Lord was speaking when he told me to get on over here."

Emma released her. "Let's sit down."

After they were settled on the sofa, Emma handed Minnie the letter.

"Are you sure you want me to read it?"

Emma nodded.

Minnie lifted her reading glasses from the chain around her neck. As she read the note a tear rolled down her cheek and she removed an embroidered handkerchief from her pocket.

"Let me pray with you." Minnie grabbed her hand.

Peace washed over Emma while Minnie silently prayed. Sometimes there were simply no words sufficient.

Later, Minnie took a tray up to Harley. While Emma waited, the clock's hand moved in slow motion, and she paced around the room. She hit the speed dial button on her phone and Casey answered after one ring. "Are you better?"

"Yes."

"I can't believe you missed the Christmas pageant."

"I'm sorry." Emma gulped. "I read Winston's letter."

Casey gasped. "Oh, honey."

"Can you come?"

"I'm walking out the door."

Emma exhaled loudly. *Thank you, Jesus, for friends.*

When Luke's vintage pickup truck pulled in the drive, Minnie stood. "It might scare the boy to face all three of us."

Casey, who had arrived minutes earlier, left the sofa. "Minnie's right. We'll be upstairs with Harley if you need us." She hugged Emma.

"Don't everyone leave me." Emma wrung her hands.

Minnie patted her back. "Casey will stay while I check on Harley."

A few seconds later, Minnie's feet disappeared at the top of the stairs when a knock sounded.

Emma opened the door to see Winston staring at the ground, his face pale, with Luke beside him.

"C–come in." Emma's hands trembled on the doorknob.

Luke placed his palm on Winston's back and led him to the sofa.

Emma sat in the club chair and twisted her activity tracker around her wrist. "Th–thank you for coming." She gulped and squared her shoulders. "This is my best friend, Casey Bledsoe."

Winston's eyes were large when he looked at Casey. "Everyone knows who you are."

"Not really." Casey beamed her million-dollar smile, and Winston looked dumbstruck.

Luke sat down on the edge of the sofa.

Winston dropped down next to him and pushed the cuffs of his green thermal shirt up to his elbows. "Thank you for having Pastor Luke get me." Winston stared at his hands, then his knee began to bounce up and down. "I heard Harley lives here."

"She mentioned she knew you," Emma said.

"The trailer park where we lived was rough, no place to leave a girl to fend for herself all the time."

"I hadn't realized there were places like that in Weldon," Casey said.

Winston shrugged. "I've lived in a lot of towns and there's always a bad part in every one."

Luke wiped his palms on his jeans. "There's no perfect place, just like there's no perfect people. Let's take a moment to pray before we start."

Luke reached to his left and took Emma's hand, and to his right he gripped Winston's.

For a split second, his large hand reminded Emma of Chris's until she felt Luke's calluses. She bowed her head and felt her nerves calm.

Luke squeezed her hand. "Father, we come before you to thank you for your love. I pray for peace and healing for all gathered today. Please give Winston courage and help him find the words to help mend broken hearts. Guide our words and spirits. Forgive us, Father, for our failings. We place our hope in you. In Jesus's name we pray. Amen."

Emma looked up and met Winston's dark tear-filled eyes.

The boy wiped his arm across his face, sat up straight, and the words tumbled out. "On the day of the fight, Josh Jackson and Clint Powers had been trying to get to me because they'd thought I'd snitched on them. It was bad timing—the police showed up the day after they offered me cash to hide their drugs in my locker."

Emma picked up her mug of coffee that had gone cold and cradled it.

"I didn't want anything to do with their crap because pills messed up my mom. I slipped into a supply closet at school to hide from them, and I thought they'd left. When I rounded the corner in the empty hallway, they were waiting for me."

"You should have told someone you were afraid—a teacher," Emma said.

Winston shook his head slowly. "Snitches get stitches. That's why I had a knife. When those guys cornered me, I pulled out the switchblade hoping it would scare them. But they jumped on me. I didn't even know when Mr. Baker stepped into the fight."

Casey moved and sat on the floor next to Emma and squeezed her hand.

Winston ran his sleeve across his face again.

"Take your time," Luke said.

"Then I saw Mr. Baker bleeding, holding his stomach, and I could see what I'd done. I dropped the knife and tried to help him."

"What about the other boys?" Emma's tears flowed.

"They run off and left us."

Emma wiped her eyes. "Thank you for trying to help him."

Winston nodded. "That was before cameras were installed, so no one believed me when I said one of them might have stabbed Mr. Baker."

Emma covered her mouth with her hand.

"While we waited for the ambulance, this is what Mr. Baker told me to tell you." The boy closed his eyes "He said, 'I forgive you. I know you didn't mean to hurt me. It's important for you to understand that I have a Savior, Jesus. If I don't make it, I'll spend eternity in heaven.'"

"That's right," Emma said. "I know Chris is in a better place."

Winston wiped his eyes again. "He said, 'Tell my wife I love her and that I'll wait for her in heaven.' He grabbed my arm and said, 'If you don't know Jesus, find my pastor at Loving Hope or my wife Emma. She's the one who helped me understand how important it is to have a personal relationship with Christ.'"

Emma closed her eyes and lowered her head, all at once convicted and warmed by these words.

"His last words were, 'Whatever happens, I'll be all right and so will you when you find Jesus.'"

Winston stopped, and Luke gave him a blue bandanna handkerchief. "The police came running and threw me in their car. That's the last time I saw Mr. Baker. I called Pastor Bob from the police station that night. He met with me for weeks."

Emma nodded. "He's a good man."

"He gave me a Bible, then Pastor Luke started the Bible study at Rocky Hills."

"I'm sorry I didn't read your letters sooner." Emma looked across the coffee table and saw not a murderer, but a broken young man.

"That's okay," said Winston. "It's taken a while for me to be ready to see you, to be able to ask you ... to forgive me." The words rushed out. "I know I don't deserve it, but ... I hope you will."

Emma wiped her face with a tissue. "I forgive you."

Winston heaved a sigh. "Thank you, ma'am." He paused. "Pastor Luke's wanted me to ask Jesus for forgiveness, but I couldn't do it until I asked you to forgive me first. I hurt you the worst."

Luke placed his large hand over Emma's and stared into her eyes. "Will you pray with me and Winston?"

Casey gave Emma a soft look as if to say to her oldest, dearest friend *You don't have to if you're not ready*.

Emma looked at Winston's hands—at the fingers that held the knife that had severed the thread of her husband's life. That broken thread had unraveled her life, but somehow, God had taken the fragments and stitched her together again. She nodded.

Luke kneeled in front of Emma and Winston. He took both their hands.

Emma took a deep breath and closed her eyes.

Luke instructed the young man: "Winston. Please repeat after me ... Forgive me, Father, a sinner—" He paused, and Winston whispered his words. "I ask for your forgiveness ... Thank you, Jesus, for suffering and dying on the cross to pay for my sins ... I place my hope in you ... You are the Good Shepherd, and I will follow you all the days of my life. Amen."

Winston repeated every word.

Luke looked at Winston. "It's not the words that save you, buddy, but the condition of your heart. You have to give up your old way of living and try to live like Jesus."

Then Luke looked at Emma. "Thank you for your generous spirit. From what Winston told me about your husband, he was a special man."

Emma nodded. "He was." She could feel her own countenance softening.

"Thank you," said Winston. "I know I don't deserve a second chance, but I mean to try to make my life count for something. I can't never do enough to make up for losing Mr. Baker, but I'll do my best."

"None of us can do enough to pay back our sin debt," said Luke. "We don't have to. Christ did that for us. If you try to live for him, you'll be okay, just like Mr. Baker told you."

"We're all going to be okay," Emma said. "This has been more than difficult, but it's been healing. I'm glad you came." She stood. "I believe that even though Satan meant evil, God will use it for good."

Casey blew her nose. "Amen."

From the top of the stairs Minnie called, "Praise the Lord." She walked down talking. "That'll teach the ol' devil to mess around with people. Young man, you're liable to lead other boys who've made mistakes to Jesus. Wouldn't that be something?"

Emma smiled. She should have known Minnie was listening at the top of the stairs. A wave of love for her life-long friend and guardian angel washed through her. She was so thankful for her friends. Her phone vibrated and she glanced at it. Her mother's name showed on the display. Whatever her mother discovered, it could wait. She would take a moment to savor this victory before wading into another battle.

CHAPTER THIRTY-SEVEN—EMMA

Emma sat crossed-legged on Harley's bed and sipped chicken-noodle soup from a mug while she told her everything about Winston's visit.

Harley listened, her hazel eyes wide. "And I slept through the whole darn thing."

"Like you would have wanted to be anywhere near such a conversation."

"Not right in the middle of it, but I can hear good from the top of the stairs."

"As I suspected," Emma said.

"What will Ms. Virginia think about all this?"

"With Mother, it's hard to say."

"Is she coming over?"

Emma shook her head no. "Mother is out of town." She should tell Harley about her mother's activities, but perhaps, it would be better not to get her hopes up. "Too bad you missed the last day of school before Christmas break."

Harley shrugged. "I already took my finals. The last day before a break is always a waste of time."

It didn't seem Harley had any friends at school. If only she had a friend like Casey. She'd have to see what she could do to help that situation. Then she paused. That was the sort of thing her mother would do. Maybe it was enough for Harley to have Mr. McCullough for a best friend. Emma couldn't think of a better role model.

Later, Emma lay in bed and stared at her ring next to the book on the bedside table. Emma picked up the wedding band, then kissed it. She left the bed and opened her antique rosewood jewelry box on the dresser and placed her treasured ring inside. Once settled back in bed, Emma picked up the novel and thumbed to the page where she'd stopped reading on the day of the accident. Then she tuned back to the first page. It was time for a fresh start.

On Wednesday morning, Emma and Becky worked on the menu for Christmas Day. Emma lifted her pen from the list. "After the candlelight service on Christmas Eve, we must go by the Bledsoe's. It's a tradition to visit Casey's family and share a glass of eggnog."

"Are you sure they'll want a stranger joining their family gathering?" Becky bit her lip.

"Casey has five older brothers and they all have kids, as well as several aunts and cousins. The more the merrier."

Emma fingered through an old wooden box filled with index cards. "This was my grandmother's recipe box."

Becky lifted a card, yellowed with age. "Look at her perfect penmanship."

"Grandmother was so elegant. It seems the harder I tried to emulate her, the clumsier I became."

"Nonsense," Becky said.

Emma phone vibrated. An unfamiliar number showed on the display. "Hello."

"Mrs. Baker?"

"Yes."

"This is Debra."

"Hi Debra. I've been meaning to call you, but I came down with the flu."

"Oh, no. I'm sorry."

"Me too, but I'm better."

"That's good. The reason I'm calling is ... well, Ms. Patsy and I drove by your house last night for me to have a look, and ... I don't think it's the place for me."

"But why?"

"I could never feel right in such a fancy place."

"We're very informal around here."

"It's not just the house. I don't know. You're educated and Ms. Patsy said a school teacher lives with you."

"Please reconsider," Emma said. "Why don't you come over for dinner tonight?" *What could she fix that might ease Debra's worries?* "Do you like chili?"

"Yes, ma'am."

"I'll pick you up around five, then we can visit before dinner."

"I guess that will be okay," Debra said.

Emma hung up the phone.

"Was that Debra?" Becky asked.

"Yes." Emma moaned. "Apparently, she and Ms. Patsy drove by yesterday. I think the house scared her."

"It is a bit over the top," Becky said.

"Do you know how to make chili?

"Yes." Becky smiled. "I'll add the ingredients to the list."

"Maybe I should invite Casey," Emma said. "She can make anyone feel special."

Becky clicked the top of the pen. "I love Casey, but she might intimidate someone lacking self-confidence."

"Phooey," Emma said. "People are always making snap judgments about her because she used to model."

"There's something I need to tell you." The constant clicking of the ink pen made Emma want to remove it from Becky's hand, but she resisted the urge because that was the sort of thing her mother would do. The look on Becky's face told her the news was bad.

"You will never believe this." Becky gulped. "The Habitat Board approved my application. Of course, it will be months before a house is built."

Emma's stomach dropped. "That was fast."

"Your mother must have pulled strings."

"She'd never use her influence to give one person an advantage over another candidate, but I don't doubt she used her position to move your application through the approval process quickly."

"I love living here, but the thought of owning my own home—I never dreamed it possible."

Emma did her best to offer a genuine smile. "Congratulations."

They worked through the rest of the grocery list, and Becky grabbed her coat. "Leslie should sleep for another hour."

"We'll be fine. I'm getting the best end of this deal."

Her phone vibrated. "It's Mother."

"Please offer my thanks to her."

Becky walked out the door and Emma answered the phone. "Finally."

"I phoned yesterday but your phone went to voicemail."

"But you didn't answer my call last night or this morning."

"You know I always silence my phone while dining. I forgot to turn the darn thing on again."

"Whatever." Emma sighed with exasperation. "Tell me what's going on. If I were a cat, I'd be dead."

"We found them."

A wave of dizziness washed over Emma and she dropped to the sofa. "And?"

"They're lovely people."

Emma couldn't speak.

Virginia kept talking. "For once, I admit to being wrong." She went into details explaining Luther's detective skills.

Guilt flooded Emma for being unhappy about the news of finding Harley's grandparents. "I ... I kn–know Harley will be happy."

"Don't tell her—yet." Virginia's tone held a hint of concern.

"B–but why?" Oh, this stutter.

"Breathe, Emma. Take a deep breath."

Emma inhaled. "I'm fine."

"We're working out details, but if all goes well, I'll be home by Friday, Christmas Eve, with guests.

"They're coming to Weldon?"

"I hope you still have an empty bedroom." Virginia sighed. "Or, I suppose they could stay with me."

"I have room for a couple, but—"

"Good. I can't think of a better Christmas present for Harley."

Emma sighed. She should be happy. Reuniting Harley with her family would be a dream come true for the child, and Becky's dream of owning her own home would soon be a reality, but her dream of filling her home with family was rapidly dissipating. Maybe she should sell out, retire, and move to the beach where it was likely Harley would be. But she knew that was impossible. Weldon was home and a thirty-five-year-old did not retire. It would require every ounce of the Christmas Spirit to put a smile on her face, but she'd do it—for Harley.

Pink rays lit the horizon on Thursday morning when Emma donned her track shoes, stretched, and then clipped leashes to the two rottweilers. Her thoughts rambled while she ran. Conversation with Debra had been stilted during dinner. After enjoying fried coconut pies, Emma had given a wide-eyed Debra a tour of the house. The only bright spot had been when Emma opened the bedroom door with the twin beds dressed in Hello Kitty bedspreads. "My girls would love a room like this." Debra's voice had been wistful.

The drive back to Freedom House had been tension-filled as Emma searched her mind for what might ease Debra's worries about living in the old Victorian. After thanking Emma for dinner, the poor girl almost ran to the front door of the log cabin. So much for the hope of filling her home with graduates of Patsy's program.

The two dogs pulled at their leashes and kept her at a brisk pace, their tongues lolling out the sides of their mouths. At last, a stitch in her side forced her to stop and she bent over double, gasping for air.

Dadgummit—the cemetery. A new saddle of silk Poinsettias sat atop Chris's tombstone. Emma appreciated her mother's habit of ordering flowers for family members' headstones, but she wished she'd let her choose the flowers for Chris. There would be lilies for Easter, and a bunch of red roses would arrive before Memorial Day.

Emma kneeled in front of the granite and fingered the letters of his name. "I've finally started to heal." The dogs panted and whined next to her. "I don't know what the future holds, but I will try to choose happiness."

A cardinal landed next to the crimson flowers in front of her and chirped. Emma remembered an old wives' tale about cardinals being messengers between the dead and the living. Of course, she didn't believe such nonsense, *but still* ... What message might she want to send Chris?

Emma spent the next hour pouring her heart out while the dogs listened, ears pricked, by her side. At last, she rubbed her sleeve across her cheek.

When she returned to the house, she shook out two more pills from the Tylenol bottle and handed them to Harley. "How are you feeling?"

Harley wiped her nose with a tissue and took the tablets. "Better."

Emma filled her in on the plan to visit Casey's family home after the candlelight service tomorrow on Christmas Eve, and discussed the seating arrangements for the dining room table on Christmas Day.

"So you're going to roast another turkey?"

"Yes, ma'am. It's already in the refrigerator. I'll put it in the brine solution in the morning."

"Cool."

"While you've been sleeping, Becky and I have been planning the menu."

"Can we have sweet potatoes?"

"It's on the list."

"And mashed potatoes?"

"If that's what you want. Speaking of what you want, I need help with choosing the right Christmas gift for you."

"I don't need nothing," Harley said. "Buster and Max are enough."

"Nonsense," Emma said. "There will be presents for you under the tree, and the chances of you liking the gifts improve if you give me a hint."

Harley stared at her hands and bit her lip. "Can I get a manicure?"

Emma squeezed her hand. "I'll call Casey. We missed our Sunday night get-together."

"Okay," Harley said. "Can we order in Chinese?"

"Of course, but focus, please. I need gift ideas."

Harley's lips disappeared. "Maybe a dog training book."

"What about clothes?"

Harley shrugged. "Maybe something nice to wear to church."

"A dress?"

Harley's nose scrunched up. "Maybe leggings and a long top."

Emma rubbed her palms together. "Okay. I'm on my way to the mall."

An hour later, after finally finding a parking space, she looked at her phone for the umpteenth time. Why hadn't her mother called with an update? It wasn't like Virginia to be so secretive. Would she really show up with Harley's grandparents?

In the mall, it didn't take her long to find a book on dog training. On impulse she grabbed the two-set volume of Julia Child's *Mastering the Art of French Cooking* and rubbed her tummy. She and Harley could learn together.

Emma also purchased several outfits from American Eagle and Hollister, hoping to please Harley. Then she purchased her a pair of stylish black ankle boots. Other shoppers jostled Emma as she made her way through the stores. She'd never left her shopping this close to the holiday, but she'd never had so many people depending on her. It might be temporary, but she'd savor every minute.

While in the toy store buying gifts for Leslie, she asked a clerk what an almost-teen of twelve might like. The savvy salesperson talked her into buying a drone, claiming it a popular gift for kids and adults.

For Casey, she purchased a new gold charm of the iconic comedy and tragedy mask as a remembrance of her directing the Christmas pageant.

Her mother loved cashmere sweaters. It was one of the few things they had in common.

She'd already purchased a gift collection of Minnie's favorite Youth Dew perfume, and weeks ago, she'd placed an internet order for her favorite salted-caramel candy from a chocolatier in Louisville.

When Emma arrived home, Harley and Mr. McCullough were working with the dogs in the backyard. Seeing the familiar camouflage coat made Emma smile. She called out to Harley. "Are you feeling better?"

"Yeah. I'm tired of being inside." Harley threw a ball to the dogs.

Emma toted the purchases to her bedroom and used gift bags and tissue paper instead of wrapping paper. Her mother would frown on this shortcut, but Emma didn't have the time nor the energy to wrap the presents in a manner worthy of her mother's high standards. Emma shrugged. *Who cares?*

An hour later, the sight of the tree filled with gift bags lifted her spirits. A Bing Crosby Christmas CD played in the background. No matter what tomorrow held, she'd make this the best Christmas ever.

CHAPTER THIRTY-EIGHT—LUKE

Luke broke down the stack of empty pizza boxes and placed them in the trash. The night would not be one he'd ever forget because Winston had shared with the group he was a brand-new Christian. He'd described the new sense of freedom he felt, and his face seemed to radiate light.

After clearing his desk of papers, he leaned back in his chair. It had been weeks since he'd last spent any length of time at the Westview Circle Church. A knock sounded on the door.

"Howdy, stranger." His boss, Pastor Steve, leaned against the doorframe.

"Hey, yourself," Luke said. "Have a seat."

The vinyl chair creaked when Pastor Steve sat down. "How's it going at Loving Chapel?"

"Good ... I guess."

"Better than that, from what I hear. Bob called me this afternoon."

Luke rubbed his beard. "Uh-huh."

"He said he asked you to apply for his job."

It seemed all the air left the room. "He did, but I'm not the right guy."

Steve gave him a long look. "This sounds like a conversation we've had before."

"You want to get rid of me?"

"You know I value your contribution to our congregation, but it's not about what I want, it's all what He wants." Steve pointed his thumb up toward the ceiling.

Luke stared at the oak paneling. It was comfortable here ... maybe too comfortable.

"You have a lot to offer Weldon that Bob can't."

Luke narrowed his eyes. He respected Steve, but he'd not listen to anyone criticize Bob. He sat up straight in his chair. "Like what?"

"Youth, energy, and a willingness to shake things up."

"It's an older congregation, and you know senior adults hate change."

"The church's survival depends on the congregation's willingness to adapt. Bob and I discussed it for a long time yesterday."

Luke's shoulders relaxed a tiny bit knowing Bob was the one pressing the issue, but still ... As much as he'd enjoyed his time in Weldon, he felt lacking in a million ways. He wished he could discuss this with Emma. She knew the church members well and might have suggestions for how to help the church grow, but he couldn't do so until Bob revealed his plans.

Getting to know Emma more deeply appealed to him but that wasn't the right reason to apply for Bob's job.

A wave of loneliness washed over him. What if she never wanted more than friendship? What if she fell in love with someone else, and as her pastor, she'd expect him to marry them? Could he preach every Sunday morning seeing her with another man by her side? His mouth went dry. And then he noticed Steve staring at him, a knowing look on his face. How long had he been out in left field?

"The look on your face tells me this is an unhappy topic. Let me pray for you," Steve said.

"I'd appreciate it," Luke said, and he bowed his head.

Late that evening, Luke couldn't stop pacing in Loving Chapel's sanctuary. He touched each pew and lifted prayers for the people who sat there regularly. Even though he didn't know all the names, he pictured their faces. At last, he arrived at the altar and kneeled. "Have thine own way, Lord."

He left the church cloaked in peace as he climbed into his old truck. Thoughts of Emma filled his head. He hoped she was feeling better. It wouldn't hurt to drive by the house. Of course, he wouldn't go in. He just wanted to see if her lights were on. Luke rubbed his beard. He was worse than a teenager. The urge to see her was so strong. He sat in the truck trying to sort through his emotions. No doubt about it, he was a goner.

CHAPTER THIRTY-NINE - HARLEY

Harley held out her hand and admired the black polish. Even though her nails were short, they almost looked pretty. They didn't look like her hands or her mom's. A wave of sadness washed through her. The antique grandfather clock chimed ten o'clock as Pepper scratched on the back door and growled.

"But you've already been out." Harley trudged to the door and Pepper howled. "Let me get my coat, you little varmint."

Emma stood. "I'll take her. You're still recovering."

"That's okay. I want to check on Max and Buster."

"They're fine. They pulled me all the way to the city limits this morning."

"But the dogs are my responsibility." Harley crammed her hand through the sleeve of her coat. When she opened the door, the bitter cold stole her breath, but it was clear and calm. She looked up to the star-filled sky. So much for hoping for a white Christmas.

Pepper sniffed the ground, growled, and took off barking. The new security lights lit up the area and she sprinted to the back of the yard. Buster and Max didn't come out of their dog houses. She called to them and the dogs howled, but they didn't exit. *Something's wrong.*

Pepper continued to snarl at a tree in the back corner.

"Leave the possums alone and get to your business," Harley shouted. "It's cold out here."

She huddled into her coat and scurried to Pepper. "You'll wake up Mr. McCullough." A dark figure stepped out from behind the shrubbery and kicked Pepper hard.

A sharp yip from the little dog shattered the quiet.

Harley ran straight into Beau's hard body and attempted to tackle him to the ground. "You leave her alone."

Beau's arm came around her like a vice grip. Her back was to his chest and his whiskey breath made her gag. "Well, if it ain't the little thief who stole my money. I've been waiting for you for a long time," he said in a gravelly voice.

His arm tightened and it cut off her breath. If she could just call out. Her vision blurred. Why hadn't she paid attention to Pepper's warning? *So much for my plan.*

Ever since she had spotted Beau lurking on the parade route, Harley had thought about how she could lure Beau so he could be captured by the police, and she could finally be free of him. She'd even talked to Mr. McCullough about her plan. But instead, Beau had surprised her. She pulled at his arm with all her strength and he cackled.

Max and Buster howled and Beau loosened his grip. "Tell them dogs to shut up." Beau's breath made her gag.

A tiny splinter of hope gave Harley courage because the dogs continued to howl.

She clamped down hard on his hand with her teeth.

Pain emanated from her skull as Beau yanked harder on her hair. She kicked him in the shin with the heel of her boot.

Buster's and Max's howls and yips continued.

"Harley! Where are you?"

Oh, no. It's Emma. Harley's heart raced.

Beau stilled, loosened his grip on her throat, and whispered. "I'll kill her if you don't get rid of her." He dragged her into the bush and limbs scratched her face.

Harley's heart pounded. She couldn't let Beau hurt Emma. "I'm okay." Her voice sounded raspy.

"It's cold out here. You'll catch your death from pneumonia. Where are you?" Emma's voice came closer.

Harley took a breath. "Run, Emma!" Beau clamped his hand over Harley's mouth and she bit him again.

Emma was upon them and gasped. "Get your hands off her!" She lunged against Beau. The three tumbled to the ground. Emma pummeled Beau with her fist, and Harley scrambled out of his reach, but he pinned Emma to the ground. The dogs howled.

"Help!" Harley screamed and she jumped on Beau's back, tears streaming down her face. But it was useless. Beau was too strong. *God, help us!*

CHAPTER FORTY—LUKE

Luke drove by Emma's home slowly. The rusted out pickup parked to the side of Emma's garage looked strange and foreboding. *What was that doing here?* Luke parked on the street and crept toward the truck. A scream shattered the silence.

Luke raced to Emma's backyard and hurtled the fence. A bent figure stood in the shadows and held what looked a rifle. Luke stopped. "Get out of the way, Harley." It was Mr. McCullough.

In the dim light, Luke could just make out Harley pounding the broad shoulders of a man wearing a dark hoodie. The man lay on top of Emma.

Luke heart raced. What to do? *Lord, help us.*

Mr. McCullough shouted again. "Move, Harley!"

Harley rolled away, and the man holding down Emma looked up over his shoulder. A patch covered one eye.

The boyfriend.

A stream of something spewed from Mr. McCullough's gun and hit the man full on the face. He screeched and wallowed on the ground holding his hand over his eyes. "I'll kill you!"

Emma scrambled away toward Harley and pulled her phone from her pocket, but her hands trembled so hard she dropped it.

Luke jumped onto the man and hit him hard with his fist. Fury flooded his body. He held his fist up again. *I'm going to kill him.*

"Stop!" Mr. McCullough shouted.

Luke vibrated with energy as he squeezed the man's throat. Rage flooded Luke's body.

"Stop. He's not worth it." Emma's tone was pleading.

Luke loosened his grip as his vision cleared, and he breathed in deeply.

The man wheezed and Luke flipped him onto his belly, and yanked his wrists behind him. Luke put pressure on the man's wrist with his knee.

"You're breaking my arms." The man rasped.

"You're lucky I didn't break your neck," Luke said.

A car with blue lights flashing and sirens blaring pulled into the drive. A policeman ran to them with his gun pulled.

"Freeze!"

As the policeman handcuffed the man who had attacked Emma, he spewed a slew of vitriolic words. He was soaked and shuddering but still looked menacing.

Emma clung to Luke. "You and Mr. McCullough saved us."

"It was all Mr. McCullough" Luke said, feeling relief flood through him.

"I called the police the minute I heard the dogs howl. I've been watching for this guy ever since Harley told me about him." Mr. McCullough stood protectively by Harley, who was shivering.

Emma trembled in Luke's arms.

The temperature hovered just above freezing. Luke removed his coat and wrapped it around her. He didn't want to ever release her.

Mr. McCullough cleared his throat. "Pepper needs the vet."

Emma removed her phone from her pocket. "I'll call him. I'm sure he'll meet me us at his clinic."

A policeman placed Beau in the back of a police car. Another policeman entered the scene. "We found a rusted out pickup on the other side of the garage. I'll bet good money it belongs to this guy."

"That sounds like Beau's truck," Harley said.

"Looks like he has a shake and bake operation," the policeman said.

"What's that?" Emma asked.

"A dangerous way to make meth," the cop said.

"That's not important right now." Mr. McCullough's voice broke. "We need to get Pepper to the Vet." Mr. McCullough held the little dog in his arms.

Luke slowly released Emma. "I'll do it. I'm sure the police will have questions for both of you." He led Mr. McCullough to the truck.

Mr. McCullough placed Pepper on the seat. "She's a tough one."

Luke wanted to comfort Emma, but he knew Mr. McCullough was right. Her dog needed the attention.

Emma stood behind them speaking into the phone. "Luke Davis will be there in a few minutes with Pepper." She paused. "Thank you." Emma disconnected. "The vet's office is across the street from the post office."

"I'll find it," Luke said.

"Thank you," Emma sniffed and hugged him.

Luke savored the feel of her in his arms. "You need to go inside where it's warm."

"Okay. We'll join you at the vet's office as soon as we finish talking with the police."

Luke drove to the clinic and lifted a prayer of thanks that everyone was okay. Then he looked at the little dog. Almost everyone. Poor little girl. He lifted another petition for Emma's beloved pet.

Two hours later, Luke stopped pacing when Emma raced into the animal clinic's waiting room right into his arms. "How is she?"

Luke smoothed his hand over her hair. "She's in surgery. A broken leg, a few missing teeth."

Mr. McCullough came into the room behind Harley. He still wore his striped pajamas under his overcoat. "Harley and I had a plan and it worked—other than Pepper getting hurt."

"I'm done with running," Harley lifted her chin. "I told Mr. McCullough about Beau so he filled his Super-Soaker with lemon juice and vinegar."

Emma untangled herself from Luke's arms. "Why didn't you let me in on the plan?"

Harley bit her lip. "I didn't want you to be scared."

"Is there anything else I need to know?" Emma cocked her head.

Harley stared at the floor. "When I ran away, I stole some of Beau's money, but I burned it last week."

"Why did you burn it?" Emma's brows furrowed.

"'Cause I didn't want my mom to get it. The money is the only reason she wanted to see me."

"Oh, honey." Emma placed her arms around Harley.

"The only thing she cares about is drugs." Harley hugged her back.

Emma gulped. "Maybe Patsy will be able to help her."

The door swung open, and they all froze. A tall man with a gray beard in jeans and a green scrub top announced, "Pepper will be sore, but she should make a full recovery."

Emma placed her hand over her heart and dropped to one of the waiting-room chairs.

"Can we see her?" Harley asked.

"She's still sedated. Why not come by in the morning?" The vet squeezed her shoulder.

In the parking lot, Emma hugged Mr. McCullough again. "Thank you, my friend."

He patted her shoulder. "You're welcome." His bent frame seemed to stand a little taller. "But it wasn't just me. I was mighty glad for the backup, Preacher."

Luke patted his shoulder. "It seems to me you had the situation under control." Luke polished his forehead. "Sadly, I can't say the same for myself. If it hadn't been for you and Emma stopping me, I hate to admit it, but I might have killed him."

Mr. McCullough looked fierce. "A normal reaction when someone you love is being attacked. That's why I used my super-soaker instead of my Glock. I didn't trust myself not to kill him."

Luke lifted a silent prayers of thanks that Emma had Mr. McCullough for a neighbor. He drove Emma and Harley home and walked them to the back door. Harley scampered inside, but Emma paused, and Luke held her. He rested his chin on top of her head. "You could have been killed. What in the world made you think you could tackle someone like that?"

She sniffed. "He had Harley. I didn't think, I just hit him with all I had."

"You need a keeper, Emma Baker."

She looked up and gave him a sad smile. "I had one, but he died trying to save a kid." She untangled herself from his arms and left him standing in the cold.

Luke rubbed the back of his neck and stared at the ground. He'd never be able to compete with the memories of her husband. If God asked him to shepherd Loving Chapel, could he settle for friendship? He gulped. *Lord, help me.*

CHAPTER FORTY-ONE—HARLEY

Every time Harley closed her eyes, she pictured Emma running toward her and Beau. What if he'd hurt her?

A knock sounded. "You awake?" Emma stood in the doorway.

"Yeah."

"I couldn't sleep." Emma came in and sat on the edge of the bed. "I wanted to make sure you're okay."

"I'm good." Harley sat up and pulled her knees to her. "I'm sorry I didn't tell you about Beau."

Emma gave her a sad smile. "Trust takes time. I'm glad you let Mr. McCullough in on your secret."

"Did you know he used to be a Ranger?"

"Yes, but I'd forgotten."

"I figured if I couldn't trust a Ranger, then who could I trust?"

Emma smoothed the coverlet. "You know ..." She gulped. "You can trust me too. You can tell me anything." Her chin dropped. "Except a lie."

Remorse flooded Harley. "I know."

Emma's brow furrowed.

"Oh, no." Harley rolled her eyes. "There's that line again." She chewed at her thumbnail.

Emma gently lowered her hand. "You don't want to ruin your manicure."

"What's wrong?"

Emma gave her a tight smile. "I just talked with Mother, and I'm worried about your Christmas gift arriving."

Harley let out a big breath of air. "It's okay if it doesn't. I promise. Having a real Christmas dinner is enough for me. Is that all that's worrying you?"

A shudder ran through Emma. "I'm still not over all the excitement. And to think, I didn't believe anything could scare me as much as the night you tried to run away."

"Sorry." Harley winced. The faint sound of the antique grandfather clock's chimes broke the silence. "Hey, it's Christmas Eve."

Emma's face looked so sad.

"I guess Christmas is when you miss your husband most." Harley fingered the coverlet.

"Waves of grief come and go, sort of like a tide. Sometimes it's a smell—while shopping at the mall I caught a whiff of his aftershave. Or sometimes it's a taste. Chris loved chicken and dumplings, so I avoid that dish." Emma shrugged. "But there are good memories too. Touching something he loved, like the paperweight he kept on his desk, can help."

"Do you think you'll ever be happy again?"

Emma patted her knee. "I am happy. Having you with me has helped me more than you'll ever know."

Harley grabbed Emma in a hug. "Thank you for letting me stay. For fighting for me tonight. If he'd hurt you ..."

Emma squeezed her tight. "Let's not think about what might have happened to either of us. Let's focus on the future and choose happiness."

"I don't know how to do that."

Emma's face fell, then she sat up straight. "Minnie says it's a choice, and I've never known her to be wrong. It goes along with Luke's recommendation to control my thoughts and pray for my enemies."

"But how do you do that?"

"When I realize my thoughts, my emotions, are going in the wrong direction, I lift a prayer. It's easy to pray for people you love, but to pray for someone like Beau"—Emma shuddered—"that takes the power of Jesus. It took Jesus's help for me to pray for Winston, and for your mom, but when I did, I exchanged bitterness and worry for peace."

"You're saying I should pray for Beau? No way." Harley crossed her arms.

"Pray for anyone who hurts you."

Would Emma really pray for Beau and for her mom when they were plum awful? Harley shook her head.

"What have you got to lose?"

Harley shrugged. "I'm not sure if I believe in God."

Emma stared at the Christmas tree, her brows furrowed again. "Have you ever spun a coin on a tabletop?"

"Sure."

"What happened?"

"It twirled for a few seconds then fell over."

"The earth spins at close to a thousand miles an hour at the perfect angle."

"So?"

"What holds it in place?"

"Gravity?"

"It's impossible for me to believe it's by chance all the planets and stars of our universe work in perfect harmony to keep earth spinning in place without God. Nature is so complex and magnificent, how could anything but a superior being have created it?"

"But if God is that powerful, then ..."

"Awesome." Emma gave her knee a squeeze.

"Yeah. Okay ... then why would he care about me?"

"Because he created you. He created us in his image. Do you enjoy baking cookies?"

"You know I do."

"They're your creation. What if I tossed them in the trash?"

"It would make me mad and hurt my feelings."

"It's the same when we don't love God, don't appreciate the world he's given, the Son he sent to save us. Don't reject Him."

Harley gave Emma a long look. It still sounded like a fairytale to her. "I still don't get it."

Emma patted her knee. "Read the Bible I gave you, and I'll pray for you to get it."

"Okay."

Emma stood "I'm going to bed. We have a big day tomorrow."

"Make that today," Harley said, pointing to the digital clock at her bedside which read midnight.

Emma ruffled her hair. "Right."

Harley couldn't stop thinking about Beau grabbing her. She'd never forget Emma and Mr. McCullough risking their lives for her. She turned on the bedside light and searched her room for the Bible. It lay on the dresser, and she traced her finger over its cover. *The Message.* All she'd done was tote it back and forth to church. After crawling under the coverlet, she opened it to the first page. *First this: God created the heavens and the earth*

It was almost lunchtime when Harley stared at her reflection in the mirror. The hem of the red-velvet Christmas dress lifted when she twirled. Minnie insisted she try it on and wear it tonight. She'd meet all Casey's family after the candlelight service. Her stomach tightened and she lifted her thumb to her mouth. She stopped and spread her fingers out in front of her again and smiled. Dark roots at the part in her hair made her cringe. It was time to get rid of the blonde, but it'd have to wait until after Christmas. A clump of hair stuck up at her crown and she licked her index finger, then smoothed it down.

Emma promised another surprise awaited her, and not to come down until called. Back and forth she paced—the black suede ankle boots sounded like drumbeats on the oak floor. *What could be taking so long?* The lights of her Christmas tree blinked and she moved to the window seat. The whole street looked like something from a Christmas card. Mrs. Virginia's Cadillac pulled in the drive. She hadn't seen her since lunch at Oak Grove last Sunday when Emma was sick. She hoped she hadn't been sick too. *Maybe Emma's been waiting for her to get here.* What could the surprise be? And why did Emma want to give it to her today when Becky insisted they open gifts tomorrow morning after Santa visited? A wave of sadness washed over. Her mom used to tell her stories about Santa.

A knock sounded and Harley jumped.

Emma stood at the bedroom door, her face pale. When she looked at Harley, her face softened. "You look beautiful."

Warmth crept up Harley's neck and she bit her lip. "My hair looks like crap."

"It looks hip, youthful, fun."

Emma's hand trembled as she interlaced her fingers with Harley's. "Close your eyes. I'm going to lead you downstairs."

"You're kidding."

"N—no!"

She's nervous. Doesn't she know I don't expect anything, don't need anything except what she's already given me, to feel like a part of a family, to have a party to go to and celebrate Christmas, like a normal person? To feel safe. To feel loved.

Harley allowed Emma to lead her down the stairs ,and they stopped. Harley sniffed and a scent from her dreams wafted on the air—she stilled. She squeezed her eyes shut harder, her pulse pounded at her temple. *It couldn't be.* Her mouth went dry.

"Harley."

The deep, gruff voice wrapped around her like a hug and washed away her fear. She opened her eyes. "Papaw," she whispered.

Red-rimmed eyes the color of the ocean met her face. Every muscle in her body vibrated, and tears rolled down her cheeks.

He wrapped her in his arms, and his whole body shook.

When she pulled away, Emma handed her a wad of tissues. "Merry Christmas." Her tone sounded over-bright.

A woman with white hair pulled back in a bun sat on the sofa staring out the window. "Nancy, this is Harley." Papaw spoke softly and led her to the woman.

The woman stared up at her and extended her hand. "It's nice to meet you. I'm Nancy West."

Papaw whispered in her ear. "It's dementia. She hardly remembers me most of the time."

Harley gently grasped her fingers. Blue veins lined the top of her hand, dotted with age spots. Her skin seemed fragile as tissue paper.

"I'm Harley. It's nice to meet you."

Clouded eyes narrowed. "I know a Harley." She looked to her husband. "Don't I?"

"This is our granddaughter," Papaw said. "Anne's girl."

The woman wrung her hands and her eyes filled with tears. "Anne's gone." She rocked back and forth, but after a few seconds, her face looked serene, and she started humming.

"It's almost a blessing she doesn't remember." Papaw turned to Harley. "But I remember everything and I never stopped praying, never stopped hoping."

"I'd almost convinced myself you weren't real. Why did Mom lie?"

"We threatened to take you away from her, and she ran."

Harley swallowed the lump in her throat. "We moved so many times."

"We stopped believing anything Anne said after she hocked Nancy's wedding band."

"She's good at stealing and lying."

"More than once we hired a private detective. He'd be on your trail, then lose it."

Nausea threatened Harley, and she hugged her stomach. "Mom would take up with a guy, then there'd be a big blow up, and we'd be on the road again." Harley squeezed his hand. "Papaw, what's your name?"

He gulped and his chin trembled. "Rick West."

"Do you live at the beach?"

"Close. Bay Minette, Alabama. I ran a bait shop and fish camp."

"In the pines," Harley said.

"That's right, honey, but we sold out and moved last year. It's all I can do to take care of your mamaw."

"Oh." Harley's stomach dropped, and she turned. Behind her, Emma, Virginia, Minnie, and Casey formed a half-circle. Their cheeks glistened.

Minnie cleared her throat. "I'd hoped you'd still be wearing the dress when your grandparents arrived."

"So you all knew."

"Mother phoned late last night," Emma said.

Harley smoothed her hand over the soft velvet and tried to smile. She had family and Papaw needed help. Poor Mamaw. But Emma needed her too. Her insides twisted.

CHAPTER FORTY-TWO— EMMA & LUKE

At six o'clock on the dot Christmas morning, Emma shoved the turkey roaster into the oven and set the timer for five hours. The turkey could cool for an hour before serving at noon.

"Good morning," Mr. West's gravelly voice made Emma jump.

"Merry Christmas!" Emma said.

"And to you. Don't guess you have any coffee do you?"

Emma grabbed a mug. "Are you kidding? No way could I be functioning without caffeine after the last couple of days."

Mr. West inhaled the steam over the cup. "Thank you."

"There's cream in the fridge." Emma slid the sugar bowl across the table.

"I like it black."

They sat in silence and savored their coffee. After Mr. West drained his cup, he cleared his throat. "I've been chewing on something all night."

Emma bit her lip. "Uh-hum."

"I have an idea." He rubbed the gray stubble of his beard. "We owe you a lot for rescuing Harley."

Emma's chest warmed. "It's more like she rescued me."

"Maybe we can work out a way to share responsibility for Harley, but it's a lot to ask of you."

"I'm all ears."

"Nancy's health's not good, and she needs more care than the assisted living facility provides."

Emma's stomach tightened. No way could she offer Nancy skilled nursing care.

He cleared his throat. "Your mother said there's an excellent long-term-care facility in Weldon."

Emma nodded.

"Tomorrow, I plan to call them to see if they might have a room for Nancy."

"So you're hoping to stay in Weldon?"

He nodded. "If they have a room, I'll find a small apartment to rent."

Emma gripped her mug of coffee. "There's little decent rental property in town. That's why Becky and Leslie ended up moving in with me after the fire." Emma sat up straight in her chair. "But I have empty bedrooms."

"I couldn't take advantage of your generosity."

"There's plenty of room, and you can pay rent if that makes you feel better. If the stairs are too much for you, you can have my suite, and I'll move upstairs."

"Oh, I couldn't ask that of you. I hated taking your room last night, but I feared Nancy might fall."

Emma reached across the table and squeezed his hand. "We can work out the details later. Let's pray Weldon Community Care has room for Nancy."

Mr. West gave a teary smile. "I dreaded the holiday. Never did I dream of God answering so many of my prayers. I almost hate to ask for one more blessing."

"Let us therefore come boldly to the throne of grace, that we may obtain mercy and find grace to help in time of need." Emma quoted the Scripture aloud.

"Hebrews. Chapter four, verse sixteen," Rick said.

Eleanor was right, Emma thought. The Lord sent us His Scriptures when we needed them most.

Luke opened the gate to Emma's backyard on Christmas morning and raised his hands as Buster and Max met him, jumping and pulsating with energy. *Some guard dogs.* He kneeled down and did his best to calm them. Buster rewarded him with a slobbery kiss. "Yuck." He ran his jacket sleeve across his face.

The enormous house reminded him of a citadel. Why would anyone feel the need to build such a structure for a home?

After the candlelight service last night, Mrs. Virginia cornered him and shared Emma's hope to fill her dining room with friends and family. When she'd introduced him to Harley's grandparents, his breathing slowed, and he sought Emma's eyes, but she'd disappeared in the crowd. It would be heartbreaking for her to lose Harley. At least she still had Becky and Leslie, but he knew Becky would be building a new house soon. Poor Emma.

"Howdy, preacher!" Mr. McCullough crossed the yard. Max and Buster yelped and shot toward him.

"Sit." Mr. McCullough spoke with authority.

The dog's rumps hit the frozen ground, and he tossed them a treat. "Good boys." He scratched their ears.

"Merry Christmas." Luke said.

Mr. McCullough clapped him on the back. "And to you."

"No Super-Soaker today?"

"It's put away, but don't worry, I'll keep my eye on your girls for you."

"My girls?"

Mr. McCullough cackled. "I'm old but I ain't blind."

Luke shoved his hands into his pockets "We're friends."

Mr. McCullough stopped laughing, and his brows formed into a unibrow. "Emma's suffered more loss than anyone should. I'd almost given up hope for her to get over losing Chris, but since taking in Harley, she's finally laughing. I'd hate to see her wounded again."

"It must have been a terrible blow for her to lose her husband. From what I hear, he pretty near walked on water."

"Not perfect, but a good neighbor and friend, gifted with kids—but Emma's Dad, that's a different story."

"She's never mentioned him."

"I'm surprised the gossips didn't fill you in."

"Gossip is not something I encourage."

Mr. McCullough shifted from one foot to the other. "First he cleaned out Virginia's bank account, then he left town with his secretary."

Luke's hands fisted. "That's low."

"Then the son-of-a-yellow-bellied-snake got himself killed in a car wreck."

"I'm not sure why you're telling me this," Luke said.

"Emma doesn't need one more bit of heartache. If you're not serious about her, keep your distance." Mr. McCullough's voice sounded menacing.

"It was Mrs. Virginia who insisted I come today."

"Someday, she'll figure out she's not the one who runs the world."

Luke gave a tight smile. "I'll not be the one to tell her."

"It'd be the same as talking to a fence post."

Harley jogged out the back door. "Mr. McCullough! Come meet my papaw."

The old man's mouth hung open, and Harley launched herself at him and giggled. "Merry Christmas."

This girl brimmed with happiness—a true Christmas miracle. *And Mr. McCullough was worried about him causing Emma heartache,* Luke thought. But the old man had a point. Standing in the house's shadow, cold seeped through his thin jacket, and he took a step back. What would Emma think about his one-bedroom studio apartment with the bare necessities?

Last night, during the candlelight service, it seemed clear to him he should stay in Weldon, but in the light of day, he remembered the reason he'd avoided romantic relationships. He didn't have a clue how to be a family man, and Emma needed a family man.

Emma poked her head out the door. "Merry Christmas, Luke."

He lifted his hand. "Merry Christmas! I stopped by to give you the greeting in person. I'm on my way to the nursing home."

Emma's face fell. "You're not staying for lunch? Mother said you'd agreed to—"

"To stop by. It feels selfish to be among a crowd when old Mrs. Wright at the nursing home won't have anyone to share Christmas lunch with."

Harley and Mr. McCullough went inside the house and Emma stood in front of him, hugging herself. "So you can't stay?"

He brushed what looked like flour from her cheek, and his thumb traced a dark circle under her eye.

She leaned into his touch, and his resolve almost melted. "You look tired."

"I've been cooking since early this morning, but I'm not complaining when I've dreamed of filling my dining room table for years."

This woman had spunk in spades. "So you're okay with Harley's grandparents showing up?"

Her brows lifted. "We plan to share responsibility for Harley. Her grandmother suffers from dementia and Mr. West—Rick—is hoping to secure a room for her at Weldon's Community Care.

"Wow. God is good." He wrapped his arms around her in a hug.

"All the time." She squeezed him back, and he inhaled her signature floral fragrance.

"Looks like I worried for nothing. One of these days, I'm going to learn to trust God with everything." He slowly released her. "Merry Christmas."

Emma gulped. "Merry Christmas."

He returned to his truck and backed out of the drive. Bob planned to announce his retirement next Sunday. Maybe, some of the members of Loving Chapel would want him to stay—but Emma's opinion was the only one of real importance to him. He scratched his head as he drove through town fighting the desire to turn the truck around and return to Emma's table. *No. She needed someone better.*

After a round of Christmas carols and lunch with Mrs. Wright at the nursing home, Luke's thoughts turned to his grandmother. If only she'd known Jesus in the same way this gentle soul did. He struggled to keep his thoughts positive as he struggled with the guilt of wanting to kill Beau Wallace. *Father, forgive me.* He knew where he needed to go next.

An invisible force pulled Luke to Loving Chapel. When he entered the dim sanctuary, a wave of peace washed over him as he made his way to the altar. The first name he lifted was Beau Wallace. Luke vowed to visit in the detention center soon, but not until the Lord softened his heart. This might take some time. He sat without speaking, clearing his mind. Intimate time with the Father never failed him.

At one o'clock in the afternoon, Emma stood at the head of the dining room table. Pastor Bob sat at the other end with Eleanor to his right. Across from Eleanor, Mr. McCullough sat next to Harley, her grandpa to her left. The detective, Luther Griggs, and her mother sat to Emma's right and left. Emma had placed Leslie's highchair across the table from Harley's mamaw, who smiled at the baby's antics. Becky sat next to the baby, an empty seat across the table from her. Sadness crept into Emma's heart as her gaze fell on the chair reserved for Luke ... but then she forced her thoughts to turn to all of the things ... and people for which she was thankful. *In everything give thanks.*

That evening, the last pink hues of the winter sun disappeared as Max and Buster led Emma home from the cemetery. Sadness for the tragedy of Chris's death lingered, but anger and bitterness no longer tormented her as she kneeled and told him everything. During lunch, Rick had mentioned his plan to find an apartment, and Mr. McCullough's face lifted. Emma had forgotten he had a mother-in-law suite that was now vacant. Mr. McCullough assured Rick, if it suited him, he was welcome to move in. The extra income would come in handy, he said, as everything seemed to cost ten times more than it was worth these days.

When Emma opened the backyard gate for Buster and Max, she noticed that light spilled from every window. She stood there in awe. God had taken the mess of Harley's broken family and given Emma a new one, with Becky as a sister, and Leslie too.

Emma rubbed her jacket sleeve across her cheek and jogged down the street. She couldn't resist the urge to give thanks on His altar.

Luke's truck sat in the church's parking lot, and Emma paused. At lunch, Pastor Bob had announced his plans to retire. He asked them to keep this news confidential—he only shared it with them early as he hoped Virginia and Emma might convince Luke to apply for the job. A shyness washed over her, and she almost turned around. The cold seeped through Emma's sweatshirt, and at last, she keyed in the security code.

Emma tiptoed to the sanctuary with only emergency lights leading her there. At the altar, she made out Luke's shape, head bowed, and she stepped backward. Her hip hit a pew and she winced. Luke's head lifted, their eyes met, Emma gulped. "S–sorry to disturb you."

He rose, pushed his palms down his thighs, and then brushed a curl behind his ear. Those curls always reminded her of Da Vinci's David and stirred her heart.

He gave a wry smile. "You've been disturbing me since the first moment I met you."

Emma swallowed the lump in her throat. "Every window of my home is filled with light, and I felt compelled to run to God, to thank him for answering my prayer for a family."

Luke's face softened. "So you've wanted a family for a long time." He stepped closer to her and she leaned in. The whiff of cedar made her catch her breath.

"My ... my whole life." Emma winced. Why would her tongue not work? "First a brother or sister, and then a daughter." Emma shrugged. "Finally, my home is filled with light and Harley's laughter."

"He's good at taking broken pieces and making something new and beautiful."

Emma placed her palm on his cheek, caressed his beard. "We missed you at lunch today." If he had any idea how every time she'd looked at the empty seat her thoughts had drifted to him, she'd die of shame. His beard was so soft. What was she doing? She jerked her hand away, turned and quickstepped to the door. *How shameful.* She'd come here to pray, not to fantasize about kissing Luke. Emma rushed away.

Just as Emma stepped outside into the cold night, Luke caught up with her and grabbed her elbow. "Wait."

Emma bit her lip, and heat traveled up her neck. Luke turned her to face him, and he wrapped her in his arms. "Don't go."

He cleared his throat and looked into her eyes. "Do you think there's room in your heart for one more broken piece?"

Emma stilled and stared into his dark shining eyes.

His hand squeezed hers, and he licked his lips.

"Y–yes."

"Now's the time to say no if you don't want me to kiss you."

Her breathing increased, she leaned forward, and touched her lips to his.

He cupped her cheeks with his callused hands and kissed her with such tenderness her insides melted, and she clung to him, savoring every sensation. His beard tickled her chin as he deepened the kiss. *Yes. Yes. Yes.* A thousand times yes, and Emma lost herself in the swirl of emotions. The world continued to spin on its axis, but Emma's world shifted.

Luke ended the kiss, and she placed her hand over her pounding heart. Her lips tingled, and it was all she could do to restrain herself from launching herself at him.

Luke dropped his head. "This is bad."

"But why?" Emma's voice sounded incredulous.

"I have nothing to offer you. You're probably the richest person in town."

Emma sighed heavily. "Grandfather left a trust fund for the upkeep of the house, but my bank account's not so impressive."

"But I grew up in a shack with a bartender for a grandmother."

"And my grandfather's most impressive talent was to get drunk and scald his family with hateful words." Emma grabbed his collar and pulled his face to hers again. Oh, this man knew how to kiss a woman. Her toes curled.

Luke's arms tightened around her, then he pushed back. "Whoa. This can't happen."

Emma had a sudden brilliant idea. "Come with me." She grabbed his hand. "Let's go for a walk. I want to show you something."

They left the shadow of the church, turned left and walked three blocks in the opposite direction of Emma's home. She stopped in front of a small white bungalow. "What do you think about this house?"

"It's charming." Luke shrugged.

"That's where Chris and I lived before Grandfather loaded us down with his baggage."

"Why did you move?"

"Chis had this idea of filling the big house with foster kids."

"I'm surprised you didn't have children."

Emma sighed and closed her eyes. "I suffered miscarriages, an ectopic pregnancy."

He hugged her. "I'm so sorry."

"If you really want a relationship with me, it's important to get that out of the way now."

He cupped her cheek and kissed her again.

This time Emma pushed back. "Are you sure? I can't carry a child to term. That part of my body is broken."

"I want a relationship with you more than anything." He gulped. "Except God, of course." Emma wrapped her arms around him, and he whispered in her ear. "You've been in my thoughts from the moment you slid your phone into your pants."

She buried her face in his shoulder. "Oh, you had to bring that up." He kissed her neck and kissed it again, sending shivers down Emma's spine. He gripped her hand and led her home. They stood on the street and watched the lights from Harley's tower change colors. Every window of her home shone brightly with light.

Luke cupped her cheeks with his cold hands. "Are you sure you have room in your heart for one more broken person?"

"I'd say this is a case where two broken pieces make a whole."

EVERY WINDOW FILLED WITH LIGHT

Their lips met, and Emma savored the moment as Luke's love filled the damaged places of her heart.

The End

ABOUT THE AUTHOR

Shelia Stovall is the director of a small-town library in southern Kentucky, where only strangers mention her last name, and the children call her Miss Shelia.

Shelia and her husband Michael live on a farm, and she enjoys taking daily rambles with their three dogs to the creek. Spending time with family, especially her grandchildren, is her all-time favorite thing. The only hobby Shelia loves more than reading uplifting stories of hope is writing them.